Praise for *The End of the World Running Club*:

'Extraordinary'   Simon Mayo, Radio 2 Book Club

'A real find'   Stephen King

'Brilliant ... superb to the end'   Lucy Mangan

'An uplifting, exciting and often humorous yarn about camaraderie, endurance and redemption'   *The Times*

'Ridiculously gripping straight from the start'   Jenny Colgan

'What sets this apart is Walker's extraordinary emotional articulacy'   *The Sun*

'A compelling read'   *Financial Times*

'Compulsively readable'   *SFX*

'Will thrill and delight ... a terrifically well-observed, haunting and occasionally harrowing read'   *Starbust*

Adrian J Walker was born in the bush suburbs of Sydney, Australia, in the mid-70s. After his father found a camper van in a ditch, he renovated it and moved his family back to the UK, where Adrian was raised. Ever since he can remember, Adrian has been interested in three things: words, music and technology, and when he graduated from the University of Leeds, he found a career in software.

He lives in London with his wife and two children. To find out more visit: wwww.adrianjwalker.com

ALSO BY ADRIAN J WALKER:

The End of the World Running Club
The Last Dog on Earth

THE
end of the world
SURVIVORS
CLUB

ADRIAN J WALKER

DEL REY

First published by Del Rey in 2019

1 3 5 7 9 10 8 6 4 2

Del Rey, an imprint of Ebury Publishing
20 Vauxhall Bridge Road,
London SW1V 2SA

Del Rey is part of the Penguin Random House group of companies
whose addresses can be found at global.penguinrandomhouse.com

Penguin
Random House
UK

www.penguin.co.uk

A CIP catalogue record for this book is available from the British Library

ISBN 9781785035739

Typeset in 13/14.75 pts Fleischman BT Pro
by Integra Software Services Pvt. Ltd, Pondicherry

Printed and bound in Great Britain by Clays Ltd, Elcograf S.p.A.

Penguin Random House is committed to a sustainable future
for our business, our readers and our planet. This book is
made from Forest Stewardship Council® certified paper.

MIX
Paper from
responsible sources
FSC® C018179

For my lifelong skipper
and crewmate, Dad

Chapter 1

'Beth, where are your children?'

If you met me you would probably think I was rude.

'Beth?'

I don't mean to be.

'Beth, you need to get your life jacket on.'

It's just that I can occasionally appear to be elsewhere. There's a distance within me. A space that opens up sometimes.

Let's say you're talking to me at a party. I'll listen. I will. I'll nod my head and smile at your story about when you met Kate Winslet in business class. (This would be back in the days when things like parties, aeroplanes and Kate Winslets existed, of course.) But there will come a time when my eyes glaze, my smile wilts, and you'll think that I've drifted away like an untethered raft.

I look around. The heaving boat, the wide-eyed crew, the passengers sobbing in terror, they're like objects in a dimly remembered dream.

Like I say, it's not intentional.

I can't feel my legs, my arms, my anything.

But it happens, and when it does it is often in the wrong moments. Like during one of your stories.

'*Beth, what's wrong? Where are your kids?*'

Or like now, when I'm standing beneath a growing shadow, and what is about to happen looms over me like a terrible cliff as if the past, present, future, and every choice I've ever made is about to crash down upon me all at once.

'*Beth!*'

But we'll get to that.

My distance has always been with me. When I was eight I was allowed to go to my grandad's social club with him after Sunday dinner. I'd sit on his knee drinking flat cola and listening to him and the other men chat over their endless whiskies and cigarettes.

Uncle Brian used to watch me.

Uncle Brian who was actually nothing of the sort, and just an old alcoholic friend of my grandad. He was a hard man with small eyes and big hands.

And he would watch me.

When I looked, he'd lean over.

'Yer awa' wi' the fairies, so you are,' he'd say.

I'd never reply, so he'd lean closer.

'What's the matter, hen? Yer awful quiet. Cat got your tongue?'

I didn't like Uncle Brian. There was something sinister about him I couldn't place at the time. But I had noticed on the rare occasions when I'd been in his house that his wife was a quiet woman, forever busy with her back turned in another room, and this somehow seemed significant.

You were wrong, Uncle Brian. I wasn't away with the fairies. I may have seemed to be but I wasn't. I was right there in the room listening to every word that slurred from the lips of those men, scrutinising their smiles and frowns, trying to understand what made them all tick.

Trying to understand what made *you* tick.

As it turned out, what made you tick, Uncle Brian, was a fondness for beating the living shit out of your wife when you got home from the pub. So that's why she was so quiet – you made damn sure the cat got *her* tongue and kept it, you evil old bastard.

Anyway. My distance might explain why I never had any friends. This state of affairs didn't bother me. I was happy on my own. I chose jeans over dresses, hid behind books and sought out corners. Like the one with the tree stump in the corner of the playground, or the one in my bedroom where I learned to program a computer my grandfather won in the pub. Or the one where I met Ed – though that was much later.

A friendless child is one thing, but when you're an adult – well, you find it's remarked upon. Especially with a mother like mine.

'You need some pals, Lizbut.'

Lizbut. I hated *Lizbut*.

'You're a mother now, you need a support network, you cannae rely on me for everything.'

I don't.

3

'I cannae be down here every weekend –'

Good.

'– helping you wi' yer bairn. I've got my own life to lead.'

Excellent. You do that. Please do that.

'You need to get out there, Lizbut. Join one of them antenatal groups or something.'

I did in the end, if for nothing else than to shut her up.

They called themselves The Survivors Club.

Carol, their leader (yes, they had a leader) explained with the jolliest of hockey sticks that this was because: 'If you can survive the first six months of motherhood, ladies, you can survive anything!'

I felt like a stalker at that first meeting, scanning them all for suitability like some postnatal Terminator looking for its mark. *Which one of you … which one of you will I befriend*. In the end, God help me, I went for the big boss: Carol herself. *What to say*, I thought as I waited for her conversation to finish. *How to win her over. It should be something interesting, something personal.*

I know, I'll tell her my fantasy.

You needn't get excited. My fantasy involved nothing more pedestrian than time, because when you have children there is none of the stuff. Certainly none of your own. I love my kids but I was surely not the only mother to slog through another precious day with her babies stacking bricks, wiping arseholes or watching that relentless pork scratching – oh, you know who I mean – and wishing I could get just five minutes to myself. Just five minutes.

Or an hour.

Or *a whole day*.

That was my fantasy – a day to myself – and that, for some reason I can only put down to sleep deprivation, is what I believed would endear me to the mighty Carol.

This is what I told her.

First, I wake up after eight hours of unbroken sleep. The bed is empty. The house is quiet. There's no sound but the twittering of birds and the distant drone of an aeroplane, so I doze for a while in the shores of my dreams. Then I get up, stretch and open the curtains. Outside is a warm, windless day with nothing to do.

Breakfast first. Poached eggs, bacon and a mug of tea that's hot to the dregs. The washing-up can wait. I'll spend an hour or two reading and then change into my gear. It's time for a run.

No phone, no watch, nothing to distract me with beeps. I take a long meander through forests and hills, around the glittering Pentlands reservoirs and back into town, across the dew-damp Meadows meadows and into the warrens of the Old Town. Good morning, Edinburgh. Happy day, my pretty city. Somewhere near the Royal Mile I'll stop at a café to read a paper with a smoky espresso. Then I'll head back. It's just me and the hills and the rest of the day to myself.

No husband, no children, no duty, just for a day.

Yes please, I'll take that. Eh, Carol?

But Carol said nothing. She just looked at me with that painted-on smile of hers, and made a noise like a constipated chaffinch.

Oh, what, Carol?

Do I not get to join your yummy-mummy Facebook group? Or sign up to your Hungry Harrison vegan recipe blog? Am I not invited for breast-milk lattes with you and your pals while you compare the contents of your moon cups?

Am I a bad mother?

There was a time when I believed I was. In those early months when I thought I was failing at everything, holding myself up to the impossible standards of those other mothers.

'Breast is best!' they'd say. But, oh, the agonising truth of breastfeeding.

'Controlled crying!' Right, when every fibre of your being is straining to comfort them.

'Sling's the thing!' But – Christ – don't hold them *too* much or you'll ruin them.

In the end I left Carol and her club to it. I hid away. I battened down the hatches and I let my distance rule. I shunned all offers of help, all those well-meaning family members with their offers of tea and conflicting advice. I shut myself away until they stopped trying, and one day I realised that I had just one job as a mother: to survive and ensure that my children did the same.

So I did. I formed my own Survivors Club, members: one. Me.

And I survived the apocalypse with a baby and a toddler.

So fuck you, Carol.

I know I wasn't really alone. I had a husband. I had Ed.

I should have been happy when he turned up at the boat. He'd made it after all. Christ knows how and he looked like hell, but he'd actually bloody made it. He'd plumbed the depths of his spirit, broken through his barriers and by God he'd found us.

Good man. Well done.

But what did that change?

This was how it had always been with Ed and me: he'd done his thing while I'd done mine, and in this case it just so happened that his thing was dragging his arse the length of the United Kingdom while mine was looking after our children in that hell of an evacuation camp. Changing nappies. Nappies I didn't have. Scavenging for clean water and food in a field of twenty thousand other hungry families, fighting the daily battle of hygiene so we didn't contract dysentery, and comforting my daughter through those freezing, wretched nights, trying to explain for the ten thousandth time why we were there, and why we'd had to leave her daddy behind, and why *no, please don't say that, please don't say that about Mummy, go to sleep, I know it's cold and that man won't stop screaming, but please, please, just go to sleep.*

So you'll forgive me if I wasn't aglow with pride when he stumbled to the rail.

It's not that I wasn't pleased to see him. I was, and I meant it when I said I'd go with him, I really did. I would have scooped up our kids and left that boat for whatever life he had planned for us on those battered shores that had once been our home. Because that's what you do, isn't it? That's what you do when you're a team.

But that's just it. Ed and I – we were nothing like a team.

Perhaps we had been once, in the early days. I still remember those moments of bliss – like finding each other's hand after our first night together, or kissing him in a flurry of snow and Salvation Army carols at Dundee station, or sitting in the bath of our Marchmont flat with our fingers interlocked, grinning over those two blue lines.

Hands. We were always holding hands. But somewhere along the way we lost our grip.

And that man who had once leaped, beaming from the train had instead trudged in from work and sunk into our milk-stained sofa without a word.

Oh, my poor hero, I would think. Did you have to spend another day pushing buttons and drinking coffee and being with other adults? Did you get to make an uninterrupted trip to the bathroom, eat an entire lunch and hear human words – actual ones, not squawks – that make sense? There, there, my brave lion. What, my day? Oh, just another storm of excrement and vomit. I'm starving, sick of the smell of my own clothes, and I feel like someone's been ironing my tits for the last nine hours. So, you know, nothing unusual.

I wanted to scream at him: *Look at what you have. You get to go out every day with a chance to do something, create something, be something. But all you do is mope. Was it really that bad, whatever it was you were doing out there?*

No. Never a team.

Nevertheless, my tears at Falmouth Harbour were real, and when he kissed me and said that he would come for me instead, my heart broke in two.

Of course it did.

But heartbreak wasn't all I felt. I felt relief as well. Relief that I wouldn't have to return to that life with him, full of its frustrations and disappointments.

Relief that I only had to carry two children, not three.

The foghorn blared, the crowd released their cheers and wails like gulls into the frigid air, and, as Ed fell from my grasp, all that distance he had somehow covered opened up again at twice the speed.

And my distance opened up too.

This distance of mine. I think I saw it in my daughter that day as we watched Britain's coastline fall away. It was cold on the deck. Arthur's face was buried into my armpit, and Alice's last tears for her daddy had already shattered into particles on the salt wind. She breathed a trembling sigh and leaned back, fingers loosening upon the battered can Ed had given her – the 'stringy-phone', he had called it. I watched her gazing back at the shore, taking in the squat nose and squint mouth, the soft drifting curls, and those heavy-lashed eyes that would one day, whether she liked it or not, see the world as a woman. Her face twitched with thoughts and I wondered whether they were the same as mine.

There's no way he'll find us again, there's just no way.

But it doesn't matter. I can do this alone.

Just like I always have.

Chapter 2

It was crowded below deck.

We were led down staircases and long, metallic corridors until we reached a large, windowless room like an auditorium, with tiers of seats and a spotlit stage at the front. The place was full of noise and bodies, and the smell of our recent encampment in Cornwall had stowed away with us.

'Ooh,' said a female voice, 'it's a bit like that cruise ship we went on, isn't it, Gerald?'

'Hmm,' said a bovine-like voice belonging to, I assumed, Gerald. 'Without the ruddy buffet, I hope. Couldn't stomach that cheese, bloody awful. Ouch, bloody hell, watch where you're going.'

Gerald scowled down at his foot, upon which Alice had accidentally trodden.

'Sorry,' I said, pushing through the crowd.

'You should take better care of your children,' he bellowed after us.

'Wanker,' I muttered under my breath.

I found a space near the back and sat down on the floor. A microphone whistled. The room hushed.

'Mummy,' whispered Alice, 'that man wasn't very nice.'

'No, darling, he wasn't.'

'Is that what *wanker* means?'

'*Shh.*'

'Ladies and gentlemen, girls and boys, my name is Captain Anders Ulrich. Welcome aboard the SS *Unity.*'

Captain Anders Ulrich – a tall man with white eyebrows and a thin moustache – proceeded to tell us about how the next few weeks of our lives were going to pan out. I got the gist of it. Cabins, water rations, food, toilets, that sort of thing, but his Norwegian mumbles were like a lullaby and I strained to keep myself from nodding off. I saw others succumb to the same fatigue.

Alice tugged my sleeve.

'Is it like that place, Mummy? Where we got our own room?'

She was talking about the barracks, of course. They seemed like a long time ago, though it had only been a few weeks.

'Yes, darling. Until we get to Cape Town.'

'And that's where Daddy's meeting us? Kip Town?'

'That's right,' I said. The truth could wait.

The afternoon and evening passed in a daze of anxiety and euphoria, as if we'd all got sunstroke and decided to drop pills. Apparently it was Christmas Day, and we were served paper plates dotted with carefully measured portions of unidentifiable meat, potatoes and gravy, with a cracker each. I sat in a dark corner next to two other families, with whom I shared some words I can't remember as I fed Arthur with a plastic spoon. Then there were presents for the children, handed out by crew members disguised badly as elves. We all tried our best to laugh.

Alice tore open her gift of a seashell necklace and clutched it with joy.

'Like a big girl,' she said, as I fastened it around her neck.

Later, when sleep crept over every word I said, the ship suddenly lurched and the lights went off. Then, after a few seconds of still darkness, they came on again and the ship powered away.

Nobody said anything, but a few quiet looks were shared.

What was that?

Afterwards we were herded to our berths. Our corridor had three toilets. We joined the queue at the end, four deep.

'Mummy, I need a wee.' Alice looked up, knees bent. 'And I'm thirsty.'

'One out, one in, eh, sweetheart? OK, well let's deal with the code yellow first. Excuse me?' I tapped the shoulder of the man in front. 'Sorry, do you think we could jump ahead?'

The man turned. His face was like a walrus, if the walrus in question worked for an insurance company, enjoyed port and had made a series of shrewd investments over the years.

'No, I do not,' he said. It was Gerald and his wife. 'We've been waiting here for twenty bloody minutes.'

'I'm sorry, it's just that my daughter needs a pee, and I just thought—'

'Well, you thought wrong, didn't you?' Gerald shuffled his great backside as if in some primal claim to bathroom territory. 'We all have needs, and just because you have children, doesn't mean you get to be first at everything.'

'Mummy, really need a *wee*.'

'But she's only three,' I said. 'We won't be long.'

'It's just like on that cruise, Mildred,' said Gerald to his wife. 'They were all at it then too, all those bloody parents.'

'Now wait a minute—'

'Hey.'

The voice came from the next queue along, at the front of which was a woman. She was younger than me and wore her hair in a black bob. 'You can go before me, if you like.'

The words, and the smile that accompanied them, were like a child's.

'Thank you,' I said, ushering Alice over.

'Don't mention it,' she said, holding the door open for us. Gerald mumbled something in the background, which our new friend ignored. She grinned down at Alice and whispered: 'He should be kinder to other people, don't you think, princess?'

'It's not his fault,' said Alice. 'He's a wanker —'

'Alice, Christ!'

The woman smirked and there were some sniggers from the queue behind.

'And I'm not a princess,' Alice went on, 'I'm a pirate, like my daddy.'

'Oh,' said the woman. Her accent sounded English, north-east, I thought. 'Is that right, pet?'

'Yes, he's coming after us on another boat. He's going to meet us at – at Kip Town.'

I shared a brief encoded look with the woman, whose smile never faltered.

'Well, lucky you.'

'Thanks again,' I said, squeezing inside the toilet. 'I really appreciate it.'

'Don't mention it. Oh, and here.' She held out an unopened bottle of water. 'For afterwards.'

'Oh, God, thanks, I mean it. I'll get you another one.'

She puckered and shook her head, then nodded at Arthur, arms out.

'Want me to take him while you do your business?'

'No, thanks,' I said, cramming into the small room. 'I can manage.'

The door shut and I plonked Arthur in the sink while I saw to Alice. He gurgled at the cracked mirror.

'Please don't use that word, Alice.'

'What word?'

'The one you just used.'

'Why not?'

'Because some people don't like hearing it, and little girls definitely shouldn't say it. It's a bad word.'

Her eyes glazed while her urine hit the water below. She searched her teeth with her tongue, waiting.

'But the world is bad, Mummy,' she said when it was finished.

My heart stalled.

'Not all of it, darling. Now come on, let's get to bed.'

The bed in question was a double bunk that shared the small cabin with a bolted-down table and chair. Arthur was already asleep, so I laid him with Alice in the bottom bunk and took the top for myself.

Soon I heard whispers, and I peered over the side. Alice had the stringy-phone to her mouth.

'What are you doing?' I said.

She looked up with bright, watery eyes. 'Talking to Daddy.'

I froze, feeling as if I had suddenly caught something fragile.

'Good night, sweetheart. Go to sleep.'

'Night, Mummy.'

I lay back, my heart turning wounded somersaults.

Chapter 3

Before it all happened – back in that world of parties, aeroplanes and Kate Winslets – being a parent meant living in a world where your worst nightmare could come true at any moment. It was a daily walk upon a crooked line. You'd be smiling, waving, having fun in a park or on a beach, but all the time you knew that the nightmare was just a slip, trip or bump away. It lurked in every misjudged step your child took, every distraction that took your attention from them, every germ in every breath. Death, disease and misadventure – and if one of those didn't get your little cherub then the hedgerows and alleyways were just brimming with eager hands waiting to grab them. And they didn't just inhabit the dark places, but the bright ones too. Teachers, priests, politicians, celebrities – seems everyone wanted to have it off with kids in those final days.

I don't know how you're supposed to deal with that. I mean, I used to love *Jim'll Fix It*. I lost count of the number of times I wrote in asking if I could have a private tour of the London Science Museum – that's right, *private* – but I never heard back. I even enclosed a picture of myself once.

Maybe he just didn't fancy me.

You knew the nightmare was there because you saw it every day. You knew that when you tucked your children in at night there was some poor soul out there who wasn't, but had been the night before. And you thanked the stars for it. You thanked the stars every night that someone else had fallen into the nightmare and not you.

Those stars, of course, weren't interested in your gratitude. They were busy making plans of their own, and before we knew it a hundred thousand asteroids had smashed the northern hemisphere into smithereens, killing almost everything in its path. And yet my babies and I were still in one piece. We had sidestepped yet another nightmare. So my relief must have been palpable that morning as I sat upon the upper deck watching Alice and Arthur play in a children's recreation area the crew had erected – a sunken pit of slides, bricks, cushions and toys surrounded by a high gated fence. Nothing could happen to them now. We were saved, and they were literally locked in a padded cage.

'I'll have three or four pints of what you're having.'

I looked up to see a black bob haloed by sunlight. Our saviour from the toilet queues the night before.

'Oh, hello. Er, I'm not … drinking anything?'

She laughed. 'You look like you're on cloud number nine, that's all.'

'Right. Sorry. I'm probably just a wee bit frazzled from yesterday.'

She shrugged. 'You just look happy, that's all. Mind if I sit with you?'

'Sure.'

I had chosen the only bench left on the deck, which unfortunately happened to be three away from Gerald. There was no sign of his wife. He had already given me one withering look when I sat down and was giving me a second as I shimmied along for Mary. She noticed.

'Made friends there, I see,' she said, and before I could speak she'd turned in his direction. 'You all right, Gerald pet?' she bellowed across, in the tone of a nurse over a dribbling geriatric. 'Happy? Do you have everything you need? I said, do you have EVERYTHING YOU NEED?'

Gerald's face puckered with affront, and he grumbled back into the battered paperback he was reading. I stifled a laugh.

'He's a flippin' old goose, that one,' she said.

'Do you know him?'

'Aye. My husband and I had the pleasure of Mr and Mrs Shavington's company for two months in Whitby.' She turned to me. 'An abandoned holiday camp. *Buttlins*, we used to call it. As in your bum.'

I hesitated, as I had already learned to at the mention of relatives who weren't visible. 'Husband?'

She smiled, understanding. 'Nathan. He's down below deck, gave him a lie-in.'

'Is that where you lived then, Whitby?'

Mary laughed. 'Christ, no, we lived in South Shields. We had to come south after the thing happened. A big one hit Northumberland, you know? Smack bang in the heart of it. Boom. Nathan said it tore the whole coast apart, and then all those floods ...' Her eyes drifted with the words, as if she had suddenly tired of them.

'Good to see the kids having fun, I bet,' she said, nodding at the play area. Alice had struck up a friendship with a boy, huddled beneath the roof of a climbing frame. 'That camp was no fun. But they're outside now, and in the sun, too.'

'Yeah, what's that all about? It's Boxing Day but it feels like spring.'

'Nathan says it's because of what happened.' She unfolded her palms to stress the nature of cause and effect. 'It's the atmosphere, you see, it's all skew-whiff now. That cloud that hung around, all the dust and that. We're still in the tail end of those things, did you know that? There's little baby ones coming down all the time, not like before, you know, but big enough to do some damage. That's why we still can't fly. And then there's all the shifting tides.' She turned to me, twin hair curtains swinging. 'Did you know most of southern Europe's under water now?'

There was something about her – the way her eyes wandered your face when you spoke, the way her sentences seemed cobbled together, as if by some extraterrestrial who had quickly absorbed a dictionary in order to fit in. She wasn't like other people. She seemed untethered, free, like a sail from a mast. I liked her.

'Do you and Nathan have kids?'

'Nope.' She drummed her knees. 'Just me and my man. I mean, *I* want some, one day, but I'm not sure about Nate. Too much going on his career.'

I looked at her, eyebrow cocked.

'Career? Really?'

She slapped a hand to her mouth and laughed. 'Sorry, you must think I'm a loon. Hard though, isn't it? You still think of things carrying on the way they were before, don't you?'

When I made no reply, she looked at me and cocked her head.

'Or maybe not?'

I searched for Arthur and Alice, aware that I'd taken my eye off them for a full five seconds. 'You can tell your man that there's never a right time for kids. If you want them, have them.'

'I shall tell him that, indeed, thank you. I'm Mary, by the way. Mary Higgs.'

'Beth. Pleased to meet you.'

'Likewise.'

We sat for a while watching the children play. A squabble of gulls that had been following the ship began to make tentative swoops for non-existent food, at which three deckhands launched a counter-attack with brooms. The crowd tittered and cheered at their efforts. All apart from Gerald, who remained disgruntled behind his book.

Mary sniffed. 'I've always thought it was a shame about seagulls.'

'What do you mean?'

'Well, look at them. Big beaks, huge wingspans, expert dive-bombers. They're perfect hunting machines, and what have they become? Scavengers. They'd rather pick through bin bags than do what they were designed to do.'

'Maybe they didn't like doing what they were designed to do.'

'We all like doing what we're designed to do.'

'You reckon?'

'Of course, otherwise we wouldn't do it. We're all put here for a reason.'

I looked away, preparing for that terrible silence that opens up between two people who have just realised they're from different planets. But Mary closed it before it began.

'Don't worry, I'm not a God-botherer.'

'I don't mind if you are.'

'Well, I'm not. What I mean is that I believe there's a purpose to everything, and we all have our own one to find – the thing we're designed for.'

'And what is it you think you're designed for?'

A strange look flitted across her face, like a bird taking flight. 'I haven't found it yet, but I can see you have. You only have to look at the way you are with your kids.'

I gave a dry laugh. 'Is that my purpose, Mary? To be a mother?'

She dipped her head like a scolded child. 'I'm sorry, I didn't mean …'

I realised I had crossed my arms. I uncrossed them, feeling bad.

'It's all right. I know what you meant. But I think you're wrong. The only thing we're designed to do is survive.' I nodded at the last remaining gull, which was hovering, open-beaked, above the three broom-wielding deckhands. 'That's all that bird's doing, surviving. Hunting or scavenging, doesn't matter.'

'It must be hard, just you and the kids,' said Mary.

'We do just fine.'

'What happened to their daddy?'

'He's still alive.'

'Then your daughter was telling the truth last night? He's really coming?'

I hesitated. 'That's his plan.'

'Right. Sounds like it's complicated.'

Suddenly there was a tremendous groan and the ship lurched. Cries of alarm shattered the silence left by the stopped engines. 'Christ, not again. Alice? Arthur?' I stood and made for the play area.

Mary's hand was still on my arm.

'It's OK,' she said. 'They're fine, look, over there.'

Mary pointed to where Alice had safely rolled against the netting. Arthur was on his side, giggling.

'Just like last night. What's going on?'

The deck vibrated as the engines restarted. Those who had stood sat down again, and the deck filled with disgruntled mutters.

'Bloody disgrace,' I heard Gerald mutter. 'Ought not to be afloat at all.'

Mary rolled her eyes at me. Then she frowned, remembering something.

'Your husband – is he the one who tried to get on at the gangplank?'

'That's him. Did you see?'

'No, but I heard someone talking about him last night.'

'Who?'

Just then there was a commotion of boots and voices from the deck above. In unison we looked up to see two men surrounded by three uniformed guards and Captain Ulrich. The sun was low and behind them, so I couldn't make out their faces, but I heard the larger of the two protesting. He had been placed in handcuffs.

Mary raised her eyebrows. 'It was him, as it happens.'

I stood up and shielded my eyes from the sun's glare. The man's hair shook as he struggled in the grip of two guards.

'Holy shit –'

'Get your hands off me you seal-fucking nob-jockeys!'

'– that's Bryce.'

'Hey! That was my arse, you bloody pervert! Get your hands off my arse! This is molestation! Are you bastards seeing this down there? I'm being fucking molested here! You're all witnesses! All o' yous!'

'Do you know him?' said Mary.

'I do. Both of them.'

'Bryce,' said the other man, just as tall but slimmer in every way. 'Calm down, for Christ's sake.'

'That's Richard.'

'Look, officer,' said Richard, attempting to take Ulrich to the side. 'I can vouch for this man, all right? He wasn't even in the camp and we weren't anywhere near Falmouth for longer than a day. He was with me all the time and I have the correct papers. There's no way he could have contracted the virus.'

There were gasps from the deck at this word. Gerald slammed his paperback shut and stood.

'Virus?' he said. 'I demand you get that man off this deck at once!'

Some other passengers shouted in agreement and the captain approached the railing, palms out.

'Ladies, gentlemen, please do not panic.' His words were like ripples in Scandinavian cream.

'Panic?' Gerald again, pudgy fists now pressed firmly against handles which I hoped, for Mildred's sake, had not been used for love in a long time. 'That bloody hippy shouldn't be aboard this ship! He could infect us all!'

'Hippy?' Bryce swung his head, finding Gerald beneath. 'Who are you calling "hippy", cobweb cock? Come up here and say that to my face you lardy old *mmph, mmph!*'

He disappeared as a third guard slapped a hand over his mouth, pulling him back.

'Well I never.' Gerald shook his head glumly. 'Bloody disgrace. Should throw the blaggard overboard right now if you ask me.'

There were more people on their feet now, each adding their own tuts of disapproval. A woman with huge sunken eyes and two missing teeth spoke. ''Ere, I thought this was supposed to be an evacuation, not a bleedin' plague ship!'

'Madam,' said the captain, 'I can assure you we have the situation under control, if you could just settle down and try not to panic.'

But the crowd had decided, and Ulrich withered beneath the might of a hundred badly formed British arguments.

'I can vouch for him too,' I said, above the din. The noise abated and all heads swung to me. Richard peered down over the railing. 'Beth? Is that you?'

'I said get off me!' Bryce wrestled free of the guards and looked over too. He grinned. 'Beth. Lovely to see you, doll. Where's Ed?'

'You ... know this man?' said the officer.

'I do. He arrived with my husband only yesterday. They were nowhere near the camp, I promise you.'

The officer looked between me, Bryce and the crowd. 'Could you come up here, please, madam?'

'Of course. I'll just get my kids—'

But Mary's hand was on my arm again. 'Don't worry, I can watch them.'

I hesitated. 'Are you sure?'

'Of course, I'd be happy to. You go and do what you need to do.'

'Right. OK. Thanks, Mary.'

She smiled. 'Take your time.'

'Still a bloody disgrace.' I heard Gerald say as I made for the steps. 'Ought to be thrown overboard. Bloody lot of you.'

Chapter 4

They looked different. The last time I had seen them was in Castlelaw Barracks, the day before the helicopters took us. Bryce was still huge but there was less to his face, and his grin was somehow like an impression of itself. Richard's skin was coarse, and there were more lines to his jagged features than I remembered. His eyes shone cobalt in the sun as I mounted the steps, and I don't think I had ever seen him smile before that moment.

'Beth,' said Bryce, still within the guards' grip. 'Where's Ed?'

Captain Ulrich spoke before I could.

'Are you sure you know this man?'

'Look at him,' I said. 'He's not exactly easy to mistake, is he?'

He looked Bryce up and down and puffed through his well-sculpted nose. 'No, I suppose not.'

'One-in-a-million, buddy,' said Bryce with a wink.

'Yes, well, Mr *One-in-a-million*, you have stowed away on a vessel belonging to *Sauver*, an arm of the United Nations, possibly endangering the lives of its passengers and crew. More to the point, you were found vomiting over the side.'

Bryce grimaced. 'I don't like boats.'

Ulrich continued. 'By rights I should eject you at the next port. Or, as your friend downstairs says –' he pushed his face towards Bryce '– *throw you overboard*.'

'You wouldnae,' he said, sizing him up. 'Nah, you wouldnae. I told you, I was nowhere near the camp, and I'm seasick, not ill. If I was I would never have got on board. There're kids here, for fuck's sake. I'm not a monster.'

The captain hardened his frosty glare. Bryce's grin drooped like a black lily.

'Tell me you wouldnae!'

Eventually the captain's shoulders fell.

'No, I – I *wouldnae*. But the fact remains you are a threat to the safety of this boat. Therefore you must be taken below deck and quarantined in the medical centre until you have been tested thoroughly.' He turned to the guards. 'Take him now, please, and ensure that he is restrained until further notice.'

'Aw, fuck,' said Bryce, kicking his heels as the guards dragged him away down the deck. 'How long do I have to be down there?'

'Five days,' said the captain. 'Maybe more. We must be sure.'

'Buckets!' he called back as he disappeared through a door. 'You'd better have plenty of buckets down there, that's all I'm saying. Plenty of buckets!'

The captain took a deep breath and turned to me.

'Mrs ...?'

'Beth,' I said. I caught a flicker in Richard's expression. 'Just Beth.'

'Well, *just Beth*, I hope you are right about your friend. Otherwise you've put everyone in great danger, including your children. Now, if you'll excuse me.'

He went to leave, but I stopped him.

'Why does the ship keep stopping?'

'A minor fault. Nothing to worry about.'

'It's happened three times already,' said Richard. 'And we've barely been at sea a day.'

The captain looked him up and down. 'Like I said, a minor fault. Some problem with the diagnostics software, I believe. It is being addressed, but as I am sure you are aware we are short-staffed. Now please, I must get back to my station.'

'Software?' I said. 'What kind of software?'

He frowned. 'I have no idea, I am not a systems engineer. But I believe we run on Unix.'

'Unix? I know that. I could … help if … if you like?'

He gave me a quizzical look. 'Thank you, but that won't be necessary. Now, if you will excuse me, I must get back.'

When he had left, I slumped on the railing, staring out at the expanse of sea that separated us from the land. 'Christ, what was all that about? "Please, sir, can I help you fix your ship?" I feel like a bloody idiot.'

Richard laughed. 'You were only offering to help. It's better than sitting down there sunbathing with the rest of them.'

'Perhaps.' I turned to him. 'How are you, anyway? How's ...' I paused again, like I had done with Mary, because I remembered he'd had a boy. 'Richard, I'm sorry, I haven't seen your son. I tried to stay with him at the barracks when the helicopters came, but he was put on a different one to us and when we landed, well, you know what the camps were like, I searched for him, but—'

He touched my shoulder, smiling. 'Beth, it's fine, I found Josh.'

'Oh, that's good news.'

'He's on board too, just below deck. Bit of a dicky tummy.'

That warm imprint of his hand was still on my shoulder. He noticed and snatched it away. 'And, er, how are you doing? Your kids OK?' He nodded down at the play area, where Mary and Alice were now sitting together, playing some invisible game with their fingers. 'I see you've got some help there. That's good.' He gave me a nervous look. 'I assume Ed didn't make it on board.'

'They wouldn't let him. No papers.'

'Damnit, I'm sorry.'

I frowned. 'Wait a minute, how did Bryce get on?'

His expression hardened. 'Seems he snuck on when all the attention was on you and your husband, which doesn't seem at all fair to me.'

He shook his head, lips tight. 'So what's Ed's plan?'

'Beg pardon?'

'I assume he's finding his own way to Cape Town?'

He spoke as if there was nothing extraordinary about the words. I laughed; a spasm of surprise.

'Are you serious?'

'Why wouldn't I be?'

'Richard, I'm surprised my husband even made it out of Edinburgh, let alone all the way to Cornwall. I can only assume it was down to your help. How did you do it anyway, did you find a car or something?'

He gave his own involuntary laugh at this.

'Car? No. We ran, Beth.'

'Ran? But that's, like, four or five hundred miles.'

'More. And it was Ed's idea. He's the one who started running.'

I stared blankly back at him, trying to conjure an image of Ed running, but it just wouldn't come.

'What about the others? The soldiers who were left. Grimes, was she with you? And that old man, Harvey wasn't it?'

He shook his head. 'They didn't make it. But Beth, I have no doubt your husband will be doing everything he can to get to South Africa. In fact –' he looked towards the front of the ship '– at this rate I wouldn't be surprised if he gets there before us. You were right to offer Ulrich help, Beth. He needs it. He's just not telling us.'

'How do you mean?'

'I was chatting to someone last night, a retired merchant seaman from Plymouth, who told me about these ships.' He tapped the handrail. 'They're not as shiny and new as they look. They've been cobbled together in a hurry, bits and bobs from other systems, hybrids basically. He thinks they're unstable, untested, not fit for sea.'

'Surely they wouldn't try to evacuate us in ships they thought would sink?'

'They may not have had a choice.'

'Well, so long as we get to Cape Town. It's not that much of a journey, is it? And we've got the rest of the fleet for support.'

He nodded ahead. 'Do you see any other ships?'

I peered ahead into the hazy southern skyline, but the trail of distant dots that had been our fleet was no longer visible. I felt a chill. 'We're being left behind.'

'Way behind. We should be at the Bay of Biscay by now, but we've barely crossed the channel. And what's more we're drifting off course. Our longitude's all wrong. We're far further west than we need to be.'

Richard had a way of talking that made me want to up my game. I found myself saying things I wouldn't normally say.

Things such as this: 'You appear very well versed in nautical affairs. How come?'

Nautical affairs.

'I used to be a wreck diver,' he replied. 'Back in the day. Did a fair bit of sailing in the Med. Boy's stuff, really, nothing serious.'

'Right.'

I looked at him, staring into the wind with those steely eyes of his. Though slim, his chest was broad and taut, and I followed the sinews in his neck down the length of his arms. It was a natural physique, one that could not have been sculpted within a gym. But it was his eyes that drew me in; they seemed to hide stories.

It felt strange to let my gaze wander over him freely like this – dangerous, yet somehow acceptable, as if I was hanging over a ravine from a safety rope. The last man I had appraised in this way was Ed as I watched him change one morning in the barracks. The view then was, well, different.

He'd put on weight in the five years of our marriage, but that wasn't the problem. Everything else was the problem. The stoop, the downturned mouth, the lethargy in his movements. In my opinion there's absolutely nothing wrong with a bit of chunk on a man, so long as he's happy. But Ed wasn't happy, and it showed in everything he did.

Richard glanced at me and I looked away, following the white trails of froth in the boat's wake.

'Better go,' he said. 'See if Josh is feeling any perkier.'

'Aye,' I said, straightening up. 'Me too, better get back to the kids.'

We stood facing each other, caught in that awkward moment where possibilities present themselves without warning. Suddenly the ship gave another lurch and he fell into me. I caught him by the elbows and we froze for a few seconds, looking at each other, trapped in our own inertia.

When the moment had passed, the engines started again and he pulled away, clearing his throat.

'It's, er, good to see you, Beth. Bye.'

He strode off down the deck, and I watched every single step he took until he'd disappeared inside.

Go ahead. Throw your stones.

It won't take much to break the glass in this house.

Chapter 5

For two days we continued south. Richard was right: we were straying west and the coast to which we should have been hugging grew further away by the hour. There was no sign of our fleet, and we grew accustomed to the ship's regular engine failures. Twice every hour we would feel the deck lurch, finding railings or doors upon which to steady ourselves and enduring the minute or two of silent drift before the engines rumbled and we were away again.

But that wasn't all. There were other things wrong with the ship. During one lurch, an old lady was hit in the hip by an unbolted canteen chair, and electric shocks from door handles and metal bannisters became commonplace. The crew seemed distracted, and occasionally we would see troops of them hurrying between decks or disappearing behind doors. We gave them our complaints but nothing was done, and Ulrich was nowhere to be seen.

Mary and I gravitated to one other, and she slipped effortlessly into a role as part-time carer. If I had to go to the toilet or back to the cabin, she would always be there to look after the kids, and it had been a long time since I had seen Alice smile so much.

'So when am I going to meet this husband of yours?' I said, one afternoon on deck.

She gave me a worried smile. 'He's sick.'

'What, like, seasick?'

'No, Nate's got the constitution of an ox. It's something else. I'm worried, to be honest, he's never ill.'

I looked around the deck. I hadn't seen Richard since our encounter on the second day, nor any sign of his son.

'Oh, fuck. Mary, you don't think ...?'

Mary shook her head. 'I meant it, Beth, he's never ill.'

'You.'

I looked up as a shadow darkened our spot. It was Mildred, Gerald's wife, looking fierce. 'It was you. Your fault. You're the one who let that beastly man on board, and now he's ill. My Gerald. He's sick!'

She sobbed into a handkerchief. Mary went to console her, but she shook her off.

'And you can get off me as well!' she cried.

She glared at her, then at me, and walked away blowing her nose.

I became aware of a hundred sets of eyes peering at me, and none of them friendly. I stood up.

'Mary, I have to go and see Bryce.'

She nodded. 'Do that. I'll watch the kids.'

I found Bryce deep in the bowels of the ship where the walls murmured with the engines like a deranged choir.

'You cannot enter,' said the pale-skinned nurse, as he pulled down the shutter to his room. 'And do not touch him. Five minutes.'

'Jesus, he's not on death row.'

'Five minutes.'

The nurse walked briskly away down the narrow corridor. I put my face to the grill. Inside was a square cell lit by fluorescent light, and upon a low bed sat Bryce, still cuffed, hunched over a bucket.

'He's got a stick up his arse that one,' he said, spitting into the bucket. His voice was as dry as sand. 'And I'd ram it further up if I could get close enough. He won't even feed me properly. Just fucking ... water, and this weird milky stuff. Tastes like spunk.' He spat again. 'Not that I've ever had the pleasure.'

'Bryce ...'

'Just, you know, that's how I *imagine* it tasting ... oh, Christ ...'

He groaned and heaved. Nothing came up.

'Bryce, what's wrong with you?'

He turned his great head and looked up at me. His hair was lank and in straggles, his eyes drawn and bloodshot. Untold years of untamed beard clamoured for space on his vomit-splattered cheeks.

He raised a smile.

'I'm right as rain, darlin'. Never better.'

'Bryce, I'm serious. People are sick up there.'

His gaze returned to the bucket. 'It's not the virus. I'm just seasick, all right? Besides, I was nowhere near the camp. We never even made it through the fence. Ask

38

Ed, he was with me all the time.' His eyes narrowed, noticing my expression. 'Where is he, anyway?'

'He didn't make it on.'

He straightened up, claiming more of the room's meagre space.

'But I saw him on the gangplank. I fucking *threw* him up there. He was with you. That's when I found my own way on at the back.'

'They wouldn't let him on.'

He watched me for a while, then shrank back to his bucket.

'Well, fuck,' he said. Then: 'He'll find you, Beth. Don't worry, I know he will.'

'That's what Richard said. Why is everyone so convinced of my husband's abilities to cross continents all of a sudden?'

'Because we saw what he was made of, that's why.'

'Crossing Britain's one thing. Crossing Europe and Africa's another. He'd need a boat, for a start.'

Bryce raised his head. 'There was a boat. At the house we stayed in, there was a boat in the garage.'

'He doesn't even know how to sail.'

He turned to me, eyes dark. 'You should learn to have a bit of faith in the people who love you, Beth. It's not every man who'd run alone through a hundred-mile canyon with a broken ankle and nothing to fuel him but crow meat.'

I shook my head, frustrated.

'Whatever, I'm not here to talk about Ed. I just need to know you're sure you were nowhere near the camp. I vouched for you, and if you've brought that virus aboard then I'm in trouble too.'

'I'm telling you, for the last time, I wasnae anywhere near it. I'm not sick, I just fucking hate –' From nowhere he gave a tremendous belch, and a torrent of vomit hit the bucket beneath him. He groaned and wiped his beard. '– boats.'

The speaker hanging above the door crackled.

'Will all passengers please make their way to deck B for an announcement. Deck B, all passengers, thank you.'

'I'd better go,' I said.

'Beth,' he said, as I backed away.

'What?'

He looked back at me through straggles of wet hair.

'He'll come. I'm telling you.'

'Whatever you say, Bryce.'

The deck was full when I returned. I found Mary and the children near the play area and stood with Arthur in my arm and Alice at my hip, ignoring the cold looks from my fellow passengers. Captain Ulrich looked down from the upper deck, a few wisps of cloud feathering the sky behind him.

'Ladies, gentlemen, if I may have your attention please.'

'What's going on?' somebody shouted.

'Yeah, why is everyone getting sick, innit?'

Ulrich raised a hand. 'Please, I understand you are worried, and—'

'My husband's shitting through the eye of a needle,' said another voice.

'Please—'

'Same with my wife. I can barely go in the cabin now, it's like the bloody Somme in there.'

'If I may—'

'It's the virus! That Scottish bloke brought it on!'

The deck boomed with dreary jeers.

This is why I don't like crowds. I mean, I wouldn't say 'people' but ...

Actually yes, people. I don't like people. There, I said it.

People are idiots. Awkward bundles of conflicting desires with a single destination: death. It's no wonder we never got anything done in the days of Kate Winslet. I mean, we thought we did, we thought we've made progress, but we could have had the internet in the fifteenth century if we'd only pulled our fingers out and stopped drowning witches for a second.

And even then, what would we have had? The internet, that's what; what happens when the world has a nice wee chat.

You only have to read the comments to see where that experiment led.

The only reason we managed to crawl to where we were before those asteroids fell was blind luck and the hard work of individuals. Geniuses and visionaries, artists and scientists, independent minds in labs and garrets – they're the ones who made the difference to history. Not the governments. Not the companies. And certainly not the crowds.

This particular crowd was ready to become a mob.

'Silence!' yelled Ulrich, his voice catapulting a register or two. The blood that had suddenly rushed to fill his face abated with the crowd's murmurs. 'There is no virus. Mr Bryce Gower has undergone a thorough physical examination, and our medical team have determined that he is not a carrier.'

'Then why is my wife—?'

'As for the vomiting and diarrhoea affecting some of your fellow passengers, this, I am afraid, is due to a bout of food poisoning.' He cleared his throat. 'The clams, as I understand it.'

'Bloody disgrace,' mumbled a voice, which had to be Gerald's.

'This is regrettable, but you are in no immediate danger. However—'

'Why are we drifting west?' It was Richard's voice. 'And where is our fleet?'

A cold silence gripped the deck. Ulrich turned in his direction. 'As I was about to say, we have more pressing matters to attend to. South Africa is no longer our destination. Please –' he held out his palms once again to the triggered crowd '– let me continue. According to our communication channels, Cape Town is no longer safe.'

'Why?' The question echoed from larynx to larynx.

'We do not have details, only that it has been … overrun.'

Alice shot me a look, fingers at her mouth. 'Mummy? What about Daddy?'

I pulled her close, stunned by her understanding, and tightened my grip on Arthur. 'It's OK, darling, Daddy will know.'

She nodded, satisfied, still pulling at her lips. How easy it is to lie to your children.

'Then where the hell are we going?' said Richard.

'Across the Atlantic to what was once Florida. We have word that a safe haven has opened up near Daytona Beach, an archipelago with plenty of room and supplies.' Ulrich scanned the crowd with a hopeful smile. 'This actually makes our route shorter by some margin, and we should arrive in less than fifteen days. Until then, please try to enjoy the journey, if you can.'

'Enjoy?' said Gerald. 'How can we enjoy it? There's bugger all to do apart from read second-rate paperbacks.' He held up the one he had been reading. 'This one's falling to bits, and it's missing the last ruddy page!'

I felt Mary bristle next to me. 'It's not a sodding cruise ship, you miserable twat. It's an evacuation. You're lucky to be alive.'

Gerald slowly turned his head in our direction. He narrowed his eyes. 'Lucky to be alive. Yes, you'd know all about that wouldn't you, *Mary*.'

They glared at each other for a few seconds before Ulrich raised those placating palms of his once more.

'Please,' he said, 'there is no need to argue, and I know how tedious long voyages can be. Take it from someone with experience!' He laughed, but it was just him, and it soon disappeared. He cleared his throat in the silence. 'The crew are already working on some entertainment for you. We will update you in due course. Thank you for your time.'

'Hear that, Alice?' I said as the crowd dispersed. 'We're going to Florida. That's where Disneyland is. Maybe you'll see a princess.'

'She told you, Mummy,' said Mary. 'She's a pirate, not a princess, isn't that right, Ally-bally?'

Alice grinned back at her, then threw me a firm salute.

'Sorry, darling, I'm sure there are pirates there too.'

Gerald passed, shooting Mary a look. She stretched her most painful smile back.

'What was all that about back there?' I said.

She shook her head. 'I don't have the foggiest. He just doesn't like me.' She smiled and raised her eyebrows. 'Can't all be friends, can we?'

'Miss, er, Beth?'

I turned to see the captain standing behind me, hands behind his back.

'Yes?'

He gave me a weak smile.

'You mentioned to me that you had some experience with computers.'

'That's right.'

'Well, some of our crew have also been incapacitated by the food poisoning, including the engineer who was working on the diagnostics system. I was wondering if you would mind taking a look?'

'Oh.' I flushed. 'Of course, I'd be happy to. Er, when do you want me to start?'

He shrugged. 'Now is as good a time as any, but I'm afraid I cannot allow children into the systems room. It is not safe.'

'Right, well, I'll need to find someone to watch—'

Mary had already taken Alice's hand. She reached for Arthur, giving me a wink as I let him go.

'Go do your stuff, I've got you covered.'

Chapter 6

Do you remember your first kiss? I do. Pete Drever, third year, in a slow spin upon the park roundabout. It was actually quite sweet – not the sweaty, ham-fisted face-gobble I'd heard some other girls describe. Pete and I lived on the same estate, so we'd often walk home through the park together, and that afternoon we found that we were holding hands, and he kissed me. It was a rare and wonderful moment of teenage spontaneity with a successful outcome; our mouths just happening to collide at just the right angle, and with just enough space between the lips to classify it as a fully fledged snog.

Loved Pete for that.

Nothing came of it, though. We stopped at the first door, not going on to explore the other rooms in the dank palace of pubescent sexuality. That would happen much later, at college, with a boy called Jamie. He was nice too, but I knew I was a little – I don't know – *late* to the party, so perhaps I was a little eager to get the job done. He seemed upset afterwards. Felt bad for him.

First kiss, first shag, what else? First hair, first period, first drink, first orgasm …

Why are these all the firsts?

Why are these the milestones we're encouraged to remember? What kind of grizzly photo album is this to carry through your life?

Why not: first genuine joke that made a friend laugh?

Easy: Knock knock. Who's there? Interrupting doctor. Interrupting doc—You've got cancer.

First sunrise witnessed alone.

16 July 1991, day after Granny's funeral, no sleep, watching blossom drift from the tree in her garden and listening to Grandad's whisky-soaked sobs downstairs.

First sentence that made your heart stop.

The Grapes of Wrath by John Steinbeck: 'And her joy was nearly like her sorrow.'

First time you closed a book and felt grief.

Wide Sargasso Sea by Jean Rhys.

First film that made you openly weep.

Dirty Dancing. Sue me.

Puberty's full of such magnificent moments; it's not just fumblings and embarrassments and awkward realisations. After the haze of childhood, we're finally coming alive, and every feeling's new and raw. It can be as wonderful as it is terrible, just like the rest of life.

I can still remember the first computer program I wrote. I was fourteen and it was on that knocked-off Amstrad my grandad had won in the pub.

'It's a heap o' shite, Bob,' yelled my granny from the kitchen. It was sitting on the sideboard, a neat beige cube next to a battered cardboard box. 'It's Christmas next week and we've precious little space as it is. I want rid o' it!'

'Aye, aye, aye,' my grandad replied, losing himself in his paper. 'Right enough.'

I peered into that musty box full of mysterious disks, cables and possibilities.

'Can I borrow it, Grandad?'

He looked at me over his paper.

'Aye,' he said. 'Course you can, hen. Till I find someone who'll buy the bastard.'

It took me the best part of an hour to carry it the four alleyways back to our house, supporting the rapidly perishing box with my knee, gripping wires in my mouth and stopping every ten paces to pick up a wayward disk. I spent all night trying to work that thing, and this is when the closest thing to Google was a monochrome fantasy on films like *War Games* or *D.A.R.Y.L.* I listened to the manual, helpfully recorded onto a C-90 cassette by the poor old train spotter from whom it had been – I now imagine – nicked, on my Walkman. I read the three magazines that had come with it, trying to understand this new language of daunting half-words and acronyms like ROM, RAM and CP/M. I typed 'DIR' and 'DATE' and felt electrified when I was rewarded with a response. And I ran BASIC, told it to print my name on the screen, then told it to do it again forever.

On Christmas Day I got a puzzle in my cracker made from four cubes with coloured faces, which you had to arrange in a row so that not two adjacent faces were the same colour. I grew impatient with it, so I snuck upstairs to sketch out the problem on graph paper. Soon I had a verbose and unwieldy program running to test every one of the 1296 combinations, and three hours later – to my intense delight – the mighty 4MHz processor had spewed out its solution. I proudly announced this downstairs, only to find that my grandad had completed the puzzle in five minutes.

But it didn't matter. I had done it, and I was hooked.

With the small stack of fivers and sellotaped coins I'd amassed from Christmas cards and the fists of the well-meaning drunks who staggered in and out of the house during the festive period, I bought a brand-new *PCW* magazine and scoured the catalogue at the back for programming tools on which to spend the rest. I stayed up late learning about functions, procedures and arrays, and becoming mildly terrified by concepts like screen memory and machine code. At the weekend I'd stay up even later, with a stash of Vimto and Wotsits by my desk and Tommy Vance's *Friday Rock Show* on my headphones. I wrote games featuring protagonists made from letters and numbers, who scurried around the screen eating punctuation marks. I built entire worlds from numbers, carved flickering ideas from fat green pixels.

I became lost in it, this little universe that was under my control, in which the worst consequence I faced was a divide-by-zero or (dear God, have mercy upon us) an infinite loop requiring a hard reset and the potential loss of code.

And it wasn't just a phase. I was still doing this two years later, at an age when the reputation of my city demanded that I spend my evenings swilling MD 20/20 and allowing myself to be fingered against some rusty, rain-soaked railings. I managed to avoid all that, thankfully.

My mother grew worried.

'You should be out having fun,' she said, whipping a tea towel over her shoulder. 'Making friends, a girl of your age. It's not right that you spend all that time up in your room.'

My dad said nothing. He knew what happened against those railings.

More than anything else I liked the feeling of being alone, and learning that being alone didn't have to mean being alone with your thoughts.

I directed all mine into the heart of that machine, solving problems the same way people climb mountains. The same way they sail seas.

I would think back to this period of my life when, years later, I attended interviews.

'And what would you say were your weaknesses, Miss Fenton? Would you say you were a team player?'

Absolutely not. I will only come and work for you if you keep those people away from me. I will require an airtight, lockable room with three forty-one-inch monitors, a top-of-the-range sound system, windows optional. Oh, and an unlimited supply of Jaffa Cakes too, please. In fact you can pay me in Jaffa Cakes; I honestly don't mind.

'Oh, totally. Team player, that's me all right. Human contact, well, it's like oxygen to me. I'd die without it.'

Listen.

I'm only telling you this because it led to what happened next. And what happened next is extremely hard for me to tell you about. Every night I live with the nightmare of what could have, what didn't and what did happen because of my actions.

So, what was it exactly that I did?

I retreated into my happy little world, that's what I did. I went below deck and set myself to the task of fixing Captain Ulrich's broken diagnostics systems. I spent all day, the next, and the next, down in that windowless room reading manuals, examining installations and poring through source code, just like I had done in my bedroom all those years ago.

They brought me tea and biscuits – not Jaffa Cakes, unfortunately – and in the safety I somehow perceived that great floating hulk of steel and aluminium provided, I broke down the problem and addressed it bit by bit. Bit by bit I fixed their system.

And all the while, Mary Higgs looked after my children in the decks above. She played with them, took them to the toilet, fed them.

Grew close to them.

And I trusted her.

Why wouldn't I?

In the evenings I would emerge onto the floodlit deck, a little dazed and groggy from twelve hours of work, and find Mary with the children.

'They've been no bother at all,' she would say. 'We've had fun, haven't we, Alice? And how are you getting on?'

'Good,' I'd reply, mind still chugging through whatever problem I had just left, and eager to return. 'Almost there, I think.'

Once the kids were asleep in the cabin, I'd stay up enjoying the novelty of a warm evening on board a ship in December. Mary and I would talk until it was time to return to her husband in the cabin. I remember I found the fact that he was still unwell strange, given that almost everyone else had recovered from the stomach upset. But I filed it away with every other little alarm bell that jangled, and forgot about it.

I told you already, throw your stones. I'm the one that has to live with it.

One evening I met Richard and Josh lying on loungers, watching the night sky. Richard sat up as I approached.

'Join us?' he said, offering an empty lounger.

'I was just going to bed.'

He frowned: 'Just for a bit? Great sky tonight, right Josh?'

His son looked between us, and I had the sense that he had just witnessed his father behave unusually.

'Hi Josh,' I said, to fill the silence. 'How have you been?'

This was not just small talk – I meant: *How have you been coping with this business of surviving? Have did you manage to cope for three weeks on your own in a camp, knowing that your mother was dead, and fearing the same for your father?*

He looked back at me, clicking two fingernails together. His features were still being manhandled by adolescence, and it was still hard to pick apart the man from the boy. I had a feeling the boy was winning.

'I'm all right,' he said.

Richard gave me a glance that told me he wasn't.

'New Year's Eve tomorrow, isn't that right, Joshy?'

He clapped a palm hard on his son's shoulder and shook it. It was a display I'd seen countless times before from my father to my brother, from boy to boy after a playground tussle, from PE teacher to the thirteen-year-old prop forward who's just crawled out from a collapsed scrum – always between males; if my mother had ever done it to me I would have leaped from my skin. The impact was just a little too hard to be comfortable, the rub just a little too aggressive to be fraternal; it was a reminder, barely encrypted in the gloomy cyphers of male communication. Pain must not be shown. Whatever it is you're feeling, bury it, just like this.

And that's what Josh did. I saw it in his eyes, some-where in the middle of his father's rough jostles he buried it; it broke my heart not to know what it was or why it was not allowed to exist.

But in its place he found a smile, which he turned to me.

'Yeah, they're putting on a film up on deck. Kind of like those outside cinema things with deckchairs and that. Are you coming?'

I smiled. 'Wouldn't miss it for the world. I'm sure Alice and Arthur will love it.'

'I'll save you a seat,' said Richard. He turned to Josh. 'Won't we, son?'

'Seat for what?' I turned at the unmistakable rumble behind me. There stood Bryce, wearing knee-length black shorts and a fresh T-shirt emblazoned with a picture of some Hawaiian sunset. His face was still pale, but the air around him suggested a recent wash.

'Bryce, you look ... better.'

'Shut up. I know I look like shite.'

'You've got less vomit on you at any rate.'

He grunted. 'Aye, which is more than can be said for my clothes. They gave me these.' He looked grimly down at his attire, picking at the fabric that strained at the extremities of bicep, chest and belly. 'Bit wee, aren't they?'

'You look fine. Really, you do.'

He sniffed and held his stomach. 'I don't feel it, but there's nothing else to come up. What's all this about seats?'

'There's a film tomorrow,' I said, 'up here on deck.'

'That right?'

'Yeah,' said Josh. 'Dad said he'd save a seat for Beth.'

Bryce paused in the awkward silence that followed, still grinning behind his beard, and gave Richard and me a look apiece. 'Did he now? Well, isn't that nice.'

I sensed it was time to go.

'I'm off to bed,' I said. 'Glad you're feeling better Bryce. Night.'

I tried to make sure Richard wasn't the last one my eyes landed on, but something made me glance at him as I left, and it felt as obvious as if I'd just sounded a foghorn.

We have limits, you see, us humans. Life can only throw so much at you before you just tell it where to go, and you find yourself reverting to easy things like finding someone attractive and liking the fact that they seem to feel the same about you.

That and neglecting your children, apparently.

I hurried away, head down, and made for the cabin.

'Night,' called Bryce in sing-song. 'See you tomorrow, if there are any seats left ...'

Chapter 7

The next day I worked as usual. Around mid-afternoon I was close to finishing when I felt my chair vibrate. The desk too, and everything on it, rattled and buzzed in a subsonic thrum. It didn't feel like the engines. It felt much further away.

After ten seconds the vibration intensified until, with a single shockwave that sent my glass flying from the desk and smashing to the floor, it stopped. With a groan, the ship rose and fell in a single oscillation, causing me to slip from my chair and more items to fall from the desk on top of me.

I heard shouts from above. I scrambled to my feet and ran up the stairs.

The deck was scattered with upturned deckchairs and broken glass. All around were people either on their backs or standing, holding their heads. I ran through the bewildered crowd.

'Alice! Arthur!'

There was no sign of them at the play area, and the bench where Mary usually sat with them was empty.

'Mary!'

I took the staircase to the upper deck, squinting in the low sun. The boat still bobbed in the wake of whatever had just happened.

'Beth, we're over here.'

Through a gap in the railings I spied Mary on a different bench. For a second I thought she was alone. My heart derailed.

But then I saw them; Arthur on her lap and Alice standing, holding her ear and looking peeved. With a curse of relief I sprang up the remaining steps and darted across the deck, pulling them into a hug.

'What happened?' I said, kissing Alice fiercely on the head.

'I don't know,' said Mary. 'One minute we were sitting here enjoying the sun, and then suddenly it felt like we'd been dropped. You know like in an aeroplane? Then we were tossed up again, weren't we Ally-Bally?'

Alice nodded.

'I hurt my ear.'

'Where?' I said.

'You did, didn't you, pet?' said Mary. 'Let Mary have a look-see.'

Mary reached for Alice's hand, but she pulled away.

'Ow.'

'Just a quick look, Alice, come on.' She reached again.

'Owww!'

'Mary, she's hurt.'

'Come on, Alice, just a peek.'

On Mary's third attempt I batted her hand away, and she flinched. Guarding her hand, she sat up straight and looked down at me, mouth shut.

'Alice,' I said. 'Can Mummy have a look?'

'It's sore.'

'I know, I won't touch, pinky promise.'

Reluctantly she let me peel away her hand, revealing a sharp graze on her left lobe. It was nothing serious. I kissed her again. 'Ouch, brave girl. Come on, let's sit down.'

I lifted Arthur onto the bench and sat with him on my knee, Alice on the other side. Arthur was gurning, watching the disoriented passengers move around us. 'And are you all right, wee man?'

He tried some noises, some *humnums* and *baggers*. He was yet to say his first word.

'Nothing fazes you, eh?'

I turned to Mary. She was still holding her hand, wide-eyed and quiet like a child before a headmistress. It was as if her emotional circuits were being rebooted. She tried a smile.

'Did he get a bump?' I said.

She shook her head.

'What about you, are you all right?'

She shook her head again, running a finger down the ligament of her index finger, the place where I had brushed her off.

'Thanks for looking after them. I'm … I'm sorry I …'

'That's OK,' she said, looking out over the eerily calm sea. There was a weight to her stare I hadn't seen before, like an unseen anchor dragging her down. 'You're her mother, not me.'

'I know, but you've done so much for me over the last few days. I feel like some, I don't know, one of those Botoxed Miami housewives who's just hit the maid –' I caught myself '– not that that's how I see you, Mary, please, oh, shit …'

Brightening, she laughed and let her hand fall to her lap.

'It's all right, I understand. I'd have done the same. And honestly, I love looking after your kids. They're wonderful.' She turned to Alice. 'We're like a little club, aren't we, Ally-Bally? We look after each other.'

I thought about Carol's Survivors Club, and how different it might have been had Mary been part of it.

'What?' said Mary, noticing my smile.

'Nothing. Thank you, that's all.'

'Don't mention it. Besides, it's given me something to do while Nate's been ill. Speaking of which, I'd better go and see if he's OK after what just happened.'

'Of course, go on, go.'

She stood and paused, as if something had occurred to her. Turning, she gave me a curtsey, hands clasped demurely. 'If it's all the same to you, ma'am?'

'Get out,' I said, laughing. 'Go and see to your man.'

With a smile, and a wink for Alice, she left.

We sat there for a while in the sunshine, thumb-wrestling with Alice and playing peek-a-boo with

Arthur, until gradually everyone had found their seats and the deck had returned to normal. Eventually the speakers crackled with Captain Ulrich's voice.

'Ladies and gentlemen, I do apologise for that, ah, disruption. We're not sure exactly what that was, but occasionally we do see certain anomalies in currents when crossing deep water.'

The words 'deep water' made my insides heave unexpectedly. I had never been this far out to sea, and the thought of all that space beneath us, filled with darkness, cold and life, gave me vertigo. Alice was at the edge of the bench, inches from the fence that separated the deck from a fifty-foot drop into the ocean. I had a flash of her tumbling in, legs and arms wheeling, curls streaming behind, no scream – a cruel flash of the nightmare lurking – and although the fence was ten feet high and unscalable, I pulled her close.

'In any case, I am happy to report that there has been no damage, and no serious injury, so you will be pleased to know that we will be continuing without delay. Thank you.'

Mary returned and sat down.

'How is he?' I asked.

She curled her lip. 'Milking it a bit now, if you ask me. But he's fine. Thanks for asking.'

'Did you hear the announcement? An "anomaly", whatever that means.'

She frowned, concerned. 'Nate said it's most likely due to some disturbance far away. A shockwave.'

'More of those things falling, you think?'

'Maybe.'

Alice tugged my sleeve.

'Mummy, when are we there?'

'Oh, darling, it'll be a few days yet, I'm afraid. But there's a film on tonight. Shall we go?'

She nodded. Just then the engines stopped, and there was the usual groan from all around. My thoughts snapped back to the work I had left downstairs.

'Why do we keep stopping?' moaned Alice.

'Because, Ally-Bally, the boat's got tummy ache,' said Mary. Glancing at me for permission, she reached across and pulled Alice over to her side of the bench. 'But luckily your mummy's very clever and she's trying to make it better. Isn't that right, Mummy?'

She smiled and nodded in the direction from which I'd come.

'*Go,*' she mouthed.

'*Sure?*' I mouthed back.

Mary held one of Alice's hands in hers.

'So, you and me'll look after Arthur, won't we? And Mummy will finish making the boat better and meet us later for the film. Sound good?'

Alice plucked at her lip and looked at me, considering the options. Finally, with a sigh too heavy for a child, she gave me a nod.

'I won't be long,' I said, 'I promise.'

*

I promise.

To this day those words still haunt my dreams and gatecrash daily activities without warning. They'll be with me forever, reminding me.

I promise.

When I had finished I sat back and rubbed my eyes. The room was still and quiet, apart from the constant hum of the engines, and I stared at the results of my last test: all positive. I ran it again: same result.

I had fixed it – there was no doubt.

I stretched and stood up, dizzy with my little victory, and left the room. The corridors were empty, but one deck up I bumped into an engineer engrossed in a clipboard.

'Excuse me, do you know where I can find the captain?'

She looked me up and down. 'Why?'

'I've been helping with the diagnostics systems, I think I fixed it, actually, so I just need—'

'Most of the crew and passengers are up on deck. The captain wanted to speak to everyone before the film.'

'Film? What time is it?'

'Almost 8.15 p.m.'

'Oh, bollocks!' It was much later than I'd thought. The film was due to start at eight, and Alice would be wondering where I was. 'Sorry, thanks.'

I found my way out onto the upper deck, where rows of deckchairs had been arranged before a pull-down screen. The place was packed, and everyone had taken their seat while the captain spoke at the front. I heard him mumbling something about new beginnings as I scanned the crowd for Mary. The lights were low, and there was little space to move, but I saw her near the front row. Alice and Arthur had a knee each.

'Madam, would you please sit down?' said one of the crew, who was manning the projector.

'I'm trying to get to the front,' I said, struggling to find a way through the tightly packed network of seats. Every movement I made resulted in a hissed complaint.

'Madam,' said the crew member, 'you can't get through that way. You'll have to stand at the back until the interval.'

'Just let me through, will you? My kids are up there.'

'Alternatively you can stand on the balcony above.'

'Why won't you just let me through? Mary!' There were more tuts and mumbles, but Mary didn't turn her head. 'Mary?'

'Madam, *please.*'

'Beth,' I heard the whisper from the row second to the back and saw the shapes of Richard, Josh and Bryce with an empty seat beside them. 'There's a seat for you here, come on.'

I took one last look in Mary's direction. I was sure Arthur saw me – one chubby silhouetted arm pointing excitedly over Mary's shoulder in my direction – but then the captain finished and in the polite applause that followed, I lost him.

'*Madam.*'

I huffed. 'Fine.'

I staggered over fifteen sets of legs to the seat beside Richard.

'You OK?' he said, as I craned my neck over the crowd.

'No, not really.'

'Don't worry.' He touched my knee. 'There's an interval in half an hour. I'm sure you'll be able to get to the front then.'

'Pipe down in front, will you?'

Gerald. Of course it was Gerald. I'd had just about enough of him, and was about to turn and let him know just how much he could fuck off, when the PA speakers gave a loud pop and the crowd yelped.

'Here we go,' whispered Richard, as the screen lit up. 'Hope you've never seen *Finding Nemo*.'

Chapter 8

I counted the minutes, ignoring the film and watching Arthur's head, which I could just make out through the crowd. It was resting on Mary's shoulder. It made me sick to be so far from them, knowing that Alice was wondering where I was or, worse, wasn't. I had never seen *Finding Nemo*, and although I'm sure it is a fine cinematic experience, I never will. Not now.

Half an hour in the speakers popped and the image disappeared.

'Right,' I said in the silence, and went to stand, but Richard put his hand on my knee again. This time there was an urgency to his touch.

'Wait.'

'Ladies, gentlemen –' it was the captain's voice again *'– please remain seated while we, ah, investigate something.'*

'What is it?' I said, adding my own question to all the others firing around me. 'What's happening?'

'I don't know,' said Richard. 'But we've stopped moving.'

'And they've turned all the lights off,' said Bryce.

Sure enough, it wasn't just the projector which had turned off. The deck was in darkness, and we were drifting beneath a cloudless sky, brightly lit by a spray of stars and a high full moon, and—

'Not all of them,' I said, nodding up to the balcony, where a wide beam of light swung.

'That's a searchlight,' said Richard.

'What are they looking for, Dad?' said Josh.

'I don't know, son.'

Some of the passengers were on their feet now, either trying to escape the growing claustrophobia of the deck or pressing crew members for answers. The crowd's energy was growing rapidly, and I felt my chances of getting to Alice and Arthur dwindle with every new upright silhouette.

'I don't know,' said the projectionist, trying to fend off a raft of questions. 'We're looking into it, please sit down.'

'Fuck this,' said Bryce, and got to his feet. "Scuse me, coming through, sorry there, darlin', didn't mean to, whoops, all right, you old pissbag, I didn't mean it.'

'What the hell are you doing?' said Richard, standing.

'I'm going to see what's what, Dick, that's what.'

Finally free, Bryce mounted the steps and leaped up to the balcony. At the top there was a walkway to another flight at the front. If I could get along to it, I could get down to where Mary was sitting. I ran after him.

'Wait,' said Richard. He followed with Josh in tow.

I made it up the stairs and was preparing to make for the other staircase when I stopped. We were on the right side of the boat and up against the tall fence was a line of passengers looking west, pointing.

'What are youse all looking at?' said Bryce, pushing in next to a scrawny, balding man peering through the mesh. 'Hey? You there, Stimpy – what is it?'

The man pointed a quivering finger at something in the distance.

I pushed in next to Bryce. I could feel him shaking beside me. Richard and Josh arrived and we each followed the man's terrified gaze across the moonlit water.

'What is that?' I said.

'That's nothing,' said Bryce. 'Just the horizon.'

'No,' said Richard. 'That's not the horizon. That's a—'

'Wave,' muttered the man, staggering away from the fence. 'Wave. Wave, wave, it's a wave, it's a wave.'

We looked closer. The black line of the horizon appeared to be expanding, with a clear white lip rising into the sky.

'How big is that thing?' said Bryce, gulping.

'Big,' said Richard. 'Possibly a tsunami. It must have been caused by whatever made that thump earlier.'

'Whatever it is it's fast as fuck,' said Bryce, 'and it's coming right for us.'

'What do we do?' I said.

'Nothing,' said Richard. 'We're perfectly safe. Tsunamis only affect shorelines, but we're in deep water so it should pass us by. All we have to do is sit tight, and whatever you do, don't –'

'It's a wave!' screamed the man.

'– panic.'

The man ran with arms flailing. 'A bloody wave!'

The word became itself, rolling through the crowd and growing with each horrified repetition.

'Stop!' cried Richard. 'Calm down, man, we'll be fine so long as we sit tight. We'll just bob up and over it.'

But panic had already gripped the crowd, and it had dispersed to do what it did best: take care of itself.

Richard turned to me. 'We'll be fine, I promise you.'

'I have to get my children,' I said, and ran for the stairs. They were still sitting in their seat with Mary. Arthur was crying and Alice looked around in mute concern.

'I'm here,' I called, waving. 'Mummy's here. Mummy's coming.'

Alice pointed in my direction – she saw me, she did – and I must only have been a few metres from them. Enough to jump, perhaps? Perhaps . . . or perhaps I could have been more brutal. Perhaps I could have pushed a few passengers out of the way, or trampled my way through to get to them quicker. But I didn't, and at that moment the lights blazed and a distorted pre-recorded message blared from the speakers.

'Will all passengers please gather at their nearest muster stations. All passengers, please gather at your nearest muster station, where you will be issued with a life jacket.'

As the message repeated a siren sounded and the crowd surged for the four staircases. A herd of bodies pushed me back up my staircase, lifting me off my feet and away from the deck below.

'No!' I cried, holding out a hand. 'Alice! Arthur!'

Alice heard me and turned. She grabbed Mary's arm and pointed up at me, face crumpling.

'Mary!' I called, struggling against the tide of people. 'Bring them to me, bring my children to me.'

There was a muster station at the top of the stairs towards which the crowd was pushing me, and another at the same place on the opposite side of the boat. Mary glanced between the two options. Then, with a look that contained what I could have sworn was opportunity, she gripped Arthur to her chest, grabbed Alice and ran for the opposite staircase.

The crowd bullied me up the staircase, and before I knew it I was standing on wet wood with a yellow life jacket in my hands. Richard gripped my shoulders.

'Beth, where are your children?'

I looked around. The heaving boat, the wide-eyed crew, the passengers sobbing in terror, they were like objects in a dimly remembered dream. I couldn't feel my legs, my arms, my anything. The distance. The distance was trying to open up.

But I wouldn't let it. Not today. The only distance that existed was the one separating me from my children. I glared at the opposite deck.

Richard looked across. 'They're over there?'

'She took them.'

'Then they're safe.'

I looked towards the bow. Ahead was a narrow walkway that joined the two sides of the deck. 'I'm going to get them.'

'No, Beth,' said Richard, pushing me back. 'That thing's going to hit us any minute.'

'I know. That's why I need to get to my children. Understand?'

'No, it's not safe.'

'Get out of my way.'

'The best idea is to sit tight until it passes, and even if we get into difficulty, then we have the lifeboats. They're submersible, see?'

He nodded helpfully at the three flame-red torpedoes.

'Richard.'

'So the worst that can happen is you'll be in a different lifeboat, that's all, until—'

'*Richard!*' The bark of my voice surprised me as much as it did him and everyone else around me. 'Get out of my way.'

He took a step back and I marched past, only to be confronted by the quivering faces of Gerald and Mildred as they fiddled with each other's jackets.

'Move,' I said. And they did.

Halfway across the walkway I saw Alice in the crowd by the opposite muster station. Her face was mangled and wet with tears, and there was Arthur crying too with one pudgy hand thrown in my direction.

Mary was holding him. When she saw me her face hardened.

I steadied myself on the railing and, forcing a smile, called to them.

'It's all right, Mummy's coming. Mary, hand them to me.'

Mary stared back. I looked around to see if anyone was watching, but they were all absorbed in their own panicked preparations. 'Mary, please give me my children.'

She bit her lip, and there it was: the slightest shake of her head, nothing more than a twitch of her neck muscles but enough to make all those half-felt instincts I had brushed aside return with the full force of certainty.

'Mary?'

I braced myself on the railings, ready to pull myself towards her, but as I did the boat gave a deep and terrible groan. The world turned, the stars spun and I was thrown back against the fence.

I fell to my knees, trying to draw breath into my emptied lungs. The ship had turned by ninety degrees and we were now moving backwards, accelerating into the mouth of the rapidly approaching wave. I looked for Mary's muster station, but she had lost herself with the children in the crowd.

'No –' I could only mouth the word '– no.'

I staggered to my feet, instantly thrown against the front railing by the boat's backward acceleration. As I pulled myself back there was a deafening snap from above, and I turned to see that a cable had sprung from one of the lifeboats. The passengers shrieked as the thick metallic cord thrashed like a skinned viper. In one furious whip the cable extended towards me and I ducked. It passed within inches of my head and returned at twice the speed, striking a crew member in the torso with a hideous wet crack.

Without a scream he sailed over the fence and out into the dark ocean, leaving a spray of blood on the yellow fence.

The stunned crowd whimpered and cowered as the cable – now tipped red – continued its violent jig.

'Beth, get up, it's not safe here.'

It was Richard again. He pulled me from the ground as the cable made another pass, and I ran back with him to our muster station.

'My children,' I seethed. 'She's got my fucking children.'

'Who, Mary?' said Bryce. 'That one that looks like Diana Rigg?'

'Who's Diana Rigg?' said Josh.

'Fucking *Avengers*, man, TV show, mind, not that piece o' shite superhero bollocks. I used to fancy her in that. Still do actually. Seen her in that *Game of Thrones*? Wouldnae mind, like, I mean if you had to shag a granny—'

'Yes, Mary!' I yelled, trying to see through the bodies to the opposite deck.

'I thought she was your pal? What's up with her?'

'She's bad news, that one. Bad news.' I turned to see Gerald, life jacket already inflated and tight around his bulging abdomen. He was shaking his head. 'Knew it from the start, didn't I, Mildred?'

'What?' I said. 'What do you know about her?'

He shot me look, grinding his teeth. 'You should never have left them with her. Never. She shouldn't even be on this bloody—'

At that moment the crowd toppled under a sudden surge in the boat's backward acceleration. We were pitching forward as the approaching mountain of water dragged us up its face.

'Hold on to the fence,' I said, grabbing the mesh. Richard, Bryce and Josh managed to anchor themselves behind me, but there were screams as bodies fell past us, gravity pulling them rapidly towards the bow.

'Help!' cried Gerald, sliding down the deck. 'Help! Mildred, Mildred, good God, no ...'

'Take my hand,' I said, reaching for him, but the momentum was already building.

'Gerald,' said Mildred, knuckles white as she gripped the fence. 'Where do you think you're going? Come back here this instant. Come back!'

Bryce stuck out a boot, which Gerald just managed to catch with one hand.

'Got you,' said Bryce. 'Now hold on, buddy, I'm going to lift you up.'

The boat groaned as its pitch rose ever greater, and spray from the sea behind now poured down on us like rain.

'Please,' whimpered Mildred. 'Please don't let go of my husband. Please don't let go, Gerald.'

'I've got you,' said Bryce, grimacing as he tried to lift Gerald's enormous weight with his left leg. 'Hold still, will you?'

Gerald struggled on the deck, legs flailing, mouth agape.

'I can't hold on. I can't—'

Bryce strained. 'Stop struggling!'

'I'm slipping, I'm—'

'Gerald, don't you dare!'

But Gerald's fingers had already failed him, and with a yelp he lost hold of Bryce's boot and shot down the slick deck, arms waving, looking for all the world like a boy at a water park. The last thing we saw was him tumbling past the next muster station, striking a fence post and spinning away at a violent angle into the darkness beneath.

'Stupid bastard,' muttered Bryce, closing his eyes and resting his head against the fence. Mildred, her hair drenched by the spray, watched the space where Gerald had been as if he had merely popped temporarily from existence and would soon reappear. But he didn't, and eventually she blinked and looked away.

I clung to the fence and scanned the opposite deck, met by a dual surge of relief and fury as I saw Mary doing the same. She was holding Arthur to her breast, protecting him from the rain, cocooning Alice against the side with her hips. Both responsibilities were mine, and I wanted them so badly I felt I might let go and leap across in one bound to tear them away.

But reality was catching up with us fast, and the noise of the spray was joined by the deep roar of water shifting beneath the hull. We must have been halfway up the face of the wave by now.

'It's all right, Josh,' said Richard, holding his son in a protective embrace. I kept my eyes on Mary. 'Just hold on.'

'Dick ...' said Bryce.

'It's all right, everyone,' Richard went on, speaking to the group. 'We'll make it over the top, don't worry.'

'Dick ...'

Bryce was glaring up at the wave. His mouth trembled. I turned to see.

'Don't worry, Beth,' said Richard. 'We're going to get out of this.'

'DICK!' Richard stopped and turned. Bryce had a raised finger. 'Look at that.'

Richard looked up. The rest of us did the same.

'I know, it's big, but like I said, these things are almost impossible to capsize, and—'

'No,' said Bryce. 'Look. At. THAT.'

Richard stopped talking. His face fell, drained of colour.

'Christ. What is that?'

The wall of water was rising fast, a hypnotic cliff face consuming the sky. And in the middle of it was something large, a drifting object, just like us and growing in size. It flashed as the moonlit caught its jagged edges, but tongues of orange flame grew visible as it approached.

'It's another boat,' I said. 'It's on fire.'

'It's on fire all right,' said Bryce. 'But that's not a boat, it's a fucking oil rig.'

'Holy shit,' said a voice, 'you're right. Where did that come from? The nearest rig must have been, what, Nova Scotia?'

Bryce closed his eyes and gripped the fence. 'Then that's where it came from, but it's not there now. It's here, and it's coming straight for us.'

We had one last remaining crew member at our muster station, a fresh-faced young man in his twenties who had just seen his crew mates slide to their deaths. It was at this moment, as the fifty-or-so passengers in his care realised that they were on a collision course with a blazing oil platform and renewed their panic accordingly, that he made a decision. Muttering to himself in hurried Norwegian, he attached his safety harness to the fence and fumbled with a set of keys, which he used to open the gate to the lifeboat. Once through, he began to wrestle with the mechanism that held our lifeboat to the ship.

'What the hell do you think you're doing?' said Richard.

'I'm releasing the lifeboat,' he replied. 'What does it look like I'm doing?'

'Don't be ridiculous,' I said, 'there's no way you can launch that thing at this angle. We'll lose it for good.'

The young man grimaced as he untethered the boat, flashing me a look of terror. 'I am the crew member. You are the passenger. It is my decision. If that thing hits us then we will sink, and then we all drown. It is my decision, do you hear? My—'

As the fastenings came free, a cable sprang loose and struck him in the face, snapping back his head. The crowd gasped and for a moment he stood like that, face turned upwards as if enjoying the cool spray. Then he slumped and fell, where he dangled from the fence by his harness.

'Christ,' said Richard. 'Now what?'

'We've got to do something,' said Bryce. 'That thing's about to hit us.'

The rig was approaching fast, huge flames spewing from one side. I noticed activity at the other muster stations, where the same plan as our hapless crewman was being undertaken. The lifeboat at Mary's station had already been released from its tethers, to a jarring cheer from its intended passengers hanging diagonally from the fence beside it. One by one they clambered aboard. With a terrible clash of horror and relief I saw Alice disappear inside, followed by Mary and Arthur.

'We have to free the lifeboat,' I said, pulling my way towards the gate. I scooped the keys from the crewman's belt as I passed his lifeless body, trying my best not to notice the deep welt across his face. 'It's the only way.'

'Let me past,' said Bryce, arriving next to me. 'Do you know what you're doing?'

I looked down at the network of cords, pulleys and levers before me.

'Of course I don't fucking know what I'm doing. Do you?'

Bryce shrugged. 'Nope. Let's try that big one with the red cross on it.'

He reached across me and, hands still shaking, yanked the lever towards the boat. With an ear-splitting snap, three of the hooks to which the boat was hanging opened and the boat fell away. Now it was dangling from a single cable. I nodded at it.

'Internal release cable,' I said, reading the sign beneath it. 'We do that one from inside.'

'Right,' said Bryce, 'well, that was a piece of piss. Now let's open it up and get in. Everybody –' he turned '– oh, fuck.'

I could already feel the heat.

'Too late,' said Richard. 'Get down!'

I looked up just in time to see one corner of the blazing rig hurtling towards the stern. I gripped the gate and ducked as it roared overhead, showering the deck with burning debris and sending more passengers spinning away. I tucked into a tight crouch, eyes shut, waiting to be skewered, crushed or burned, but in place of death was a curious silence and I looked up to see it had passed. What's more, our pitch was levelling out; we were no longer at an angle.

Bryce, Richard and Josh looked back at me.

'We're OK,' I said. 'It missed us. Let's get in.'

I unlocked the lifeboat's hatch using the keys I had taken, and a sharp light came on inside. The remaining passengers, wide-eyed and bedraggled, crawled into the cocoon, and as I shepherded them in I checked the progress of the other boats. We were the last on the starboard side, and my gut heaved when I saw Mary's drop.

I ushered the last passenger – a stocky, weeping man – inside.

'Are you ready?' said Richard. Josh shivered beside him.

'You two first,' I said, and as they prepared to board I looked out across the water. We were on top of the wave now, and a clear rolling summit stretched away from us on either side. The moonlight picked out shapes; our oil rig was not the only prize the wave had claimed on its journey. A whole fleet of giant mangled structures – ships, trucks, planes and what looked a tower block snapped in two – was being carried upon its crest like an upturned box of toys.

'Hurry,' I said, but as Josh reached for the hatch a terrible thud shook the air, followed by a sound like a hundred trees falling at once.

The cable snapped and the lifeboat fell, just as Richard pulled his son back onto the deck. There were screams from inside the hatch, and we watched the terrified faces fall into the murk below, framed in their yellow light. The capsule hit the water and spun, hatch down, but before we could see its fate we were lifted from our feet and hurled along the deck.

Scrambling to our feet, we saw what had caused the impact; as the rig had rotated, a huge, flaming girder had swung into the boat's bow and torn it from the hull. The air was filled with a sudden burst of heat as the front end exploded, and we began to pitch forward once again, only this time head first into the water.

Moments passed. I scrabbled for something to grab, dimly aware of Richard, Bryce and Josh's cries as they disappeared above me. I was slipping down the deck, accelerating as the boat plunged beneath the wave, faster and faster until the freezing water engulfed me.

When I emerged, gasping, I found myself in a flaming, junk-strewn maelstrom. My life jacket had inflated and I bobbed helplessly on the still-rolling wave, trying to orientate myself. I was some distance from the ship, which was now vertical, stern in the air and sinking fast. Shouts and screams punctured the night. One of the lifeboats – possibly ours – was sinking too. A woman clung petrified to its hull as water gushed into the open hatch. My heart hammered, my body shook with the cold.

'Al ... Alice! Arthur!' I cried into the darkness. I scanned the swirling wreckage for signs of other boats. I couldn't see. My mind reeled. My breath clouded before me. I was freezing to death. It was winter in the Atlantic ocean. How long did I have? Minutes? I heard a voice calling.

'Beth!'

I grunted at the sound of my name and tried to paddle round to see its source, but as I did a wave rolled over me, dragging me down for more empty seconds beneath the black water.

Up again. I was somewhere else now.

'Beth!'

I turned again. Something else was coming, but not a wave this time; something hard and jagged. It swept by, crested by a breaker, and snagged my right leg as it passed. I felt a painless dislocation somewhere south of my waist, which my mind put to one side. I couldn't feel my hands. My lungs were like rocks.

'Alice!' I strained the word. 'Alice, where are you?'

'Beth!' My name again. A deep growl from the murderous night. I paddled with hands that belonged to someone else. I wasn't in this water. This was someone else's nightmare, not mine. 'Over here!'

Bryce. The silhouette of his shaggy mane, then his terrified grimace lit by the flames. He was spread out upon some kind of raft, a wide metallic sheet. There were other figures too, face down or clambering onto it. Josh pulled Richard up from the water, and he flopped down like a landed eel.

'Swim!' roared Bryce.

I swam. But something was wrong. My kicks didn't work as they normally did. It was like running in a dream, the synchronisation all wrong, the geography of my body distorted. Some part of my mind contemplated why, but not too deeply. I dug with my arms instead. Those arms that belonged to someone else.

'Swim, Beth, come on!'

OK, I thought, *I'm swimming. It's not as easy as it looks ... Alice. Arthur. Christ, where are you?*

Sobs arrived. My sobs. *Not now, swim.*

But my body felt like some flimsy counterfeit of itself. Each stroke barely dragged me an inch towards the raft. I tried to concentrate on Bryce's urgent face, but it kept disappearing from view, and I realised it was because I was closing my eyes.

How easy it would be to just do that. Just close my eyes and let myself drift away. Just like Leo ... oh, Kate, why didn't you just take turns on that raft? ... No pain, no memory, no—

Another voice. A cry in the dark. A familiar cry. Arthur.

My eyes shot open. My muscles sprang into life, all moving at once. Through the wreckage beyond the raft I saw a lifeboat, its hatch still open. Arthur's cries were coming from within.

At once my body was mine again. I plunged my arms in and swam with everything I had, kicking with whatever mutilated machinery existed beneath. I heaved myself through the water, passing the raft, ignoring Bryce's calls to turn, and as I drew near to the lifeboat I saw a figure in the hatch helping another on board.

Mary.

She looked up as the legs of her rescuee disappeared inside, and froze when she saw me.

'Mary,' I spluttered as I swam the last few metres. 'Mary, help me.'

Behind her was a full boat, and from somewhere within the clamour inside Arthur wailed. And Alice too – I heard her, to more crushing relief I heard her too.

Mary stared down at me from her safe perch. The hatch was high above the water. I held out my arm.

'Mary, please.'

She put her fingers to her mouth.

'I was trying to help,' she said. There was that voice of the chastened child again, trying to get itself out of trouble.

'I know,' I said. The cold was taking me again, now that I had stopped. My limbs were disappearing. 'Thank you, thank you, Mary. Now lift me up, help me on board.'

I strained my arm as high as it would go. She hesitated, looked inside, then back at me.

'Please.'

Finally she reached down.

'Take my arm,' she said. I grasped her wrist as she grasped mine, and I felt myself leaving the water.

'Oh, God, thank you, thank you, Mary.'

She was holding me in two arms now. My feet were clear of the surface, my head almost at the hatch. I reached up with my other hand. Soon I would see them.

But Mary stopped.

'Mary?' I said, dangling. Her stare seemed to penetrate me, reaching down into the ocean's darkest places. Then her eyes turned to me, and in one swift, businesslike motion, she unfastened my straps and unhooked my jacket, tossing it to one side.

'Mary, what are you doing?'

With surprising strength she pulled me close.

'Looking after your children,' she said, 'that's what.'

I had barely registered what had happened before I hit the water, and this time I sank straight down, with no hope of bobbing back up.

I watched the surface disappear, and nothing flashed before my eyes but the possible futures of those little hearts above me. Where would they end up? Would they be looked after? What would they be told, what would they believe, what would they become? I grasped for something hopeful. At least that they might survive. Perhaps they would remember me, perhaps they wouldn't. Either was fine so long as they were happy, so long as they were safe, so long as nobody hurt them.

Cradling this thought like a pearl, I prepared to close my eyes and open my lungs to the frigid sea, and the last thing I saw was a black explosion at the surface, haloed in orange flame.

Chapter 9

I felt time passing without me. The world turned. People spoke, wept, shuffled about.

Sounds became familiar.

Bryce's mutters.

Richard's heavy sighs.

Argument, frustration, the dull thump of water against flat metal.

And beneath them all was the roar of shifting tides, like leviathans churning beneath my skin.

Somewhere we met searing light and pelting rain, though my eyes remained closed, and I had a sense of my body being moved like furniture.

But me? I was elsewhere.

The world became quieter, darker, stiller. My thoughts persisted, but in some other place; a room locked away from the world.

And suddenly here I am in our little back garden. Look at this – it's summer, the tree's in blossom, and a mobile of mirrors hangs from the lowest branch, glinting as it turns in the breeze. It's been one of those impossible days where everything has gone to plan. Sleep, food, weather, everything. I'm sitting on a step with a glass of lemonade. Lemonade – when had I last enjoyed that simple pleasure? The fizz and chink of the ice. It's warm and quiet, and running bare-foot on the grass before me is my beautiful daughter. She's laughing, waving a windmill on a stick. Arthur's waddling after her, giggling at the colours, and behind him, all tanned and happy with his shirt open, is my husband, Ed.

There's nothing wrong. Everything's right.

I stand and walk to him. He turns and smiles, and I put my arm around his neck for a long kiss. When it's finished I look down at Alice, who's grinning up at me. I can't hear her, but her mouth says '*Mummy*.'

The sun glints in the mobile. I turn to look, and in one oblong mirror I see my face. Only that's not my face ... that's not my face at all. It's hers.

Mary's.

'Alice.'

I sat bolt upright, looking left. I was on a hard bed beneath a rough blanket in a small square room made of stone. The air was hot and damp, clogged with an earthy smell that reminded me of museums. A tissue-thin blue paper gown hung limply from my shoulders, and my body felt thinner than usual, my joints more noticeable, torso more concave. On the wall to my left was a window with no glass – just a square hole that had been cut into the rock. There was a dungeon-like feeling to the place, and I had the sense that I was high up, as if in some medi-eval tower. Warm rain blew in, laced with the smell of ozone and wet foliage. I heard cracks and shouts from far away.

'Hello.'

I turned to see a woman in a nurse's outfit standing by the door. Her voice was familiar, but her face was in shadow. She was holding a bucket and flannel.

'Where am I? Where are –' I gasped, winded by a sick surge of memories. '– my children.'

I threw off the blanket and swung out my legs.

'Don't.' The woman dropped what she was carrying and stepped nimbly from the corner to steady me, but my right foot had already touched the ground and I howled with pain. I fell back on the bed, retching, though nothing came up. 'You have only just had the plaster off.'

'What plaster?'

'I was just about to give you a bed bath, actually. It's been a while since your last one, I'm afraid, and I would have done you sooner only we've been so terribly busy, what with everything going on out there.'

Swimming back from nausea, I focused on the woman above me. Her face was thin and lightly wrinkled, and a brittle sadness inhabited her eyes.

'Mildred?'

She nodded. 'Yes. You broke your leg in the wreck. Don't you remember?'

'No, I don't remember anything after ...' I broke off again, paralysed by another flash of memories. Arthur's cries, Mary's hand, that look in her eye, falling into the freezing darkness. 'What happened?'

'Some of the wreckage hit you. We saw it from the raft. I can't believe you managed to swim all that way. It was ... well, let's just say you didn't look pretty when that man pulled you aboard.'

'What man?'

'The great big hairy one. Briggs, or whatever his name is.'

I remembered the dark shape in the water and the flames above it.

'Bryce.'

She nodded. 'That's the fellow. He dived in and pulled you out.'

'Who else was on the raft?'

'It was more like two rafts, actually. Two platforms joined beneath the water. We thought it might have been a part of that terrible oil rig. We kind of –' She turned a finger in the air, and a smile flickered on her mouth. '– spun around each other as we drifted. Like a dance, I suppose. Anyway, you and your saviour, Bryce, were on one section with five others, including that tall man with his son, what was his name ...?'

'Richard.'

'That's right. Funny, you'd think I would remember their names.' She blinked and looked away. 'I was ... well, I suppose I was a little distracted. I didn't join in much of the conversation. Gerald always did most of the talking for us.'

I lay still for a moment, staring at the stone ceiling. Then I sat up and placed my feet upon the floor, gently this time, experimenting with the pressure on each leg.

'Be careful,' said Mildred. 'I'm sure the doctor said you shouldn't be putting too much weight on it to begin with.'

I pushed harder, ignoring the stabs of pain.

'Especially after you've been unconscious for so long.'

I stopped and frowned at her. Another splutter of cracks sounded somewhere in the distance.

'What? How long have I been unconscious?'

Mildred tightened her lips, flustered. 'You contracted a terrible fever. You came in and out of consciousness that first night, but you were never properly with us after that.'

I glowered at her. 'How long, Mildred? And where are we?'

'We ... drifted for a few days. We tried to follow the lifeboats west, but the current from the wave was too strong. And Richard was wrong; nobody found us. Nobody.'

I gripped the bed.

'You lost them?'

She looked down at her hands.

'I'm afraid so.'

My insides seemed to move of their own accord – heart spluttering, guts shuddering, lungs pumping short, sharp breaths.

'Try to calm down,' said Mildred, touching my shoulder. 'You mustn't get upset.'

I knocked her hand away.

'My children were on those boats. She ... she *took* them.'

Mildred's face hardened.

'Yes. I saw what she did. We all did.'

'You and Gerald were with Mary in that camp, weren't you?'

She gave a swift nod. 'Yes.'

'You know something about her, don't you? What is it?'

She searched the walls, the ceiling, floor, eyes dotting about like pinballs until finally they gave one last roll at the ceiling.

'Oh, God ...'

'Mildred.'

'All right, all right.' She expelled a long breath through her nose, then walked to the window and looked out. The strange cracks continued, like axes hitting wood.

'Gerald wanted to tell you,' she said, 'but I made him promise not to. I felt sorry for her, truth be told. She hadn't done any harm, not really, and after what had happened it just didn't seem fair.' She paused, giving me a half-smile over her shoulder. 'We never had children, Gerald and I. We almost did, but I'm afraid I lost her quite early on. I'm sure it was a girl. We were only young. It upset me terribly, and Gerald didn't speak for days. It was a dreadful time for us. I know it happens a lot, and that it's not like losing a real child, and I'd heard that most couples keep trying, but ... well, I just don't think either of us had it in us to withstand another loss if it happened again. So we decided not to. We just lived our life, Gerald and I.'

She turned and gave me a full smile this time, eyes glistening.

'And it was a wonderful life. It really was. A wonderful, safe and untroubled life with the man I loved. I never worked, apart from volunteering at the nursing home, and I had my bridge club and coffee mornings, cruises in the summer to look forward to, and my husband to look after. The man I loved.' The smile faltered. 'And I know what you're thinking; women aren't supposed to do that kind of thing any more are they? It's weak, it's not *feminist* enough, giving up your life like that for a man. But I'm afraid I just don't care. I loved my life, and I loved my Gerald.'

She sighed and turned back to the window, placing her fingers delicately on the stone ledge. A breeze disrupted a strand of mousey hair that had escaped from her nurse's cap.

'What I'm trying to say is that I may not have ever experienced a mother's instinct, but I do have some idea of what it's like to lose a child. That's why I didn't tell you.'

'I don't understand. What did she do?'

'We were given rooms to live in. In the camp at Whitby. Nothing more than cubicles, really, like swimming pool changing rooms with beds. There was absolutely no privacy; you could see under the walls and hear everything. Gerald and I had been in there for two weeks when Mary arrived. She had a little baby with her. Well, needless to say Gerald made it clear to her right from the off: "'I hope we're not going to be kept awake by crying at all hours!'" And Mary replied: "'I'm a single mother, and my daughter is only five months old. I'd appreciate a bit of understanding.'"

Mildred looked at me.

'*My daughter*, that's what she said. *I'm a single mother.*' She shook her head. 'As it turned out the baby wasn't any trouble at all that night. But the next day something very strange happened. In the queues for the canteen we heard a woman scream, and she came running to the queue with her arms outstretched exclaiming, "My baby, my baby!" and "Mary, you found her!"'

'It was Mary she was running to, you see. And then this man came running too; the woman's husband, we supposed, and it was clear that they knew her, and that they believed she had their baby. I remember the look on her face, hunted, like a cornered animal. There was a moment when I could have sworn she was going to run, but she didn't. Instead she turned on a smile and handed over the baby, and embraced the woman and her husband, telling them where she'd found her and that she was fine, and how lucky it was that they had bumped into her. The couple were so happy to have found their little girl that they didn't ask any more questions, and Mary gave her up, just like that.

'Well, Gerald and I were horrified. "Single mother", she had said. "My daughter." He went to speak to the couple later that day. We didn't tell them what she had said, but asked them how they knew her and what have you. They said they'd known her from before, they'd been friends with her and her husband.'

'Mary's husband. Nathan – he wasn't with her?'

Mildred shook her head. 'There were terrible floods. He drowned in them. And they'd had a little baby of their own who had drowned too.'

A chill ran through me.

'Why didn't you tell me?'

'Because I felt sorry for her, and I thought that maybe we'd misunderstood her. Gerald had a way of talking that ... well, I thought perhaps he had made her nervous and the words had come out wrong – he could do that, could Gerald, he made people nervous.' She faltered with doelike eyes. 'I don't know. I just saw her with your lovely children and she was so good with them ...'

There was a crutch by the bed. I snatched it and stood, immediately collapsing. Mildred caught me.

'Please, you shouldn't be moving about so much.'

'She took them.'

'I'm sorry. I never once imagined that she would do such a thing. And we were on a boat. What could happen on a boat?'

'Tell me where we are.'

'I ... I'm sure she wouldn't hurt them. I'm sure they're safe.'

I glared down at her, dizzy with a sudden rabid urge to grab her by the throat. 'I am their mother and so long as they're not with me, they're not safe. Now tell me where we are.'

Her jaw trembled. 'Like I said, we were taken east for a day or two, after which we somehow found our way into the Mediterranean.'

'What?'

'We were in bad shape – you especially. We had no food or water, and a couple of the others didn't make it. There was a terrible storm that tossed us from pillar to post. I thought for sure we were going to die, but then –' she turned to the window, from which yet another round of snaps and bangs could be heard '– then we were saved.'

'Who saved us?' I gripped her shoulders. 'Mildred, tell me where we are!'

'We're in Gibraltar,' she said. 'It's been twelve weeks since the SS *Unity* sank.'

'Please, come back. You shouldn't be walking on that leg yet.'

Using the crutch, I hobbled down a narrow, stone corridor lined with cells like the one in which I had awoken. They were hospital rooms, and each one was occupied. Some patients were bandaged and unconscious, while others groaned or screamed as they were restrained. Mildred scurried after me.

'I'm fine,' I said.

My leg was like rubber and protested with every step, but the pain was silenced by a furious flood of adrenalin.

Gibraltar?

Twelve weeks?

They could have gone anywhere in that time. I had to get out. I had to get to Florida. Right now.

'Beth, please,' said Mildred.

'What is this place? Are these people from the wreck?'

'No. They were here when we arrived.'

'Why are there so many injuries?'

'If you'll stop for a second, I'll explain.'

'I don't have time to stop, *Mildred*. I'm in fucking Gibraltar, and thanks to you my kids are with some lunatic on the other side of the Atlantic.

'Thanks to me? *I* wasn't the one who left my children with a stranger, thank you very much.'

'Where the hell is Gibraltar anyway?'

I turned onto a second wider corridor, then followed it onto a third. The air was fresher, the light brighter. The sounds from outside grew louder with every step.

'Bottom of Spain,' mumbled Mildred. 'It kind of just dangles there, a bit like a tonsil. Used to, at any rate. Very muggy. Maggie says the floods—'

'Used to?' I smelled warm plant life, as if we were in a jungle. There were more people on this corridor, busy with their heads down, and some gave me strange looks as I passed. I felt naked in my flimsy gown. 'Where are my clothes?'

'Maggie has them.'

'Who's Maggie? And why are we still here after *twelve weeks*?'

I turned another corner and stopped. At the end of the corridor was a short flight of steps leading into an oval room with one wall missing. The empty space was curtained by creepers and foliage, and beyond was a wide vista of sky, sea and distant mountains. I walked towards the stairs. The room was carpeted with a huge mosaic rug and furnished with antique furniture – chests, cupboards, a square table and three desks. At one of these sat Josh, nervously scribbling notes on an A4 pad.

At the second desk stood what I thought was another young man, but soon realised was a shaven-haired girl of about seventeen staring down at a series of papers. She wore grey cargo pants and a military green vest, and had a fierce, fine-featured face with dark skin. In one hand she held a walkie-talkie.

The third and largest desk was empty, but behind it stood a woman examining a huge map on the wall. She was striking – tall, dark-skinned, in her fifties, wearing a short-sleeved checked shirt tucked into khaki shorts. Her greying black hair was swept into a loose ponytail.

There was also a monkey on her shoulder. It screeched when it saw us, and the woman turned.

'Aha,' she said. Her smile revealed a large gold tooth. 'You're awake.'

The strange cracking noise from outside was now accompanied by the occasional concussive thud, which shook dust from the ceiling overhead.

I reached the stairs and used the banister to help me down. Josh looked up.

'Hi, Beth,' he said.

'Josh, where's your dad?'

'He's upstairs with Bryce in the radio room.' He turned to the woman at the map, with a look of deference. 'Can I go and tell him?'

With a smile, the woman nodded. Josh left his desk and ran out, avoiding the glare of the girl with the walkie-talkie.

'I'm impressed to see you walking,' said the woman.

'I tried to stop her,' said Mildred from the top of the steps. 'The doctor said she really shouldn't be on her feet.'

The woman appraised me with her hands on her hips. I could have sworn her monkey did the same. 'She looks fine to me,' she said. 'Obviously made of strong stuff.'

Mildred cleared her throat. 'I should probably get back to the hospital.'

'Yes,' said the woman. 'Go now, I can take care of her.'

Mildred attempted a strange and flustered curtsey before abandoning it and abruptly about-turning. Her heels echoed down the corridor.

'You are Beth Hill,' said the woman. 'I've heard all about you. My name is Maggie Navaro.' She gestured to the desk. 'And this is my daughter, Dani.'

As the girl glanced up, the walkie-talkie crackled and she brought it to her ear.

'Yes?' she said, turning away.

'She helps me run things around here. It's a kind of mother–daughter operation, if you like.'

'Operation?' I gazed round the strange roughly hewn walls covered with maps and plans. My head began to swim. 'What kind of operation?'

'Try to relax, you've been through a lot.'

'I don't have time to relax. I need to ...' My head swam. 'I need to leave. I need to get to Florida. How do I get off this place?'

She gave me a smile of pity and shook her head. 'Oh, darling, if only life was that simple.'

Another terrific crack shook the ground and I walked to the open wall.

'Why?' I said. 'And what the hell is that noise?'

'Careful,' she said, coming to my side. I pulled back a vine and looked out, immediately hit by a swell of vertigo. We were hundreds of metres above a choppy grey sea, standing within the face of a sheer cliff. To our left, the cliff tapered to a steep, forested hill, which led down to wide marshland dotted with stone structures, wooden jetties, and sandbagged turrets. Beyond, a huge network of sailing boats were lashed together around a vast, dilapidated cruise ship. It was far bigger than the

Unity and crawling with vegetation, with scorched holes torn in its hull like the open sores of a beached whale.

Between the ship and the cliff, a skirmish was playing out beneath a haze of mist and smoke. The cracks and thuds were from guns, and I saw figures wading between the structures close to shore. Somewhere further out was their enemy, and I saw the occasional flash and puff of smoke from a crumbling tower block.

'What the hell is happening out there?' I said.

'I'm afraid you've stumbled into a war, Beth Hill,' replied Maggie.

Chapter 10

An urgent voice crackled on the girl's radio, obscured by shots and yells. She exhaled audibly and muttered something back.

'They can't get past Eurotowers,' she said. *'Again.'*

Maggie turned.

'Tell them to return. Pull back. I'm not going to waste any more lives or ammunition on that idiot this afternoon.'

'They need something to draw the fire. If we send down another—'

'Pull them back, Dani. That's an order.'

The girl stared back for a few moments, jaw set. Finally she scowled and marched from the room, muttering the order into the radio.

Maggie sighed and shook her head. 'My daughter is her mother's child.'

She turned to me and smiled. I shivered on the stone floor, though the air was hot and thick with moisture.

'Come on,' she said. 'Let's find you some clothes.'

'I've lived in Gibraltar all my life. Born here, raised here, never left. It's the finest place in the world.

A country where everybody knows each other – not many can boast that, no?'

Maggie led us through the maze of stone corridors. Her stride was immense and I struggled to keep up with my new limp. The monkey watched me from her shoulder with what I was sure was amusement.

'I ran a shop in the Old Town selling electronics, curiosities, knick-knacks and what have you. It was just me and Dani. Her father was ... a long-forgotten mistake, shall we say.'

'Where are we, exactly?'

'Where are we? We're in the Rock, my darling. Right in the middle of it. Over thirty miles of tunnels dug by the British over three hundred years of its bloody wars.' She slapped the rock. 'These walls have kept garrisons safe since the eighteenth century. They've seen fourteen sieges, countless battles, and a million lives lost on the land and sea beneath. It's a living fortress, and now it's ours. Pretty good place to live when the sky falls, no?'

Her laugh – a friendly but maniacal cackle – echoed from the stone. The monkey added its own screeches, hopping excitedly onto Maggie's other shoulder.

We climbed some steps and reached a doorway, behind which was a huge cavern filled with tiers of seats, like a concert hall. Stalactites hung like gnarled fingers from its roof, and at the front was a stage stacked with crates.

I hovered at the top, still shivering.

'They used to play music here,' said Maggie, with a disinterested sniff. She led us down some more steps to the stage. 'Orchestras and what have you. Now it's our supply store. When we heard those things were coming, the military – there was a base at the top of the Rock, no? – they packed this place with food, clothes, blankets, fuel, you name it, and opened the tunnels to the population in the town below. Many came up, but most preferred to stay in their homes.' She gave me a flat, disparaging look. 'They thought they would be *safer* there. Can you believe that? Not me. Me and my daughter, we came straight up here, and anyone with sense came too.'

We reached the stage and Maggie began searching through the boxes. She found a crate of water and pulled out a bottle, tossing it to me. I emptied half into my mouth in one gulp, eyes bulging with relief. Some spilled from my mouth.

'Careful with that,' she said with a frown. 'We don't have an endless supply.'

I froze and took another more careful sip.

'That's better.'

Maggie began sorting through a stack of crates further along.

'Everything was rushed. The army was needed elsewhere, God knows for what, so they had no time to evacuate us. They left us in the dead of night. We watched their trucks roll across the border from the top of the Rock, and never heard from them again.

Can you believe that? This Rock, the military strong-hold that's stood for centuries, abandoned overnight.'

She opened one crate and selected from the stack of neatly pressed fatigues inside a vest, some trousers and the most heavy-duty set of bra and underpants I had ever seen.

'Here,' she said, tossing them to me. 'For you.'

I caught them, nearly falling over with the impact. She waited.

'Go on then, girl, get dressed.'

I slipped off the coarse gown and struggled into the clothes. Maggie searched another box.

'We were right to take shelter in the Rock,' she said, 'because when those asteroids fell –' she broke off, examining a pair of polished black boots '– we heard it all over the radio. They peppered the south coast of Spain, took out most of the major towns and cities, Gibraltar included. There were terrible fires. No survivors. Not one. The buildings, the airport, the harbour – almost all that reclaimed land burned down or sank beneath the waves. Then another hit the rock itself, tearing off a chunk that killed half of us inside and exposed a huge section of the tunnels. Here, these look like your size.'

She handed me the boots and a pair of long green socks, and watched as I struggled to pull them on. I had the sense that I was being assessed.

'We sheltered in here for two weeks with the bodies, waiting for the fires to go out. When they finally did, we emerged into a very different world. Our homes beneath were destroyed, and our friends and relatives were all dead in the rubble. But that wasn't all. The water had risen. It encircled us. Spain was flooded for miles, and La Línea, that poor little town that had been our only border with Europe for hundreds of years, now lay beneath the Mediterranean Sea. We were no longer connected to the mainland. We had become an island.'

I finished tying the laces of my boots and stood. The rush of blood to my head made me stagger, and she caught me.

'Easy there,' she said, but I brushed her off.

'I'm fine,' I said, looking down to see Maggie's monkey with one paw on my leg. He was looking up expectantly. 'Why do you have a monkey?'

'Colin's not a monkey,' she said. 'He's a Barbary ape, and he obviously likes you. Which is a good sign, no?'

She made a kissing noise and the creature found her shoulder in two light bounds. She rewarded him with a smile.

'Most of the other apes were killed in the strike, of course, but—'

'Maggie,' I said, no longer able to endure Alice and Arthur's faces swimming into my mind every few seconds, 'thank you for rescuing me, and for looking after me, and for the clothes, and the boots, but I really need to go. My children have been taken from me, and I need to find a way of getting to them. Now.'

I gulped, wobbling, my throat dry again. She looked down at me, her face all grim concern.

'I told you, my darling, it's not that simple.'

'Why?'

She looked me up and down.

'You're weak. You need to eat. Come and I'll explain.'

'They came from all around,' said Maggie. 'Refugees from a flooded Spanish plain.'

We were in a brightly lit room full of long tables – one of the mess halls, Maggie explained. There were others in there too, all in the same fatigues as me, looking over and sharing whispers as they ate. Dani sat alone a few tables down, grumpily hunched over her bowl.

I wolfed the food in front of me. I had no idea what it was and I didn't care; it was fuel and my body accepted it. Perhaps it already knew before I did that leaving Gibraltar was going to take everything it had.

'They carried their possessions in plastic bags on their backs,' said Maggie. 'Wading, swimming, pushing their children on rafts. We were the highest point in many miles – their only sanctuary – and we took them in. The idea of thousands of Spanish people wandering freely across the border and taking sanctuary in this rock would have been laughed at once.' She shrugged. 'But I suppose multiple asteroid strikes have a way of making territorial disputes somewhat trivial.'

I licked my plate and pushed it to one side. She gave a quizzical smile. 'You were hungry.'

'Who's down there?' I said, wiping my mouth. 'Who are you fighting?'

She paused, then leaned on the table.

'When I said that everything had been destroyed beneath us, that wasn't entirely true. There was a cruise ship in the harbour, the one you saw down there earlier. They arrived every week in the summer, full of rich old Brits, Yanks, Dutch, Germans and what have you. They'd come in their droves and blunder about the town with their caps and cameras, getting in everyone's way. Good for trade, of course, but . . .' She broke off, noticing my look of impatience. 'There were still people on board the ship, and it was by pure luck that they survived. When we found them we offered them shelter in the Rock, but they refused it. They were terrified. They didn't want to leave the safety of their boat. They had some food and water, sanitation, comfortable beds, and they were sure they would be rescued. "Someone will come for us," they said. And they were right, someone did. Unfortunately for them it was Tony Staines.'

'Who's Tony Staines?'

Maggie's gaze drifted to the row of high windows. 'It was a cold day when we spotted that line of boats in the east. Late September and the wind was up. There must have been fifty of them, maybe more, and apart from the refugees and the cruise ship holidaymakers they were the first people we'd seen for months. A party of us made our way down to Europa Point to greet them and found they'd already dropped anchor. We had no boats of our own because, apart from that great monstrosity in the harbour, everything that floated in Gibraltar had been smashed to pieces and dragged away by the tide, but we had a small raft made of palettes and empty fuel barrels that we used to paddle out to that boat of his. The *Black Buccaneer* he calls it – his pride and joy.'

She stopped and shook her head.

'I had a bad feeling about him from the start. Red nose of an over-imbiber, stretched belly of an over-eater, smile of a crocodile. "Well, greetings to you, madam,"' he said, waving his hat like some old-fashioned gentleman. Honestly. Nobody should be that polite and happy when you've just survived the end of the world, and those men skulking behind him ... I'd seen their sort a thousand times before with their bald heads and tree-trunk arms, the wrap-around sunglasses, red faces and oily grins of men on holiday to do nothing but drink, I—'

She stopped again, mid-fume, and turned to me.

'I'm sorry. It's just that I trusted him, you see, despite all the signals. Do you understand?

I paused. 'Yes. Yes, I do.'

'It's my mother's fault, God rest her soul. She always taught me to give people the benefit of the doubt.'

'What happened?'

She ran a tongue over her front teeth.

'I swallowed my misgivings and invited him in. I took him and some of his men up to the Rock, and they sat in that very room in which you met me, with candles lit, eating our chicken, drinking our wine and telling me their stories. There was a point to what I was attempting, you understand; he had boats and we did not. There is only so long ten thousand people can live isolated on the Rock, after all. We had to find supplies from somewhere, and I thought perhaps, if we joined forces, we could reconnect with the outside world. He laughed when I suggested this to him. It was a terrible laugh, a counterfeit, and when I heard it I knew at once that it came from a man to whom treasures like joy or kindness or love were alien. And I knew I had made a terrible mistake.

'When the laugh was over he wiped his mouth and stood up, his henchmen quickly following, and he told me he had no intention of "reconnecting with the outside world", as I had put it. He wanted nothing to do with the outside world, never had, and that it was a damn fine thing those rocks had rained down upon it, because now we could all live as we were supposed to. Hand to mouth, port to port, free as the sea to do as they pleased. "I have almost everything I need at sea, Miss Maggie," he said, "and everything else is right here."

'At this point I was ready to bolt, but there was already a blade at my throat. "You've done a fine job," he said, "but I believe I'll be taking things from here." Before I knew it I was being dragged away down corridors that were suddenly full of his men, all of them armed and bullying our people out of the place in which they had found safety. Children, families, old men and women. I tried to plead with him, offering him half of what remained in our stores if he left us alone, but he just laughed again. As it turned out, I needn't have bothered.'

'Why, what happened?'

Maggie turned to her daughter, still eating at her table.

'Because, unlike me,' she said, loud enough for her to hear, 'my daughter never trusts strangers.'

Dani looked over, saying nothing.

'She had seen Tony too,' Maggie went on, 'and his boats and his men, and she'd watched his ambush from an adjoining corridor, where she'd prepared one of her own. We had our own guns, you see, from what was left of the military barracks. Tony wasn't expecting it, and before he knew what was happening two of his men had been killed and they'd been forced under heavy fire back down to their boats.'

She smiled at her daughter, but Dani's face was deadpan.

'We shouldn't have pulled back today, Mother,' she said. 'We had him on the back foot. We could have pushed.'

'It was too dangerous, Dani. You know it was.'

The girl pursed her lips, nostrils flaring.

'We have to make sacrifices, can't you see that? Or we'll never get off this place.' She slammed her hand on the table, and the room hushed. 'Never!'

With that, she stormed out.

Maggie watched her daughter leave, then turned back to me.

'As you can see, my daughter and I share somewhat different views on our home country. Anyway, we thought we'd seen the back of Tony Staines, but he had no intention of giving up so easily. He moved his boats to the harbour, and set up that floating ... *shanty* town of his behind the cruise ship. It's under his control now.' She leaned forward. 'That bastard has kept those poor souls trapped in there and held us siege for the past five months, and he's showing no sign of giving up. We cannot leave.'

'What about from the other side of the Rock?'

'It's a sheer cliff face now after those things hit us. We tried one night. We built two rafts and lowered them down with ropes, but one of them fell, killing three people on the rocks below, and the second was ambushed a quarter of a mile from the shore. Staines has boats stationed all around, waiting for us.'

'Then how did we get through?'

'You were lucky. You rolled in on a ferocious storm that kept them to the harbour. If it hadn't been for that then you'd be in his care now, and I guarantee you his care is not as good as mine.'

At that moment I heard footsteps and looked up to see Richard at the canteen door. He smiled at me with relief.

'Beth,' he said, 'how are you doing?'

He looked tanned and well fed, less wiry than he had done on the boat.

'I'm fine,' I said, as he hovered at the door. 'Richard, I need to talk to you.'

Maggie stood up. 'I'll let you catch up with your friend.' She clicked her fingers and her monkey, who had been gathering scraps beneath the tables, hopped back onto her shoulder. 'Come and see me later so we can discuss your living quarters, and what kind of job we can give you. Richard tells me you're good with computers, no?'

I turned to her.

'Job? Maggie, I don't think you understand. I'm not staying here. I *can't* stay here, and boat or no boat I'm leaving, even if it means wading out to sea.'

She fixed me with a look of bland amusement, before finally turning to Richard.

'Come and see me when you're done,' she said.

When she was gone, Richard turned to me. 'It's good to see you up, Beth. I was worried about—'

'Josh said you'd been in the radio room.'

'That's right,' he said, a little cowed by my interruption.

'Is that what you do around here? Is that your *job*?'

'Amongst other things. But it's mostly Bryce that does it. Beth, don't think for a second that we haven't been trying to get off this place ever since we arrived. We know what happened to your kids, we all saw it, but the fact is we're trapped here. I wish it wasn't the case, but it is.'

I got up from the table. I was getting used to a new way of moving, avoiding certain positions in which the pain was worse. I walked to the door where Richard leaned.

'Is Bryce at the radio now?'

'Yes, it's in a room near the old munitions store.'

'Take me to him. Take me to him now.'

Chapter 11

The munitions store was high in the Rock near the southern summit where the barracks had once been. Richard led me up some winding stone stairs dotted with roughly cut windows that offered views across the empty sea. The sky and water were reflections of each other. Above us was a colourless grey, but black and bouldering clouds gathered over the Atlas Mountains on the African coast. A storm was coming.

We reached a short corridor, whitewashed and brightly lit from windows with real glass. At the end of it was an archway sealed by a dark oak door – the munitions store, I presumed, and halfway along was another smaller door at which Richard stopped. He gripped the handle.

'Is this it?' I asked.

'Yes. But listen, about Bryce ...'

'Richard, I don't have time for this.'

'I know, it's just ... look, he's changed. A bit.'

'What do you mean *changed*?'

'He ... well, he's met someone. Here. Just to prepare you.'

'Right, whatever.'

I pushed past him and opened the door. Inside was a wide room with oak beams and long windows that flooded the chalk-white walls with light. In one corner was an iron bed neatly made with pressed sheets, and in the other was an ornate antique desk upon which sat a complicated-looking radio set. Standing in the middle of the room was a large and rather beautiful black-haired woman in a red skirt and white blouse, who was sweeping the sanded wooden floor. Behind the radio sat Bryce.

At least, it was someone who looked a bit like Bryce. He looked up as I entered and raised both eyebrows.

'Beth, you're awake. How are you, darlin'?'

I paused.

'Fine,' I said, taking in his face, which I had never seen and was, to my surprise, a lean egg-shape. His beard had been trimmed to a respectable half-inch fuzz of black, and his hair was slick and swept back into a – I had to look twice to be sure – topknot. Perched on his nose was a pair of half-moon spectacles.

'How are you?'

He beamed. 'Wonderful. Just wonderful. Come in, come in, please. You too, Richard.'

I caught Richard's eye as he shut the door behind him.

'I tried to warn you,' he muttered.

'What's that smell?' I whispered.

'I think it's a joss stick.'

Bryce got up and marched around the desk. 'This –' he held out a hand to the raven-haired woman with the broom '– is Carmela.'

The woman smiled at his approach, her caramel skin flushed with a kind of hungry pride. She was the same height as him, and therefore not dwarfed by his presence like most others. He put his arm around her waist and kissed her cheek. She bowed her head in my direction.

'*Hola.*'

'Hello,' I replied, looking between the two of them. 'Pleased to meet you.'

Bryce sighed.

'Carmela only speaks a little English,' he said, 'and I speak even less Spanish. But that doesn't matter, does it, my little wood pigeon. We talk to each other in other ways.'

'*Mi guapo,*' she said, stroking his cheek. '*Mi hombre.*'

Bryce gazed into her deep brown eyes.

'Amazing thing, love, isn't it? No need for words. No need for conversation. We communicate just by looking at each other, knew it from the moment I opened my eyes in that bed and saw her looking down at me.' He turned to me. 'Carmela was working in the hospital when we washed ashore here. Nursed me back to health, didn't you, pigeon?'

Moments passed as they looked at one other. Richard cleared his throat awkwardly.

'Bryce,' I said.

'Aha?' he said, turning. His eyes were glazed like a drunk's.

'My children. I need to find them.'

His face fell and he released Carmela's waist.

'I'm sorry, Beth. What am I thinking? Talking about my happiness when you're ...' He turned to Carmela, speaking slowly, 'Carmela, this is the one I was telling you about. From the boat.'

Carmela watched his lips, then threw a hand to her mouth and turned to me.

'*Tus niños? Oh! Pobre mujer.*' She ran to me and pulled me into a fierce embrace. '*Pobre, pobre mujer!*'

'OK,' I said, eyes bulging. 'OK.'

She pulled away. Bryce approached.

'Beth, I've been on that radio every day and night for the past six weeks trying to contact them. I try every channel, up and down, I say the name of the boat, your name, the names of the children, where we are and what happened, but –' he shook his head '– there's nobody there, Beth. The airwaves are dead. Nobody's responding.'

'*Nada,*' said Carmela, fiddling with her sharp-nailed fingers and searching the ground. '*Nadie nos escucha ... estamos solos. Estamos solos!*' She stamped her foot.

'It's true,' said Richard. 'I've been trying too, it's like ... everyone's just packed up and left.'

I looked at the radio.

'Does it even work?'

'Aye,' said Bryce, 'it works all right. There's a fifty-foot antenna on top of this roof, and I know for sure it's transmitting because we can talk to people on our own radios down there on the ground.'

'So we know it can reach at least as far as ... what, the harbour?'

'Aye,' Bryce nodded, 'at least.'

I walked to the ancient desk and placed a hand on the warm, chrome radio casing.

'I want you to send a message, Bryce.'

'Darling, I told you, I've been sending messages every day. Nobody's—'

'To him, Bryce. I want you to send a message to him.'

Bryce walked to my side.

'I could try,' he said, rubbing his beard. He smelled of citrus and coconut. 'But Ed would already have picked up all my other calls if he'd been listening. And I don't even know if that boat had a working radio.'

'I don't mean Ed.'

'Who, then?'

'Tony Staines. I want you to tell him I'm coming down to the harbour.'

'Absolutely not.' Maggie dismissed me with a wave of her hand. 'No way.'

We were back in her open-walled office. It was early afternoon and the rain had grown heavy. Thunder growled in the distance. Richard, Bryce and Carmela stood behind me, and Dani was at her mother's side, arms folded.

'I have no choice,' I said. 'I need to get off this island if I'm going to get my children, and the only way I'm going to be able to do that is if I have a boat.'

'And you think that bastard down there is just going to let you have one?'

'Maybe, maybe not. Maybe he'll give me safe passage to somewhere that will.'

'Safe passage?' Maggie laughed. 'You really don't know who you're dealing with, child.'

I took a step towards her. She was taller than me but not by much, and I glared up at her. 'You listen to me. I'm not your child and I never asked to be on this Rock. My children are on the other side of the Atlantic Ocean and I've already been here too long. I won't spend any more precious time waiting while some ridiculous argument I have no part in plays out. I'm going down there, and I'm going to talk to him like a human being, and I'm going to ask him for his help. Do you understand me?'

She glared back at me. I caught something in her daughter's expression behind; a shiver of admiration soured with envy.

'I understand you,' said Maggie, slowly and deliberately. 'I understand you very well, and I'm sure I would want to do the same in your position. It's you who doesn't understand. You could spend a hundred years trying to talk to that man like a human being, but he still wouldn't listen. He'd just wait patiently, looking back at you with that crocodile's smile, and then he'd just take whatever it was he wanted from you.' Her eyes wandered my face and she lifted a lock of my hair. 'You're a very pretty woman, so I have a feeling I know what that might be.'

I brushed her hand away.

'I don't care what he wants. He can have it if it means I get a boat.'

'And what then? You think you can just sail off into the ocean? Have you ever even sailed a boat before?'

'It can't be that hard, and anything's better than sitting here while my –' I gulped and shut my eyes '– while my children are over there. Please, let Bryce send the message, and for God's sake let me go.'

A moment's silence passed. Then Richard spoke.

'If you're going, then I'm going too.'

'Aye,' said Bryce, stepping forward. 'Me too.'

'That would only make it more dangerous,' said Maggie. 'With two bodyguards, you wouldn't even make it down to the town.'

I turned to them.

'She's right,' I said. 'Richard, you're a tall man, and Bryce, even with –' I waved a hand '– whatever this is, you still look like Lemmy and Hagrid's love child. No offence.'

'None taken.'

'It has to be me on my own.'

Maggie's eyes hadn't left me.

'You are a brave woman,' she said at last. 'And it makes me furious that you need the help of a cruel man. But I cannot let you go, it's too dangerous.'

'It's not your choice!'

'It *is* my choice. This Rock is under my care. Besides, you're not the first to go blundering down there trying to find another way out of this situation.'

'What do you mean?'

Maggie scowled.

'Ernest,' said Dani. 'He was one of the refugees who came in from Spain; a doctor. He worked in the hospital, and he didn't agree with my mother's ... *approach* to the situation.'

'Approach?' said Maggie, affronted. 'The only approach I've ever taken is to care for the people of this Rock in the only way I know how.'

Dani sneered. 'You mean by waiting for that bastard to attack us every two days?'

Maggie sighed and shook her head at the ceiling. 'By holding him back until that cruise ship runs out of supplies or he gets bored. There's no way he can beat our defences. He'll tire eventually.'

'Ernest didn't think so.'

'No,' said Maggie, pacing, 'he didn't, and he went bouldering in there against my wishes, in the dead of night, to broker a "peace deal" with that maniac. You can guess how that went down. Staines launched another attack the very next day, and we haven't seen Ernest since.' She turned to me. 'If you go down to that harbour asking for help then it will only provoke another attack. I won't risk it.'

Dani gave a sullen pout. 'You won't risk anything. You never have.'

'Child,' said Maggie, bitterly, 'you have no idea what it's like to have something in your care. It's not that easy to take risks when lives depend on you.' She touched a finger to her daughter's hair. 'Or even just one.'

Dani brushed off her mother's hand and went to the window, where she glared out at the sullen afternoon.

'What about Staines?' I said to Maggie. 'Surely he must have taken casualties too?'

'That's part of the problem, no? We have no idea how many men are down there, or what ammunition they have. We've never been able to get close enough to look.'

Dani pushed away from the window and paced the floor, smacking a palm with her fist. 'If we launched a proper attack on the harbour rather than messing about in no-man's land, do some *real* damage ...'

Maggie rolled her eyes. 'You know that's not possible when we don't know what's down there. His entire set-up is completely invisible to us. Even from up here we can't see how things fit together. It would be like walking into a minefield.'

'We have to try, Mother, we can't just sit here.'

'We wait, regroup, plan a proper attack on Eurotowers.'

'What about our supplies? How much time do we have? Three weeks? Less?'

'We'll ration them. We just need to sit tight.'

'What we *need* is to grow a set of tits.'

'And *you* need to watch your language, young lady.'

I limped to the missing wall, crutch squeaking, and pulled back a vine. The afternoon was growing dark and the clouds seemed to twitch with lightning, like a boxer's muscles before a fight. An orange glow rose from the harbour water behind the cruise ship. I thought I could hear music.

'You need to know what's down there,' I said.

'Exactly,' said Maggie. 'And we don't. So that's that.'

Dani joined me at the window. 'We would if you told us.'

Maggie threw up her arms. 'And what's she going to do, shout back up the Rock? Take a walkie-talkie in with her?'

I looked at Dani. She smiled. 'Not a walkie-talkie.'

'A wire?'

Dani turned from the wall of shelves. We were deep in the Rock now, far beneath the scrubbed, bright warmth and dope-shop aroma of Bryce's radio room. Down here was dark wet stone and cold musk. It was a store room of some kind, three walls of shelves piled high with boxes of nuts, bolts, cables and spare parts.

'No,' she replied, holding up a small silver disc no bigger than the button on a blouse. 'There are no wires, see? It's a wireless microphone transmitter.'

Richard took the disc and held it to the light of the bulb hanging from the ceiling.

'This is not a good idea,' he said, inspecting it like a jeweller with a counterfeit diamond.

'Though it pains me to say it, I agree with Dick,' said Bryce, hanging by the door with Carmela. The pair of them had been inseparable since I'd met them in the radio room, with some part of their bodies always touching. If a hand left a shoulder, another would reach for a hip, or a knee would search for a companion. I felt a sudden fierce envy at how easy it was for them to touch each other. Only inches separated them from the one they loved – my children, whose touch and smell I was already missing like a limb, were an ocean away from me.

I took the disc from Richard.

'How does it work?'

'USB-charged,' Dani said. 'You squeeze it to activate, after that it'll run for about three hours before it dies. It'll pick up any conversation in a twenty-metre area and transmit it up to one kilometre. I'll be down in the town receiving it with this.'

She held up a battered smartphone attached to a small white box with an aerial.

'What do I do with it?' I asked.

'Drop it somewhere busy, anywhere there's conversation like a canteen or a mess hall.'

Richard shook his head. 'No. No, no, no, this is *not* a good idea.' He turned to Maggie. 'What good will it do you anyway?'

'We can use it to trace Beth's location and pick up any information about their set-up down there.'

'What if they find it on you?' said Richard, turning to me.

I shrugged. 'Then I'm in trouble.'

Bryce stroked his freshly manicured beard, shaking his head.

'No, I don't like this. *Ed* wouldn't like this.'

'Well, Ed's not here, is he?' I snapped. 'Just like he's never here, and never was. This is my choice and it's the only way, so you can either help me or get out of my way. Now, will somebody tell me how to get down from this *fucking* Rock.'

Chapter 12

Bryce said his goodbyes and, still stroking his beard as if a cat was dangling from his chin, he disappeared with Carmela up to the radio room in an attempt to warn Tony of my impending visit. Maggie and Dani led me from the storeroom down some deep tunnels. My crutch technique was improving and I swung my leg for momentum in a bid to keep up with their swift strides. The ape looked back at me, claws clasped together and a wary, judgemental glint in his eye.

Richard and Josh followed. Richard muttered something to his son in a tone set somewhere between encouragement and frustration.

I tried to concentrate, to plan what words I would say to this supposedly dangerous stranger I was about to confront, and imagine what kind of journey awaited me if I was successful. But I couldn't think of anything for long. Only them. Only moving forward. I would swim that sea if I had to.

Eventually we emerged from a small opening in the Rock. We were not yet at ground level, and a rough track led down into the northern section of what had been the town. The now vertical rain carved grooves in the dirt.

Maggie handed me her torch and pointed down the track.

'Take Main Street until you reach the wall, then follow it until you come out at the car park.'

Main Street, the wall, the car park – they were all just dark clusters of rubble.

'Where am I heading?'

'That tall building. It's an old block of flats called Eurotowers. It's one of their lookouts, so it's where they'll first see you. Take these.'

She handed me a folded white rag and an unlabelled bottle.

'The rag for when you reach Eurotowers, the bottle for when you get inside. I happen to know the man likes rum.'

I tucked the rag in my belt and the bottle in my pocket. 'Thanks.'

'And take this as well.' Maggie unfastened a chain from her neck and held it out for me. A crucifix dangled from her fingers.

'Oh,' I replied. 'No, really, I'm not religious.'

She smiled. 'That makes two of us.'

She pressed the short length of silver at the top of the cross, and a long, thick needle sprang from the base with a click. She turned it, gleaming, for me to see. Then, with another click, the needle returned. She fastened it round my neck.

'OK,' I said. 'I'm going now.'

As I turned, Richard grabbed my arm.

'Beth, you don't have to do this.'

I pulled his fingers gently from my wrist and looked at Josh.

'You should know better than anyone that's not true.'

The track was steep and I pushed my crutch hard into the slick dirt to stop myself slipping. As my distance from the Rock grew, so did my sense of its immensity. It loomed over me, swarming with shadows and vegetation that clung like rope-less mountaineers to the merciless crags. A plume of cloud drew out from the jagged tip of its northern face. It seemed to be permanently attached, like a parasite, a slippery aide soothing the brow of its troubled king.

And down one side of this giant wedge was a scar. From north to south, a gouge that exposed the innards of the Rock like freshly sliced flesh. Tunnel segments ran like veins, and caves gaped like open wounds. I thought I saw Maggie's room high up near the north face, with strips of dull light between the vine curtains.

Thunder rumbled. I walked on, becoming sodden by the rain. It was warm, but not in a pleasant way, not in the way of a sun-baked Mediterranean town, or even in the humid, scent-filled way of a tropical jungle. It was a dense and poisonous heat, as if the mountain behind me was crushing everything beneath it, including the air itself. Isolated, oppressed, claustrophobic – that's how it felt, and I've never believed in ghosts or ghouls or witches, but there was something about the place that made me think about what it meant for a place to be haunted. Something wasn't right.

Or maybe it was just me.

There was something wrong with my heart, you see. It wasn't working properly. Where before it had beaten, now it stuttered. Where before I had barely considered this thing in my chest, this muscle that kept me alive without requiring any effort on my part, now I was aware of it all the time. It cried for me like a baby. It fluttered and flopped like a broken bird beneath a window. And it hurt. Real pain too, not the metaphorical kind but a jagged sting. Perhaps my heart really had stopped that evening on the *Unity*, and hadn't properly started since.

I was in the town now, or what was left of it. I had only seen glimpses of the devastation left behind after the strike, like when we were rescued from our cellar in Edinburgh, or from the grimy helicopter window on the way to Falmouth. Broken buildings spinning beneath, upended planes smoking in the distance. Always from afar. This was the first time I had ever seen it up close.

Main Street was a slim shopping parade of three-storey, smashed-fronted buildings that still held clues to what they had once been. The charred and empty shelves lining the entrance to a jeweller's, and the fragments of rings and necklaces now sprayed into dust with the glass that had once housed them. The blue, uptight logo that could only have been a bank's now hanging skew above a slashed and tattered awning. A dusty stuffed bear straddling a ballerina puppet, the puppet's jaw dropped in alarm, arms bound by its own strings.

Mist clung to the cobbles like spiderwebs. It reminded me of one morning in my student days in Leeds, when I had woken early and gone out for milk. Nobody was awake, and the terraced street upon which I shared a house was deathly quiet. An eerie fog hung over everything, withholding and compressing the sunlight so it had felt like I was walking through a dream.

Then I had passed a burned-out car, and a second further up. The shop had been shut. I found out later that there had been riots the night before. I had slept through them.

Everything seemed to taper towards the end of Main Street as if the buildings were being driven down into rubble. When finally they disappeared altogether, I saw that the wall Maggie had described was actually the ground which had been torn up. A deep trench lay on the other side of it, stretching from the water's edge up to the northern face of the Rock.

I followed the wall, picking carefully through the bricks and glass. I was close to water now; I could hear it lapping against rock ahead, and there was something else too. Music. Huge and over-produced, a woman's voice soaring over synthesisers and sizzling, cavernous drums. A saxophone solo. I was sure I recognised it. It was coming from the harbour where the grey wedge of the cruise ship now appeared through the gloom. There was orange light behind it, the source of the music, I supposed.

I felt something in my torso – not my heart's struggling pang, but dread, as the reality of what I was about to do finally became apparent.

I am not particularly good at walking into new situations. I get nervous before doctor's appointments. I do not find sport in argument or take pleasure in negotiation. The truth is I just don't understand how people work. I am neither driven nor able to make secret assessments of a rival's weaknesses or recall things I might have against them. I don't have any rivals. Anyone who opposes me, who wants to get one over on me, who wants to get more of the cheese than me – fine, take it, I don't mind. Anything to prevent the need for confrontation.

I cry. I actually cry if I have to talk to somebody when I'm even just a wee bit pissed off. The corners of my mouth pull down, my stomach flips and my eyes fill up with tears. I can't help it.

I'd be the world's worst hostage negotiator, and if I ever tried to talk someone down from a building then I'd probably end up holding their hand and jumping off with them.

I'm shit at talking to people. Basically, I'm no good at being human.

And yet I had just managed to confront Maggie without a thought. I took some dim comfort in this, because whatever I was about to do had to work. For Alice and Arthur.

As I neared the water's edge another shape emerged from the mist, a degraded tower block to the left of the ship. I had just realised that this was Eurotowers when I heard a shot and the sea-wet mud before me exploded. I yelped and froze, dropping the bottle, which broke upon a buried breeze block. The treacly contents oozed into the mud.

'Damn it.'

I stared at the place where the bullet had hit the ground, only a few metres from me. Then I looked up at the tower block. There was movement between the broken windows.

'Don't shoot,' I cried. My voice made dull echoes from the wet stone. I yanked the white rag from my belt and waved it above my head. 'Don't shoot! I'm not—'

Another shot, closer this time. I staggered back, nearly falling but steadying myself with my crutch. The music played on from some time and place in which gunshots and mud-soaked rum did not exist.

'Please!' I shouted now, waving the rag violently. 'Don't shoot! I'm not armed, I just want to talk!'

There was silence. The music had stopped. From somewhere deep in the murk came the cold cry of a gull, then lumbering footsteps on metal.

Silence again. Then a voice.

'Put that down.'

I turned in its direction. The silhouette of a large man with a gun strapped over his shoulders stood between me and the ship. He seemed to be floating on the water.

I held the rag higher so he could see. 'I'm not armed. We radioed a message.'

'Put that down,' he repeated.

I paused, then tossed the rag in the dirt.

'Not that,' he said, his impatience inflated by the rubbery vowels of a Birmingham accent. 'The stick.'

I looked down at my crutch.

'It's a crutch. I broke my leg.'

He lifted the tip of his gun, just a little.

'I said, put it down.'

Letting my good leg take my weight, I dropped the crutch in the mud. There I stood like a heron, my bad leg barely touching the ground.

'Come on then,' he said.

'I–I can't walk.'

"Course you can. There's a jetty here. Come towards it.'

Scanning the ground, I took a few hops towards the figure. I had already hit water when I saw the wood slats of the jetty in the mud ahead, but on the next hop I accidentally balanced on my bad leg. It was just a touch, but enough to make me collapse with a cry onto the wet wood.

I lay there whimpering and clutching my leg. I heard tuts and mumbled words of irritation from the figure at the other end of the jetty. When the pain had receded sufficiently for me to consider it, I grabbed the wood and pushed myself up till I was standing once again. Then I tested the pain's biting point by gradually exerting more pressure upon my bad leg.

'Come on, hurry up, will you?'

After a few more tries I found my leg would take my weight, at least for a moment, and in this way I limped along the ramshackle jetty. The shadow became visible as I reached the end. He was a fat, white man with a bulky nose, a wide, guppy-like mouth and swollen dark-ringed eyes. His tongue seemed to take permanent residence in the space between his lips, giving the impression that he was stuck at all times between thought and speech. He had an enormous chest and shoulders, but it was hard to tell what was what; fat, bone or muscle – there was no clue. He could have been a skeleton swimming in blubber for all I knew.

'Hello,' I said, annoyed at the tremble in my voice, the tightness in my throat. I thought of Alice and the pressure relented.

He smiled – not a pleasant experience – and looked me up and down.

'O'right,' he replied cheerfully.

I watched him. He watched me back. He was either dim-witted or playing with me. Probably a bit of both.

I thought of Alice again and straightened up. I let both legs take half a body each. Though the pain was intense, I withheld it, and in return it helped me concentrate.

Another roll of thunder arced above us.

'We sent a message,' I said. My voice was clearer now. 'On the radio.'

He blinked.

'You're the one who wants to speak with Mr Staines?'

'Aye.'

'Are you Scottish?'

I frowned. 'Aye.'

He seemed pleased with himself.

'Thought so. Thought I could hear an accent.'

I cocked my head. 'So?' I said.

'What?'

'Can I speak with Tony?'

He looked over his shoulder then back at me, as if trying to reach a decision we both knew he'd already been told the outcome of.

Finally he rolled his eyes.

'Follow me,' he said, turning.

I followed him along a series of other jetties to a network of wooden platforms lashed together around the cruise ship. His bulging shoulders swayed as he walked, like a grizzly in the throes of a dart's sedative.

We passed the bow of the ship. It seemed deserted, though I thought I could see figures moving behind the dark portholes. It was almost dark by the time we reached the other side, and our way was lit by flaming torches lining the walkways. There were wooden railings which I used to take the pressure off my leg. Another song had started, this one a gruff-voiced blues club number. I didn't recognise the voice, but it made me think of sweaty men with open shirts and pained expressions.

The network of walkways was as long as the ship, and stretched almost the same distance out into the harbour. It formed a series of mooring points for vessels of all kinds – yachts, speedboats, fishing trawlers – each lit by its own torch. They had made a new harbour for themselves behind the cruise ship, but unlike other harbours I had seen, the boats were unkempt and filthy. There were figures on board, drinking and mumbling with each other around stoves. Occasionally there was a cackle or a roar of laughter which stopped at my approach. Heads turned, eyes glinting with menace as they tracked my limp past. At one boat somebody got up and stepped onto the walkway in front of me. He was a wiry man, long-haired, smoking a cigarette with that face that makes it seem like every drag is a source of incredible pain. He positioned himself so that I had to brush past him. More figures followed his lead, putting themselves in my way so I had to negotiate my way through and around them. At one boat I met two girls, hips cocked, and as I passed one held her nose.

'Phwoah, fucking hell,' she said, wafting her nose. 'Smells like something died in her fanny.'

She slammed into my shoulder, and I just managed to catch hold of the side rail before toppling into the water. I stooped over the side, catching my breath as lazy laughter came from the boats around us.

'Christ, don't bend over,' said the girl in her Essex snarl. 'That's even worse.'

More laughter. I could feel them all around me. I was scared now.

I thought of Alice, straightened up and hopped around to face her.

'I'm not looking for trouble,' I said. The laughter died with disappointment. 'I just want to talk to Tony.'

Her eyes glinted like scraps of tinfoil. She curled her lip and let me pass.

The walkways led to a central covered platform surrounded by flaming torches. It was the source of the music, and now I heard voices too. My guide waddled on, and as we approached the entrance of the platform two figures – guards, I guessed from their guns – turned. One was female, thin-lipped with hair like Styrofoam, and the other a stocky, broad male with two missing incisors on the last drags of his cigarette.

My chaperone made a clicking sound with his cheek and tongue.

'O'right?' he said.

'This her?' said the bullish man.

'Yeah. She's Scottish.'

The woman looked me up and down. 'Checked her?'

My guide shrugged. 'She 'ad a stick. I made her leave it.'

She rolled her eyes. 'Fucking hell, Grot.'

'What?' said Grot.

136

'Jesus,' said the other guard, flicking his butt in the water. 'You were supposed to radio it in, dickhead. That's why you've got a *radio*.'

Grot gave another shrug. 'Didn't see the point. She only 'ad a stick.'

'Who else was in Eurotowers?'

'Mark, Stacey and Beans. I'm not a fookin' idiot, am I?'

'And what were they doing when you were letting people through the line?'

'Mark and Stacey were shagging, and Beans was taking a dump. And anyway, I didn't let her through, I *escorted* her through. Like a prisoner, you know? There's a difference.'

'You're a dickhead, Grot.'

'I am not.'

As the pair argued the woman beckoned to me. 'Come here. Raise your arms.'

I did as she asked and she swung back her gun, patting me down. Ears, neck – her fingers ran over the crucifix but not for long – shoulders, breasts, waist. I held my breath as she checked the rim of my belt, where the transmitter was hidden, but she passed it unnoticed and moved onto my crotch, bum and legs. I flinched as she patted my right leg, and she froze, hands still on the spot. Her eyes flashed up at me.

'What?'

'Nothing.' A tear escaped. 'I broke my leg. That's why I had a crutch.'

She blinked. Still looking at me, she checked the same spot more carefully, kneading her fingers into my flesh with excruciating precision. Every muscle tightened as I bit back the pain. I whimpered as more tears followed the first. When I was just ready to crumple, she finally moved on. Shins, then ankles. She unfastened my boots and put them to one side so I was standing, dripping in my socks.

Satisfied, she stood.

'Fine, you're clear.'

Grot and the guard were laughing about something now, sharing a match for a cigarette.

'Get back to the Eurotowers, Grot,' said the woman. 'You know the score.'

Grot tutted and puffed his cigarette.

'All right, Jules,' he said. He gave the guard a wink. 'See youse later.'

With that he waddled off the way he had come.

I was still holding my arms outstretched, right foot raised so only my toes were touching the ground.

The woman gave a bored frown. 'Put your arms down, girl. You look like a fucking scarecrow. Come on, inside. Stay here, Ollie.'

The guard sniffed and turned back to his sentry, and I followed the woman, limping. Beyond the rough wooden archway was what looked like an outdoor beer garden. Tables and benches lined the slatted floor, through which the sea was visible, slapping the wood with every surge of the tide. Along one end of the platform was a long bar, roughly hammered together with timber and metal. Car bonnets were embedded in the wall behind rows of discoloured bottles and glasses, and what looked like bus seats skewered with spikes formed stools along its front.

The music blared from a mismatched collection of speakers in one corner, from which a series of cables fell like black intestines to a box on the floor. The blues song had faded out, replaced by something tuneless and synthetic. Every table was full of people drinking. At first I only saw men, and mostly of the same kind. The way they were built, the way they talked, their accents, the way they smiled, the colour of their skin – not white at all, but red and swollen with sun and beer.

It's not right to judge people on appearances. It's not right to assume a political stereotype just because someone happens to be fat, bald and white, and happens to be drinking a certain kind of beer with a certain swagger, and making a certain kind of expression. Inside every sunburned, shorn scalp I saw that evening there could have been a whole world going on to which I would never would be privy – subtleties of thought and emotional depths that would forever be theirs alone. So it wouldn't be right for me to snap them to a grid of behaviours in the same way I believed they did to others.

But I did. I definitely did. And the Union Jacks plastered over the bar did nothing to help.

And as I hobbled from table to table, I noticed women too, more and more of them, and darker skins, though in lesser number.

Each table's conversation ceased as I passed it, the men's expressions ranging from glowers to leers, the women displaying only bored menace. The guard led me to the middle of the bar, where a group was gathered around a tall man with his back turned. He wore a blue linen shirt, shorts and sandals, and was talking animatedly about something to the group, who looked on, rapt. One saw me approach and nudged his elbow.

He turned.

Blue wolflike eyes, tanned skin and a shock of white hair greeted me. He was in his sixties, I guessed, and a small paunch pulled at the otherwise taut and leathery torso dusted with soft, white hair. His face was frozen in the half-smile of his story, hands in mid-gesticulation.

'Hi,' he said, with a baffled tremor of his head.

'Hello,' I said.

He glanced at the tall, dark-eyed girl standing on his right, who sauntered to the speakers near the end. A moment later the music had stopped. The whole bar watched us in silence.

Tony turned fully to face me, face frozen in an overly worried frown.

'Is this her, Julia?' he said to the guard, almost a whisper. 'The one from the radio missive?'

Julia nodded. 'Apparently so.'

'Right, right, and I suppose you've done all the, you know, necessary checks and what have you?'

His accent was hard to place. Definitely the plummy end of English, but softened by a West Country roll.

Julia looked at me. 'She's clean, I've searched her.'

'OK.' He looked at me, bringing his hands together. 'OK, well that's good.'

He glanced around the group, then back at me.

'Never can be too careful these days. What's your name, my darling?'

'Beth.'

'Beth.' He looked around again, hands still together. 'Just Beth?'

'Beth's fine.'

'Right, well, I'm Tony.' He bowed his neck towards me, speaking quietly. 'But you knew that, didn't you?'

I nodded. The words he spoke, though dressed up in kindness, came out as cold and measured, a razor blade concealed in every consonant. I could feel myself trembling with nerves. If only they didn't make it to my lips.

'Thank you for ... for ...'

He shook his head and tutted.

'You're absolutely soaked,' he said. 'You must be freezing.'

'I'm fine, really ...'

'No, honestly, you'll catch your death! Ernest?' He snapped his fingers and blew an incredibly loud and well-practiced whistle, looking about. 'Ernest, where are you?'

From behind the bar came a man in a faded yellow polo neck. He was younger than Tony, with thinning black hair and wide, hound dog eyes.

'Ernest, there you are. Get this young lady a towel, will you?'

The man gave me a wary glance.

'Ernest.'

Ernest snapped to attention.

'Yes. Anything else?'

'And something to drink. Would you like something to drink, Beth? What's your poison? Beer, spirits? Me, I'm a rum drinker – never to excess, you understand, one in the morning, one in the afternoon, two in the evening. That's my rule. One of them, anyway. You have to live by rules, don't you think?'

I was fighting to stop the tremble rising through my body.

'I ...' was all I could muster.

Tony shook his head again, frustrated with himself. 'I'm babbling,' he said with a laugh, 'please, ignore me. Now, what would you like?'

'Just water, thank you.'

Tony turned to Ernest. 'Water for Beth, please, Ernest.'

Ernest nodded, gave me another glance and hurried away, tripping on the same stool. A second later he returned with a tea towel and an unopened bottle, which he handed to me with shaking hands. Sweat lined his stubbled upper lip.

'Thank you,' I said.

'My pleasure,' said Tony. He smiled and put his hands in his pockets, watching me. I noticed that the rest of the bar was watching me too. Tony cocked his head. 'Don't wait on our account, Beth.'

I patted my neck and hair with the towel as Tony and the rest of the bar watched in silence. I felt exposed, as if I was undressing in front of them. Then I opened the bottle and drank from it. Once I had started, I found I couldn't stop, and when I came up for air the water was finished. Tony broadened his smile and beckoned for the empty bottle.

I gave it to him.

'Did Maggie send you?' he asked.

I went to reply but he held up a hand.

'Before you answer, you should know that I place a huge amount of value in the truth. So please, don't lie to me.'

'I wasn't going to. Maggie didn't send me. In fact she didn't want me to come at all.'

Tony looked up.

'Really?' He glanced at one of his cohorts at the bar. 'Why do you think that was?'

The pain in my right leg was becoming a distraction, and my left leg was starting to quiver with the additional weight. The transmitter beneath my belt felt five times its size, and I was convinced everyone in the room knew about it.

'She thought it was too ...'

'Too what?'

'Too dangerous.'

He tutted and rolled his eyes, waggling the bottle.

'Dangerous. Charming. I've only ever been open and honest with that woman, and she calls me "dangerous". Can you believe that?'

I realised he had directed the question at me.

'I don't know,' I said. 'I've only just met her.'

'How so?'

'I was on the raft that came in twelve weeks ago.'

Tony's eyes widened. 'Really?'

'Yes. I was on an evacuation boat that sunk in a tsunami. My children—'

'You were one of the poor souls who washed up in that terrible storm?' He turned to the group around him. 'Do you remember that storm, Danny? Cheryl?'

Danny and Cheryl nodded without a word.

'Good God,' he said. 'You poor thing. We tried to get to you, we really did. But those waves, atrocious, weren't they, Cheryl? Our harbour was almost washed away, and then I saw that *woman* and her bandits dragging you in and I thought *poor things. Poor, poor things, if only we'd got to you first.* You could have been safe here with us, rather than in that godforsaken Rock up there.' He cast a dark look up at the hulking shadow beyond the cruise ship. 'What were there, eighteen, nineteen of you?'

'I don't know, I was unconscious. I broke my leg, went into a coma. I've only just woken up.'

He pulled his head back, startled.

'Only just woken up?' He looked around for support. '*Only just woken up?* And the first thing you do is wander down into a war zone. You've got balls of steel, Beth! Balls of steel.'

There was laughter at this, I presume because women don't have balls. Tony's face lit up.

'Please ...' I began. My hand had travelled to my belt without me noticing, and I let it fall quickly. Tony, still enjoying his laughter, didn't notice, but I thought I saw the tall girl's eyes narrow at the movement. Tony finally quelled the room with a downturned palm.

'Apologies, apologies, they're an excitable bunch. What was it you wanted to say?'

'My children were taken from me. When the boat went down, somebody took my children.'

'Who?'

'A stranger. She knew I was alive but she took them anyway.'

'What kind of monster would do such a thing?'

'And now –' my heart did its stunned bird routine '– now they're on the other side of the Atlantic, and they must ... they must think I'm dead. I need to get to them. I need to find a way across ...'

A sudden wave of dizziness overcame me and I stumbled forward. There were gasps as Tony caught me.

'Easy there, I've got you. I've got you. Cheryl, get a chair, love, would you?'

Though my vision was a mess of moving parts, my mind was still alert and as Tony fought to keep me upright, I slipped my finger beneath my belt and retrieved the transmitter. A chair leg scraped on wood, and I found myself being manoeuvred into a low seat. Blood thumped as my vision steadied. Tony was now crouching before me.

'This has been a most upsetting time for you, hasn't it, Beth?'

I nodded, overwhelmed by the sour reek of cheap aftershave and cigar smoke.

'Well, I'm here to tell you I understand.' He placed a hand on the knee of my good leg and patted it. It was an inch from my own hand, in which the transmitter was still clasped. 'I understand what upsetting times can be like, and I understand what losing your children is like.'

'You do?'

He nodded, face a parody of concern. 'I do, because it happened to me too.'

His hand was still on my knee. He noticed me looking at it, but he didn't snatch it way. He left it there for one second, two seconds, three, before finally retracting it and standing.

'I'm a father, Beth. Still am, as far as I'm aware.' He took a long, deep sigh. 'Worst day of my life when she took them from me. My wife, you understand, not a stranger like in your case. Mind you, it's almost worse when you do know the person, isn't it?'

I said nothing.

'I mean, I know I deserved it.' He made a boyish smirk of guilt. 'Playing away from home and all that, not very clever. But all the same, it was a dreadful feeling having my son *taken* from me. What right does anyone have to do that? Not just to me, but to the boy as well? She was robbing him of his father.' He shook his head wanly. 'Stupid bitch.'

He lost himself in the middle distance for a few moments before snapping back to attention. He shrugged.

'Anyway, dreadful feeling, like I say. I felt like my heart had been ripped out, you know? Do you feel that, Beth? Like your heart's been ripped out?'

I nodded. 'That's why I need to—'

But he had already started to pace, and his eyes were following the trajectory of his own thoughts, not mine.

'For a while I didn't know what I was going to do. I was a child's father, after all. I had a job to do. And fair enough, maybe I didn't get to spend as much time with him as I would have liked, and maybe I travelled a lot, and yes – ' he made an *irk* face '– the whole thing with the affairs and what have you, *guilty*, but that didn't change the fact that I was his father, did it? I still had to be there for him, tell him how to be a man and all that. But now that had been taken away from me. It was like I'd been sacked. Anyway, I did all the usual things, you know, pleading, begging, crying, then screaming, shouting, making threats, other things . . .' he trailed off. 'But then I stopped. I stopped because I realised something. These feelings I had, they were for me, not my son. They didn't help him. My boy would go on living without me, that was the truth. They're adaptable things, children, even at five years old, and I knew he'd be just fine. He might be sad at first, but in time he'd get over it. So I stopped. I stopped feeling those selfish things and I got on with life. I let him go. And that was the greatest gift I could give us both. I returned to my instincts, the things that made me *me*, not those pressures we feel as a parent. *Me*. And by Christ it worked. Overnight I was a different person. I was free.'

He stopped pacing and crouched down before me. The transmitter felt as if it was burning a hole in my palm.

'What I'm trying to say, Beth, is that you shouldn't let these feelings you're having right now –' he tapped my ribs just above my right breast '– in here cloud your vision. You need to let go.'

I stared at him, hairs on the back of my neck standing on end, and shook my head.

'I can't do that.'

'Of course you can't,' he said with a smile. 'You're a mother. Your children have been taken from you. You feel an unbearable pull, Beth, don't you, you're on a mission. A quest!'

He grinned at me. A cold wind from the sea sent a shiver down my neck. Suddenly I wanted nothing more than to drop the transmitter and run.

'I just need some help.'

'Help? And how can *I* help you, Beth?'

I glanced around at the expectant faces.

'I–I need a boat.'

There was a moment's silence. Tony blinked, and from the far end of the floating platform a woman released a single, stifled hoot. Tony stood and turned to the tables.

'A boat,' he said. 'She wants a boat.'

The place erupted with laughter, jeers and stamping feet. I took my chance and felt beneath the chair, where I found a gap between the wood and the seat. Squeezing the transmitter to turn it on, I pressed it between the gap and returned my hand as quickly as I could.

Tony quelled the baying crowd.

'Quiet!' he roared, and gradually the noise abated. 'Bloody animals, the lot of you. This poor, brave woman has been through hell and you're laughing at her. Would any one of you do what she's doing in her position? Fresh from a coma, broken leg, come and face a stranger on the other side of a battlefield and ask for help? Well, would you? No, didn't think so, you bunch of scruffy cowards.'

He stood before my chair, appraising me.

'This woman has come asking for our help, and I for one am touched by that, I really am.'

'I'm sorry, I know you're ... busy with all that up there. But there's nowhere else I can go. You appear to have all the boats.'

He nodded. 'That I do, Beth, that I do. And tell me, what were you, er, hoping to offer in return for one of them?'

My gaze dropped. 'I–I don't have any money.'

'Money?' He pulled a face. 'I don't want money. It's worthless. Always was.'

He crouched at my feet again, gripping the chair just inches from the transmitter.

'So I'll ask again, what can you offer me in return for one of my boats?'

I looked directly at him. There really is nothing I wouldn't do for my children.

'I'll do anything you want me to, if you can get me where I need to go.'

The crowd erupted again with filthy jeers and hammered tables, like rampant chimps. Tony silenced them with a deafening whistle.

'Quiet!' He was serious this time. 'Shut the fuck up, the lot of you.'

His expression had darkened.

'I may be a lot of things, my darling, but I'm not that.' He stood and turned to the floor, raising his voice. 'Nobody here is. Understand?'

There was silence. He went on.

'No, I don't want money, and I don't want *that*. What I want, Beth, is trust. Pure and simple. I want you to put your trust in me, just like all these ... *enlightened* men and women have.'

The wood squeaked as he walked between the tables, placing a hand on every shoulder he passed. 'These have been some fairly bleak and desperate times, and you're not the only one with a sob story, Beth. Each and every one in this little haven of mine has a tale that would make your hair stand on end.

Myself included. But we've survived, haven't we? We've come through it, and we've done it by trusting each other. Not by payment, not by false promises, but through trust and loyalty. That's what makes the world go round now, that's the currency in which we trade. And we're all fucking millionaires.'

Whistles, cheers and claps filled the air as he returned to my seat.

He beamed and opened his arms like a preacher to his congregation.

'Friends,' he said. 'We're nothing without our friends, Beth. Wouldn't you agree? So. If you want a boat, if you want help to get to your children, then that's my price. Trust and loyalty. Friendship. Can you give me that?'

For the first time since the *Unity* my heart found its rhythm; a flutter of hope.

'I already told you, I'll give you anything if you help me find my children.'

He smiled with wonder. 'A mother's love. Indestructible. Now, I'm going to make you a promise, Beth: you put your trust in me and I'll give you a boat. I'll even sail it across that ruddy ocean myself if I—'

He stopped. His eyes had landed on the crucifix around my neck. He reached for it, and it took all my effort not to flinch.

'What's this?' he said, lifting it.

'Oh, nothing,' I said, taking care not to rush my words. 'It was a gift.'

'You're religious?'

I shook my head. 'No. Not really.'

He nodded, then removed it from my neck and placed it around his own. I noticed that there were three or four other necklaces there too.

'Then I'll take this,' he said. 'As a symbol of your promise.'

He stood and turned his head to the Rock. His expression darkened. 'As I was saying: you'll get your boat. All I ask is for a little patience while Maggie and I sort out our differences.'

'How long will that be?' I blurted out. 'I can't wait, and I don't need your help to sail it. If you had something small, something you wouldn't miss, even just a dinghy, I could leave now.'

A flicker of annoyance crossed his face. 'You wouldn't make it out of the Straits. It's not just ocean between here and America, you know. Scoundrels roam these waters now; outlaws, pirates, people who would kill you as soon as look at you. You need a crew and safe passage, Beth. Without that, you're dead in the water. Patience, as I said. Patience. Now.'

He brought his hands together with a gentle clap.

'Ernest, take our guest to her quarters, would you? There's a good chap.' Ernest resurfaced from the shadows. 'It's late and I'm sure she's tired.'

Ernest hesitated. 'Quarters?'

'The eastern brig is empty,' muttered Tony. 'See she's secure. Oh –' he grabbed a broom that was propped against the bar '– and take this. It's not quite a crutch but it should help. Must be terribly uncomfortable, hmm?'

I remained in my seat, the silence of the bar broken only by the relentless slap of seawater beneath us. Ernest hovered nearby as Tony looked around, awkwardly. 'It's late, Beth. Good night.'

Chapter 13

'What are you doing here?' said Ernest in a Spanish hiss. There was a strained quality to his voice, like an old man struggling with shopping bags. 'Did Maggie send you?'

I limped after him with the broom lodged painfully in my armpit. It was darker out here on the furthest edged of the floating network, and the noise of the bar was behind us. We passed boat after boat until we reached a hut of some kind, where Ernest stopped and fiddled with a set of keys. A guard patrolled the walkway. Ernest grinned as he passed, but the guard dismissed him with a sneer.

'You're the one she told me about,' I said, once the guard was gone. 'The one who came down to try and reason with Staines.'

He huffed and muttered, rattling his key in the hut's lock.

'*Reason*, that's a joke. There is no reasoning with Tony Staines. Why did she send you?'

'She didn't. I came down of my own accord.'

'Why?'

'To ask for help, like I said.'

'That story about your children, it was true?'

'Yes. Why would I lie about—'

'So you really came to ask Tony for his help?'

'Yes.'

The door opened into a small, dark room. 'Then I'm afraid you made a terrible mistake. Get inside, please.'

Reluctantly, I stepped through the door. My head grazed the rough wood of the ceiling.

'What is this place? How long do I have to stay here?'

'That is not up to me.'

'What happened to you? Why did you come down here?'

'Because someone had to. It was madness staying up there in that Rock, watching our supplies dwindle and our casualties mount up while he sat down here having parties every night, biding his time. There was no chance of us winning, no chance at all. I begged her to see sense, to go down and broker some kind of a deal, give him what he wanted so that we could get off that place. But she was too proud, and too naive. She had never left that Rock of hers, she didn't know men like Tony Staines. I did. So I came down instead, I slipped past our guards one night and swam the flooded tunnels to the shoreline. Tony's men picked me up and took me to him, just like they did with you, and he paraded me in front of his audience, just like he did with you, and he listened to what I had to say, just like he did with you.'

He looked bitterly at the sodden floorboards. The room swayed with the tide.

'What did you ask him?'

'I asked him to let the people in the Rock go free. In return he could have the place, so long as he gave them safe passage to the mainland. He told me that his terms were the same as they had always been. The people of the Rock were free whenever they felt like surrendering, but that there would be no need for their safe passage. He would take care of them once Maggie had given over control. Then he gave me a choice ...'

He broke off, fiddling with his keys.

'What kind of a choice?'

'I could either go back to the Rock and tell Maggie the terms that she already knew or stay with him. Be a part of his tribe. *Trust* him. I chose the latter. I couldn't stand to go back to that place again. And now I'm stuck here.' He kicked the frame of the door. 'Doing his chores, laughed at by his men. I'm a prisoner.' He glanced up. 'And now you are too.'

'I have to believe there's a chance he'll be true to his word. It's the only hope I have right now.'

Ernest's eyes caught a fierce glint. 'You need to listen to me. There is no hope. You cannot believe a word that comes out of Tony Staines' mouth. All that stuff about trust? It's horseshit. He's a narcissist who only cares about the size of his pile and how many people he has under his control. He wants that Rock as a base, a place he can rule and store his loot. I'm sorry, I wish I could tell you otherwise, but there's no way he'll take you to your children. He's a power-mad lunatic.' He sighed and rubbed his brow. 'And Maggie cannot beat him.'

I looked out at the twin shadows of the Rock and the cruise ship.

'Why doesn't she fire directly on his base?' I asked. 'She has the upper hand, being so high.'

'Why? Because of that bloody great cruise ship out there. It's a human shield. He keeps all those poor bastards locked inside and Maggie knows it.'

'Ernest, is there anything you know about his set-up? Anything at all that might help Maggie?'

He shrugged. 'I know the layout, the patterns of the sentry shifts at Eurotowers. But—'

He froze as the guard passed the hut.

'You have to stay here,' Ernest said in a deliberate tone, watching the guard's progress, 'until Mr Staines decides what will happen to you. There's a bed in the corner, I'll bring you water, and some ...'

He turned back, the guard gone, and leaned close.

'Why? What good is my knowledge here?'

'There's a transmitter underneath the chair I was sitting on in the bar. Maggie is listening to it.'

Ernest's eyes widened, two terrified moons.

'What ... how?'

'They gave it to me when I left. If you can find a way of speaking nearby then maybe the information could help her. Ernest?'

But Ernest was backing away. 'No ... no, you've made a terrible mistake.'

He closed the door and snapped the padlock shut. I looked out through the small rectangular window. 'Ernest, please, you have to try.'

'No. A terrible mistake. Terrible.'

He made off down the walkway, keys jangling.

I sat on the cot bed in the dark, trying to ignore the rowdy jeers and slurred murmurs coming from in the bar. It was late – after midnight, I guessed – but the party was showing no signs of stopping. Tony's atrocious music blared from the speakers and his voice rose over everything as he regaled the crowd with stories. And that laugh of his – Maggie had been right; it was a foul thing, like the cries of some prehistoric birdlike beast drowning in oil.

It was cold and the blanket they had given me was thin, but I pulled it to my chin and turned to look east through the hut's slatted walls. The sea churned beneath a low moon. It had never seemed so dark and terrifying, but all I could think of was plunging into it. I knew exactly where my children were. I could feel them pulling at me like a pole at a compass. The distance would be nothing, the pain inconsequential compared to what I felt now, trapped and useless in this cell.

These are the times when people pray, and this is the kind of place in which they do it; this dark cell with a figure in its corner, out of luck and options.

But I've never got the hang of prayer – mine ends up sounding like awkward, apologetic poetry – and besides, it always feels like a lottery to me. For every prayer that's answered, after all, a million more are tossed aside. Just like *Jim'll Fix It*.

I tried that night. I tried to pray.

God, I need my children back. God, what, why, who and however you are, I need my children back or I'm going to suffocate. My heart is going to crumble into dust and I'm going to …

But I couldn't finish it. I couldn't enter the safety of my children into a lottery that guaranteed more heart-break and disappointment than it did joy and relief.

So I hoped instead.

I hoped that Ernest was wrong; I hoped that Tony Staines was nothing more than a scoundrel who would find it in his heart to be true to his word, and that he wouldn't ask too much in return. I hoped that I would be out of this cell and across the sea before I knew it. I hoped that Mary was just a desperate mother who had lost her child and made a bad decision, but that she would care for my children nonetheless. I hoped that Alice and Arthur were safe, even if they were upset, and I hoped they wouldn't be angry with me when I found them.

I hoped I would see Ed again.

That one was a surprise.

What was he doing right now? Was he moving, getting to where he needed to be? Or was he stuck somewhere in the dark like me?

I remember watching him flounder in that cellar (another dark place in which I had failed to pray), trying to be the husband and father who looked after his family, who knew how to survive. It had reminded me of that camping trip he'd insisted on us taking, the one where it rained constantly and nothing worked. He had tried to cook sausages in the pouring rain and I wanted so badly to tell him that sausages didn't matter, that I didn't need a hunter for a husband or even a man who knew how to work a camping stove. All I needed was for him to be near us. To be present.

But I didn't, because I thought it might make things worse. That's how fragile I thought him; that he might shatter under the weight of a single kind word.

The moment I realised I was smiling about sausages, there was a commotion from the bar. The music had stopped abruptly, replaced by the sound of sharp voices and scuffling boots. I hopped to the door and peered through its slot. Shadows moved quickly. It was a struggle of some kind, but I couldn't see who or what it was between. The guard on my walkway had stopped and was looking in the same direction.

I called to him.

'What's happening?'

In the distance Tony Staines spoke in calm, measured tones.

'Never you mind,' replied the guard, ambling off to get a closer look.

Tony had stopped talking. After more scuffling and a terrified cry there was an eerie silence in which a flame was lit.

Then Ernest began to shriek.

I staggered away from the door and sat on the crib.

So that was hope.

Chapter 14

Sometime later, once Ernest's howls had finally ceased, there were footsteps on the walkway. I sat up. The guard mumbled something, to which a familiar voice responded with a knowing laugh. The padlock shook, the door opened, and in walked Tony Staines.

His silhouette filled the frame.

'I *am* sorry to disturb you,' he said. He sounded drunk, his voice swaying with the brig. 'Really I am.'

I gripped the crib's frame. 'What did you do?'

He raised his arms in a half-hearted flap.

'This must all seem very ... *barbaric* to you, I suppose.' He huffed a sad little laugh and sat down beside me. I shuffled away, knuckles tightening. 'But believe me, I don't want to be here any more than you do. I'd much rather be out there at sea, moving on, getting stuff done, know what I mean? Out there, where there isn't anything to get in your way. Best thing about the sea, in my opinion. No borders, no walls, no rules. Just you and the horizon.'

He gave a deep, satisfied smile and turned to me, teeth flashing in the moonlight. Wood smoke now overpowered the stench of rum and cheap aftershave. The smile drained.

'I wasn't always so enamoured with it. Sea that is. I was a City boy through and through back in the day. Worked in finance. Yup. Big cheese. Made a lot of dough, and I mean a *lot*, know what I mean?' He wagged a finger. 'Not just for me though, no, for other people too. Other people with money, that is.'

He gave a deafening bray of that terrible laughter and squeezed my left knee. I felt sick.

'No, no, honestly I loved my job, loved it. And do you know the thing I loved most? Every single thing I did had an immediate consequence which you either paid for or profited from. Simple as that. I loved the City, loved the life, the clubs, the cars, the lunches, the suits, the free tickets, girls, all that bollocks. Thieves, they used to call us, yup, s'true. And you know what? They were right. We *were* thieves, thieves and scoundrels through and through and we knew it. *I* knew it.'

He turned to me as if his neck was a spring.

'But what I didn't realise then was how much honesty there is in theft. Understand? No. You don't. See, I loved money. I did. Then one evening – forget what it was, some charity fundraiser, PR stunt for the firm – this woman talking to me – pretty little thing in her twenties, some sort of writer I think – asked me: "What is money?" I laughed and told her: "Money's the meaning of life, sweetheart, haven't you heard?" But she smiled sweetly and asked me again: "Seriously, how would you describe money to an alien?" *Stupid girl*, I thought, and I laughed her off and went to talk to somebody else.

'But it stuck with me, that question. It stuck with me for weeks, like gristle in a molar. I couldn't stop thinking about it, kept me awake every night. I mean, I knew what the accepted definition of money was – I'd done a bloody masters at the LSE, for Christ's sake – but somehow I couldn't get my head around what it actually *was*. Right proper puzzle.

'Then one morning I was paying for a coffee, and I looked at the tenner in my hand and I saw it. That little sentence: "I promise to pay the bearer on demand", and I realised, that's what money was; a promise. It was one of those –' he mimed a cranial explosion '– moments, you know? Road to Damascus kind of things. Suddenly I realised that all those little bits of paper and metal that used to make our little world go round, before those wonderful great things fell down and levelled everything for us, they were all just promises, Beth. Promises we had no intention of keeping. When you give a man a fiver for some of his spuds, all it means is that he doesn't trust you to do him a favour in return. That's all money is, Beth, a measure of our lack of trust in one another.'

He slumped forward with his elbows on his knees.

'So that's when I realised that straight-out theft was more honest than monetary trading. If all money represented was how little trust we placed in each other, then why not just cut to the chase? You have something I want, I take it, and you do the same. Simple. The most watertight contract there is. That's why you can always, *always* trust a thief.'

He took a long breath, after which he seemed steadier, as if sobered by the oxygen.

'Do you trust me, Beth?'

I faltered. The muscles in my neck tensed. 'You're a stranger. The last stranger I trusted took my children.'

'Ah, yes. Quite true. Should have trusted your instincts, am I right? Hmm.' He stood, no longer swaying, and put his hands in his pockets. 'Do you know what my instincts told me this evening? They told me that our friend Ernest was acting a little strangely after he returned from locking you up in here. Clearing things away that didn't need clearing away. Glasses, stools. Chairs.'

My chest tightened. Tony removed his right hand from his pocket and held it up. Between his finger and thumb was a silver disc.

'Maggie's idea, I presume?'

I let my heart deal with itself, breaths pumping furiously. I could lie, I thought, say I'd never seen it before, but at this stage I doubted it would matter.

'What did you do to him?' I said at last.

He shrugged, examining the disc in the moonlight. *Roasting*, they call it. It involves a sack. I believe the Native Americans used to be quite fond of it. I generally prefer to keep out of these things, but I got involved this time, thought it was important to, you know –' his eyes flashed '– send a message. Wonder if Maggie saw it? We'll know soon enough, I suppose; my boys are heading up there now.'

I shook my head. 'You're insane.'

He snapped his fist tight around the transmitter.

'Funny,' he said. 'That is *precisely* what my ex-wife said right before she took my son away. And you know what? Maybe she was right. But sanity's overrated, Beth. Highly overrated.'

He tossed the transmitter through the window, where it plopped in the water outside.

Just then there was a flash from beyond the bar, and a sharp report of gunfire. Tony turned, as if he'd merely heard the chime of a doorbell.

'Hey up, there we go, looks like things are happening. I'll leave you now, Beth. I'm sure you have a lot of things to mull over. Bye-bye.'

He skipped out onto the walkway.

'Lock that door,' he barked at the guard, 'and keep an eye on her.'

He disappeared back along the walkway, leaving the guard to secure my door.

'Tell me what's happening,' I said, rattling the doorframe. 'Let me out of here!'

The guard turned his back, blocking my view. 'Shut up, you Jock whore.'

I peered through the triangle of space between his lumbering arms. Dot-dash flashes traced the darkness between the ship and the sky, making the clouds pulse like veiny wombs. The Rock was in darkness, unprepared for Tony's attack. They would be taken. And then what? Did Ernest's grisly fate await me too?

Suddenly the ocean behind me seemed more inviting than ever.

I scanned the floor for boards I could pull up, but they were all bolted tight. The walls were the same, and lashed with chicken wire outside.

'Stop it,' said the guard. He poked the barrel of his gun through the slit. 'Unless you want an early checkout.'

Maybe I did.

'Maybe I—'

But before I could finish there was a tremendous explosion. The guard ducked and ran to the other side of the walkway. In the distance, a cloud of flame and black smoke billowed high above the walkways. It was a building; the only one left standing between here and the town. Eurotowers.

The guard gripped the railing, giving little roars of disbelief at each new explosion and puff of smoke. I staggered back, found the bed, picked up my broom. If he came for me, I'd be ready.

'*Hey.*'

I looked about. The whispered voice seemed to have come from beneath me.

'*Here.*'

In the far corner, through a gap in the wood, I saw a pair of eyes in the water.

'*It's me.*'

Using my broom for support, I got down on one knee and peered at the apparition floating beyond the wall.

'Richard?'

He put a finger to his lips. His head was clear of the water and there were others behind him floating like beach balls in ink. The flames from the fallen tower cast shadows on their faces.

'How—' I began.

'*Shh.*' He nodded at the guard on the walkway above, still transfixed by the flames. There were shouts in the distance now, and the direction of the shots had reversed. Tony's men were under fire. 'Keep your voice down. No time to explain. You have to get the guard's attention.'

'What? Why?'

'We can only get onto the walkway from the side he's standing on. He'll see us and fire. Get him over on this side.'

'How?'

'I don't know, use your imagination.'

I stood and put my face to the window.

'Hey,' I said. He ignored me.

'Hey you,' I said, louder. Still nothing.

I took a breath.

'It's fire, mate, FIRE. Next big thing, you dickless wanker.'

He was already at the door. I heard ripples beneath us.

'I'll show you dickless,' he said, rattling his keys in the lock. 'I'll show you fucking dickless ...'

The lock sprang off and the door burst open, and there he stood like a stooped, misshapen monolith. But he barely had time to sneer before a shadow rose behind him. His head snapped back and his hands leaped for his throat, around which a rope was suddenly looped.

'There, there, sweetheart,' said the figure, tightening the rope. 'Nighty night.'

The guard dropped to the floor in a heap of cloth and muscle, and Bryce stood dripping above him. Three figures emerged from the water at the walkway's edge. Richard, Josh and Carmela. Bryce picked up the dead guard's gun and held out his hand.

'All right there, darlin'? Are you ready to get out of here?'

Chapter 15

We followed the maze of walkways south, keeping our heads low. Eurotowers was now an inferno, flames and smoke spewing from each tiny window as tight gunfire rattled on the ground beneath. Most of the guards had run to join the skirmish, but some still patrolled the walkways and we had to duck at every turn.

'What's happening?' I said.

'Maggie launched an attack,' replied Richard.

'But I thought—'

'After you went in, we all sat in Maggie's war room listening for a signal. We heard nothing for ages.'

'Sorry to hold you all up,' I muttered. 'Had a few things on my mind.'

'Wasn't criticising, just explaining. Anyway, it made Maggie nervous.'

'Aye,' said Bryce, 'so she started up her pacing, you know how she does.'

'I've only just met her, so not really.'

'Christ, she's always at it.'

'*Mierda*,' said Carmela, shaking her head.

'And when *she* gets nervous,' said Josh, 'so does her monkey.'

'I fucking hate that monkey,' growled Bryce.

'I believe the feeling's mutual,' said Richard. 'Wait – everybody down.'

We ducked behind a railing. On a walkway parallel to us was a guard about to turn.

'Can you get him from here?' whispered Richard.

Bryce, frowning, turned. 'Are you talking to me?'

'Of course. You're the one with the gun.'

Bryce looked at the guard, then back at Richard. 'That's a terrible idea, Richard. It would only attract the attention of the other guards.' He tapped his head. 'You've got to think these things through, bud.'

Carmela gave a creamy smile and kissed him on the cheek.

'Love you, darlin',' said Bryce, with a wink.

Richard stared dumbly at them for a few moments before shaking his head. 'He's gone now anyway, let's go.'

We shuffled across to the next walkway.

'It's an ape,' I said.

Everyone turned. 'What?'

'It's an ape, not a monkey.'

'Right,' said Richard. 'Anyway, Maggie had given up, and Bryce and I were ready to come and get you.'

'It wouldn't have worked.'

'Maybe not, but we would have tried.'

'Would you?' I glanced at Richard, embarrassed at the rise in my voice. 'Go on.'

'But then we heard a crackle. It was you talking with Staines. We didn't get much at first, just a lot of nonsense about money and trust —'

'Fucking bullshit merchant if you ask me,' said Bryce.

'And a few drunken conversations in the bar. Then, about half an hour after you'd gone we heard another voice. It was Ernest, right up close, talking directly into the transmitter. He was babbling, telling us everything. The layout, numbers, weak points, strong points, where you were being held, that Eurotowers had a skeleton shift that night, that their ammunition was kept in two stores and that the closest one was almost gone.'

'Aye,' said Bryce, nodding up to the cruise ship. 'Second one's up there on that ship with the walking dead. Poor old bastards.'

I looked over the walkway maze to the cruise ship, it's flanks flashing in the flames and gunfire from Eurotowers. 'Ernest told me he was using them as a human shield.'

We turned left.

'That's right—' Richard began, but stopped short as we almost bumped into a guard. He halted, staring madly between us.

'Hey—'

Before he could lift his gun, Bryce stepped forward and drove his forehead into the man's nose. With a sickening crack and a squirt of blood, he fell backwards and lay still on the planks.

'That was close,' said Bryce.

Carmela took the abandoned gun and slung it over her shoulder.

'*Mi alma,*' she said, kissing Bryce's bloody forehead. We walked on. Richard continued.

'The main thing that Ernest told us was that Staines doesn't get his supplies from the cruise ship as Maggie had thought. They ran out weeks ago. He's been bringing them in from up the coast ever since.'

'So he was never going to run out.'

'Exactly. Maggie didn't say anything for a few minutes after that. She just sat down, head in her hands, until finally she stood up and ordered the attack.'

'That fucking monkey went ballistic,' said Bryce.

'Ape,' corrected Josh.

'Ape, monkey, whatever, it's a bastard, oh fuck—'

We froze. A guard had turned onto our walkway. I put out my palms, but she had already raised her gun, the barrel now a dark spot in the centre of my vision.

My breath left me. I felt surprisingly calm. Somewhere inside me a cold assessment of my impending oblivion was being calculated, like a blackjack player totting up her chips at an empty table. All things considered, it reasoned, things could have been worse. At least I wouldn't die like Ernest.

The guard pulled the trigger.

It clicked.

For a second nobody moved. The guard checked her gun and tried again. Same result.

'It's jammed,' said Josh.

Carmela looked at Bryce and, with an almighty screech, ran down the walkway with her arms outstretched and her sodden dress flapping behind her like the wings of a rabid hell-swan. The guard cowered in horror as Carmela descended on her, hurling her forehead into her face.

The guard dropped to the floor. Carmela hovered, swaying, and joined her a second later.

'Pigeon!' yelled Bryce, running for her. We followed and Bryce helped her to her feet.

'Are you all right?'

'*Bien, bien,*' she said, finding her balance. '*Estoy bien.*'

Bryce kissed her.

'Use the top of your head next time, darlin',' he said, tapping his scalp. 'Top, understand? Much better.'

'*Si,*' she said, smiling, '*como un toro, si? Entiendo, mi alma, entiendo.*'

We looked down at the guard's unconscious body. The sounds of the battle intensified, shaking the wood upon which we stood.

Richard breathed a sigh.

'Anyway, long story short, we came to rescue you.'

'How did you find me?' I said.

'The sunken tunnels,' said Josh. 'They lead straight out into the water.'

'The ones Maggie said were unsafe?'

Josh shrugged. 'They weren't that bad.'

I caught him glance at his father, and Richard smiled. I looked around, trying to orientate myself. The walkways were clear of guards and the harbour was a short dash away, closer to the battle but lined with the yachts and speedboats I had seen on my way in.

'I need to get to a boat,' I said.

'That's why we're here,' said Richard.

'You're coming with me?'

'Of course. Finish the journey, right, Josh?'

Josh nodded. I turned to Bryce. He shifted uncomfortably.

'Much as I prefer dry land,' he said, looking up at the Rock. 'Gibraltar's not really my cup of tea.'

Carmela machine-gunned something in Spanish and stood tall, looping her arm proudly in his.

There was another explosion at the harbour and the sky lit up. Cries and flailing limbs filled the air, and we ducked as burning debris rained down upon the walkways. One of the boats had caught fire and another was on its side. Half of the harbour walkway had been torn away and bodies floated face down in the exposed water.

'Good God,' said Richard, 'Maggie's throwing everything she's got into it.'

'Quickly,' I said, 'while we have the chance.'

We zigzagged across the walkways, aiming for the eastern end of the harbour where there were fewer guards.

'What do we take?' I said.

'Something small and fast,' said Richard. He pointed at a bullet-shaped white yacht. 'Like that—'

Before he could finish there was another explosion, and the boat he had been pointing out was torn in two. We fell to the ground and covered our heads. Now the harbour was in three sections.

'Shit,' I said, as I pushed myself back up with my broom. 'There'll be nothing left at this rate.'

Just then we saw figures running through the smoke that shrouded a walkway to our right. Bryce and Carmela turned their guns.

'Don't shoot,' said Josh. 'It's Maggie.'

Maggie and Dani emerged from the smoke, hands raised. Their faces were black and smeared with sweat, and the face of Maggie's ape, Colin, was just visible from his hiding place behind her neck.

'Are you all OK?' said Maggie, looking us over. 'Beth?'

'We're fine,' I said. 'Just trying to get to the harbour.'

'Hi Dani,' said Josh. Dani dismissed him with a gritted jaw.

'What's happening?' said Bryce.

Maggie smiled, eyes shining. 'We've taken the ship. Eurotowers is falling. Staines' men are all over the place.'

Colin chattered and screeched. Dani raised her chin. 'Bastard's running scared. I told you, all we needed was a concerted attack, Mother.'

Maggie rolled her eyes. 'You did, but let's leave the I-told-you-sos for later, shall we? The fight's not over.'

Dani maintained her fierce grin.

'We fired mortars on the harbour to draw Staines' attention away from the ship. He loves his boats, so he'll be going there now. Follow me, we can approach from the other side.'

We reached the harbour and crept along the water's edge. All the attention was on the opposite end where the flames licked from the burning boats and figures lay struggling. I heard the familiar voice of Tony Staines barking orders in its upper registers.

'What about one of these?' said Bryce, referring to one of the three expensive-looking unguarded boats to our right. 'They look all right.'

'Gin palaces,' said Richard.

'Sounds good to me. Let's take that big fucker there.'

'They don't have sails,' I said.

'So?'

'So they run on diesel, and we don't know how much they have, or whether we'll be able to find some more. We need to be able to rely on wind power.'

'Right,' said Bryce. 'Makes total sense. Oh, by the way, small question: does anyone actually know how to sail?'

'I did some when I was younger,' said Richard.

Bryce sighed. 'Of course you did. Don't know why I asked. How about that one, then?'

'Too big,' said Richard. 'Difficult to manoeuvre.'

'That one,' I said.

Near the centre of the harbour was a black-hulled yacht with a two tall masts. It was squat and sturdy-looking with sleek lines and a proud-tipped bow.

'Yes,' said Richard. 'That'll do nicely. What is it, forty foot? Big sails, stable hull, perfect.'

'No guards either,' said Bryce. 'It's ours.'

'That's Staines' boat,' said Maggie with a warning tone. 'The *Black Buccaneer*. If he sees you, he won't let it go so easily.'

'Then we'd better be quick,' I said. Just as I moved off, there was a sound behind us.

'Oi,' said a voice, 'turn around, all of you, very slowly.'

We turned and found ourselves face to face with three guards, their guns raised. The one in the front smiled.

'I could smell you a mile off,' she said, with a nasty smile. 'Smelly cunt.'

The two men behind her smirked.

'Put your hands up,' said one. 'Go on.'

We raised our hands.

'What are you going to do?' I said.

'Take you to Tony, that's what I'm going to do.'

'Why? Look around you, Tony's lost.'

'Not yet he hasn't, and anyway, what would that matter? Doesn't make me your friend, or your prisoner.'

'Just let us go, will you? Please? I need to find my children.'

Her eyes glinted. 'I don't give a shit about your kids. Now shut up, turn around and move.'

I got mugged once in Edinburgh. It was broad daylight on a busy weekend afternoon in the

Grassmarket, with plenty of people about. I was unlucky. I happened to turn up the wrong street and found myself alone with three young men. One took out a knife. It was only small, and he offered me the blade like a cigarette. His hands were shaking. 'Geez yer purse,' he said. That accent, the nasal whine of an Edinburgh schemie, so skewered with violence that it was almost more threatening than the knife. I wondered if he'd ever actually used it. Like this girl who stood in front of me. Her voice was all in her throat, all hard and taut like a throttled gull. I doubted she could make a soft vowel if she tried. And I doubted she had ever fired a gun.

My mugger had been chewing his gum furiously, and his breath was ripe with the tang of marijuana and Juicy Fruit. He spat at my feet and shook the blade at me. 'And yer phone too, eh?'

I had always wondered what I would do in that situation. Do the sensible thing and give up the goods without a fight? It was a pain getting all your cards cancelled, and your whole life was on your phone back then, wasn't it? Email, Facebook, Twitter, all logged in. Who knew what they'd be able to do with all my passwords before I managed to get to a computer and change them?

Scream for help? I could hear the crowds move happily on the street behind, unaware of my plight. Would anyone come before I was stabbed? Probably not.

Or take a chance? Refuse. Hit them, kick them, call their bluff. Surely nobody *wants* to stab someone else, not in broad daylight. But then again ...

I decided to do the right thing that day. I emptied my pockets without a word, hands shaking, and gave it all up. My mugger smiled, kissed two fingers and placed them on my cheek. I couldn't get rid of the smell of Juicy Fruit for weeks. But at least I was alive. I had been sensible.

'Oi, smelly cunt. Did you hear me?'

That day in Gibraltar's sunken harbour, with a tower burning behind me and gunfire thundering in the distance, I wasn't feeling particularly sensible.

With a sideways glance at Bryce, I took a step towards her. I was taller than her. She bristled.

'If you don't mind me saying so, sweetheart,' I said, hardening my own accent into a cold Dundonian drawl, 'you seem worryingly obsessed with my genital hygiene. Perhaps you should focus on concerns a little closer to home.'

Her eyes squeezed together in puzzled disgust. 'Whatchoo talking about?'

'What I'm talking about, sweetheart, is that I can always take a bath, but there's absolutely bugger all you can do about that space between your ears.'

I swung my broom up with all the force I could muster, striking her on the chin. Her head snapped back, stretching the sinews of her throat, and there, finally, was that soft vowel. A childish *'Huh!'* of surprise. Her gun went off, a single shot fired above our heads as she fell back into the guard behind her. He caught her, lost his balance and fell, by which time Carmela had run head first into his chest and the second guard's neck had received the full force of Bryce's gun butt. He grasped his throat with both hands and fell to his knees. Bryce relieved him of his gun and kicked him into the water, where he floundered, gasping for breath. Meanwhile, I disarmed the stunned girl while Josh and Richard did the same with the guard who lay beneath her. They struggled to their feet, the male bent double and the girl holding her bleeding chin, looking back at me like a child caught playing truant.

'Now, piss off,' I said. And after a moment's hesitation, they did just that.

Carmela stood shakily next to Bryce, holding her head.

'*Como un toro*,' she said.

I turned. Maggie looked back at me with bemused admiration.

'See, Mother?' said Dani. '*Tits*. That's what you need.'

We dashed to the *Black Buccaneer* and clambered aboard. By this time great cheers were rising up near the cruise ship, and figures ran about on its deck, some with blankets around their shoulders, others with guns helping them. The blaze from the harbour was spreading towards us, sending smoke across the deck.

As we unfastened the mooring ropes, Richard busied himself at the helm, which was tucked into a cavity in the middle of the boat behind the tallest mast. Inside was a confusing array of dials, levers and winches from which thick ropes drew out to the sails.

'We're going to have to use the engine to leave the harbour. Fuck, he's not left the keys.'

Passing the helm, Bryce felt beneath a wooden shelf.

'Keys,' he said, dropping a set into Richard's hand.

'Thanks,' said Richard, looking at the keys in surprise. 'Bryce, you need to lift anchor.'

'Whit?'

'You need to pull the anchor up, the winch is on the starboard bow.'

'The what's on the what now? Speak fucking English!'

'The big windy metal thing at the front of the floaty thing on the right-hand side! Turn it!'

'Thank you!'

Bryce marched off up the deck. Richard began sorting through the keys.

I heard a furious, strangled voice from the end of the harbour.

'Staines is coming,' I said. 'Richard?'

'I hear you,' he said, fumbling through the keys. 'Going as fast as I can. Bryce, are we up?'

'How am I supposed to fucking know?'

'Is it still winding?'

'Yes.'

'Then keep winding and tell me when it's stopped. Ah, bingo.'

Richard inserted the key into the ignition and turned it. He gritted his teeth. 'Please be fuelled.'

The engine spluttered. 'Fuck.' He turned it again. This time it caught and the deck rumbled. 'Yes! Bryce, how are we doing?'

'The windy thing's no longer winding.'

'Good, lock it and we're set. How are we doing back there?'

Josh pulled the last mooring rope aboard. 'All done, Dad.'

Maggie picked up two of the guns we'd just taken and turned to me. 'This is where we leave you. We'll deal with Tony.'

'Thank you, Maggie, for everything.'

'Good luck, Beth, I hope you find your children. Now go, before he gets here.'

She smiled, but as she did there was a whistling sound followed by a dull thump. Maggie twitched, as if she'd been jostled in a crowd. Colin jumped, nearly falling from her shoulder. Her eyes widened and she gave a tight gasp.

'Mother?' said Dani, steadying her. Maggie looked down at her chest, where a patch of blood was already appearing below her right shoulder. The ape inspected it, reaching a paw, but jumped clear just as she toppled forward onto the deck.

'Mother,' cried Dani, falling to her knees and cradling Maggie's head. 'She's been shot!'

Colin scrabbled from the mayhem and beneath a seat. Maggie's eyes were open, and her expression had hardened into a serious frown. She drew long breaths in and out of her nose. 'It's OK,' she said. 'I'm OK.'

'Shit,' said Richard. 'What do we do? Beth?'

Tony's voice was drawing ever closer, his sharp footsteps audible on the planks.

'We need to go,' I said. 'We need to go now. Maggie?'

Maggie looked up at me, eyes bulging. '*Go*,' she mouthed. '*Go*.'

I turned to Richard. 'Do it. Now.'

Richard pushed the throttle and we pulled away. The sudden movement sent another shockwave of hope through my chest; the bird beneath the window had fluttered to its feet.

'It's all right, child,' said Maggie, wheezing, with one hand trembling on her daughter's cheek. 'I'm all right.'

We were passing the end of the harbour when her eyes flashed to me. 'What happened to Ernest?'

I looked up at the platform upon which a small fire still burned. Hanging from a rope above it was an egg-shaped bundle of sackcloth, charred and slowly turning.

'He's dead,' I said. 'Tony murdered him. I'm sorry.'

Maggie blinked.

'Is he there? Does he see us?'

I looked back at the expanse of burning harbour, shrinking now beneath the shadow of the Rock.

Silhouetted against the flames stood Tony, looking back with his hands in his pockets.

'Yes,' I said. 'He sees us.'

Maggie looked away. 'Then you'd better find a way of making this boat go as fast as it can. Because he'll be coming, mark my words.'

A breath of cold wind swept over my face. *I don't care*, I thought. *Let him come.*

I was moving again, and so was my heart.

Chapter 16

Of the long list of tortures for which you're told to the prepare when you have children, sleep deprivation ranks top. Awaiting you on the other side of labour, you are told, is a four-walled hell of permanent consciousness from which the only respite is those fraught periods during which your infant sleeps and you end up cleaning the house anyway.

What they don't tell you is that once you've survived this ordeal, sleep is never the same again. It's never as deep, never as restful, never as fulfilling. It becomes a baggier and more neurotic version of itself. Just like you.

Sleep used to be a bottomless pool into which I would nightly plunge. Now I only ever dabble my toe.

That's how it is for me anyway, and that's how it was on the boat when, as Gibraltar became a distant smear of smoke on the eastern horizon, and Dani and Carmela had carefully lifted Maggie below deck, I curled up on one of the deck's benches and closed my eyes. When I opened them it was light, and I could smell coffee. I was beneath a blanket.

Richard came into focus, leaning at the helm with a mug in his hand. He seemed to be shrouded in steam, which I realised was actually mist.

'Morning,' he said, and gestured to a battered metal mug on the floor. 'I made you a coffee.'

I sat up and put a hesitant hand to my leg; the pain was not as bad as I had expected, so I explored it further, kneading the flesh as I straightened my knee and gradually eased my way into the discomfort.

When I was done, I picked up the mug and took a sip. It was a hot tangle of tastes.

'Thanks.' I pulled the blanket around my shoulders. 'And for this.'

I picked up my broom, which I'd left on the floor, and got shakily to my feet. Richard watched me, uncrossing his legs in a signal that help was there if needed.

'I'm OK,' I said, crossing to the helm.

He nodded at the coffee. 'Didn't know how you took it.'

'Black's fine,' I said.

'Good, because there's no milk. Or sugar.'

I took a bigger sip. This time my taste buds unravelled the mystery.

'There's rum, though, I gather?'

He smiled. 'Thought it might help, under the circumstances.'

I looked at the flat water behind us. Fragile mist hung over it like pale blue tissue paper. I scanned it for ripples, disruption, any sign of a boat. 'And what exactly are the circumstances?'

'Don't worry,' said Richard, draining his cup. 'I've been watching for him. There's nothing.'

'What time is it?'

'A little after 6 a.m. We've been motoring for three hours.'

'We're drifting. Why is the engine off?'

'Because I wanted to conserve fuel. Besides, there's a little wind, so I thought we'd try a sail. Want to help?'

'Bow, stern, starboard, port.' Richard pointed around the boat. 'Helm.' He tapped the wheel and jumped up onto the deck. He offered me his hand and pulled me up too.

'Mainsail.' He tapped the tight, blue roll of sail above the cabin and pointed ahead. 'Jib. Some vessels have a third, but we just have the two. Keeps things simple. Oh, and these are lines.' He rubbed a palm along a taut rope and looked up. 'Mast, obviously. Winches, boom, cabin, deck. That's it, basically.'

I looked around the deck. I had been on boats before; the *Unity* of course, and the canoe I'd capsized on a school trip to the Lake District which had required me to be dragged, half drowning to shore. Then there were the overnight ferries to Orkney for our annual family holiday, full of sliding, seasick drunks.

But yachts were part of a different world; one of cashmere jumpers, white teeth and bulging bank balances. It was a world in which the act of raising a sheet of canvas and expecting the wind to carry you safely in the right direction was no more presumptuous than, say, taking over a company or buying a third Range Rover for your child's nanny. It was a world which I knew existed, but in which I could never hope to exist.

I looked up at the towering mast.

'So … you just raise the sail and it goes?'

'That's the idea. Fairly simple principle, apart from when you put it into practice.'

'How do you mean?'

'It's like everything. Sometimes you have to improvise.'

He looked around as if he'd suddenly forgotten where he was.

'Right, gentle south-easterly, calm seas, let's try the jib.'

I looked at him. 'Sure. My thoughts exactly.'

Standing with my shoulder against a cable, I helped Richard unroll the jib's heavy canvas cover.

'How's Josh?' I asked.

He took some moments to answer. I already knew this about Richard – he took time to consider his words before answering, like a Scrabble player shifting tiles. It made what he said seem more robust, as if stamped with a mark of quality assurance.

'He's coping,' he said at last. 'And with everything that's happened it would be wrong to expect more of him.'

'How old is he, fifteen?'

'Almost sixteen.'

I paused and tried his trick of thought before speech.

'And how is his father?'

He tugged at a fastening and shot me a conspiratorial smile.

'That's a different matter.'

'You lost your wife, didn't you?' The words came too quickly and he turned his attention back to his fastening. 'I'm sorry, I didn't mean—'

'It's all right. Yes, Gaby died in the strike.' He paused, staring at the knot. 'Christ, it seems like such a long time ago now, but it's not even a year.'

'You must miss her.'

Stop.

I have to explain something to you.

I woke up on a boat I'd helped steal from a maniac's blazing harbour after my children had been taken from me when my ship went down – a ship on which we had been bound for a foreign country because the planet had been pulverised by asteroids. All of that: it happened.

So it must seem strange that I'm leaning casually on this stolen boat, having a gentle chat with a handsome man about grief and loss and feelings.

But that's how it goes. The world is a nightmare, it always has been, and we crave safety. That's why we snuck to the caves and built fires. We seek comfort in anything: the taste of instant coffee laced with rum, or the pallor of a sea mist, or a simple conversation. When the nightmare comes for you, you don't want to become it. You want to sneak from it.

But don't think for a second that this conversation existed in a vacuum. Despite the mist's cocoon and the untroubled sea and our quiet voices, my insides were shifting like molten lava, and my stomach heaved with that same repeated reality: I had been separated from my children, and the best I could hope for was that it was only by a mere ocean.

'Of course I miss her,' said Richard. 'Every day. I never even got to say goodbye to her. But ... I feel terrible about this, but do you know what the hardest part is? She did most of the work with Josh. She always had done, from baby to boy, but now it's up to me. And I don't have a clue what I'm doing.'

'Parenthood's never easy. Anyone will tell you that.'

'Maybe, but perhaps if I'd spent more time with him in the early years then I'd be more capable now. I didn't, though. I was always at work. I thought that was my duty, you know? Bring in the money, get us a big house, keep us financially secure. Gabs ended up taking on the rest. The feeds, the nappies, cleaning ...'

He broke off, aware of the sudden intensity with which I was tugging at a knot.

'Just a few nappies, eh?'

'I didn't mean ...'

I stopped and looked up.

'You're raising a child, Richard, not just keeping it fed and watered. You're teaching it how to live, how to be around other people, how to be happy. All it takes is a bit of time. A bit of presence. You just need to be in the room.'

'I know.' He harshened his tone, the words bitten off. 'That's what I'm trying to say. I wish I *had* invested the time more than I did the money. I wish I *had* been more present.'

I returned to my knot,.

'I'm sorry,' I said. 'I don't know why that made me angry. My head's all over the place.'

'It's OK.'

Neither of us spoke for a while, and we concentrated on the last few knots.

'All I'm trying to say,' he said at last, 'is that it's even harder now. I don't just have to teach him how to be a child, I have to teach him how to be an adult. A man. In a world like this.'

I released the last knot and found my makeshift crutch, standing back from the cable.

'There's no manual for parenthood,' I said. 'Sometimes you have to improvise.'

Smiling, Richard pulled away the cover.

'Speaking of which,' he said, 'shall we?'

I stood at the helm as Richard fed a rope through a winch.

'What do I do?' I asked.

He pointed up at the mast. 'See the weather vane at the top? That tells you the wind direction. You want to point the boat into the wind, so go hard to port.'

'What?'

'Turn left.'

'Right.' I turned the wheel. The boat obeyed, and its hull slapped with little waves of encouragement.

'We're moving,' I said, excitedly. 'The boat's moving.'

'Indeed, now watch the vane and stop when it's pointing straight ahead.'

I peered up at the wavering black arrow, turning the wheel back as it found its centre.

'Good. Now tell me you're ready.'

'Pardon?'

'I'm skipper, you're crew.'

I gave him a stony look. 'Is that right.'

'So you have to tell me you're ready.'

'Fine, I'm ready.'

'Good. Hoist the jib!'

He grinned and wound the winch. The wheel began to knock as the wind explored the lifting canvas, but I held it tight. Richard tied off the line.

'OK, try a little starboard.'

'That's right, right?'

'Right.'

I turned the wheel. The sail flapped violently as the wind finally found it.

'Christ,' I said, freezing.

'It's OK,' said Richard, 'keep going.'

I turned slowly, allowing the wind in, and gradually we began to move.

'Holy shit, it's working.'

Richard shrugged. 'Told you it was simple.'

We were away. We weren't moving at speed – perhaps not even as fast as we had been under the engine – but the experience was incalculably different. I felt the tug of the wind in everything, as if the boat had suddenly woken up. It had merely been an object before, but now it was alive and happily surrendering itself to its master. It was moving us, closing the distance, and I loved it.

I felt a pressure in the wheel.

'Steady,' said Richard. 'Watch for lee helm.'

'Who's *Lee Helm*?'

He laughed. '*Lee* means away from the wind. The helm's going leeward. Keep it steady by turning into it.'

I did as he said and the pressure relented.

'Excellent. You'll make a fine helmsman.'

I blinked in the fine spray rising from the hull. The mist was rising, and to the right I could make out the dull outline of a coast. Richard folded his arms and raised his chin, closing his eyes.

'I've missed this,' he said. It was to himself, I think.

Suddenly there was a piercing scream from below deck. Richard jumped and opened his eyes. We looked at each other.

'If that was Bryce,' he said, 'then we're in trouble.'

'Take the helm,' I said. 'I'm going to see.'

We swapped positions awkwardly, and I poked my head inside the hatch. Josh was in the galley – the small kitchen at the front of the cabin – attempting to cook something in a skillet while shooing Colin from the shelf above. Bryce was nowhere to be seen, but Carmela was with Dani and her mother, who lay on the table with her mouth open and her eyes rolling. I stared down in horror. Carmela loomed over the mess of gore that was her shoulder holding a pair of bloody tongs, in which something hard was pincered.

She inspected it grimly, saw me and grinned.

'*La bala*,' she declared, and dropped the bullet in a bowl beside her.

'Is she all right?' I said to Dani.

'I don't know,' she said. 'We think it just hit her shoulder.'

Carmela, who had threaded a needle, took a deep, business-like breath.

'*Listo*?'

Dani gripped her mother's hand and nodded. Carmela dove in, point first.

As Maggie arched her back and howled, the door beside the kitchen opened and out staggered Bryce. His hair had regained a little of its wildness, his face was pale and dark circles hung beneath his eyes. He froze as he spotted the DIY operation in the corner.

Colin screeched. Josh shook the skillet. 'Who wants eggs?' he said.

I slammed the hatch as Bryce heaved.

'What's going on down there?' said Richard from the helm.

'You don't want to know. It's better up here.'

He nodded to the coast. Though mist still covered the millpond sea, we could see details on the land. What appeared to be a floating town rose from the gloom with stained white turrets glinting in the sun.

'Where are we?' I said.

'Looks like Cadiz.'

'They might have better communication there, someone who can contact *Sauver* and tell them what happened.'

'Worth a shot. Let's take a closer look. Here.'

He gave me the helm and adjusted some lines as I took us starboard. Soon we were cruising towards the coast, but the mist thickened as we drew closer, and a boglike smell hung in the air.

'Ease up,' said Richard. 'Don't get too close, we don't know what's beneath this water.'

I turned to port and Richard let down the jib, although the wind had almost disappeared anyway. We were back to calm water, but not as it had been before. There was an oiliness to it I didn't like. Something was wrong.

'What's that smell?' I said.

'I don't know, but it's not good.'

He rummaged in a cupboard next to the helm and pulled out a pair of binoculars, which he held to the skyline, elbows extended like hawk wings.

'What do you see?' I said.

'Yep, pretty sure that's Cadiz. That's the harbour, and that's ...'

He stopped.

'What is it?'

Slowly he took the binoculars from his eyes, face pale, still looking into the mist.

'Richard?'

He shook his head. 'It's nothing. There's nothing. Come on, this water's too dangerous, let's go.'

'What did you see?'

'I told you: nothing.' He busied himself with the lines.

I lunged for the binoculars but he grabbed my wrist.

'Beth, believe me, you don't want to see.'

'Just give them to me.'

After a pause, he relented, released my wrist and offered me the binoculars. He turned away as I put them to my eyes. A fuzzy image shook of burned towers and shattered turrets.

'I don't see anything but damaged buildings.'

'Good, then let's go.'

'Some burned out cars, no sign of any people, wait ...'

I froze and backtracked, stopping on what looked like a harbour wall.

'Beth, please ...'

I steadied my hands. The details came into focus. In the centre was a tall flagpole upon which two flags were raised. The first, halfway down, drooping and tattered, was the Spanish flag; the second, billowing fiercely in the fog-drenched wind, was black and scrawled with white paint. A white face with a drooping mouth and two crosses for eyes.

Lining the harbour wall on either side of the flag-pole was a series of sticks. There must have been at least two hundred of them skewered into the ground at odd angles, and on each was a severed animal head. Sheep, goats, dogs, pigs.

And humans.

My throat tightened. Shaking, I roamed through the sticks. Swarms of flies buzzed between the faces of men and women with lolling tongues and ragged hair.

Then I noticed that between some sticks were smaller ones. My brain caught up with my reflexes a little too late, and before I could snatch the binoculars away I saw something. It was just a glimpse, but enough to burn itself into my memory. It's still there to this day, and I won't talk about it, not even here.

I shut my eyes, gritted my teeth, tried to open my throat.

'It's all right,' said Richard, placing a hand on my shoulder. 'It's all right.'

I handed him the binoculars.

'Come on,' I said, returning to the helm. 'Let's keep going. It's not safe here.'

Chapter 17

After Cadiz we sailed in silence. Neither of us wanted to talk. We let the wind pull us steadily along, making sure we kept as much distance as possible from the coastline, and gradually we left that boglike smell behind us.

'Staines said there were people in these waters,' I said. 'Bandits, that kind of thing. Maybe that's who did that.'

'Pirates,' said Richard. 'I met some once.'

'When?'

'On a wreck dive in the South China Sea. Stupid, really, it's a dangerous place but I needed the money. Luckily for me they were only small fry, just swung their guns at me, took my valuables and left me floating. One chatted to me as they were going about their business, asked me about my family, showed me a picture of his daughter. I just grinned and went along with it. He waved when they left.' He turned to me. 'A different breed to whoever did that back there.'

The hatch opened and Josh poked his head out.

'Hi,' he said.

'Hello, chief,' said Richard. His voice took on a friendly, sing-song tone, the same way mine did with

Alice and Arthur. 'Motherese', I'd heard it called, some evolutionary means for parents to connect with their infants. Except Josh was fifteen.

'You all right?'

Josh nodded and pulled himself out onto the deck, shutting the hatch behind him. 'How's it all going down below?' I asked.

'Pretty rubbish,' he replied. 'Maggie's unconscious and Carmela's looking after Bryce. He's locked in the toilet being sick.'

'It's called the "head" on a boat, Josh,' said Richard. Josh bobbed his head, a nervous twitch I'd seen him do before. It was as if he was ducking from the correction.

'What about Dani?' I asked.

'She's just sitting there. Won't talk to me.'

'Never mind, eh, mate?' said Richard. 'Plenty more fish.'

Josh flushed. 'I didn't mean—'

'You want to watch that girl anyway, she's a feisty one.'

He gave him a wink. Josh ducked it.

I looked between the two of them – Josh's eyes wide and wandering, Richard's grin straining at the seams. Finally I took a breath.

'Dani's probably just upset after what happened. Maybe it's best to give her some space, Josh. People need that sometimes.'

He gave me a sheepish smile.

'Richard,' I said, 'why don't you let me take over the helm and you can show Josh around the boat. Show him the ropes, so to speak ... oh –' I stopped '– that's where that comes from. How about it, Josh?'

The boy's interest peaked.

'Dad?'

'You're sure?' said Richard to me.

'Aye, go on. This is a piece of cake anyway.'

'Right, well ...' Richard gave me the helm. 'Keep it on that heading for now, OK?'

I leaned in. 'Just talk to him normally. He's your son.'

He nodded, patted his sides and followed Josh down the deck.

'Right, Joshy, this is the mainsail and that there ...'

I watched them for a while. Richard pulled ropes and turned invisible winches, miming the various exertions required for sailing. This physical realm was where he seemed most comfortable. *In order to be a man, you must pull that, push that, move like this.* He hadn't shown me any of those things on my brief introduction to sailing – everything had been in the abstract – and as I watched Josh nod his head and try his best to please his dad by doing the things he wanted him to do, and Richard try his best to train his son in skills he thought he should know, I wondered whether this model, when multiplied by billions of fathers and sons over countless centuries, might just have produced some unwanted side effects.

But I suppose he was just trying to teach him how to sail.

And what did I know, anyway? The eldest of my children was three, and I had yet to start teaching her about real life. She currently lived in a fiction, a half-fantasy world I had conjured for her in which dinner times, cars and train timetables existed alongside tooth fairies and an overweight elf who gave you presents if you were good. It wasn't the real, visceral life in which dreams rarely came true and your body bled monthly.

At least, I hoped she still lived in that fiction. My heart sank when I considered the alternative.

A thought struck me.

'Richard, what's the date?'

He looked back from the mast. 'Fourth of April. Why?'

I let my gaze travel west.

'It was Alice's birthday yesterday.'

The wind changed and Richard showed us both how to *turn about*. The mist persisted, holding back the sun. Josh sat on the foredeck while Richard joined me at the helm.

'Florida's what, five thousand miles?' I said. 'How long will that take us?'

'Three weeks if we're lucky. The Atlantic's not a difficult crossing but there's nowhere to stop, and if we've just passed Cadiz then we're already going in the wrong direction. I've been hugging the coast in the hope that we'll find somewhere to load up on supplies for the journey.'

'Do you know how much we have?'

'I had a quick root through the cupboards. A few tins, packets, not much, but food's not the problem. The water tank's full but I don't know how clean it is, and it has to hydrate five of us for the best part of a month. That's if we can find somewhere safe to drop Maggie and Dani off. I'm sure they don't want a one-way trip to Florida.'

I watched the coast stream by. The thought of going in the wrong direction sent a shiver of panic through me. Suddenly the mist seemed to close in.

'I don't want to wait any longer. I want to get going.'

'I understand, but Maggie's been shot. She needs proper medical attention.'

My pulse quickened. 'She can get it in Florida.'

'In three weeks? Four? What if she's infected?'

Richard jumped as I slammed my fist into the cabin wall.

'It's not my fault she was shot. Or that she took it upon herself to get into a siege with a lunatic. My children were taken from me, and I can't wait around any longer.' I flung a finger west. 'They're out there, Richard. They're somewhere out there with a delusional child snatcher who tried to kill me, and every second I'm apart from them weakens the chance of me ever seeing them again. Right now this boat is my only hope, do you understand? I'm on my own, Richard. It's just me.'

'It's not just you, Beth.'

The ladder rattled and the hatch opened again. It was Maggie. She looked weary and bruised, and her left arm was in a sling. Richard extended a hand but she brushed it off and pulled herself up with her good arm.

'That's better,' she said as the fresh air hit her face. 'It's rather close down there.'

I shared an awkward glance with Richard. She noticed and smiled.

'It's all right,' she said. 'I heard you.'

'I'm sorry.'

'Don't be.'

'Are you all right?' I said, nodding at her sling.

'I'll be fine. Carmela is a good nurse.' She explored her shoulder delicately. 'If a little enthusiastic. How about you? Your leg?'

'Better than yesterday.'

Dani sprang up the ladder and shut the hatch.

'How's everyone else?' said Richard. 'Bryce?'

'I haven't seen him,' said Dani.

'Although we have *heard* him,' said Maggie.

I turned to Dani. 'Did you have any luck on the radio?'

'Yes. I got through.' Her face lit with a rare smile. 'The Rock is safe, and the cruise ship too. The passengers have been helped onto land, they're shaken but they'll be taken care of. Everyone's moving down from the Rock now, reclaiming the town and the harbour. Staines and what remains of his men are gone.'

'So there is much work to be done,' said Maggie. She looked at her daughter. 'We need to get home.'

Dani folded her arms, avoiding her mother's gaze.

'I understand,' I said. 'But how? We can't sail back. Staines may have left the Rock but nobody saw which way he went. You said yourself there's a fair chance he's on our tail.'

'Of course. I was thinking we would travel back by land.'

'We've been trying to find a safe place to stop,' said Richard, 'somewhere to drop you off, but we're not having much luck. Cadiz was … not safe.'

Dani released an impatient huff.

Maggie's eyes narrowed. She turned to her daughter. 'And what do you suggest?'

'We should push west immediately.'

'*West?*'

'Yes. I want to go with them.'

Maggie scoffed, then paused. 'You're serious.'

'Yes, Mother, I am.'

'Don't be ridiculous. We need to get home.'

'No,' said Dani.

Maggie gritted her teeth. 'Yes.'

'Why? What reason do we have to return?'

'I told you, we have work to do. I have a responsibility to those people.'

'What work? And what responsibility? Who put you in charge, anyway?'

'It is our home, child.'

Dani's mouth twisted. She took a step closer Maggie. 'Home. An island cut off from everything. It might be your home, Mother, but it's suffocating me. I want to see more of the world, and if we go back now . . .' her breaths came hard and fast 'if we go back now then we'll never leave. *Never.*'

Maggie watched her daughter for some time. Then she turned to me. 'Drop us off at the next available place, please.'

'If you walk off this boat, Mother, then I'm not following you.'

'Child,' said Maggie.

'I mean it.'

'Watch out!' Josh sprang up from the foredeck. 'Dead ahead, there's something in the water.'

Richard ran to the bow.

'Good God,' he said. 'Beth, hard to port, now.'

The hull creaked as I turned.

'What is it?' said Maggie, craning her neck. 'What's happening?'

'Richard?' I called, but he ignored me, darting about grabbing ropes. 'Josh, pull that line. No, not that one!'

Josh stumbled as his father yanked the line from his grasp. Richard pulled another and the jib began to fall. 'Well, help me then!'

He ran to his father's aid, clumsily pulling at the rope behind him. Soon the jib had fallen and we began to lose speed. Richard crouched on the starboard side, catching his breath and peering into the water.

We slowed up, drifting again.

'Look at this,' he said.

I left the helm and made my way to the bow. Floating in the water just metres from us was a huge, long cylinder, the size and shape of a fuselage. It had once been white but was now a rusty, weed-smothered green. Josh joined us at the guard rail.

'What is that? A plane?'

We bobbed along its length.

'No,' said Richard, pointing ahead. 'Look.'

Another shape drew out of the murk – a towering blade rising diagonally from the water, hanging with weed.

'It's a wind turbine,' I said. 'How the hell …?'

But as I spoke more shapes appeared. Pale, broken cylinders with bent and rusted blades. The sea was full of them, either upended or floating like the first.

'Behind you,' said Maggie, who had taken the helm. She stared upward, port side, where an upright turbine loomed over us, half submerged in the water. A gull perched upon a horizontal blade.

'That one's still standing,' I said.

'It's not the only one,' said Richard, nodding beyond at the array of blades now emerging, like stopped clocks from the mist. Richard shook his head. 'It's not possible. They never built any wind turbines in these waters. They were all on—'

'Land,' I said.

Richard paled. 'The water's risen. We've drifted too far north.'

'Dad,' said Josh, looking directly ahead.

'Shit,' said Richard, scanning the water, 'we need to head back.'

Josh raised a finger. I went to his side and followed his gaze. 'What do you see, Josh?'

'Dad ...'

Richard began to gather lines. 'Not now, Josh, this water's shallow and this boat has a *very* deep keel.'

More shapes appeared, these ones moving.

'Dad ...'

'I said not *now*, Josh.'

'Richard!' I snapped. 'Look.'

He dropped the rope and came to the side, peering out.

'What is it?'

There in the mist was a grassy lump no bigger than a small truck. A rickety wooden structure stood on its prow, and near the water's edge sat a figure.

'Maggie,' I called back. 'Do you think you can steer us a little to the right?'

Steadily we drifted towards the lonely hill. The figure looked up at our approach. It was a woman. She had knotted hair and a mud-caked shawl which she gripped tight with one hand, and with her other she dangled a crooked rod and line in the water. Her face was scored with age. She watched us with suspicion.

As we drew near there was a ripple in the water and a short raft emerged from the distance, paddled by a boy. He wore shorts and nothing else, clawing his scrawny arms at the water like a surfer battling through a reef. His face was drawn and he had the bulging eyes of hunger.

He clambered from the raft, tripping on a tuft of earth and sitting beside the old woman. She drew her shawl around him, placed her rod down and pulled something from the stone beside which she sat. It was a small fish, perhaps a sardine. She gave it to the boy, and there was a deliberation to the act that stung me. It made me think of all those times I had fed Alice and, more recently, Arthur – experimenting with vegetables, mashed lentils, chicken, the various concoctions designed to persuade my children to nourish themselves against their will, and invariably destined for the bin. But this was different; the fish was a prize, a body of hope that was not to be wasted.

The boy cradled the fish in his long fingers, looking up and down its body as if its geometry held as much nourishment as its flesh. Then, delicately, he ate it, head to tail.

We were metres from them now, and the suspicion on the woman's face was tightening into fear. She picked up her rod as if it was a totem and pulled the boy closer.

Maggie spoke.

'*Buen día señora –*' she smiled at the boy '*– señor.*'

They made no reply, so Maggie spoke some more, a soft and rattling thread of words I couldn't understand. The woman made some noises back, though they didn't sound like sentences. As they conversed the mist revealed more shapes behind – more lumps, some far bigger than the woman's, others merely perches for gulls. They stretched into the distance, an entire archipelago of grassy islands with figures moving on each one.

We had passed the first island now, and as we continued to drift the old woman croaked something, repeating it with a flick of her hand as if she was shooing us away.

'What is she saying, Maggie?' I said.

'She's warning us away. These waters aren't safe for boats.'

'Well, we knew that,' said Richard, returning to his ropes. 'Come on, let's turn back before—'

There was a jolt and Richard fell face first onto the coil of rope. Josh and I steadied ourselves on the cables. The bow of the boat had suddenly twitched to starboard, as if yanked by an unseen rope.

'Christ,' said Richard, getting to his feet, 'what was that? Did we hit something?'

'I didn't feel anything. Are you OK, Maggie?'

'I'm fine, but I think this wheel is trying to tell me something. It wants to go that way.'

The bow twitched again. We were moving.

'It's a current,' said Richard. 'Look.'

He pointed to the water as he made his way back to the helm. The calm surface was riddled with twists like eddies in a brook.

I turned to Josh. 'Stay at the front, Josh, will you? Tell us what's ahead.'

He nodded and took his place at the bow while I followed Richard back to the cockpit. He had already taken the helm from Maggie's hands.

Another twitch. Maggie fell, crying with pain as her shoulder hit the bench. Dani helped her up.

'Are you all right?'

'Yes,' she said, wincing, 'but are we picking up speed?'

'Damn right we are,' said Richard, glaring ahead, 'we're caught in it. Shit.'

'Land!' Josh shouted from the bow. 'Loads of it.'

We were being dragged into the archipelago, thrown between the currents that encircled each island. The inhabitants looked up as we passed, stopping whatever they were doing – shifting timber, rocks or fish – and watching us, half-naked and scratching their heads from their shore. With each one we passed we seemed to gain speed and lose more control, until it felt as if we were helplessly navigating a river's rapids.

Richard attempted a starboard turn, but a dull thud travelled up through the deck.

'No.' He centred the wheel. 'No, we definitely hit something that time. I can't turn, we don't have enough space.'

'Try the engine,' I said. 'Put it in reverse, see if we can slow down.'

Richard turned the ignition and the engine spluttered awake. He pulled the throttle back. The motor strained but the current still pulled us on.

'It's not powerful enough.' He switched off the engine. 'We need to use the sails. Here, take the helm.' He pointed at Dani. 'I need your help, come with me.'

Dani scrabbled after him.

'What do I do?' I called.

'Just keep us as far away from the islands as possible. I'm going to try and use the mainsail to slow us down. Josh, keep a look out, Dani, help me untie this sail.'

As they went to work on the fastenings, I stiffened my grip on the helm, trying to quell its spasms as the water coaxed it from port to starboard. A heavy thud rocked the hull and for a second I lost control of the wheel, but Maggie jumped up and caught it. Together we drove it back to its centre.

'Josh,' I cried, catching my breath, 'how are we doing?'

'I don't know. It looks like we're heading into … it's like an alleyway or something.'

Two taller islands appeared ahead with a thin strip of water between them. Their high banks formed a gulley into which we were being dragged. We passed through its entrance and into the shadow of its walls.

'Stop,' I called to Richard and Dani, who were still unfastening the mainsail. 'We're slowing down.'

They both stood and looked up in awe at the eerie mud-faced cliffs through which we were now passing. The current still pulled us, though less violently now, and we followed its slow bends left and right.

'We could turn here,' said Richard, 'and I think there's enough wind to sail us out, especially if we use the motor too.'

'We'd still have to negotiate that current again. I say we keep going.'

Richard hesitated, eyes dotting around the boat. Then he looked back at me.

'All right,' he said. 'Your call, skipper.'

Chapter 18

The gulley ran for miles. I stood at the helm allowing the soft current to carry us between its crags while Josh watched for obstacles at the bow. It felt like we were in deep water again, no thumps or cracks from the keel. A light wind blew from the stern but we kept the sails down.

Richard disappeared below deck to scour Staines' maps for a possible position. Dani helped. Maggie brought me black tea.

'You suit that wheel,' she said, placing a mug in the cockpit's holder. She pulled a tobacco pouch from her shawl pocket and deftly rolled a cigarette with her one good hand. Colin sprang from her shoulder and began clambering between the ropes.

'I don't know about that,' I replied. 'I do like the feeling, though. There's something, I don't know, *real* about it.'

'Real? How so?'

I paused, trying the trick of thought before speech.

'I'm steering the boat, but only by so much. There's no illusion that I'm in control. I'm just doing my best.'

She lit her cigarette and took a long drag.

'Spoken like a true mother,' she said on the outward breath.

'Dani seems ... strong,' I said.

She raised her eyebrows and tapped her ash. 'She's always been her own person, even when she was little. Fierce. I used to call her my *warrior*.'

'Was it always just you and her?'

'Mm-hmm. Her father doesn't know about her.'

'Who was he?'

She shrugged. 'Some soldier. English. A bad idea, like I said. He was only in the barracks for two weeks before being shipped off to Afghanistan. Never came back.'

'Doesn't she ever wonder who he is?'

I sensed a bristle of irritation. 'Why would she? I raised her, did everything for her, made her the woman she is today.'

She looked away, and I decided to stop talking.

'What about you?' she said after a short silence. 'You're separated from your husband, no?'

It was my turn to bristle. 'Not exactly, we're just not in the same place. He couldn't get on the boat. Bryce thinks—' I stopped. 'Actually, it doesn't matter what Bryce thinks. I just want to get to my children.'

I kept my eyes ahead, but I could feel her watching me in that unabashed manner that only children and people over fifty-five can manage. Those ages inhabit some realm of unlearned wisdom, I'm sure of it. Something else happens in between.

'You're a brave, strong woman, Beth. And take it from me, you can do what you're about to do without help.'

I glanced at her.

'What is it you think I'm about to do?'

'Rescue your children. Find a safe place for them. Raise them on your own. Am I wrong?'

The words crept over me like the mist.

'Not easy waters, I'll grant you,' she went on, 'but you can navigate them without the help of a man.'

The hatch shot open and Richard's long frame emerged. He brandished the map.

'I think we know where we are and how to get where we're going.'

Maggie gave me a flat look. 'Well, that was unfortunate timing.'

'What?' said Richard, looking between us.

'Nothing,' I said. 'Tell us where we are, *number one*.'

He gave me a curious look and spread the map on the cockpit shelf.

'Here.' He pointed at a hill range north of Cadiz. 'I went over it several times with your daughter, Maggie – she's quite the stickler for detail, by the way – and we both agreed ... finally ... that we absolutely have to be between the summits of these two hills. It's the only thing for miles that resembles this gulley, and there are – were, at least – tonnes of wind farms along this coast. If we're right, it means that if we follow the current then we'll leave it about five miles from what used to be the coast. All we need to do then is take a rough bearing and head out into the Atlantic.' He glanced around the map, rubbing his stubbled chin. 'I think.'

'That doesn't make sense,' I said. 'How can the water be so high around here when it was only, what, ten metres in Gibraltar?'

Richard looked at me. 'I don't know how much you experienced of Britain, Beth, but we saw a lot when we ran through it. Crumbling coastlines, craters that stretched to the horizon, canyons where cities used to be. Those things tore the country apart, and from the looks of it they did the same here; there's every chance this coast sank.'

'Sank? Is that even possible?'

He looked grimly back at the map. 'It would explain the tsunami that took the *Unity*. If continents are breaking apart at the edges then anything could happen.'

I chewed my lip. 'OK, well, we don't have much of a choice now anyway. We follow this and then head south-west. We can try to find our bearings again when we're out in the Atlantic.'

'Good idea.'

I looked at him. 'Is it?'

'I don't know, Beth. I know a bit about sailing, but next to nothing about nautical navigation. I'm sure we'll work it out, though. Someone had to once, right?'

'No manual.'

He smiled. 'No manual.'

217

I turned to Maggie. 'Maggie, this is your last chance get back on dry land. Shall we drop you and Dani here?'

She gave a flat smile and shook her head. 'It would appear that I no longer have a choice in the matter. I think we're coming with you, if that's all right.'

'Of course.'

Her smile fell and her head turned. 'What's that noise?'

'What noise?' said Richard, walking to her side.

She held up a finger. 'Shh.'

In the distance there was a low humming; a growl drawing near.

Richard turned, his jaw set. 'That's an engine.'

My pulse raced. 'It's Staines,' I said. 'I know it is. How far?'

'I don't know. A mile?'

I fumbled with the ignition. Richard swung past.

'Don't, he'll hear it, and anyway, we're going to need more than that if we want to outrun him. That sounds like a much bigger engine than this lawnmower. Josh?'

'Yeah?'

'I need you to raise that jib.'

Josh eyed the two sails.

'One at the front, Josh,' I said. 'You pull the cable at the bottom and lash the—'

Richard broke in, 'He knows how to do it, don't you, Joshy?'

Josh went to work on the cable while Richard called down the hatch.

'Dani, I need your help with the mainsail. Quickly.' Dani darted out and attacked the cover's knots. Richard shouted into the now empty cabin. 'And it would be really fucking useful if you could lend a hand some time, Bryce.'

There was a distant groan. Richard slammed the hatch shut.

'What do you want me to do?' said Maggie quietly to me.

'Er … er … just keep a look out behind, Maggie, please. Tell me when you see them.'

'OK,' she said, smiling. 'Don't worry, keep calm.'

Keep calm, I thought, as she went back to the stern. *How can I keep calm?*

I watched the three at work on the foredeck.

'Josh,' I said, weakly. 'How's the jib?'

But he didn't hear me. He'd stumbled and lost his grip on the cable.

I could do that, I thought. *I know how to do that.*

'Christ, Josh,' said Richard. 'Dani?'

'What?' She was struggling with a knot.

I'm good at knots. I've got stronger fingers than her. I could untie that.

'Go and help Josh, will you.'

Dani gave a frustrated yell and threw down the knot, stomping over to where Josh was fumbling with the cable. 'Give it here!'

Josh fell back, lost for what to do. Richard glanced at him.

'Well, come and help me, then!'

Josh, pale-faced, crawled over the deck and felt his way along the canvas.

'What do I do?'

'Just untie that flaming knot!'

I turned.

'Maggie, any sign?'

'No, but it's definitely getting louder.'

I could do that too, I thought. *I could do all of this*.

'What's the wind doing, Beth?' shouted Richard.

'What?'

'The wind! What direction is it blowing in? I can't see from here.'

'Oh ...'

I looked up at the swinging vane.

'Getting closer,' said Maggie.

'Er ... coming from the right, I mean left.'

'What?'

'Port.'

'Right.'

The mainsail was free now. Dani had released the cable and raised the jib.

'Done!' she yelled, as a gust of wind pulled us ahead. I battled to control the helm as the boat threatened to swing into the starboard wall.

'Good, now take this line, Josh and ... no, not there, oh for God's sake.'

With another rasp of frustration, Dani strode over and snatched the line from Josh, threading it through a winch.

'That's it, now turn,' said Richard. 'The boom's going to swing out starboard. Josh?'

Josh was crouched against the guard rail, hugging his knees.

'Fine. Dani, ready?'

'Yes.'

'I see them,' said Maggie. 'I see them, they're close.'

'Shit, Richard?'

'OK, turn that winch. Josh, we could do with your help.'

The mainsail began to rise. Josh watched it from his self-imposed cocoon.

'Josh!'

'They're gaining on us,' said Maggie. 'Looks like they're in one of those gin palaces we saw.'

My imagination was suddenly assaulted by the figure of Tony Staines looming somewhere behind me. I turned. In the distance a vulgar, fat boat motored through the mist, and standing on its prow with his hands on his hips stood the man himself.

'It's him,' I said. 'It's him.'

Suddenly a gust took us and I turned to see the mainsail billowing halfway up its mast, with Richard and Dani on the deck. In the shock of movement I lost my grip on the helm and it span violently to the right.

'Port, Beth, port!' shouted Richard, scrabbling to his feet. But the boat had already found its path and now shot diagonally across a thin section of gulley. Before I could compensate there was a sickening crunch as the boat hit land, where it creaked and stopped.

I froze, hands still on the wheel and staring madly ahead at the patch of soft earth into which we had become lodged. The mainsail flapped uselessly. The pitch of the engine behind us dropped.

'I'm sorry,' I said, but nobody heard.

Richard had stopped giving orders and grabbed a long hook with which he was attempting to push the boat away from the land. Shakily, Josh wiped something from his cheek and found a hook of his own to help with, leaving Dani in mute struggle with the winch.

'Beth,' said Maggie, backing away from the stern.

Staines' boat had drifted to a stop about fifty metres from us, and he watched us, half smiling from the prow. There were five others visible on the boat, one at the helm and the rest on each side of the deck, guns raised.

Dani had joined her mother's side. With her eyes on Staines she carefully reached into a seat cavity and pulled out two guns, one of which she gave to her mother. Maggie shook off her sling and the pair crouched, taking aim.

Staines' voice jarred the silence.

'You appear to have hit a spot of bother.'

Nobody responded. Josh and Richard struggled with the hook.

'Yeees,' Staines continued, 'extremely big keel, the Salar 40. Makes it damn near impossible to capsize but an absolute *bugger* to manoeuvre, don't you find? Of course, if you'd taken this beast you'd have been right as rain. No sails to worry about, big engine, oh, and plenty of fuel on board too. Quite sufficient for an Atlantic crossing. As it is, you're stuck with that old bird.' His tone darkened. '*My* old bird. I do hope you haven't damaged it.'

Maggie raised her head. 'This isn't your boat, Tony. It never was. You stole it, just like everything else.'

'Maggie,' he beamed, 'good to see you as always, but I'll have you know I paid for that vessel fair and square. It cost me forty-six thousand euros, which was pretty much all the money I had left after that bitch cleared me out. So you *might* say it holds a certain sentimental value.'

'We have two high-powered rifles aimed directly at you, Tony,' said Maggie.

'And I have four at you.'

'My daughter's a crack shot. She could pierce your fuel tank before you knew it.'

He smirked. 'My men would kill you in a second.'

'And risk damaging your precious boat in the process?'

His smile withered, replaced by a scowl. They were drifting closer now, and beads of sweat were visible on his ruddy skin.

'Take it,' I said.

His eyes flicked to me. 'What?'

'You take your boat back and we'll take that one. Then we go our separate ways.'

Tony removed his hands from his hips. He shifted his weight between his feet and frowned, as if considering the offer – and for a second I honestly thought he would take it – but then a hollow, lifeless look took hold of him and his hands dropped to his side.

'If only it were that simple, Beth.'

'Why isn't it?'

'Because my boat wasn't the only thing you took. A few hours ago I had an army, almost two hundred loyal men and women under my command. But thanks to you and that little device of yours they're all either dead or on the run. You've left me with nothing, Beth. Do you understand? Do you know how that feels, to have everything you value taken from you in one fell swoop?'

My jaw tightened. 'Yes.'

'Then you'll know exactly why I'm not of the mind to just let you go. You've ruined me, Beth. And I'm taking that very personally.'

He stopped, distracted by something behind us. The men behind swung their guns.

'Keep two on them, you idiots,' he hissed, gripping the guard rail.

I turned. In the water was another boat.

'Get down,' said Richard, pushing Josh to the deck.

We watched in bewilderment as it glided through the still water towards us. It was small and worn with a single mast, to which a collapsed grey sail hung. The hull was green and barnacled, streaked with age, and ropes dangled from the deck into the sea. Its cabin windows were grimy. One was cracked. There was nobody on board.

It drifted past and veered right, where it came to rest against the opposite bank like a paper boat against the edge of a duck pond.

'Get me a hook,' said Tony, holding an arm out. 'There might be supplies.'

With his attention on the boat, I turned to Richard.

'Can you get us free?' I said. 'This might be our only chance.'

A strong breeze rattled our sail.

'We'll try,' said Richard. 'The wind's picking up too, and it's with us. Josh –' he held his son by the shoulders '– do you think you can push us away from the wall while I get the sail up?'

Josh took a breath, nodded and scrabbled back to the front with his hook.

A burst from Tony's engine pushed them across the gulley. He stretched his hook over the side and the little boat's sail seemed to flap with alarm in the strengthening wind.

I felt our boat move and turned to see Josh's delighted face.

'I did it!'

'Bloody good work,' said Richard, grinning. He had loosened the sail and was winching it up. Cables rattled. He turned to me, nodding at the sky. 'When that wind hits us the boom's going to swing to port, so keep her steady.'

'There won't be enough time,' said Maggie. 'One of their gunners is still aiming at us.'

'Then we'll fire first,' said Dani.

I heard Tony's voice. His hook was inches from the boat's guard rail. 'Almost ... almost there.'

'Hurry,' I said.

Something glinted above the stranded boat, a moving object catching the light. It was a canister of some kind, spinning from the cabin in a short arc and landing with a *thunk* Tony's feet.

'Oh,' said Tony, looking down. 'What the hell—?'

Many things happened at once. First, the stranded boat's engine roared to life, and it reversed from the bank in a 180-degree turn. I saw movement through the cabin windows – a figure darting – and suddenly the loose sail seemed to spring up the mast in three swift strokes. A hissing sound came from Tony's boat, followed by cries of alarm. Blue smoke plumed from the canister that had landed on his deck, and he and his men scrabbled about, diving for cover. A gun went off. One of them jumped overboard, and soon the boat was engulfed in a thick cloud. At this moment a terrific gust of wind inflated our sail, and that of the little boat. We were pulled away, but the other boat was faster.

As it passed, a figure popped out from the cabin. It was a man, ferociously thin with a shock of unkempt hair and tattered clothes.

He wore an eyepatch.

'Ed?'

The corner of his mouth twitched, and he tracked me with one wide wild eye.

'Follow me,' he said.

'Christ almighty,' exclaimed Richard.

I stood, unable to move and uncertain of what I had seen. But before I could process anything more, the helm tugged. I held tight this time, battling it starboard to keep us on course. Another shot rang out from Tony's boat and Dani returned fire with two sharp cracks. The gin palace's engine started again.

'What's happening back there?' I called back, pressing my shoulder against the helm.

'He's coming after us, but I can't see properly.'

I found the binoculars and then threw them back at Maggie.

'They're still in the smoke. Wait ... I think ... they've stopped. They've come aground!'

We were moving now, but Richard was back to shouting at Josh. They were struggling. The boom was still loose and I had to duck twice as it swung over the cockpit.

The little boat scudded ahead.

Ed scudded ahead.

My head spun. I gripped the helm.

Finally the boom locked into place and our mainsail bulged, hurling us on. I navigated the gulley, heart in my mouth – but alive! – and knuckles white. I glanced back every few moments, but no great boat loomed behind, and gradually the walls shrank and the gap between them widened, and the air became fresher and full of salt, until finally we sped out onto the open ocean and I wondered at how my chest wasn't bursting and at how close fury was to joy.

Chapter 19

Some hours later we slowed and dropped anchor in open water. The coast was far behind and the sky had cleared to the dark blue of late afternoon, revealing the night's first stars. Without a word Ed jumped across and pulled me to him. I shut my eyes and held him tight. I didn't recognise his body – the feeling of his ribs and spine, the hardness of his bearded chin – but through his unwashed stink I caught his scent and breathed it in.

I felt like I was somehow watching it all, standing baffled and awkward like the others, or staring down from the mast like a crow.

I pulled back. My eyes were red raw.

Richard stepped forward.

'Ed,' he said, pumping his hand. 'It's you. It's really fucking you.'

There was a kind of horror in Ed's face. He avoided Richard's eyes as if he didn't trust what he was seeing.

'Good to see you too,' he said, letting his hand fall. 'Richard.'

'Bryce told me about Harvey.'

'Bryce?' said Ed. His eye twitched.

Richard glanced at me. 'Yeah. I'm sorry.'

Ed looked away.

'How did you find us?' I said.

'I heard you on the radio. There was a girl's voice. She was trying to contact … I don't know, *Malta*, or somewhere.'

'Gibraltar,' said Dani. 'That was me.'

'That's right,' said Ed, hesitantly. 'Gibraltar.' He picked up a rope and began coiling it absent-mindedly, eyes roaming the deck and landing on anything but the faces around him. 'I heard where you were going, who was on board, your rough location. I heard your name. I'd just made it past Portugal and I was about to cross the straits, so I was in the right place.' He dropped the rope and raised his arms weakly. 'And here I am.'

'How long have you been travelling?'

He shrugged, mouthed something to himself. 'Three weeks, give or take a day.'

I looked at the battered boat next to us.

'In that thing?'

'Yes. From Falmouth.'

'But you don't know how to sail.'

'Neither do you. What happened? Why are you on this boat?'

'The *Unity* was hit by a tsunami. It sank.'

Terror bloomed in his eye.

'Where are the kids?'

I shook my head. The terror swelled. 'They're alive,' I said quickly, to quell it. 'But we were separated. They're in Florida.' I looked at the deck. 'As far as I know.'

'What do you mean, "as far as you know"?'

Richard backed away. 'We should probably, um ...'

'Maybe that's a good idea,' agreed Maggie.

'Somebody took them,' I said.

Ed frowned, his eyebrow folding over its patch like a slug on a lettuce leaf. 'Took them? How?'

I clenched my jaw. 'She was looking after them for me. I couldn't get to them in time. She took them.'

He shook his head, mouth agape.

'How ...' he began. 'How could you be so careless?'

The first and only person I ever hit was Emily Lamond. We were six years old and dressed as mice for the school Nativity. She didn't like me because her mouse mask kept falling off and mine didn't, so she bit me, and I walloped her right in the face. I burst out crying before she did.

I had never hit anybody since.

Ed hit the deck – literally – and I howled at the pain in my fist. I shook it, glaring down at him.

'How dare you?' I screamed. 'How fucking dare you!'

He sat up, stunned, cupping his nose.

'I've been looking after our children since that cellar hatch slammed shut – no, since way before then, waiting for you to stop moping around having your mid-life crisis. Is that done yet, by the way?'

He went to speak but there was no way I was letting him, and neither was there any way to think about these words before they burst from my mouth. I was a river that had finally burst its banks.

'I'm not finished!' I paced, cradling my throbbing knuckles. 'I begged you, Ed, *begged* you not to go on that salvage run. We had sex, remember? I even let you put your finger up my arse. I fucking *hate* it when you put your finger up my arse! And you know what? You still went, didn't you, you still went out and pretended to be a fucking soldier. And don't even think about telling me it was because you felt a *duty*, don't tell me you were trying to *feed your family*. You went out there because it meant you didn't have to spend time with us inside. Just like you always have done. And because of that we got separated and I had to look after our children alone. Just like I always have done, Ed.'

I bent over him, tears shaking from my cheeks.

'You have no idea what I've been through. And you have no idea how I'm feeling. My heart feels like it's been torn out, chewed up and stuffed back inside me. It doesn't work properly, Ed, it stutters and jumps and I think I'm going to die. Every minute I'm away from them it feels like I'm one minute closer to death. It's agony, Ed. And then you come waltzing in on your shitty little boat, the big fucking hero, and tell me that I'm careless?'

I'd run out of words, so I breathed at him for a bit, made a noise like a strangled chicken, and took myself downstairs.

*

The hatch opened. I'd been down there in the dark for about half an hour, fiddling with my nails at the table. There was no sign of Bryce or Carmela; they had consigned themselves to the bedroom at the front.

Ed stood halfway down the ladder, blocking the light. It was evening now and the sun was sliding to the horizon.

'I'm sorry,' he said, hanging there. 'I know it wasn't your fault. It could never have been your fault. I'm sorry.'

'It's all right,' I said, clicking my nails.

'Can I sit with you?'

I glanced up. Nodded. Returned to my fingers.

He took the bench opposite, tracing a line on the wood.

'I had already said goodbye to you,' I said.

'What do you mean?'

'I mean: I thought I was never going to see you again. So I said goodbye. It was one night in that awful camp. Nobody slept, the kids were awake every hour crying with the cold, and I didn't believe we were ever going to get on a boat. It didn't seem possible, there were so many people, you know? I thought we were going to be left behind. And you – the last time I'd seen you, you'd been leaving for Edinburgh on that stupid fucking salvage run, where there were people with guns, and I just thought ...'

'Thought what?'

'I thought you were dead. And thinking about the possibility that you might not be just made things more difficult. It's like I was hanging on to something that wasn't real, and it was holding me back. I had to get moving, Ed. For the kids, you know? Do you know how that feels?'

'I know exactly how that feels.'

'So I let go. I said goodbye to you, and cried up at the moon in that freezing compound, and that night I slept well. The next day we got our papers. We were going, and you weren't going to be with us. I buried you, Ed. You were dead.'

He leaned forward. 'But I'm not dead. I'm here. I found you.'

'I know. And don't think I'm not glad. It's just … now I've got to dig you up again.' I sat back. 'I can't really explain it. I'm sorry.'

He looked down at the table. 'Did you tell Alice I was dead?'

I shook my head. 'No. I was trying to find the right time.'

'What happened on the *Unity*?'

I told him, and afterwards he nodded, rubbing his beard.

'Florida, then?'

'That's the plan.'

He drew a long breath through his nose, then frowned and sniffed.

'Why does it smell of sick down here?'

The door to the bedroom flew open.

'Have we stopped?' said Bryce, standing in its frame. Any remnants of his brief foray into hygiene were gone, and his hair hung in straggles, peppered with objects I could not and had no inclination to identify. He wobbled, scanning the cabin, eyes landing on Ed.

Ed folded his arms, seeming to shrink into himself as he had done with Richard. He didn't meet Bryce's eyes as he approached the table.

Bryce looked between us, breathing heavily.

'Told you he'd make it,' he said to me. He slapped Ed on the shoulder and went upstairs. Carmela followed.

'*Hola*,' she whispered as she passed.

'What's all that about?' I said. 'You were the same with Richard. I thought they were your friends?'

He chewed his lip, arms still folded, staring at me with that same wild look in his eye.

'You can ...' he mumbled, 'you know, *see* them, then?'

'What do you mean *see* them. Of course I can, why wouldn't I?'

He nodded, rubbing his tongue around his teeth.

'Right,' he said, with a sigh. 'That clears that up, then.'

As the sun set we sat up on deck, eight of us around the fold-out table. Maggie lit some candles she'd found in the cabin, and we shared three tins – potatoes, peas and a meat stew – with a bottle of Staines' sickly rum. The sea was a hard glass beneath a spray of stars.

I sat next to Ed, our legs squashed together and his hand on mine.

'The hardest part was getting the boat down,' he said. 'The path from the house had crumbled away so there was only scree. They had an old Citroën—'

'Who?' I asked.

'The people. The couple I found in the house, the ones I buried with Harvey.' Bryce and Richard dropped their heads at the name. Ed took a breath. 'Anyway, there was no fuel in it, of course, but I managed to push it as far as the slope. Then I kind of let it slide down, steering it as best I could. I hit some rocks, lost control a few times, but I made it. After that I took it for some practice runs around the bay, learned what all the ropes did. There were charts in the house, a few books on sailing. I got pretty good –' he glanced at Bryce, '– better than I was at running, anyway.'

'That's not difficult, Edgar,' said Bryce. 'You run like a girl.'

Dani bristled. 'You think girls can't run, no?'

'Just a turn of phrase, sweetheart. I know fine well girls can run.' He lost himself in his glass, and some memory or other. 'Fine well.'

'I took as much food and water as I could from their house. They had a whole store full; "preppers", I think they would have been called once. After that it was just a case of plucking up the courage to set out.'

'Where did you go?' said Richard

He shrugged. 'South. Navigated the channel best I could, almost hit rocks off Finistère so I kept clear of the coast after that.' He looked up suddenly, as a streak of light traced across the sky. We watched as another one followed.

'I heard they're still falling,' I said, breaking off at the bitter memory of my first conversation with Mary. 'Although that might not be true.'

'It is true,' said Ed. 'I saw three hit the sea off Bordeaux. Just small, but enough to whip up the water enough that I had to drop anchor in a bay. Scared the shit out of me. I spent a couple of nights below deck thinking it was all going to happen again, you know? After that I lost my confidence a bit, so I thought I'd try getting to dry land, talking to someone, maybe finding someone who could help me. But the coasts ... they're not safe. And not just because of the rocks.'

'We've seen it,' said Richard, looking at me.

Ed nodded. 'It was everywhere. Almost everywhere, at least. I found a small village in Portugal that had somehow avoided the trouble. I stayed up drinking white port with an old fisherman who told me about Cape Town. He's the one that gave me that smoke canister. "Not much," he said, "but you might need it." Pushed on after that.' He looked at me. 'Couldn't stop thinking about you arriving there, and what might have happened.'

Ed toyed with his glass, the rum untouched.

'That was only a week ago. It seems like longer. Then I picked up your call on the radio, decided to brave the coast again and –' he raised a palm, looked at me '– here we are.'

Nobody spoke for a few moments. Then Bryce grabbed the bottle and filled everyone's glasses.

'Here's to Ed,' he said, raising his. Everyone followed.

'To Ed.'

Somehow my toast came later than everyone else's, and the sound of his name – flatter than the rest – hung there in the silence. I held my breath.

Bryce made a noise of disgust and stared at his glass. 'This stuff's rank. Reminds me of my fucking prick grandad.'

I exhaled, glad of the distraction. 'You feeling better, Bryce?'

'Aye, I'm fine when we're no moving. What about you?'

'I'm all right.' I looked at Ed. 'Broke my leg.'

There was another silence. This time Bryce broke it with a great inhalation.

'You know, personally, I'm quite partial to a finger up the old arsehole. Is that just me?'

I held my brow. 'Jesus.'

Maggie gave a hoot.

'For fuck's sake, Bryce,' said Ed.

'What? Just saying, bit of bum fiddling never did anyone any harm. Right, darlin'?' He looked at Carmela, who shrugged and said something that sounded like agreement. 'See?'

'Right,' said Richard, draining his glass. 'Enough. Time for bed. We take watches, OK? Two men at a time—'

'Men?' said Dani.

'Two *people* at a time, swapping every four hours. Bryce and Carmela, you can take the first.'

'Brand new,' said Bryce.

'Then Maggie and I, if you don't mind, Maggie?'

'By all means.'

'Ed and Beth next, then Josh and Dani. OK, kids?' Josh smiled at Dani, who rolled her eyes.

'Where do we sleep when we're not on watch?' she said.

'I'd, er, say use the front room, darlin',' said Bryce, 'but I wouldn't recommend it.'

'There are two bunks in the back.' Richard turned to me. 'And Beth's with Ed in his boat. Right, Beth?'

'Of course,' I said.

Of course.

That night we tried to huddle in the single bunk below deck on Ed's boat. We tangled and untangled, trying various combinations of limbs and awkward spoons. Ed's touches were hesitant and hovering, each with a tacit request for permission. Eventually we gave up.

'You take the bunk,' he said. 'I'll sleep up on deck.'

'Sorry. It's my leg. It still hurts when I lie down.'

'I know. Good night.'

'Ed.'

He stopped at the cabin door. 'Yeah?'

'I'm sorry I hit you.'

He shrugged. 'I deserved it. Night.'

When he was gone I tucked my chin into my neck and closed my eyes.

There were thumps and mumbles from the other boat. Bryce and Carmela had started their watch and were talking, each in their own language, and laughing at small things. I remembered how easy it was at the beginning of relationships, how much you forgave the other for the trips and stumbles in what they did and said, and how your touches were delicate for different reasons.

Ed whispered from outside. 'We'll find them, Beth. We'll get there, I promise.'

'I know,' I said.

I know.

I know because that's what I'm doing.

Chapter 20

When I woke, Richard and Maggie were just finishing their watch. Richard handed Ed and I cups of coffee across the guard rail, one of Maggie's roll-ups hanging from his lip.

'I'm going to stay up,' he said, blowing smoke into the cold morning air. 'Get things moving on the *Black Buc*. Wind's still in our favour so we should use it while we can. I'll take the helm, Josh and Dani can take sheets, right Joshy?'

He turned as Josh emerged onto deck, rubbing his eyes and nodding.

'You two OK on the –' he arched his back to see the stern '– what's your boat called, Ed? I can't read the name.'

'I changed it,' said Ed. 'She's called the *Elma*.'

He took a sip of coffee, avoiding my eyes.

Richard paused. '*Elma*. Nice. So, are you two OK on the *Elma*?'

I looked back at Richard. 'Yes, but we don't know where we're going.'

Richard smiled. 'I plotted a rough course last night. Want to see?'

We followed Richard below the *Black Buc*'s deck, where he had spread out a map of the Atlantic.

'We're dealing with somewhat limited technology,' he said. 'We have a compass, of course, but nothing like a sextant. There's a Raymarine, but obviously that's no use to us.'

'What's a Raymarine?' I said.

'A charting tablet,' said Ed. 'Kind of like an iPad for a boat. It uses GPS, so—'

'No satellites,' I finished.

'Exactly,' said Richard. 'Useless. Plus it's out of charge. But anyway, who doesn't like a good old-fashioned map, eh?'

He grinned and leaned over the crumpled chart. A curve of twine stretched across it, tacked with pins.

'Pretty simple,' said Richard, smoothing the paper. 'We left the gulley here, and maintained roughly eight knots for four hours on the same heading, which puts us about here.' He tapped a spot somewhere beneath Portugal. 'Which means ...'

Ed leaned across. 'That's not where the gulley was.'

'What?'

'The gulley was here.' Ed tapped a spot a centimetre or so north of Richard's marker. Richard frowned, inspecting the map.

'No. No, it was definitely here. That's the only thing that looks remotely like the landscape we passed through yesterday.'

Ed gave an awkward laugh, and I sensed Richard bristle. 'That's because the landscape you passed through looks nothing like the map any more. The whole coastline's different. Believe me, it's there.'

Richard hesitated, scanning the map. 'How can you be sure?'

'Because I've been following it for days. I have my charts as well.'

'What does the course look like if we move the starting point?' I said. 'Just to see.'

Reluctantly, Richard reached for a new pin and drove it into the sea where Ed had pointed. Ed corrected it, placing it a half centimetre to the right and attaching a new piece of twine to show the new heading. Richard's jaw clenched.

I rolled my eyes. 'That doesn't seem to make much difference.'

Richard huffed. 'Not on the map, but on the sea it would make the difference of a thousand nautical miles. If we take the wrong heading now we could end up in South America.'

'Can't we adjust as we go?' I said.

'Sure,' said Richard, 'if we were on land. We'd have something to take readings with and from; land-marks, hills, forests, etc., but we're at sea. We have no GPS and the only other way to navigate would be to use a sextant, which we don't have, and even if we did I'm fairly sure nobody would know how to use it.'

'So we're sailing by instinct,' I said.

I turned to Ed. 'How did you make it down here?'

'I had the coast to guide me.' He gestured at the map. 'I'm positive that's where we are.'

'Right,' I said. 'It's just ...'

'What?'

'Well, you don't exactly have an A1 track record in navigation.'

'What do you mean?'

'That holiday we went on to Cornwall, when you didn't want to take phones or a sat nav or anything. Remember that day trip to Land's End?'

'What about it?'

'Ed, we ended up in Devon.'

'That was different.'

'How?'

'Because *I* was different.'

He looked about awkwardly.

'The point is,' said Richard, a little gruffness entering his tone, 'we need to be sure *now*. Every mile we cover on the wrong heading is one more mile that takes us away from where we want to go.'

My eyes drifted along the twine. 'What are these things?'

I touched a series of marks some distance into the ocean. Richard peered at them.

'The Azores,' he said. 'Why?'

'They're between the two twines. How long will it take to reach them?'

He shrugged. 'Five days, six, depending on the wind.'

'Would they be visible from either route?'

'Well, theoretically, I suppose ...'

'Then we'll know. If we pass to the north of them then Ed's guess is correct, if we pass to the south then it's Richard's. Once we know we can adjust our course.'

Richard sniffed, straightened and folded his arms. After a deep breath, he nodded.

'All right with you, Ed?'

'Sounds good to me.'

'Good. Then we'll start with your route. Let's go.'

As Ed and I prepared the *Elma* for sail, I asked him about the name.

'*Elma*, then. Where did that come from?'

He gave me an encrypted look. 'You don't know?'

'Why would I?'

He shrugged and tossed the dregs of his coffee overboard. 'I'll tell you one day.'

I dropped the rope I was coiling. 'Tell me now.'

He winked as he passed, making for the mainsail. 'One day. You're on the helm, all right?'

Following Ed's bearing, we set out, the two boats side by side with their sails inflated proudly. The sky was clear and bright, the sea sparkling, and a strong, steady breeze blew us south-west. I could almost feel the depth of the water drop beneath us. The waves seemed bigger somehow, darker, wilder, their faces like shark fins worrying our bows.

I kept to the *Elma*'s helm while Ed worked the sheets on the foredeck. He moved nimbly, moving around the sail on all fours with his trousers rolled up and his shirt hanging loose. You might have said he looked healthy, were it not for the darkness beneath his eyes, or the way the only one left darted this way and that as if tracing invisible bullets. There was a wildness to him, but whenever I thought of what experiences might have led him to this state, I found my distance growing. Strange. I just couldn't latch on to him, no matter how hard I tried.

But we buzzed along, each of us performing the duties of our role with the occasional shout or nod.

I learned about the *Elma*, about how she worked and fitted together, drawing the same pleasure as I did whenever I examined a piece of software. That bit fits there, connects to that, which, when pulled, does that ...

Same principle.

Her sail and rudder: those were her interfaces; the sea and the wind were her data. The only task was to position them so that her software – her shape and weight – processed the information in such a way that you got the intended result: velocity.

But her helm felt loose and plasticky in comparison to the *Black Buccaneer*'s, and occasionally I looked up from my task to watch the bigger boat's progress. Dani and Josh worked the sails while Richard manned the helm, and Maggie kept watch at the bow with Carmela, somehow managing to keep her black roll-ups dry in the way that only a seasoned smoker can. Bryce was, once again, nowhere to be seen. I felt a longing to be back on that deck, behind its grander helm and beneath its towering mast, even though I had only been on it for a day.

We like things. Other things, new things; it doesn't take long. It's a wonder we stick with anything.

Maggie shouted something back at Richard, and he raised his head in laughter I couldn't hear.

'Are you OK?' shouted Ed from the bow.

'Aha,' I said, with a nod.

Squinting, he looked out to sea.

Days passed. The wind stayed strong and the sky remained clear; *providence*, they would have called it once. We made the most of the conditions and sailed for as long as the light permitted; though we were doing well, none of us felt comfortable navigating in the dark. A routine developed and each boat had its own responsibilities. The *Buccaneer* was where we sat and ate in the evening, and where we kept most of the food. The crates of water – we had discovered to our dismay that the *Bucaneer's* tank was almost dry – stayed on the *Elma*, where it was cooler. We kept our nightly watches, and if it was our shift when the sun rose, whoever else was waking would offer to take over the *Elma* for us. But I always said no. I didn't crave sleep, and whenever it took me it was rarely for more than a few minutes.

One night, during one of these half-sleeps I woke to see Ed's face near mine.

'What is it?' I mumbled, blinking.

He kissed me. A long, soft touch of our lips. He stroked my hair. There was a hunger in his eye.

'Ed, I can't ... my leg.'

'It's OK,' he said, standing. 'I love you, that's all.'
My leg was fine.

Sometimes I would wake up at night and sit at the bow while Ed slept at the stern. There was a carton of cigarettes on the *Elma*; seventeen faded packs of Dunhill into which I dipped on these occasions and smoked, facing east, scanning the water through the blue haze.

There was no sign of Staines, though my neck ached from turning to check. I told Ed about him, and about how I had gone down to ask for his help. He said I was brave and foolish, but that he hoped he would have done the same. There were others like him, now, he went on to tell me. Others who had crawled out of the woodwork after the strike, like cockroaches claiming their new lawless world.

We had to be careful, he told me. And I told him I planned never to be careful again, at least not until I saw our children.

One night, as Dani and Josh took watch on the *Black Buccaneer*, I crept up for my midnight smoke. This time Ed woke and found me.

'Didn't know you smoked,' he said, sitting beside me.

'Normal rules no longer apply.'

'Can I have one?'

I tossed him the pack. He lit one and nodded across at the other boat.

'What do you think those two are talking about?'

I looked over at two starlit figures huddled together near the helm.

'Josh and Dani? Don't know. I didn't even think they were talking.'

'Do you think they're ... you know.'

'No, but I'm sure Richard would like it if they were.' I turned to him. 'He was telling me he's found it hard, with Josh, you know, after his wife died.'

Ed nodded slowly. 'I can imagine. Especially being Richard.'

'What does that mean?'

'Well, you know. He's fairly old-fashioned, isn't he? Men are men, women are women, all that. Must be a shock to the system having to take that responsibility, right?'

I put my cigarette out and turned to face him fully.

'And I suppose you'd know all about that.'

'What do you mean?'

'Fatherhood. Responsibility. That's something you have some experience in, is it?'

I think I had some expectation of him trying to defend himself, stammering, trying to form excuses, but instead his expression seemed to close in, like a machine returning to a default state. He blinked, the cigarette still trailing smoke beneath him.

'You're entitled to say that, but don't for a second think I've not been poking that wound ever since Edinburgh. I know I let you down and I know my faults, and believe me when I tell you I've had many long nights to think about them. But I'm not going to spend the rest of my life telling you I'm a born-again father. I have changed, Beth, it's true, I really have, but that doesn't mean I'm perfect. I'm still going to make mistakes, just like you.'

My hackles rose.

'Me? What mistakes did I make?'

He looked away, rolled his tongue around his teeth, looked back.

'I was miserable, Beth. In Edinburgh, that's the truth of it. I hated my job, hated the world, hated my responsibilities and drowned it all in a lifestyle that only made things worse. I was a miserable, self-absorbed wanker who didn't know when he had a good thing, and it took what happened to make me see otherwise. But when I look back on that time ...'

He trailed off.

'What?'

'It's like you disappeared. As soon as Alice was born, you went inside of yourself—'

'Ed, don't you dare.'

'It's true. I couldn't find you. You were ahead of me, you knew what you were doing, what had to be done, and I didn't. I just didn't, and when I tried to help, stumbling about trying to find nappies and pass you muslin sheets when you were breastfeeding, I made mistakes. And every mistake I made just put me one more step behind. You never told me what you needed.'

I shuffled away from him. 'You should have known what I needed.'

'How could I? I had no manual.'

'Neither did I! How do you think I managed? You have no idea how hard it was back then.'

He stood, abruptly.

'No. I don't. Because you never talked to me. And by the time Arthur came along you had everything locked down. You had your own routines, your own methods, even your own way to talk to them. It was as if you didn't need me any more. Everything I did was wrong.'

'That's a fucking cop-out.'

'It's the truth, Beth. I felt redundant.' He turned and leaned on the guard rail. 'So I drifted too.'

I stood. 'You've always been drifting, Ed.'

He nodded. 'True. But I thought I'd stopped when I met you.'

He turned to meet my eyes, but I looked away and went to bed.

Chapter 21

The next day, our seventh since leaving the coast, I woke from my imposter of sleep to more activity than usual. There were shouts from the other boat and Ed's footsteps rattling on the deck above. Rain was battering the *Elma*'s windows, and the little boat swayed and bobbed in the unsettled water.

'Morning,' said Ed, as I poked my head out. He didn't look up from his reorganisation of the water crates.

'Hi.'

I looked at the *Black Buccaneer*, where Richard and Maggie were unfurling the mainsail as Dani and Josh went about their now usual morning chores at the foredeck.

'Top of the morning!' called Richard. 'Look at this, eh? Proper weather!'

The blue sky had filled with oily black cloud and the wind had lifted, abandoning its calm breaths for furious gusts. The two boats concertinaed on the swilling sea.

'We're going to try to make the most of it today. Push ahead. But don't worry, I'm sure you'll catch up.'

'We won't need to,' Ed called across. 'You've not seen the *Elma* in action yet.'

Richard laughed. 'Good luck!'

'No sign of Bryce, I suppose?' said Ed.

'Nope, but Carmela's in the kitchen. Oh, speaking of which, only fair to feed you first. Here –' he tossed two paper packages across '– bacon sandwiches.'

I caught the hot greasy wrapper. 'How the hell did you get bacon sandwiches out here?'

'Bacon's actually jerky, and Carmela made bread if you can believe that. It's a bit doughy, but bloody lovely. Come on, eat up, you've got a race ahead.'

Ed took a seat by the helm, and we worked our way silently through the dry, salty paste.

'I've had worse,' said Ed.

'Like what?'

'Rat. Dog food.' He adjusted his eyepatch. 'Crow.'

I nodded, pursing my lips. 'I ate something I was told was cheese in the camp. It wasn't cheese. I can still taste it.'

Ed swallowed. 'I'm sorry. About last night.'

'I'd rather not—'

'I mean it. Beth, part of the problem is I don't know how to express myself. Especially during an argument. I think of better things to say after I've said them.'

'You seemed to know how to express yourself last night.'

'What I was trying to tell you was that –' he looked around my head, like a mystic inspecting my aura

'– there's stuff in there, in your brain, that I have no idea about. You're cleverer than me, Beth.'

I rolled my eyes. 'That's not true, Ed.'

'It is. You know it is. You're cleverer and more capable at most things than me, and that's the truth of it. When we first met and you talked about your work, I felt embarrassed. I had no idea what you were talking about, and yet you spoke with such passion and energy. And then Alice came along, little Alice –' he trailed off, looking at his bare feet '– and you were the one who stayed at home with her, while I went out to do my work. There must have been times when you went spare.'

'I didn't. I mean, sometimes I used to think about . . .' I shook my head, held my cheeks. 'Ed, it doesn't matter. None of this matters. I just want to find them.'

'We're going to. I know we are, do you know why?'

'Why?'

He slapped the wheel and fixed me in the eye. 'Because you're the one at the helm.'

I don't know why I felt like looking away. Maybe it was the patch, or the wildness in his eye, or maybe it was because I couldn't remember the last time we had looked at each other for longer than a moment. But whatever it was, I pushed through it. I held his gaze, and slowly it became easier.

Then I noticed he was frowning.

'Why are you looking at me like that?' he said.

'Like what?'

'Kind of, I don't know, *wobbly*.'

'I'm not wobbly. I've just never looked at someone with an eyepatch before. Where do I focus? Bad one, good one, which?'

He winked, or blinked, I couldn't tell.

'This one's fine. Now, are you ready?'

We let the *Buccaneer* leave first, watching as the wind slowly took their jib. Then came the mainsail, billowing at first then inflating like a puffer fish and sending them starboard. By the time Ed hoisted *Elma*'s single sail, they were well ahead of us.

'This is hopeless,' I said, as the pitiful rag flapped above us.

'Have a bit of faith, will you? They're bigger than us, so they can't tack as quickly.'

'What do you mean, "tack"?'

'You'll find out. Now, ready? A little to port.'

'Ach, whatever – holy shit!'

The sail snapped solid and we shot ahead. He tumbled onto the deck, laughing and grasping for a rope to pull himself up.

'That's it! Now, we're lec– '

'Lee helm, I know. Starboard right?'

'Right.'

I slung the wheel starboard, feeling the bite where wind, hull, sail and water met, and as I kept it there, our speed increased.

The spatters of rain became a cloud through which we sped. Ed gripped the rope and released a manic laugh into the spray, and as the *Elma* scudded after its prey I could no longer resist the smile that pulled at my cheeks.

We chased them for hours. The wind buffeted, a strong north-easterly surge disrupted by unruly gusts from the south. Sometimes it felt like we were closing the gap, others it felt like there was nothing we could do to beat them. At times I panicked as the distance became too great to see them clearly, fearing we would lose them, and then what?

Then we would be alone. Just me and Ed.

I told myself that my discomfort at this thought was because they had most of the food, but I knew there was enough aboard the *Elma* to last us.

By midday we were closing the gap again, but we soon realised that they had stopped and weighed anchor. Richard was dangling his legs over the side as we pulled up beside them, mouth full of another doughy sandwich, as Josh and Dani high-fived behind. Maggie sat cross-legged by the helm with Colin on her lap, smoke seeping from her smirk. They all cheered at our approach.

'Don't feel bad,' mocked Richard with a wink. 'Bigger boat, bigger crew. You didn't stand much of a chance.'

The sky was clearing. I squinted up at him.

'Day's not over, smart arse.'

He grinned. 'That's the spirit.'

We ate lunch. Bryce, more drawn than he had ever looked, came up on deck and sat forlornly at the bow for a few minutes before Colin came to bother him, and he returned to the cabin like a beleaguered troll beneath its bridge. Ed spent the time looking at the sky, watching the clouds clear.

'Wind's changing,' he said. 'Can you feel it, Richard?'

Richard sniffed and pulled a face. 'Perhaps. Nah, this bugger's not going anywhere.'

'Any idea where we are?' I said.

'Well, we've covered more water this morning than we did all yesterday. We should be nearing the Azores any time now, so keep a look out. Got that, Joshy?'

Josh gave one of his ducks in acknowledgement, coiling a rope at the brow. An impatient gust of wind rattled the guard rail.

'Right,' said Richard, jumping to his feet. 'Everyone ready?'

We pulled away again. This time the wind had lost all its distractions, and as soon as the sail popped I had to battle to keep the bite. After an hour or so, Ed took the helm while I sat and massaged my leg, watching the *Buccaneer* race ahead yet again.

'I told you,' I said, 'there's no way we'll catch them.'

'Faith, Beth, faith.'

'Aye,' I said, with a tight-lipped smile. 'Faith.'

He took a long breath as he braced the helm. 'I always wanted a dog. Did you ever want a dog?'

'What, in our house? It was way too small. There was barely enough room for us and two kids, let alone an animal.'

He smiled. 'Maybe. Still, would have been nice. I used to love watching them play at the park. Remember? Where we took Alice to the swings.'

'Ed, what the hell are you on about?'

He glanced up at the mast. 'There were a couple of greyhounds, remember them? They used to tear across the grass, feet barely touching the ground. Alice loved them. None of the other dogs could catch them, they were just too fast. Apart from one. Remember?'

'Aye. That brown one. Its owner ran the pub in Colinton.'

'She was fast, but not as fast as a greyhound, right? So she used to cut them off. Clever thing. You could see her working out their trajectory, then she'd take the shorter route so she caught them on the way round.'

Another glance at the mast.

'Why are you talking about dogs?'

He smiled. 'Always wanted a dog. Here, take the helm.'

'What, why? What are you going to do.'

'We're going to tack.'

'What's tacking? Ed, tell me—'

'Just keep her steady.'

He loosened a sheet and the boom swung port. 'Follow the wind. Turn with it.'

I spun the wheel. 'What are you doing? We're going to lose speed that way.'

'For a while, yes.'

I watched as the *Buccaneer* sped off to the right, following the bearing we should have been taking. 'Ed, we're losing them!'

But his eyes were on the sky, and the weather vane that twitched at the top of the mast. 'Not for long ... ready?'

'Ready for what?'

'The wind's about to change. I know it ... almost ...'

'Ed—'

'Now! Hard to starboard!'

In a rattle of ropes and winches the boom swung back, immediately inflating again with a tremendous gust from behind. Suddenly we were speeding towards the *Buccaneer*'s starboard side, and as we approached we saw their mizzen flap, and the mainsail flag as it lost the wind. Figures scurried about on the deck to Richard's desperate orders.

'Christ!' I cried out, shielding my face from the spray. 'How fast are we going?'

Ed whooped. 'No idea!'

I have no idea what we did that day. I'm sure a thousand experts would have held their heads and cursed us for the way we manhandled those ropes and sails, but whatever we did, it worked. We let the wind push us across the water at speed. We sailed.

We crossed the bow of the *Buccaneer*, waving as Richard tracked us, mouth agape. Josh waved back from his lookout point at the bow, but was distracted by something beyond our sail.

Eyes wide, he pointed ahead.

'Land,' he cried. 'That's land ahead!'

It took another hour before we reached the Azores, during which time the sun had dipped and the wind had changed so much that the race was forgotten in place of survival. Ed grinned all the way in; we were approaching the islands from the north, which meant he had been right. He glanced at me to acknowledge this, and I couldn't help smiling back.

The land Josh had spotted was a long and hilly island which we identified on Richard's chart as Terceira. The landscape was rural, and the shapes of fields dotted the plains beneath the tufted crags of hillocks in the west. About two miles out the two boats drew side by side, slowing, and I scanned the coast using the *Elma*'s binoculars. There was a small town in the east swarming with gulls, like flies over meat.

'What do you see?' said Ed.

'Nothing I like.'

Maggie, Josh and Dani were already taking down the *Buccaneer*'s three sails.

'We'll motor from here,' Richard called down. 'There might be rocks. You lead. Take care, go slow.'

Ed started the *Elma*'s engine and we chugged ahead with me at the bow, binoculars in hand. The *Buccaneer* thrummed behind us. Another mile in and the town revealed little more than a few boats in its harbour. One was on its side being picked at by gulls.

'Any sign of life?' said Ed from the helm.

'No. Wait!' I sat up. 'Stop.' I waved behind. 'Stop your engine!'

The two motors spluttered out and we drifted. Ed came to the foredeck.

'What is it?'

I handed him the binoculars. 'See?'

He peered ahead. A spray of jagged points rose from the sea ahead, submerging and resurfacing from the choppy tide. They spanned as far as we could see around the coast.

Maggie leaned over the bow next to us, cigarette half rolled in one hand.

'What are we looking at, Beth?'

'Rocks. Everywhere. It's not safe.'

'There's something else around them too,' said Ed. 'Froth, or nets, maybe. I can't make it out, but whatever they are there's no way through. Perhaps we could try the southern coast.'

Maggie looked west. 'The sun's going down. Another hour and it'll be dark. We could stop here for the evening, maybe check it out in the morning.' She lit her cigarette and called back. 'What do you think, Richard?'

'Fine with me.'

'Beth?'

I was tired. My leg ached, and my arms felt like rock from hauling the helm. I felt as if we'd clawed our way across an entire ocean, but more than anything else I had a bad feeling about the island.

I wonder – if we'd gone south, if we'd found a way onto the island, would things have been different?

'Yes,' I said. 'Let's rest here.'

Chapter 22

By the time we'd anchored, coiled ropes and stowed the sails, the last strings of sunset were throwing their amber light across the island's fields and hills. A low full moon made shadows of its crags, and the land sank into a brooding black mass beyond the glow of our deck.

We were floating beside an unknown quantity surrounded by rocks, but that did little to dampen the mood; we had come far and fast, and it felt like we could do anything. We sat on the *Buccaneer*'s deck by Maggie's candles, talking about the day with mugs of tea and Carmela's bread fried in oil with the rest of the jerky. Bryce was still below deck and Carmela chose to eat hers at the bow, looking out over the moonlit water. I felt sorry for her – the language, Bryce and whatever had drawn her to flee to the Rock – but I knew enough about solitude not to disturb her.

Besides, I didn't want to leave the table. Spirits were high and it felt good to talk about something positive that had happened – the past had been something I had steered from for so long. I caught Ed's eye occasionally, and I found I didn't look away. Richard noticed, and looked away, smiling.

After dinner we performed our daily provisions check, shelling peanuts from a bowl while Colin stood eagerly upon Maggie's shoulder, catching every one we tossed at him. Maggie marked a list as Dani scoured the *Buccaneer*'s cupboards and Josh did the same on the *Elma*, armed with a flashlight he held between his teeth.

'Plenty of water,' he called. 'Five crates, few more spare bottles. Eight packets of flavoured rice ... five tins of hotdogs, three tins of ... bleurgh ... burgers ... why would you put burgers in tins? ... two packets of dried bananas ... one of Rice Krispies. Some crackers, few packs of noodles ...'

'Seven tins of beans,' said Dani, 'four of tomatoes, two of potatoes, one crate of water, four packets of mashed potato, some of Carmela's bread ... that's it, I think.'

Maggie mulled over the list as Colin chattered. 'I'd say that should do us for another week at least, if we're lean. The main thing is water, of which we have plenty on the *Elma*.'

Josh clambered back and Dani returned from the cabin. Maggie threw down the list.

'Now who's for some rum?'

We gave a dreary cheer. Although we had grown used to the sour taste of Staines' rum, it wasn't something we craved. Richard pulled a bottle and glasses from the cavity beneath his seat, still sticky from the night before.

'Come on,' he said. 'Drink up.'

He went to pour but Ed stopped him.

'Shouldn't we wait for Bryce and Carmela?'

Richard sighed and sat back, popping a nut in his mouth. 'Jesus, do we have to? He's been down there all week. How long can one man be seasick?'

There was a rattle from beneath the cabin and we turned. A thump, a grumble, the sound of glass, then a groan.

'Ooo …'

But the groan rose and became something else.

'… Oooo ya beauty!'

Bryce burst from the cabin, brandishing two bottles. With gritted teeth, he looked around the deck, hollow eyes trying their best to gleam in triumph.

'Fucking whisky! Found it in the hole behind that bastard's bed.' He clambered up, snatched the glasses from Richard's hand and began pouring frantically. 'Better than that shite, eh?'

'Feeling better, then?' said Richard, looking up in disbelief.

Bryce glanced at him, trying not to spill. 'Told you, didn't I? Fine when we're no moving, bright as a button. But as soon as we're off – cannae help it, can I? Maggie?'

He offered her a glass, but she waved a hand.

'No, thank you.'

He grimaced. 'And how about your monkey?'

Colin bared his teeth and chattered.

'We'll stick with what we know, I think. But enjoy.'
She stood, scooped the rum from the table and took
it to Carmela's seat at the bow.

'Suit yourself.' Bryce sat down. He raised an
eyebrow at Ed and Richard. 'Remember the last time
we drank whisky?'

The three of them shared a smile and raised a toast
to a place or a person with some old lordly name I
can't remember – and went on to talk of things that
seemed far out of time and mind.

Whisky – never a fan. Perhaps it's because my dad
drank it. He never knocked us about or anything
like that, but my brother and I both knew when the
bottle was open, and by nine years old I had learned
to tell how many glasses down he was by the pitch
and slur of his voice, the speed with which his head
swung to the door when you came in from playing,
and the weight of his eyelids. These cues gave me
my first inkling that this man – this hero who made
bicycle obstacle courses in the garden for us out of
planks and oil drums, who never seemed to eat,
who read thick books about wars and politics, and
around whom my cousins, brother and I would sit
on Christmas Eve, fighting for the best patch of
carpet to hear him read his Robert Burns poems –
was only as good as the clarity of his blood. He said
things he didn't mean and didn't remember, became
sullen for no apparent reason, surrendered himself
to the liquid's will.

In short, he was not a constant. And that, I realised, was true of everyone.

I still like a drink. It's just that I like to *like* a drink, and for most that doesn't seem to be a prerequisite – from the clutched throat of the first attempt to the creased face after the fifth shot, to the vomit sprayed body in the gutter – pleasure is optional.

Just take a drink.

So what do I like? I like thick red wine with a T-bone steak, gin and tonic on an aeroplane, frosty beer on a hot day. That's all good. What I don't like is losing control. I know I'm not a constant (PMT, hello) but I have no desire to rediscover that truth on a nightly basis.

I had seen Ed lose control. Like my dad, he never turned on me, but he turned on himself often enough. His eyes bulged when he drank that first glass in the evening. There was no pleasure there; just an unwanted parasite being sated, a prophecy being fulfilled.

I watched him from the corner of my eye on the *Buccaneer*'s deck, swilling my own un-drunk whisky and wondering if I could detect the signs – the ones I'd learned to watch out for in my dad – but he seemed wrapped up in the conversation with Richard and Bryce, about crows and dog food, and old men in big houses.

And I noticed his whisky was un-drunk too.

I grew tired of the stories and went to visit the head. Sitting, cramped, on the squat toilet, my foot throbbed. The numbness extended from my toes to the middle of my calf, but pain had now coalesced around my big toe and arch. My cargo pants were around my ankles, and from their shadows I thought I could make out a discolouration to the flesh. It was darker than a bruise. I considered inspecting it but decided against it, finished up and left.

As I left the head I bumped into Richard.

'Sorry,' he said, with a gasp. The whisky had unsteadied him. 'Didn't meant to startle you.'

'That's all right. You didn't.'

'Are you OK?'

'Fine, I'm just—'

'That was something today wasn't it? The wind! Christ, I haven't enjoyed myself like that in *ages*.'

'I'm just glad we covered the distance.'

'And you and Ed were flying! Really caught us at the end, there, fair play to you. You and Ed ...'

He trailed off. It was dark but his eyes were visible, expectant, in a shaft of moonlight. I used the pause to break free.

'Well, best be off—'

'Wait.' He blocked my path and put a hand to my shoulder, where it remained, fingers twitching.

And just like that, everything changed.

Amazing how a few mumbles and a badly placed hand can change a feeling. It would be wrong to say that my affections for Richard had been *growing* since the *Unity*, but they had been gathering, like a collection of emotional components finding a mechanism with which to become something bigger. That was true.

But in the dark of that cabin they broke apart, instantly replaced by something else; not fear or mistrust, but disappointment, in myself and in him.

'What is it, Richard?'

He worked his jaw and throat. 'Er ... I ... er, sorry, not very good at this. I don't know what to say.'

'Then don't, Richard. Don't say anything.'

He stammered and rushed. 'But ... but, I feel like if I don't at least say *something*, then I never will. And I don't think I'd be able to stop thinking about it. Beth—'

'Richard, please don't.'

'No, I just ... I just want to say that –' he gulped '– talking to you, *being* with you, it's the first time in a long time that I've felt close to anyone. It's made me feel alive, you know? And I just think you're ... I just thought ...'

'Thought what?' I removed his hand from my shoulder. 'What exactly did you think? That we were going to fall into each other's arms? That you were going to save me, is that it? I don't need saving, Richard. I never have.'

'I can see that. That's not what I meant.'

He shrank, folding like a flower at dusk. Feeling bad, I recalibrated.

'You're an attractive man, Richard, don't get me wrong. And yes, I'm not denying I like being around you too, which, if you knew me at all you'd realise was a fairly big deal because I don't … I don't …'

I exhaled, letting the sentence die and looking up at the shaft of cold moonlight. I was remembering something – the party where I had first met Ed. It was years ago, some stupid thing of a friend from work, and I'd had just about all I could stand. I was about to pour my second glass of champagne into the pot plant and slip out before anyone noticed, when he sat down next to me. He looked desperate.

'Right,' he said, scanning the room, 'I'll make a deal with you.'

'Pardon me?'

He turned to me.

'A deal. I can't take this any more. They're playing Whigfield. You kill me, and I'll kill you, all right?'

A smile pulled at my lips. 'How?'

'I don't fucking care. Push me out of the window.'

'We're only on the first floor.'

'Then make sure you impale me on the fence.'

'That might not be enough to kill you. Did you see those pictures of that guy who got stuck on a fence by his jaw? He had to stand there for hours while they cut this huge iron railing from his mouth.'

He nodded happily. 'That sounds great. Perfect. Do that. Anything but this.' He leaned forward. 'Anything but fucking Whigfield.'

I laughed. A great big laugh. And he smiled.

'I'm Ed. If you can't kill me, I'll settle for a conversation.'

'Beth?' said Richard.

I took a deep breath and turned back to him. 'If you want to feel close to someone, there's a young man up on deck who needs his father.'

He hovered, eyes darting about, and a for a split second I thought I could sense the trajectory of his thoughts, and that he was going to make a clumsy lunge for me. I prepared to dodge the pass, but it never came. Instead his face creased in tears.

'I miss her, Beth,' he said. 'My Gaby ... I just miss her.'

I put my arms around him, and he held me back, sobbing into my shoulder.

'Everything all right?'

Ed's silhouette filled the hatch. I let Richard go and he wiped his eyes. With a last smile at me, he sighed and turned to leave, placing a hand on Ed's shoulder at the ladder.

When he was gone, Ed gave me a frown.

'What was all that about?'

I smiled and shook my head. 'Nothing. Absolutely nothing.'

I thought it best to leave Ed, Richard and Bryce to their conversation, so I took a blanket and went to the bow. Carmela was checking on Bryce, so I sat down beside Maggie. Stretching out before us was dark water cut by a single jagged blade of moon.

Maggie looked over her shoulder as I sat down. The men were throwing nuts for Colin again.

'It's as if they can smell it,' she said.

'Smell what?'

She scanned me, heavy-lidded, as her gaze returned to the water.

'You know. *Availability.*'

I pulled my blanket tight. 'I don't know what you're talking about, Maggie.'

She gave a weary sigh. 'Everybody always knows what everybody is talking about. There's never any confusion in these matters. You know what I mean; it's written all over your face, and his.'

I paused, working my jaw. 'If you're talking about Richard, then you're way off the mark.'

'Nobody would blame you. He's an attractive man, and I know that your husband has been somewhat ... *absent* ... so—'

'You're wrong.'

'I don't think I am.'

I turned to her. 'Yes, you are, Maggie. You are wrong. You've only known me for a couple of weeks. You don't know what I've been through, or how I feel about things, and you don't know the first thing about my marriage. In fact, you've never been married. You don't know what it's like; it's not just a straight line, it's lots of fragments all cobbled together, the good parts and the bad parts of your lives all mashed up together, and sometimes it's hard to stay as close to each other as you were at the start. What's that horrible expression? *Love isn't gazing into each other's eyes, it's looking in the same direction?* Well, sometimes it's just being in the same room. Same house. Same bloody country.'

I paused, thumbing the blanket's hem.

'And yes, sometimes there are reminders that maybe you could have chosen a different path, and sometimes, when you're not quite *in the same room*, it's nice to feel that someone else might want to come in, you know, for ... a cup of tea. Or something.'

It was dark but I could tell she was smiling.

She turned to me. 'Sometimes it's best just to speak plainly.'

I shrugged. Sniffed. 'Haven't felt wanted for a while. Nice to feel it, doesn't mean I want to do anything.'

She took a long breath and nodded once, slowly and firmly. 'Then maybe I was wrong. But you were too.'

'How?'

'I *was* married. Once, when I was very young. Way before Dani's father.'

'What happened?'

'Same room? Child, we weren't even on the same planet.'

There were footsteps from behind and Carmela arrived. We made room and she sat between us, her wide shoulders hunched as she looked down at her lap.

'*Que pasa*, Carmela?' said Maggie.

Carmela sighed and turned her velvet eyes to me.

'I try English,' she said. 'I learn some. A leetle, from –' she looked back at her fingers '– Bryce.'

'Is Bryce OK?'

She sighed. 'Is … difficult. He is a proud man, a big man.' She flexed her torso in imitation, then shook her head. 'Think everybody must believe he a big man. But –' she turned back to me '– he not that big man. He leetle, like a child.'

For a brief moment the suspicion that she was talking about a specific part of Bryce must have become apparent in my expression, because Carmela quelled it with a hand – extremely strong and large – on my arm.

'Not leetle like that, Beth. No.' She smiled pleasantly. 'That actually very big. He is … is difficult for me to say.'

I placed my hand on hers and she heaved a sigh. 'It's OK.'

She smiled, embarrassed. 'I am nob jockey.'

Maggie let out a laugh.

'Pardon?' I said.

'Nob jockey,' said Carmela. 'Is what Bryce teach me. Means … I don't know …' She fanned her palms and made a childish face, and I had a sudden sense of Carmela's life; the software of a shy girl running on industrial hardware.

'Silly?' I said.

'*Si*, Beth,' she gripped my fingers in hers. 'Silly.'

'We don't think you're silly. Tell us.'

She looked out over the dark water. 'I live on a farm before. Five brothers, all older than me, and my father. My mother dead.'

'I'm sorry.'

She shrugged. 'Is not you. Donkey kill her in face. My father was hard man. He teach us all how to work on the farm, and I do the work of my mother. In the house.' She made a box of her hands to show us. 'They work out house, I work in house. That is how it is. And I watch them through window. They outside. I inside.' She narrowed her eyes, remembering. 'They hard with each other. *Hard*. If hurt, no cry. If something heavy, no say cannot carry. Carry anyway.'

She turned to Maggie.

'No talk, only work. You know? No...' She faltered, trying to find the word. '... like ...' She slumped, letting her limbs flop like a marionette.

'Weak?'

'*Si*, weak.' She returned to her fingers, memorising the word under her breath. 'One day, I make bread and watch through window. Is hot day, and I see my brother very tired. They take water to field because big ... er ... *car* ... er ...'

'Tractor, darling, tractor,' said Maggie, touching her hand.

'*Tractor, si*, is too hot. They try cool it down. But my brother *tired*. Hot. I see him, he cannot walk properly and he drop bucket. My father sees, and he walks to him, and –' she straightened her back, hardened her jaw and swiped at the air '– hit him. *Very* hard. My brother's head turn like this. I drop the bread on floor and I do not pick up. Just watch. My father stare at him. Is like he want him to do something, cry, but my brother does not cry, my brother look at ground and my father walk away. When he gone I run. I run outside and my brother, yes, then he cries, and I go to him to … *hold* him, tell him it OK.' She turned to me. 'He has no mother. Only father and me. So I think I *hold* him like mother did. But no. He push me away, and he says: "Do not tell father. Do not tell father that I cry. And he walk away too."'

She looked down, folding her frame around a picture only she could see.

After some moments, she shrugged it off and sniffed.

'I don't know why men like they are,' she said. 'Why Bryce like he is.'

I shared a look with Maggie that told me she had as little clue as I did.

'Are you worried, Carmela?' I said. 'Are you worried that he's sick?'

She fixed me with a look of intense frustration.

'He not sick,' she said, shaking her head. She poked her fingers down her throat. 'Bleurgh. No. Not sick.' She gave a last glance behind, brow softening. 'He *scared*.'

'Scared?' I said. 'Bryce?'

Carmela nodded. 'Scared of water. Scared of sea.'

Maggie and I looked behind. Bryce was red-faced with whisky, grinning as he recounted some story with Richard and Ed sniggering along.

'Right …' I said, turning back. 'So why did he come?'

'He didn't have to,' said Maggie. 'There's no reason for him to go to Florida.'

Carmela smiled, neck elongating with pride. 'He come for me. I no want to stay in Spain. But for his friends as well. For you and Richard. And Ed. He always say he see Ed again. And now he does.' She smiled and gathered her skirt. 'I go shitter now.'

She left Maggie and I to the moon.

'I told you,' said Maggie, when we were alone. 'Men just make things more difficult. It is much easier to do things alone.'

We looked out at the sea. The wind was still firm, muttering the same words it had been screaming all day, and the light from the rising moon spilled around us like milk. Everything was perfectly visible. The island, however, remained in darkness.

'This is the last land we'll see for a long time,' I said. 'If you want to stop here, you should do it now.'

Maggie ran her tongue along her cigarette paper. 'There are no lights. No fires. There's nobody there. And if there is then they're either dead or they don't want to be found.' She turned to me. 'I think, for better or worse, I'm with you for the long haul.'

Richard's voice broke through the men's laughs and mumbles at the stern. The whisky had given his tone a rowdy edge. 'Hey, Joshy. Josh.'

We turned to see. Dani and Josh, clearly bored with the men's conversation, had broken away and were sitting on their own with their legs dangling over the side. Their voices were close and hushed.

'Josh!' Richard threw a peanut shell across the deck, connecting with his son's ear. Josh broke mid-whisper and turned.

'What?'

'What are you two talking about,' said Richard.

'Nothing,' said Josh.

Richard tossed another nut in his mouth.

'Right,' he said, munching through his grin. 'Thick as thieves, you are.'

'Whatever,' said Josh, turning back. Dani put a hand on his wrist and stood up. Leaving him alone, she wandered up deck to where we sat.

'Idiots,' she said, glaring out at the water. 'They have no idea how to talk.'

'What *are* they talking about back there?' said Maggie.

'*Running*,' said Dani with a sneer. 'And people. Places. Beating the clock, whatever that means.'

'Old men with their war stories,' smiled Maggie, face clouded with smoke.

The wind picked up and I felt a chill, suddenly gripped by an urgency I knew I had only been keeping at bay. I stood, looking out at the dark island and the thousands of miles of sea that stretched beyond it.

'We don't have a clock,' I said. The three looked up at me.

'What?' said Maggie.

'There is no clock to beat,' I said. 'Not this time. The clock's already stopped.'

There was a sound and the three of us froze. It was tinny music; a simple hi-hat rhythm, warbling organ, and a bass thumping along beneath it all. We looked around, trying to locate it. Maggie stood too, cupping her ear.

'Is it coming from the island?'

'No. Sounds like it's closer, like it's behind us ... *shh*!' I turned to the men and hissed: 'Quiet!'

They stopped mid-sentence, mouths agape, eyes beginning the same dance as ours as they too heard the music.

Bryce frowned. 'Why am I hearing fucking Creedence?'

Ed stood, looking at me. 'It's coming from your direction.'

'No, it's not,' I said. 'It's coming from you.'

We stood in silence, listening as drums and a clean guitar joined the mix. As the penny finally dropped, we turned simultaneously to the cabin door.

The singer began to holler his lazy lament, closely followed by a trailer-park quartet.

I descended into the darkness of the cabin with the rest peering behind. The only light was the red LED of the radio, from which the song crackled. As I approached it, sideways and gingerly, another voice joined in the chorus. It was male, out of tune, a terrible imitation of Californian twang, like a child playing soldiers.

I paused at the radio, watching the light, listening with dread. The song faded out, but the voice remained.

He blew out an enormous sigh. *Ah, I tell you what, they don't write 'em like that any more do they? Bloody genius, love it.* Love *it.*' There was a thump, a *'Fuckit'* and the sound of liquid pouring. Then another sigh. I put my ear as close as possible to the receiver. There was a motor in the background, and distant voices. *'Beth?'*

I jumped away.

'Are you there, Beth?'

Hesitantly, I reached for the receiver. Ed joined me. 'Beth.'

But I had already picked it up.

'What do you want?'

There was a pause.

'Ahhh,' croaked Tony. His voice was slurred and ruddy with drink. *'Finally. I was beginning to think you'd got into trouble. Sunk my boat ...* drowned. *You haven't, Beth, have you? You haven't drowned?'*

'You know I haven't.'

'Yes I do.' He inhaled, exhaled, slurped. *'Yes I do.'*

'I'm hanging up now.'

'We had a little bit of trouble, truth be told, Beth. Ran aground a bit, took bloody ages to get ourselves free. It was dark when we finally got back on course, so yes, we lost a bit of ground, I'd say. Lost a bit of ground ... or is it water? Ha. Do you lose water?' His voice trailed off into liquidy mumbles, and I was about to replace the receiver when he spoke again. His voice was darker. *'Found it again, though. Ground, water, whichever it is. We're catching up*

with you, Beth. Where are you? Must be approaching the Azores by now, aren't you?'

I froze.

'Oh,' said Tony. *'Maybe actually* at *the Azores? Wow, well done.'* He clapped his hands. *'Bloody good work! You must have got that wind today, right? It's been a while since she's let rip like that, the old girl, bet she enjoyed it. Expect you've discovered her preference to lee port by now, right?'*

He waited.

'Beth,' whispered Ed. 'Leave it, turn it off.'

'Who's that?' said Tony, his voice suddenly closer. *'Is that the one who was on your boat? Or is he the one who threw that smoke canister onto my deck? Looking forward to meeting him, I can tell you. Looking forward to meeting all of you, as it happens. Won't be long now, Beth. Won't be —*

Ed switched off the radio. I made for the deck, pushing through the others who were listening at the ladder. I looked around, heart thumping. The wind was still up, the moon bright, we could see everything.

'He's behind us,' I said. 'He's coming.'

'How far?' said Maggie.

'I don't know, but he was in the same wind as us today, and he knows we're at the Azores.'

'Why the hell did you tell him that?' said Richard.

'I didn't fucking tell him, he just knew. I don't know how.'

I ran to the stern and stared out at the eastern horizon. There was nothing but black and stars. I turned.

'It's bright tonight, and the wind's still strong. We could sail.'

Richard shook his head. 'It's too dangerous, especially with these rocks. We don't know what the rest of the islands are like.'

'Then we go around them.'

'Beth,' said Maggie, 'you said it yourself, this is the last dry land until we reach Florida. There might be supplies on there, fuel, water.'

'Fuck the supplies, we've got plenty between us. '

Richard rubbed his neck. 'I agree with Maggie. It wouldn't take long to search that town. We could get up early.'

I faced him. 'Listen to me. I don't want to go onto the island. I don't want to go on one of your scavenging trips. I feel *stupid* that we've even been sitting here chatting and eating fucking nuts and drinking when we could have been pushing on. That's what I want to do – push on. No stopping, just moving. I won't eat, if that helps. I won't eat, not until I find my children.'

The deck was silent.

'You stay, then,' I said at last. 'We'll go. Maybe it's better that we do this on our own anyway. Right, Ed?'

I turned to him. Looking back, I think I was expecting some hesitation, but he was already on his way to the *Elma*. 'Right.'

Richard breathed a sigh. 'And wait here for that maniac to catch us up? No thanks. Come on, everyone, let's get ready to sail.'

Dani and Josh immediately snapped to their tasks, while Maggie tidied away the table and candles.

Richard turned to Bryce, who was still sitting on the bench. His face had turned white. 'I'm going to need everyone's help though. All eyes ahead to watch for obstacles. OK, Bryce?'

Bryce looked up, and gave the smallest shake of his head. 'I can't, Dick. I'm sorry.'

'I help,' said Carmela. 'Bryce OK on his own.'

Richard clapped his hands. 'Right. We're going to motor round the coast and hope the wind's still strong enough to carry us west. Chop-chop!'

Ed started the *Elma*'s engine, and as we motored away he took the helm from me.

'You've had whisky,' I said. 'It's safer if I drive.'

He glanced at me with one steely eye. 'I didn't touch a drop.'

Chapter 23

We left the Azores in the opposite fashion to how we arrived – in darkness, afraid and uncoordinated. Our anchors snagged on weed, our ropes and muscles were stiffer, our movements sluggish. By the time we finally pulled away I was sure I could hear the drone of a distant engine beneath every zip, clang and rattle the two boats made.

After a hurried scan of the chart, we made a plan to pass south between the island's west shore and its neighbour, São Jorge, a sliver of land far enough away not to pose any problems. We followed Terceira's northern coast, keeping our distance from the rocks. The *Buccaneer* roamed ahead, and Ed and I stood silently at the helm listening to Richard's frustrated rumbles and slurs across the water. Bryce had retreated to his room, and Carmela was attempting to help Maggie but seemed only to be getting in her way. Josh's nerves, and the dark, made his fumbles worse than usual, and even Dani moved with less confidence.

'It's not too late to turn back,' said Ed.

I turned to him, our faces clay-white. I wanted to test him; a strong and familiar urge, I realised, though

I couldn't decide whether it was to prove him wrong or right.

'Do you want to?' I said.

'No,' he replied, looking straight ahead. 'I want to keep going, with you.'

'I'll sit at the front then,' I said. 'Keep a lookout.'

I picked up my broom and pulled myself up onto the deck. As I did I brushed his shoulder and I sensed his hand reach for me, but I had already passed before it could make contact. I glanced back with an awkward half-wave of acknowledgement. He smiled in understanding and I found my way to the stern, where I looped my legs through the guard rail.

I was secretly relieved to be away from the helm. My foot and ankle were both buzzing like live wires, and the prospect of standing through the night was not something I wanted to dwell on. I stretched out my leg, massaging the thigh and trying in vain to work the blood into an even flow.

I knew there was something wrong. It just wasn't a priority, though part of me suspected it wouldn't be long before it was.

We were still only halfway along the northern coast when I felt us veering to port.

'Why are we turning?' I called back.

'We're not.' The engine strained. Ed braced himself against the wheel. 'There's a current; a strong one.'

The *Buccaneer* was banking in the same direction, and the water was marbled with thick eddies.

'Something ...' Maggie's nervous voice drifted across. 'There's something ahead.'

I strained to see past the bigger boat's hull, but there was only a dark patch in the water.

Maggie made a noise. 'Oh – oh, my goodness.'

Just then, Dani shot across to the starboard side and ejected an arc of vomit over the side. She held her mouth, still heaving, then stifled a sob.

Josh and Richard stood looking over the starboard side.

'Don't look,' he said, but it was too late.

We were passing by an enormous clump of what looked like rotten green weed, timber and tangled netting. A small cloud that had been smothering the moon drifted away, and in the fresh light we saw the entirety of the object. Human bodies were embedded in the weed. They were not yet skeletons. What had been flesh and clothing hung in tatters from torsos, limbs and skulls, and we could see quite plainly the features on every face that passed. One – a woman's – sat waist-deep in the wet, furry matter with her arms before her and her head lowered, as if reading in bed. One of her eye sockets still had an eye, looking sadly down at the space where the book should have been.

I pulled in my legs. The current was dragging us towards it.

'Ed. We need to go starboard, now.'

'The current's too strong, the engine's not powerful enough to escape it!'

'Then I'm raising the sail.'

'Too dangerous, the wind's strong and if we lose control then we'll plough straight into the rocks.'

'We don't have a choice. Carmela?' I called across to the *Buccaneer*'s stern.

'*Si?*'

'Tell Richard and Maggie –' I performed a hoisting mime '– I'm raising the sail.'

'*Si*,' said Carmela, and hauled herself across to the helm.

Progress with the sail was slow, my lower leg having resumed its vibrations, but I managed to raise it and the wind took it. The current, outraged, fought back. The *Buccaneer* was already clear, its mainsail carrying it away without protest, but the *Elma* was now stationary, caught in a furious tug of war between the opposing wills of wind and water. The hull groaned and the mast creaked. The floating graveyard lurked near, seeming to call us to it and the rocks beyond.

'Beth? Beth, what do we do?'

I looked at it all – the balance of forces within which we were snared. The wind was constant, free of gusts. The water, however, was full of moving parts. I gripped the guard rail, following the moonlit contours of the current's swirls around the boat.

'We have to go nearer,' I said. 'Let go. Hard to port, when I say.'

'But we'll—'

'Ed, trust me.'

He paused, but not for long. 'OK.'

'Now.'

I let the boom swing, Ed released his grip, and the little boat spun helplessly towards the weed.

'Please,' I said, watching the current's course. 'Please.'

As I had hoped, the current veered sharply to the right, rocketing us away from the weed. I let the boom swing starboard once again, and locked it with my feet against the cabin wall. I cried out in pain as my leg jarred.

'Starboard, Ed. Now!'

The wheel spun, the boat lurched, and with a fresh gust of wind our course was locked. We were free of the current and I could feel the island's monstrous grip relinquishing as we sped towards the *Buccaneer*.

I tethered the mainsheet.

'That was amazing,' said Ed.

I looked back, breathing hard, and smiled.

'Are you OK?' he said.

I smiled, nodded and crawled back to the stern. My leg felt better stretched out, so I lay on my front like a sniper, with pools of water cooling my neck as I looked ahead. There was a storm on the horizon. Distant flashes of lightning reflected in the water, as if the sky and the sea were locked in an embrace, sharing a memory.

I must have slept because night became day without me noticing. I lifted my head. We had stopped, and all around us was a flat, yellow-green haze of sky and sea. The horizon was obscured but one half of it was engulfed with black, flashing cloud. There was no wind. The water was deathly calm. Its surface steamed like the reedy banks of a pungent lagoon. The *Black Buccaneer* floated alongside us, sails down and empty decked, like a ghost ship.

Ed was still at the *Elma*'s helm, heavy-eyed but awake. He leaned with his forearms on the wheel.

'You've caught the sun,' I said. 'You look brown.'

His brow twitched. 'You don't.'

'Thanks.'

'No, I mean it. You're pale. Do you feel all right?'

No. I did not. The cold prickles on my skin were not just because of the moisture in the air. The painful shivers in my back were not because I had been lying outside all night. I could no longer feel my toes. Not a fizz.

But I didn't want to talk about it.

Apart from a brief period in Arthur's first six months when I believed he had every condition known to medical science, I am the opposite of a hypochondriac. It's not that I'm in denial; I'm well aware of the biological cataclysms ready to drag me and my loved ones into the grave as soon as possible, and I'm not suggesting that mere positive thinking is going to save me from them. But there's one thing I'm certain of – you give something a name, you start talking about it: it exists.

And right then, whatever was going on south of my sock did not need to exist.

'I'm fine,' I said. 'You should get some rest.'

'No, I'm all right. You go.'

'There's no point both of us being tired. One up, one down, remember?'

We used to say this after Alice was born. You take shifts, one sleeps while the other's awake.

'Besides,' I said, looking around at the still water, 'doesn't look like there's much happening right now.'

Ed pushed himself from the helm, smiling. 'One up, one down.'

As he passed, our shoulders brushed and I pulled his neck towards me, kissing him on the soft, stubbled flesh between his ear and jaw. He breathed out, and it felt like something departed him. Or us.

There was a noise from the other boat, and Richard emerged from the cabin with a steaming mug in one hand and the chart in the other.

Ed squeezed my wrist. 'Wake me when things pick up, OK?'

I nodded and he went below deck.

Over on the other boat, Richard slurped coffee with his head buried in the map.

'Where is everyone?' I called across.

He didn't look up. 'Asleep.'

'Any idea where we are?'

He blew out in frustration. 'It was hard to keep track of our bearings last night, but I've got a fair idea. The currents around those islands took us all over the place, and we must have been sailing for three hours before the wind fell, after which we just drifted.

I think our bearing needs to adjust by ... two degrees south.'

I checked the compass and scanned the horizon.

'That puts us right into that,' I said, nodding to the storm clouds in the west.

'Yes, I'm afraid it does ... Beth?'

'Yes?'

He kept his eyes on the map and his voice low, like somebody making a passing remark while reading a newspaper.

'I'm sorry. About last night. I'd like to blame it on the whisky but that's no excuse. I was thoughtless and clumsy, and I'm sure it –' he puffed again '– whatever *it* was, was the furthest thing from your mind. Please, forgive me.'

He gripped the map tight, and his jaw tighter.

'There's no need,' I said, 'there's nothing to forgive. So don't think on it.'

Only then did he look up.

'Christ,' he said when he saw me, 'you don't look well.'

I held up a hand before he went further.

'Just tired,' I said.

'Are you sure? You look like death on a plate. Come on.' He put down his mug and chart. 'Let me make you a coffee, at least.'

'I can do it. You keep looking at the chart. I'll come across if that's OK; I don't want to wake Ed.'

We tethered the boats and I clambered over the guard rail, ignoring the numbness in my foot as I scaled the ladder down into the cabin. Below deck was dark and stifling, full of snores, so I moved quietly in the galley.

'Morning.'

I jumped and nearly dropped the kettle.

'Jesus, Bryce. I didn't see you.'

He was sitting in the shadows with his great arms stretched over the table.

'Sorry.' His voice was like gravel. 'Just needed to get out of that room.'

'Why don't you go out on deck?'

He shook his head, folding his fingers together.

I put the kettle down. 'Bryce, what's going on? I know you're not really seasick.'

He said nothing, looked away.

'Bryce, you can tell me. I won't think any less of you.'

He stared into the corner for a while, then, finally he released a mountainous sigh.

'It's the water, all right? I just don't like the water.'

'You can't swim?'

He shook his head. 'I can swim just fine.'

'Then why?'

He gave me a nervous glance. 'Remember *Piper Alpha* – the rig that burned?'

I remembered. The deathly quiet in our kitchen that morning when I came down for breakfast. My father at the table, face the same colour as the ash in the tray before him. Wondering what was going on,

why my mother was weeping, and then seeing the
television, the weary reporter and the flames in every
picture.

'Of course.'

'Aye, well,' said Bryce, 'my uncle died on it. I watched
it all from home. Never been the same around water
since. I thought I was getting better, on the *Unity*,
you know? Getting used to it. And then that bloody
great flaming rig came and ... Christ.'

He shook his head.

'Bryce, that's nothing to feel bad about.'

He slammed his fist on the flimsy wood.

'I can't go out there, Beth. I can't help you. I can't
help Ed. I want to, but ...'

He fumbled with his fingers, then stood and clumsily made for his room. I stepped in front of him.

'Bryce, stop.'

'What?'

'I don't know what happened between Edinburgh
and Falmouth, and to be honest I don't want to. But
I do know that before Ed met you he could barely
drag himself to the shop for a packet of fags, let alone
across a country.'

'I told you, you should have more faith in him.'

'I do. I do now, at any rate. And it's down to you.
He's never had a friend, Bryce, not in the time that
I've known him. So thank you, and just remember
that we're your friends too.'

He looked down at me, those dark brown eyes
casting more shadow than they did light, and placed

a hand on my shoulder. 'Aye,' he said, loping back to his room. 'Aye.'

The door shut, leaving me alone in the dark, snore-filled room. I filled the kettle and lit the stove, but as I waited for the water to boil, there was a crackle from the radio. The LED was still on.

Another crackle.

Music.

This time I recognised it; it was the same song I had heard walking into Tony's camp that night – piano, pizzicato, a female voice …

Tony's voice joined it as verse swept into rapturous, sizzling chorus.

'Oh, my goodness, what a tune.'

I stared at the blinking light. The kettle began to roar.

'I honestly don't know what happened to music,' said Tony. *'I really don't. They say most great artists only have one honestly great piece of work in them – the* Macbeths, *the* Mona Lisas *and the Ninth Symphonies and what have you – I wonder if that's true of musical genres? Did pop peak in the mid-eighties? Certainly feels like it to me, Beth. Jesus, I mean just listen to it; all those synths, the reverb, the sax solo – makes me feel like rolling up my suit jacket sleeves. Know what I mean, Beth?'*

The kettle began its nervous whistle, and I took it from the hob, switching off the burner.

'Beth?'

I limped between the bunks and sat down before the radio. My back was to the rest of the cabin, so all

I saw was a dark void with a red dot in its centre, from which Tony's voice seemed to be emanating.

He sighed. I can't explain it, but he knew I was there. I could feel it.

'I was twenty-two when this song came out, just starting out, house share in Fulham, hadn't made my money yet but happy as a pig in shit. Friday nights at the King's Arms, Saturdays in Notting Hill, brilliant days. This song takes me right back there. That's what they do, songs, connect you to times, places, things that happened ... people, though ... they're different. I find them harder to connect with. Don't you?'

For a few moments there was silence, and I had a sense of him sitting in a similar darkness, staring at a light.

'Do you ever wonder how you're going to die, Beth?'
My throat tightened.

'I do,' he went on, 'all the bloody time, if I'm honest. People don't talk about it, but they should. Do you know, I read that there are people alive today who will live to see a thousand. Medical science, drugs, treatments and what have you, will ensure that their ends are violent. A thousand, Beth, can you believe that? What would that do to you, I wonder? Eh?'

He broke off. There was heavy breathing, something liquid in the background. His voice deepened.

'How do you think ... you're going to go, Beth? Be nice to be able to choose, wouldn't it? Me, I'd choose the ocean any day. Ker-sploosh, just like that – succumb to it all. The slow drag of the deep, drowning, or maybe ...

maybe being eaten. Sharks. Lots of them in the Atlantic. They have razor-sharp teeth, so I've heard, and sharp blades don't hurt as much as blunt ones. Apparently if you're stabbed with something sharp enough you won't even feel it ... 'course, sharks would pull you apart as well, so I suppose that would be painful, but –' he exhaled long and slow *'– pain, once you're in it, you become it, don't you? Are you in pain, Beth? How's that leg of yours?'*

He broke off, and once again I heard the same wet sounds in the background, punctuated by the odd word, like an old man mumbling to himself. I thought he'd finally given up and was about to leave the radio when he spoke again, this time with an angry shudder.

'You took everything from me, Beth. Everything. And I—'

A hand reached over my shoulder and snatched the receiver.

'You talk too much.'

I spun round. 'Ed?'

Ed breathed furiously into the receiver, finger on the button. 'In fact you sound like an old boss of mine. He talked too much as well. He could talk for hours and never say anything, he just loved the sound of his own voice. Just like you.'

There was a moment of silence.

'Who's that, then?' A smile had crept into Tony's voice. *'Is that ... is that the smoke man? The* Great Soprendo?' He cackled. *'Yes, I think that's who it is.*

Who are you, then, and where do you fit into all of this?'

'Put it this way,' said Ed, 'you want to know how you're going to die? You're listening to the answer if you get in the way of us finding our children.'

A long pause. *'Us? My goodness—'*

'Yes, us. Me and my wife, and believe me, mate, you do not want to get in her way right now.'

I could almost feel the smile slip from Tony's lips. *'I remind you of an old boss, do I? Well, I'll tell you something – I got a look at your face in that gully, right before you threw that smoke canister, and you remind me of someone who used to work for me too. Feeble around the gills, weak in the jaw, just the kind of man who has a boss. Not a man who can do things or exert any influence the world, not a man who can change the tide.'*

'I don't want to change the tide, dickhead, I just want to find my kids.'

Ed slammed down the receiver and flicked off the radio.

'I think it's best we keep that switched off from now on, don't you? Now, are we going to use that storm or not?'

The others took little convincing. We woke them – Maggie, Josh, Dani and Carmela; Bryce's absence was now taken as read – and they listened in silence as Ed and I told them our plan. They did not need to follow; they could stay, or sail north or south to avoid the storm and hopefully lose Staines in the process. But we were going in.

It was clearly a dangerous plan, but it was also the only rational one. Behind us lay danger and old water; ahead lay our children, and an atmospheric cauldron boiling with the energy that might deliver us to them.

When we had finished, Dani and Josh shared a look and began wordlessly preparing the ropes. Richard slapped Ed on the shoulder and Carmela kissed my cheek. Maggie went below deck to clear the cabin, wincing as she descended the ladder. It was clear that her shoulder was troubling her, and on the last rung she offered me a hollow smile that only bore out her reluctance to be there.

I'm sorry for what happened, truly I am, but what else could I have done?

Chapter 24

I had never realised how different the same ocean could be before. I don't know why. The land shifts with the seasons, after all. Hillsides bloom and die, summer-dulled cities ignite in winter sun; weather changes everything. That's why strangers talk about it. 'We're living within a beast,' they're saying, when they remark upon the wind tearing at the orchard, or the rain soaking the fields, 'a beast with its own mind and feelings, and we're at its mercy. How do you think the beast is feeling today?'

The same is true of the sea. It has its own mind and feelings, and on this particular day its mind was distracted, its feelings muddled. We moved through still, uncertain water in a sticky yellow haze. There was a sweltering density to the air, like a car's heater stuck on full during a heatwave.

We itched and fanned ourselves, aware that we were drinking more water than our rations allowed. But there was something else too – an occasional sharp smell that made me nervous. It felt as if we were inside a fever, and this is what I put my own symptoms down to. But the truth was the sweat on my brow was as much due to what was going on inside my body as outside.

The haze worsened. I steered, keeping close to the *Buccaneer*'s starboard side. Maggie stood at its bow, frowning, chest out like a figurehead.

I called up to her.

'Can you see something?'

'I think so. I don't know what, though. Some detritus floating ahead. I think we should slow down.'

Richard shut off the *Buccaneer*'s engine and Ed did the same with the *Elma*.

'Take the helm,' I said to Ed, and made my way to the bow.

The water was treacle thick and marbled with oily rainbows. There was a gloop. At first I thought it was a fish, but from the haze I saw something turn upside down and bubble from a hole. Lying on my front, I reached out with my broom and lifted it from the water.

'What is that?' said Ed.

I stared at the loose fabric, wilting over my crutch like a lily. 'It's a hat. For a wedding or something.'

'There's more,' said Maggie, pointing. 'Look.'

I let the hat fall and looked ahead, where more objects were becoming visible. Plastic bowls and cutlery, an ornate bathtub, an upturned child's chair and count-less sheets of paper that stuck to our hull. There were numbers on them, and scribbles down their sides.

'Do you think this is from a wreck?' said Ed.

'No,' I said. Tin cans and empty plastic bottles bobbed between the larger objects, and countless crisp and sweet wrappers clung together beneath the surface like plastic weed. 'It's rubbish. Trash.'

'We need to find a way round it,' said Richard. His voice was distant. 'Too dangerous to motor through it – that stuff could mangle our props. Where are you going?'

I looked across, noticing that the *Buccaneer* had drifted from our side.

'Nowhere,' said Ed. 'We're dead ahead. Where are *you* going?'

'We're not – oh, fuck.'

Below the littered surface, a slow stream of rubbish was moving right to left.

'There's a current,' I said. 'Heading south.'

The *Buccaneer* was now ahead of us. We were moving further apart.

'Don't worry,' said Richard. 'Maybe it'll take us out of this mess.'

As he spoke, his voice grew ever more distant. The *Buccaneer* became a mustardy outline in the haze, and before we knew it, it was gone.

'Richard?' I called. 'Maggie?'

But there was no answer. We bobbed alone in the stagnant water.

'We should follow them,' said Ed. 'Why hasn't the current taken us too?'

'Because we're stuck in this stuff.'

A dam of paper and plastic had built up against our hull. I tried to push it away with my crutch.

'Maybe motor just a bit to get us ahead?'

But as Ed reached for the starter, we heard a roaring noise ahead. It started quietly, from starboard, and grew as it moved towards us.

I hobbled back from the bow.

'What is that?'

'I don't know but it's coming this way.'

With a sudden crescendo, a huge shadow pulsed in the distance and disappeared to port. Soon the noise was gone, but a wave rippled out from the wake of whatever had passed, knocking away the rubbish at our hull. Now free, the *Elma* drifted ahead, and the current took us too.

'I don't like this,' I said. 'Ed?'

'I know, I know, I'm going to back us out.' He started the engine, but there was an almighty thud and the boat rocked. The engine spluttered and wheezed, smoke streaming from its cavity beneath the deck.

'Fuck,' said Ed, shutting it off.

'What's happened?'

'The propeller's jammed.'

The *Elma*'s speed slowly climbed. We swung our heads to starboard, from which another sound was approaching. This time it was closer. There were voices.

'Is that …?'

'It can't be, they went port.'

But the *Buccaneer* burst from the fog, and Maggie, wild-eyed and waving, screamed at us. 'Get back! Get back!'

They swept past. Dani and Josh were flat against the deck, and Richard and Carmela strained at the helm, fighting to steady the wheel.

'Motor out!' yelled Richard. 'It's not—'

But they had disappeared into the haze once more, and the *Elma* was following.

'Ed, try the engine.'

'I am, it's not starting.'

'Keep trying.'

I clung to the guard rail as Ed turned the starter, watching our helpless passage into the swirling current. It seemed to stretch ahead, lanes of rubbish moving in different speeds but all in the same direction.

'It's no use,' called Ed. 'What about the sail?'

'There's no wind.' I turned and faced him. 'It's too late. Ed, hold on to something.'

He grabbed the helm and I wrapped my arms around the mast. The *Elma* suddenly swung to port. My broom fell and span across the deck, where it balanced on the side. I reached for it but the distance was too great. The current surged and I gripped the mast with everything I had as water sprayed across the deck, showering us with dirt, plastic and all manner of sodden, stinking debris.

'What the hell is this?' screamed Ed above the roar.

'I've no idea!' I closed my eyes as a plastic bag hit me square in the face. I pulled it away and squinted ahead, but as I did the mast tilted starboard, and I had to brace myself against the cabin wall. I glanced at the guard rail.

'My crutch – no!'

But the water had already taken it. I watched it spin away, lost in the refuse through which we were now thundering.

'We're banking starboard,' said Ed. 'Hold on!'

The *Elma*'s mast pitched ever more to the right. Gravity pulled me and I prepared for what I was sure would be a plunge into the mess below, but we steadied at a 45-degree angle.

As the little boat sped on, the haze began to clear and a searing shaft of sunlight hit the deck. It spread, pushing its way through the murk until it had illuminated the water around us and everything beyond. With a lurching horror, I saw what was causing the current.

'We just need to hold on until whatever's causing this stops,' said Ed. 'It can't go on forever.'

'I think you might be wrong about that – look.'

We were clinging to the outer rim of an enormous whirlpool, a vast man-made maelstrom of plastic, metal and cardboard heaving clockwise around a deep vortex.

Ed renewed his grip on the wheel and stammered: 'Shit.'

The world spun around us. I tried to get a sense of the scale of the thing. Was it fifty metres across? Double that? I couldn't fathom it. That box bobbing in the foam could have been a truck, that splayed book could have been floorboards for all I knew.

All I *did* know was that, whatever it was, and however big it was, we were heading directly into it. The swirling centre was a deep black hole sucking everything into it.

I scrabbled against the mast, kicking from the drop. 'Ed! Hard to port, hard to port!'

Ed slammed the helm and the *Elma* obeyed with a plucky spring to the left. The mast straightened a little, but we were still within the lip of the basin.

'More, Ed!'

'There's no more, that's it! We need something to pull us out.'

'Try the engine again.'

He tried. A stinking foam sprayed over us, and I wiped the putrid film from my face.

'It's still jammed,' said Ed. 'Can you raise the sail?'

'I told you, there's no wind.'

I tried anyway, easing myself down towards the cleat where the rope was tethered, its loose end flopping like an eel in the brown froth rapidly covering the deck. I reached down for it with one arm looped around the mast. My leg screamed under the extra weight and another wave of dizziness overwhelmed me. For a moment gravity seemed to disappear and I thought I'd let go, but my senses returned and I found that I was still there, hanging on with my left arm as my right swam unsteadily beneath.

'Careful,' said Ed. 'Hold on.'

He jammed a boat hook in the helm to lock it and clambered along the port side towards me, the *Elma's* camber requiring him to hang from the guard rail, slipping his feet against the slimy wood.

'Hurry, Ed.'

'Hold on.'

I reached for the rope again, the tendons in my neck and shoulders straining. I felt a twang above my collarbone, and at the same moment a fleet of boxes were suddenly whipped up from the water and hurtled across the boat. One struck me in the head. Luckily it was empty – just a rhombus of damp cardboard – but the impact was enough to daze me again, and this time I lost my grip on the mast.

'No!' I screamed. The world slowed as gravity took me. I slipped down, flapping with my arms, trying to find anything to hold on to. The mast was out of reach. My fingers found taut rope, but it was greasy with foam and it sprang uselessly away. My eyes locked on the *Elma*'s stern as a shadow passed over me; I was beneath the basin's rim now and into the darkness of the maelstrom. I scrabbled at the deck, fingernails scratching, clawing, breaking, bleeding . . .

'Got you.'

The shadow disappeared and I was in sunlight again. With his other hand looped over the guard rail, Ed had caught my wrist and hauled me up. My neck felt like it was on fire as the recently shorn tendons now found themselves yanked in the opposite direction. Dizziness again, and a rush of bile this time, but I pushed it down and wrapped my other arm around the mast, locking on.

'I'm up,' I said. 'You can let go.'

He released me and clung on with the free hand. For a moment I registered the shape of the *Black Buccaneer* on the opposite side of the whirlpool, bucking and jolting like a toy.

'I'm going to untie the rope,' said Ed.

'Ed—'

'Just hold on.'

'Everything's slippy, the rope, the deck, everything.'

'It's OK.'

He let himself slide towards the cleat. Without thinking I stuck out my boot. 'Hold on to my ankle.'

He did so, and I screamed at the sky. The flesh of my foot felt like soft clay being squashed in an anvil, as if muscle and bone were no longer connected. But there was a border to the pain that chilled me. Everything around my toes had a dreadful, empty numbness.

'Are you all right?' said Ed.

'Just do it. Untie the rope!'

Ed whipped the rope from the cleat and clambered back up with one filthy end between his teeth, lunging for the mast. He clung there as we both caught our breath.

'Pull together,' I said, the taste of my own stomach contents now forming a terrible cocktail with whatever foul sludge the ocean was hurling at us. 'OK?'

He nodded, and we both fumbled for the rope with our free hands.

'Ready?' I said. 'Heave.'

Together we pulled, but our palms slipped down the slick surface. We each let off a curse.

'Try again.'

But it was no use. It was like trying to open a jar smeared with oil.

'We'll need to use the winch,' said Ed.

We looked down at the starboard deck where the winch was positioned, not more than a step away from the water.

'I could reach it,' he said, desperately scanning the deck for a safe route down.

'You'll never make it. There's nothing to hold on to.'

He looked at me. 'I could hold on to you.'

Our faces were inches apart, and as the water roared around us and the sea hurled its endless, salty filth, a strange intimacy hung between us. I looked into his one good eye, lashes dotted with foam, imagining I could see the whirlpool behind me reflected in its iris, and moved my hand slowly up the mast towards his. Our fingers were almost touching. There was barely a spider's leg between them.

With a sickening thud, the boat lurched and I gripped the mast with both arms. Ed did the same. The *Elma*'s bow had hit something, and now she was sliding like a car on ice.

Ed opened his mouth to speak, but before he could something dark seemed to flap above us and there was an ear-splitting crack.

'Watch out!' I yelled, ducking as we were showered with splinters. A machine-gun of snaps, whips and twangs sounded above us, followed by a groan and a screech as half the mast was torn away.

'Shit, no!' cried Ed. 'No, no, no!'

The broken pole disappeared behind us, twiglike against the roiling black clouds with its cables and ropes flung hopelessly behind it. This was it. The engine was jammed and now we had no means to lift a sail. The whirlpool would take us. I closed my eyes, pressed my forehead against the mast and wept. Ed did the same.

There was a thickening to the sound of roaring water and a dimming to the light which I took as a result of our descent into the basin. I didn't look up. I didn't want to see what we were heading into. *Just let it take us*, I thought, and I hoped something would knock me unconscious before I was subjected to the pain of drowning. My fingers searched for Ed's again. I thought, *At least … at least …*

But Ed's fingers weren't there, and when I opened my eyes I saw that that he had turned around with his back to the mast, and that the change in the sound was not due to our descent into the basin at all.

'Beth, look!'

Something was near us. Something was above us.

'Hold on, we're going to throw you some ropes.'

It was Dani's voice. She was leaning over the guard rail of the *Black Buccaneer* which, although it was just as caked in sludge and slime as the *Elma*, had its mainsail up and full. Richard was at the helm, bracing port, and I sensed he was holding the boat on a course from which it wanted to break. It had escaped the basin and was surfing its rim, ready to burst from the maelstrom's orbit.

Maggie was at the helm with Richard, holding on, for they were pitching like us, and behind Dani's urgent face Josh swung a rope as Carmela lashed it to a cleat. With a single glance at his father, he hurled it, but it landed in the water far from us.

Richard made a noise of frustration and Josh scurried for the rope, slipping as he went.

Dani leaped to his side. '*It's OK*,' she mouthed, followed by something else I didn't see. Together they gathered the rope and Dani stood back. This time he threw it higher, and it landed just over the *Elma's* guard rail. Dani's face flashed with fierce celebration, and Josh – he couldn't help himself – looked behind again. But Richard was set upon his own task.

Ed snatched the rope and pulled until it was taut.

Dani cupped her hands around her mouth. 'We can't pull you in, so you'll have to tie it around your waist.'

'Then what?' he called back.

'Jump in. We'll haul you up.'

He scanned the water above us. 'Are you fucking serious?'

'It's the only way, Ed,' I said. 'This boat's useless now, we have to get off it.'

He looked at me, rope gripped in both of his hands.

'Hurry up!' said Josh. 'We've only got one spare rope.'

'Right,' said Ed. 'Right. You first.'

Before I could protest he had looped the rope around my waist and tied it in a crude but tight knot. He turned back to the *Buccaneer*. 'We're ready.'

He helped me around the mast until we were both at the guard rail, and my gut heaved as I looked down into the swirling mass of rubbish. I swallowed vomit.

'Beth, you have to go. Jump. Now.'

I looked up. Dani was screaming into her hands. 'Jump!'

I glanced at Ed, and there was something about the smile that flickered in his eyes I didn't like. It was too peaceful.

'I'll throw it straight back,' I said.

He nodded. 'I know you will. Now go.'

He shoved me, and with a yelp I dived beneath the black foam. My mouth filled instantly with the vile liquid, and I belched up warm vomit that washed around my neck. The water stung my eyes and my body was pounded by object after object, boxes, bottles and scraps trying to find a way around or through me. I felt I was going deeper, but suddenly the rope tightened and I surfaced, finding myself gasping for breath and flat against the *Buccaneer*'s hull. I vomited again, this particular ejection disappearing down my front, and pushed with my good foot against the side of the boat. I looked up, squinting. Carmela was pulling me up, face set and serious, the sinews in her arms working like machinery beneath the bare skin. Before I knew it my belly was on the guard rail and

I was tumbling onto the deck. Josh and Dani helped me up.

'Ed!' I looked back, noticing with horror that the *Elma* had moved a little further away. The basin was claiming it.

Ed stood with both hands on the rail. He still had that smile – too peaceful; it didn't belong here. I met it with a firm grimace. 'We're throwing the rope.'

'It's too far,' he said, with a shake of his head. 'It won't reach.'

'Yes it will. I'm throwing it now.'

'Beth—'

'Shut the fuck up, Ed. I'm throwing the rope and you're catching it.'

'Beth, you have to go.'

The water roared between us, along with a fresh wind, readying itself to carry the *Buccaneer* to safety.

I looked back at Ed. For a moment I felt nothing – an emotional vacuum while my mind decided what to fill it with.

Grief? Love? Gratitude?

No. As it happens, rage. Furious, white-hot rage.

'Edgar Hill,' I screamed across the widening void. 'There's no *way* I'm letting you off that easy, do you hear me? No way. So hold out your hands and catch this rope, all right? Do you understand?'

His smile had fallen. He opened his mouth to say something.

'I said, do you understand?'

He nodded, and slowly raised a hand, but as I lifted the coiled rope something stopped him. A look of dumb horror took over his face.

I froze. 'What is it?'

But I think I already knew.

'The water,' said Ed. 'Most of what we have is on the *Elma*.'

'Oh, shit,' said Dani. 'He's right. We didn't move any across before we left last night.'

'It doesn't matter,' I said. 'We'll manage, we'll have to. Ed?'

But Ed had already crawled along the handrail and dropped into the cabin. A second later he emerged with two crates balanced precariously on top of each other.

'Can you carry them across with you?'

He nodded. 'I'll try.'

The gap was widening. There was no more time.

'OK, here comes the rope.'

I hurled it and Ed caught the end with one hand. The crates almost fell but he steadied them on one knee as he wrapped the rope around them and his own waist. After another rough knot, he nodded at me, clutched the water to his belly and, with one last look at the broken boat on which he stood, jumped in.

The rope snapped tight almost immediately as Ed was submerged. I braced myself against the guard rail and leaned back. Again came that freakish, deep pain in my foot, and the pulpy numbness where my toes should have been.

The *Buccaneer* weaved dangerously back towards the lip.

'I can't hold her much longer,' said Richard from the helm. 'She'll be dragged back in if we don't head out of the current now.'

'Help me!' I cried back, and Carmela arrived behind. We both heaved, arm over arm, and eventually Ed appeared, gasping and spluttering through the tumbling froth. His patch had been torn clean off and I caught a glimpse of the empty socket; a dark, puckered place where his other eye had been. Carmela roared as we pulled, and soon Ed's waist was clear. The water was still there, but it had slipped down so only the lip of the outermost crate was gripped to his belly. Both hands were on the rope, so if they slipped then he wouldn't catch them. He fumbled for them as he swung out, but by the time his hand found them he had hit the hull. The impact knocked the crates from their fragile harness.

'No!' he cried, catching one in his left hand. The other hit his boots, where it balanced for a second, then fell and was gone. 'Shit!'

Now he was holding on to the remaining crate with one hand and the rope with the other. He was almost at the guard rail.

'Here!' he yelled, scrambling with his feet against the side and hauling the crate up to where Josh was standing. Josh grabbed the crate, but it was a little too low and he only managed to hold on to it by puncturing the plastic with two fingers.

'I have to go!' said Richard. 'Do you have him?'

'Yes,' said Dani, 'we have him, go.'

'Wait,' I yelled back, but it was too late. Richard had slammed us to port, and as the *Buccaneer* was finally allowed to let rip, Ed swung away left, losing his grip upon the crate and the rope. Carmela and I fell backwards with the slack rope flying through the guard rail, but as he fell Ed managed to grip the side of the boat with one hand. There he hung, legs dragging in the foam behind, as Josh hung over the guard rail with two fingers curled tightly through the crate's plastic cover.

'Don't let go!' we all said at once, and while I didn't know for sure where everyone else's command was directed, I knew where mine was. I sprang up and reached down for Ed. 'Give me your hand.'

He looked up at me, one eye wild and the other in its permanent, mangled squint. 'I can't,' he said, wheezing.

I glanced to the left, where Josh was still hanging over the side with a string of drool dangling from his mouth as he watched, in wide-eyed horror, the plastic stretch from his fingers like molten wax. The crate was almost in the water. Dani came to his side and reached down to help, but her arms weren't long enough. Dimly, I heard Richard yelling out commands from the helm, but I looked back to Ed.

'You can.' I stretched further, shoulder, elbow, wrist and fingers reaching the limits of their length. I found his eyes and looked into them as deeply as

I could, even the wreck on the left. My voice trembled, and not just under the strain of my ready-to-pop joints. 'You can, Ed. You can and you will. Give me your hand.'

His fingers were bloodless, as white as the hull, and slipping from it, but with a sudden jolt he brought his right hand up and grabbed mine.

We held each other – not wrist-to-wrist, but hand-to-hand.

I gripped tight, he gripped tighter, and I pulled with everything I had until he was on the deck. As we tumbled together in a heap, I heard a shriek from Dani and a cry of woe from Josh, and a splash as the crate of water disappeared in the waves behind us.

'Christ, Josh, no!' shouted Richard, as his son fell back, eyes open and mouth shut in mute horror. Richard hit the wheel, cursing some more. The maelstrom was already disappearing to starboard, and the noise of the water was being replaced by the steady rush of wind and the thrum of the halyard. Josh put his head in his hands.

I looked at Ed.

'Are you all right?' I said, barely able to breathe.

'Yes,' he replied, examining his head and, when he realised his patch was gone, covering his eye in shame. I pulled it gently away.

'It's all right,' I said, and though my body was howling with pain, my throat burned with recent vomit and everything seemed to swim in and out of focus, I managed a smile. 'I'm your wife, remember?'

Chapter 25

We sailed hard until the wind died, by which time the sun was sliding towards the horizon. The water was clear of debris, though it was still tinged a strange orange that matched the air. Everything was gloopy and hot, and we were nearer than ever to the flashing, black clouds in the west.

Shaken and silent, we dropped sail and drifted, facing the storm.

Richard paced the deck, rubbing his stubble with one hand while the other was fixed to his hip, elbow bent like a pair of garden shears. Occasionally he glanced at Josh, who sat at the bow with his hands around his legs, looking away from us all.

Maggie sat at the stern as Dani changed the dressing on her shoulder. Her face was grim and set, and I could sense that the friction between them had reached a point of no return.

'Is this what you wanted?' she muttered. 'Is this the adventure you were after?'

'Shut up, Mother. Sit still.'

Colin scurried up and down the starboard deck, seemingly searching for a way off the boat.

Carmela was below deck performing a stock check; a useless exercise, since we already knew exactly how badly we were fucked. But I suspect she was doing it to keep her mind off Bryce's continued self-confinement.

Ed had made a new eyepatch out of a red scarf Carmela had given him. He was scanning the chart at the table behind the helm, shaking his head and dragging his finger over imaginary lines spanning thousands of miles.

And me? There was not much of me left by that point. My head spun, my vision drifted, my throat hurt and my mouth was filled with the taste of my own sick and whatever had been in that water. I felt as gloopy and unreal as the sea, and my shot mind presented me with a continuous loop, an old and scratchy cartoon like *Popeye* or those first Mickey Mouse shorts. It was of me melting into the ocean like rancid butter in hot oil.

The boat began to rock. The storm was approaching.

Ed stood up suddenly. 'This isn't right. We're way off course.'

'What?' said Richard absently, still pacing and rubbing his chin.

'That whirlpool took us far further south than we should be.'

'Nonsense,' said Richard. 'We've been heading west.'

'No, we haven't.'

'We have.'

Richard strode to the chart. 'Let me see.'

'Look –' Ed pointed '– we were here, the storm was there. So we must be here.'

Richard snorted. 'How the hell do you work that out?'

Ed narrowed his eyes for a moment, then snatched back the map and flattened it on the table. '*Because*, the storm was moving south. Fast.'

'No it wasn't.'

'Yes it was.'

As they argued, Dani and Maggie continued their own snippy exchange. Josh, mute, kept his eyes on the storm.

Richard raised his voice. 'Ed, I've been watching that storm all day.'

'Really? Have you been marking our bearing against it? Counting off the miles? Triangulating?'

Richard scoffed. 'This isn't a Scout hike, Ed.'

'That's a "no", then. Look, we need to adjust our heading to account for our shift. I'd say 260, or more like 263. If we don't then we'll end up in Venezuela.'

'Bullshit, we'll end up in Florida like we always would – 263 will take us all the way up to –' he scanned the map '– New York. Or even fucking *Maine*.'

Carmela crashed around downstairs. I sat with my back to the guard rail, watching the waves lick the hull below with more and more appetite. The haze in which we sat became a fine spray, which I realised was rain, and I closed my eyes, trying to pretend it was a garden hose on a summer's day. But all I could think of was a burst water main after an inferno.

'I told you,' said Maggie. 'We should have stayed. The world isn't *safe*, Dani. It's not now and it wasn't before. We had everything we needed, but you didn't listen to me. You never *listen* to me.'

With a rasp of exasperation, Dani stood and leaned on the guard rail at the stern.

'Go on,' said Maggie. 'Go and sulk.'

More thumps from downstairs. The deck clanked and rattled as the waves grew ever more ravenous.

Carmela appeared from the cabin. 'We have not lots water. Not for every person.'

'No shit,' spat Richard.

She pulled back her head and rattled off a few lines of affronted Spanish. Richard ignored her, returning to the chart.

'Ed,' he said, 'you're not thinking straight. The one thing we have to go on is the storm, and the storm—'

'The storm has moved. You've not been paying attention.'

Richard straightened. 'Paying attention? I've been captaining a bigger boat with a larger crew—'

At this, Dani spun from the stern. 'Really? Who made you captain?'

Josh huffed from the bow. 'He's always captain.'

Richard, already derailed by Dani's retort, turned to his son. 'What's that supposed to mean?'

Josh turned, glowering. 'Exactly what it says. You always take charge. You're always telling people what to do.'

Richard looked around the deck, bemused and insulted. 'Well, someone had to.' He strode to the hatch and shouted into the cabin: 'And it's not as if I had any fucking help!'

Carmela barked back, consonants like shrapnel.

Maggie looked up. 'You think just because your hairy friend isn't up here you've had no help?'

He sighed. 'You know that's not what I meant.'

'Yes it is,' said Josh.

'Just what is your problem, Joshy?'

Josh stood, fists clenched, and made his way down to the helm. The boat rocked, stern to bow, but he kept his footing.

'Don't call me *Joshy*. And my problem is you. You think you've got all the instruction manuals, don't you? You think you know how the world works better than anyone else. Like this –' he flicked a hand at the chart '– you're not even prepared to consider the possibility that Ed might be right and you're wrong. Even when he was right before. That just wouldn't make sense to you, would it? In what universe could you ever be wrong?'

'Josh, what has got into you?'

'I told you. You have. You never listen. To me, to them, to anybody.'

'That's not fair. I'm not the one—'

Richard stopped and closed his mouth.

'Go on,' said Josh, 'say it. I'm not the one who dropped the water.'

'Josh, please.'

Josh gave a snarky fake sneer. 'That was *Joshy*. My son, who can't catch properly, even though he's supposed to, because he's a *boy*, isn't he? What a fucking embarrassment, eh, Dad? What boy can't catch? Especially after you spent all those hours in the garden trying to teach me how to play rugby.' Tears were streaming from his eyes now, fists clenching and unclenching. The rain was no longer just a spray, and fat drops of it formed puddles on the deck. 'Did it ever occur to you that I never wanted to play rugby? That there were other things I was interested in? Things that I couldn't tell you about, because you didn't think they were … *appropriate* for your son to like?'

Richard narrowed his eyes, speaking softly. 'What things, Josh? I don't understand.'

'No, you don't, because you never listened. Mum did. And she knew a lot of things you didn't.' At this, his mouth began to quiver and bend. 'I wish she was here. I wish she was here and not you.'

Richard's face fell, and Josh stumbled back up the deck. Halfway up he slipped in a puddle and fell. Richard held out a hand but Josh, with his head turned, got to his feet and continued on his way more slowly.

Richard fell into the seat behind him, hands on his knees, and for a while nobody spoke but the weather.

Eventually I got to my feet, my head Catherine-wheeling with the rush of blood. I could feel nothing beneath my left knee but a dull and painless throb.

'The storm's almost on us,' I said. My voice was brittle and high. 'We need to decide what we're doing.'

Richard's eyes were glazed and trained on the deck.

I turned to Ed. 'Ed, are you sure that we are where we are?'

He took a breath and nodded. 'I'm sure.'

'How sure?'

'I promise you. We need to adjust our heading north: 263.'

Richard said nothing. I looked over the chart, then turned to the rest of them.

'I believe my husband. We need to head further north. Does anyone object?'

There was silence, then Maggie spoke. 'What about water?'

'We have some. We can ration it.'

'It won't last. How many more days do we have? Seven? Ten? We're still closer to the Azores than we are to America. We could go back.'

Colin lapped at a puddle on the deck behind her. I was about to speak, but Ed suddenly jumped forward and grabbed the set of plastic brandy cups from beneath the seat, setting them out on the table. They began to fill with rain. 'We're about to head into a storm. If we're lucky then we can catch some water along the way. We still have bottles, buckets, basins. Josh?'

Josh turned, wiping an eye.

'Do you think you and Dani can be in charge of that?'

Josh glanced at Dani. They both nodded.

'Good. I'm sorry that you're involved in this, all of you, and if we still had the *Elma* then I'd suggest we split up and go our separate ways, but unfortunately we only have one boat.' He turned to Maggie. 'And we need to find our children. Do you understand?'

Having had his fill of rainwater, Colin hopped onto Maggie's shoulder, curling into the crook of her neck. She reached up to stroke him, then nodded at Ed. 'OK. All right, Ed.'

'Then it's settled?' I said.

Everybody nodded. So that was that; we would head further north.

And it was then, almost immediately, that things went south.

'Are you all right?' Ed said to me as we cleared the deck. 'You look green, and your limp's getting worse.'

'I'm fine. Just tired, and I feel sick after swallowing that water.'

'You should get some rest.'

'You know I can't.'

He nodded and went to untie the jib.

'Ed?'

He turned. 'Yeah?'

I nodded at Dani and Josh, who were busy securing bottles and cups to the guard rails. Dani had lashed an empty water canister to the deck and placed a funnel in its spout. 'Good shout on the water.'

He was about to speak when a flash lit the sky, followed by a deafening crack. We cowered instinctively, then straightened as the thunder rolled east.

'We'd better get these sails up,' said Richard, crouching over a winch; it was the first thing he had said since Josh's bruising words, 'before the wind picks up.'

As if in retort, a terrific gust of wind tore across the deck, rendering the next few seconds into a blur of disasters.

'No!' said Josh, as a bottle was whisked from his grip. The boom swung starboard, knocking Carmela off her feet, and the rope Richard had been securing whizzed through his palm. It snagged, something snapped, then whipped clean away into the wind. Richard howled and stood, gripping his wrist and holding up his hand, from which two fingers had been torn clean away. Blood streamed down from the broken stubs as he staggered back. The boat's pitch was sending him dangerously towards the guard rail.

'Christ,' said Ed, scrabbling to steady him. 'Get him below deck.'

Richard screamed again, staring at the space where his fingers had been, and Maggie, wincing and holding her shoulder, left the helm and hobbled to his aid, dragging him to the hatch just as the wind hurled another gust. The free boom swung like a madman's axe over our heads. Carmela, stunned, was just getting to her feet, but I managed to leap across and flatten her before she was hit again.

'Beth,' said Ed above the now howling wind. 'The helm!'

The wheel was loose. Leaving Carmela on the deck, I fell down into the cockpit and braced myself against it. The compass was spinning like crazy – 320, then 200, 220 … 263, that's what Ed had said. I steadied the wheel, trying to find the magic number, but with every wave we were tossed another ten degrees from it. Ed was struggling to secure the boom, the mainsail's halyard now flying in the wind, whipping back and forth from stern to bow.

'We need that rope!' yelled Ed, looking wildly about for help as he braced himself against the cabin wall. Dani was flat against the deck, but Josh was already inching out across the guard rail. The rope straightened, then curled and darted back. He made a grab for it but missed, almost sending himself over the side.

'Josh!' called Dani. 'Get back!'

He turned. 'I need your help.'

She looked back, terrified, but then a fierceness gripped her and she slithered across. The deck was now awash with rain and seawater, and she slipped the last few feet, landing in a heap by his legs. He helped her to her feet.

'Just hold on to me, OK?' he said.

She nodded and wrapped her arms around his waist, pinning him to the mainstay. The boat tossed and turned and the wind tugged at the wayward rope, keeping it just out of reach. Then, as if tiring of the game, it threw it back towards the bow. Josh leaped, catching the rope in one hand and pulling it back in. He handed it to Ed, who grinned and slapped his shoulder.

I blew out my held breath and returned to the compass. We had already been shifted by twenty degrees, but slowly I inched it back to the magic 263.

The measure of my trust in Ed: 263. If he was right, it would take us to our children.

The boom was finally secure and the boat's pitch softened. Ed, Josh and Dani began to unfurl the great mainsail while Carmela, still stunned and holding her head, made for the hatch, from which we could all hear Richard's cries of pain.

The compass had steadied, along with my breathing and pulse. Things began to settle. A shot of sunlight streamed through a gap in the cloud, and we bobbed for a few moments in this window of peace.

But the window closed as quickly as it had opened. The sunlight winked out like a light, swallowed by cloud, and another crack of thunder shattered the air. Fresh wind slammed into us with a torrent of rain that sent Ed, Josh and Dani sprawling on the slick deck. The boat tossed and groaned, the compass spun, and from somewhere above came a terrible snap. There was a flash, and I looked up to see that a stay had broken from its tether and was now as loose as the rope had been, swinging wildly about the deck.

It whiplashed across the foredeck and back to the stern, and I ducked just in time to miss the heavy steel hook rocketing overhead. It was intact at least.

The sea had renewed its raucous swill and the wind played along, provoking the waves to toss the boat like a cat with a mouse. But the *Buccaneer*'s keel was long, I remembered Richard saying, and wouldn't be pushed around so easily. It seemed to dig hard, gripping the water with unseen claws.

The cable was still loose. It had passed me by and was now heading for Ed, Josh and Dani.

'Get down!' I screamed as it whistled towards them.

Ed was almost on his feet, but Dani yanked him down. With every swing of the boat the cable built momentum, until it was zigzagging across the deck with no discernible pattern. There was no way to predict where it would end up next.

The wind roared. Ed shouted something. I wiped the water from my eyes and saw him point below deck.

'*Not safe*,' he mouthed. '*Not safe*.'

The three of them shimmied towards the hatch. I looked at the compass – 190 now. Knowing it was useless – the next bit wave would throw us off course – I eased our heading back to 263 and I followed them, tumbling down into the cabin and shutting the hatch behind me.

The cabin was hot and wet, full of a dozen different stinks and bodies gasping for breath. Richard was groaning, his face creased with pain as Carmela tried to stop his recently de-fingered hand from bleeding out. She was bleeding too from the fresh welt the beam had delivered to her head. Maggie was next to her, clutching her shoulder, eyes shut tight.

It was growing dark outside. The roar of rain on the cabin roof was deafening.

Ed peered through the window. 'We have to secure that cable. If we can't raise the sail then we've no chance of negotiating the storm.'

It whizzed past the glass. Ed ducked, and there was a crack as it hit something; the mast, I thought.

'It's going to break something,' I said. 'We'll be stranded. We'll drift.'

Ed turned from the window. 'I'm going out there.'

'Don't be a bloody fool.' Richard grimaced, face streaming with sweat. Carmela was tying off a bandage. 'There's no way you can catch a loose cable, and even if you did, it would maim you or knock you clean over the side.'

'I have to try.'

'The only thing we can do is wait it out and hope it doesn't do too much damage before the storm passes.'

I looked out at the dark, flashing sky. 'That's not happening any time soon.'

Ed and I shared a look.

'I'm going out,' he said, making for the hatch.

I followed.

'I'm coming t—'

Suddenly I was on the floor. My nose was flat against the wood.

Ed and Dani pulled me up, and all at once I was back on the seat. The side of my face stung.

'What happened?' I said.

'You passed out,' said Ed.

My vision pitched and swam like the boat.

'You don't look well,' said Dani, putting a hand to my forehead. 'You're burning up too.' She wrinkled her nose. 'And what's that smell?'

'Christ, not you as well.' My words slurred. 'I haven't had a bath for a while, all right?'

'No, it's not that. It's something else.'

I looked up at Ed.

'Ed?'

'Stay here.'

He turned and clambered up the ladder. Screams of wind and rain burst in as he opened the hatch, cut short as it slammed behind him. Richard shook his head at the space where he had been. 'Bloody fool.'

Finding some balance, I got up and made for the seat opposite. Through the window I watched the hunched figure of my husband stagger into the wind. The cable flashed as it passed him and he swiped at the air, slipped and fell. My fingernails bit into the window's rubber seal, and for a few moments he stayed where he had fallen. The cable passed twice, goading him to try again. Steadily, he pulled himself up. He swung twice, ducked, and on the cable's third pass the hook struck his head with a sickening crack that I could feel through the hull.

'Ed!'

His face whipped round as if he was an extra in some Hollywood brawl, but rather than stagger back and fall, he retained his footing and clutched the side of his head. Inspecting his hand, he sank to his knees and crawled back to the hatch.

'Are you all right?' I said, pushing back from the window and standing shakily on the tilting cabin floor. The hatch vanquished another scream of wind and rain and Ed slid clumsily down the rungs, holding his ear. He was pale-faced, drenched and panting. A dark trickle of blood ran through on his fingers.

'It's OK,' he said. 'But Richard's right –' he dropped his gaze '– there's no way I can catch that thing.'

'But we have to,' I said. 'We have to or—'

There was a crash. One of the windows shattered. Dani screamed as glass showered the cabin floor and the cable's hook darted, tongue-like, in and out of the hole it had made. We all fell against the opposite wall. Rain poured in through the gaping wound, drenching the seats and making an instant river of the floor.

'We have to stop it!' I screamed, getting to my feet.

'Beth, no!'

It didn't feel like I was walking. It felt more like the boat was ushering me with its sway towards the ladder, but that was OK because it was where I wanted to go. I had pushed past him, put my foot on the first rung – my left, and with the pressure came the nauseous yet pain-free swell of bile in my throat. It was as if my foot and gut had bypassed the usual chain of command and were talking to each other on a direct line. I was no longer in the equation. I pushed harder and saw only the black outline of the rung before me. My vision fizzed. Gravity released me for a second. It really did feel as if I could float away into nothingness, and that scratchy cartoon loop of me melting like butter played up again, only this time the butter was burned and bubbling, and more images joined it too, each with that same rubbery, black-and-white style: Ed strolling down a street on bouncing legs with his thumbs in his lapels, whistling through overgrown blood-soaked lips; Alice reaching for a heart-shaped balloon floating just out of reach, like that graffiti by the artist who nobody knows, except this was a real heart, fresh and pumping and torn from a chest, dripping down its cord; Arthur, grown into a boy, skinny, in rags and sitting in a dark corner, munching feverishly on a bone, his teeth making a click-clack, click-clack, click-clack noise with every bite; and a dead bird on the ground, neck broken, crosses for eyes, maggots crawling from its backside, but still whistling. Somehow still whistling. A terrible tune.

I felt hands on me, heard a voice – my own – screaming '*No!*' Then felt the thud of a plastic seat on my back. Thunder roared like laughing gods. The sky flickered and flashed and for a second I saw the whole horizon lit up. The clouds were right upon us, unearthly, thick and billowing like smoke from an enormous forest fire.

I felt a sudden calm, though the cabin was still filled with screams and voices and I couldn't move because of the limbs holding me down. My cartoon loop fell away and I stared into those clouds and I swear I saw a face in them. It was a woman's face, impassive and beautiful, wordlessly asking me to stop.

Give up, she seemed to say. *Give in. There's no hope here, so stop searching for it.*

As I stared at it, an enormous crack of thunder shook the boat and the door to the front berth burst open. There stood Bryce, legs apart, grim-faced and paler than ever.

'Tell me what I have to do.'

Nobody spoke. He glared around the room, eyes popping from their sockets.

'Well?'

'There's a cable,' I said. 'Loose, outside. If we can't secure it then we're done for.'

Bryce looked at the broken window and took a long, shuddering breath.

'Right,' he said, and stepped into the cabin.

'Bryce, stop,' said Richard, struggling up from where he had fallen.

Bryce looked down at him. 'What is it, Dick?'

'There's no way you can catch that thing. If it hits you it could kill you. Ed just tried, look at him.'

'Richard's right,' said Ed. 'It's faster and heavier than you imagine. Even for you, Bryce.'

Bryce looked at Ed, narrowing his eyes. 'Got a wee clip, did you?'

Carmela stood up and walked steadily to Bryce.

She said nothing, just looked at him eye to eye. She wasn't there to stop him. Instead she reached into the galley and pulled out a large pot, which she presented to him. He took it by the handle and looked it over.

'Good idea, pigeon,' he said with a devilish grin. Then he turned to the shelves above and found a long, thick screwdriver and a mallet. Laying the pot on its side, he drove the screwdriver into the metal, roaring with every blow, until he had made two holes side-by-side.

Inspecting his work, he tossed the tools to one side and placed the pot over his head. Two bright eyes peered out through the jagged holes.

'There. Job done.'

Carmela smiled with pride as he marched to the ladder. At the first rung, he stopped and looked down at the cupboard to his right. With another roar, he tore its door from its hinges and held it by the handle like a shield. Then, grabbing a boat hook from the bucket on the floor, he climbed outside.

I don't know exactly how he did it. By the time he was outside I was fading again. The cartoon loop had returned – my burned melting butter routine now joined seamlessly by Ed's jaunty whistle, Alice's grab for the beating heart and Arthur's bone-gnawing in the corner – and everything else stuttered in and out of focus, making no sense.

I heard thumps, clangs and crashes outside, punctuated by Bryce's gruff yells as the cable lashed at him. I heard the others' calls of encouragement, saw them cower and *eesh* at every failure and then, at some point, raise their hands and cry for joy. At this I remember seeing Bryce's silhouette against the lightning-bright sky, cable in one hand and guard rail in the other as wind and rain lashed the wildly rocking deck, but I couldn't have done. I could barely see my own fingers in front of me by that time. Could barely feel my own bones, think my own thoughts, feel my own feelings.

And when he was inside again, and the cabin seemed to be at the end of a long corridor, full of figures moving, voices chattering, shoulders being slapped. And then all faces turning to me. Ed's voice above the others, his face a million miles away.

'Beth? Beth, wake up. Christ …'

Chapter 26

Drifting away. Into the void.

Again.

Why?

Why now, when I need so much to be awake? When I need so much to be up and moving about, getting things done. Getting to my children.

Where's Ed?

I could have sworn I saw his face just then.

Oh, there it is again. Whistling, and I'm like butter and my children are cartoons leaping for internal organs and clacking their baby teeth on animal bones like a typewriter.

Phew. Thought I'd lost them for a second.

Thought I'd lost them. There's a joke.

The sky lady laughs. Big, black bellyfuls of mirth.

Fuck off, sky lady. I've had enough of you. Hear me? Enough of you, right? You're not ... you're not ...

Wait. Am I drunk? I've not been drinking. Is that my sick?

Just a bit higher, Alice. Go on, sweetheart, you can get it. Aw ... too bad. Next time, baby, next time.

Num-num, Arthur. Num-num.

Ed, what the fuck is that tune? It's a piece of nonsense, that's what it is. It's a ... it's a ...

What's that ... pain? Oh, aye, I've got plenty of that thanks. Too much, if you want to know the God's honest truth. God is honest, isn't he? I mean, he wouldn't lie, would he?

Would he?

Please, God. Please, whatever wherever however whenever whoever you are, please, send me to them, send me ... first class ... recorded delivery ... got to sign for it, love ...

Is it whoever *or* whomever? *I can never remember.*

That's some more sick for you right there. Hey, wait a minute ... I know that face. That's Richard. I like him. Handsome. Sigh. *Tut, stop it, you harlot, you're a married woman. Disgusting.* Married.

What, Ed? What's going to be OK? Everything? Oh. Right. That's OK then. Tickety-boo.

What's that? A stick? What stick?

This one you're putting in my mouth. Right.

I can't bite down any harder or it'll split my lip.

Why am I ... am I drunk? The room's spinning.

Where am I?

What year is this?

Who's the president, God damn you!

Ha ha!

Oh, I do tickle myself sometimes I really do ... right, sorry, bite down, sorry. Crunch. Ow.

What are you doing there, Dani? Dani? I wouldnae take that boot off if I were you, darling, it's not pleasant down there. Like that lassie said, bit of a smell – 'cept you don't keep your fanny in your boots, do you? I don't, anyway.

What's that you're holding, Carmela? Looks sharp, careful now.

Keep trying, sweetheart, jump!

Num-num, Arthur, there's a good boy!

Ed, shut the fuck—

Reality slaps me in the face. It's like I've surfaced from a freezing lake, gasping for breath. Pain. Pain has torn me back from delirium for no other reason than to remind me of its presence. Searing, screeching, tugging, twanging, tearing agony in my foot. Something's moving against it, catching on flesh and bone, pulling at tendons.

I howl to the heavens. I can't get up. I'm being held down and I can't speak because there's a stick in my mouth. I bite down hard, I'm *supposed* to bite down hard, so I do, and I think of all my teeth breaking and decide it would be preferable to this pain, whatever it is.

Carmela's beneath me, pumping her arm, face a grim, sweat-drenched picture of determination. There's a spray of blood that hits her lip, but she ignores it. Even though it's not her blood.

It's mine.

She speeds up. Her eyes widen. The pain reaches a level I didn't think was possible. You should pass out before this point, should you not? But no, the pain has done the opposite; it has woken me up to *remind me it exists.*

There's a thump. Vomit gloops from my mouth. Carmela fumbles for something as Dani holds a hand to her face. I think I see Bryce turn and heave. Ed's hand is on my brow, like it was when Alice was born and I had completed the final push and there she lay, a bloody thing upon the bed beneath us.

There is a bloody thing upon the bed beneath us.

'There we go,' he says, smiling, 'there we go, you did it, you did it. I love you, I love you, I'm sorry, I'm so sorry, there you go, there you go.'

So there you go.

Chapter 27

When I woke, my body seemed to speak to me as if it had been waiting by my bedside. *Don't move too quickly*, it said, so I didn't. I was lying on one of the pull-down bunks. I looked around the cabin, saw other bunks too with lumps on them; three figures lying with their backs turned. It was hot. The air was moist and pungent with salt, old breath and unwashed human flesh.

The boat was hardly moving, though I heard it creak. The broken window had been patched with plastic and duct tape. Occasionally the plastic flapped, inflating inwards like a broken lung, before returning again. Through its grimy surface I saw a sickening bright blue sky.

'Hello?' I croaked.

None of the figures responded. I watched them, straining to see if they were breathing, but I couldn't tell. I decided to risk movement, starting with my hands which were curled into claws at my chest. I unfurled one, then the other, and the fingers responded with just a brief stab of discomfort. So far so good. I tried my neck. Stiff, sore, but I managed to turn it and lift my head from the flattened pillow.

I raised myself up on my elbows and looked down at my legs.

Thirty-eight years on the planet makes you used to certain things. The shapes, sounds and feelings reality presents to you on a daily basis, those little maps of the world we take for granted and only notice when they change are or gone. Like the smell of your own house. Or the way the streets fit together in your town.

Or the fact that when you look down, you see both your feet.

My first instinct was grief. It was as if I'd been told that someone I knew had died. Tears appeared. My left foot was missing. *My* foot. A bandaged stump was all that was left of it. I began to weep and shake, but as the tremor reached my calf I froze, eyes and mouth suddenly wide open. I clawed for the pain, making no sound but a gasping croak followed by a deep, trembling groan I was sure I had never made before. I clutched my calf, letting more groans come, slow and measured, as if through bellows.

When the pain had gone I opened my eyes. One of the figures had sat up in its bunk. It was Josh. He looked back at me over his shoulder, eyes swollen, skin pale.

'Are you all right?' he said, struggling to speak.

I shook my head slowly. 'What happened?'

He swallowed and pushed himself up. 'You had ... you had gangrene. Carmela said it was probably because you had been moving about when your leg hadn't healed properly. The blood wasn't getting to your foot, so it went –' he looked at the stump '– it went black. It was pretty gross.' He looked up at me. 'It gave you that fever. Carmela had to cut it off with a hacksaw. I'm sorry.'

I stared at him, trying and failing to take in what he had just told me. Instead I looked down at the stump, willing it to sprout a new foot.

'How long?'

'What?'

'How long have I been out?'

'Two days,' he said.

'Where are we?' I said.

Josh shook his head. 'I don't know. The storm blew out in the morning after –' he coughed '– Bryce fixed the cable. Since then there's been no wind. We've been drifting, I think.'

He fell back into the bunk, his coughs answered by more from the other bunks; Dani and Richard, I thought.

'What's wrong with everyone? Josh?'

Josh made no reply. He had turned back to the wall.

I sat motionless for some moments, staring at the space left by my foot. I had heard that people still felt the presence of body parts even once they'd been amputated. Flesh ghosts. That was almost true. I felt the presence of something all right, but it wasn't flesh, or bone, or muscle, or tendon. It was more like – something incendiary. A tripwire. An unpinned grenade of pain hovering below the stump, ready to explode at the slightest twitch.

There were thumps overhead and I looked up. I thought I could hear voices mumbling.

I glared back at it, my new enemy made from empty space, attempting to tell it what had to be done. With dreadful care I lifted my leg from the hammock and quickly swung my right over with it. The muscles in my back, stiff with disuse, protested, but the stump had the monopoly on my pain. Their petty arguments were nothing.

I stiffened as if shot through by a jolt from an electric chair, but the pain gradually subsided. Whimpering, wiping my mouth of drool, I let my right leg take the weight of my body and stood.

A wave of vertigo rushed through me and I staggered against the ladder. I scooped up the boat hook Bryce had used to rescue the wayward cable from a nearby seat. It was longer than my lost broom but it fitted beneath my armpit and took my weight. Resting my head against the ladder, I closed my eyes and placed my right foot on the bottom rung.

It took me three attempts. The first time the boat hook slipped off the first rung and I landed on my right foot. The second time I managed two rungs before I slipped, this time my stump missing an open cupboard door by a hair's width. I froze in horror, trembling, watching it hang, until I found my breath and tried again.

But on the third rung the hook slipped again, and this time my stump hit wood.

Whether it was due to temporary unconsciousness or the fact that my mind simply deemed those several seconds of my life as unnecessary, I don't know, but I found myself in shock on the cabin floor, staring at nothing with my heart pumping a sparrow's beat, unable to make a sound.

There were shuffles from the hammocks, but nobody moved. Once the pain had subsided I got to my feet and inspected the three lumps in the dark. The fetid air caught in my nostrils.

I wanted to get out. I had to get out. The seven feet of ladder towered above me like a cliff face in cloud.

On the fourth attempt I made it. It must have taken five minutes, thirty seconds per rung, before I finally flopped out onto the deck like a landed fish. I lay there gasping, waiting for the rushing feet and cries of alarm I was sure would come. Ed, Bryce, Carmela, Maggie – but there was nothing, just bright, hot sun bearing down on my neck. Though better than down below, the air was still not fresh. There was a staleness to it, like compost or boiled turnip.

I heard mumbles and looked up. Maggie was at the cockpit. Her hair was loose and matted and she had removed her shirt so that all she wore was a discoloured bra digging into the reddening skin of her back. I could see scabs on her shoulders and the filthy bandage protecting her gunshot wound flapped idly in the breeze. She was poring over the chart which, even from my position on the deck, was clearly upside down, and occasionally she would look up, scan the sea, mutter something, and return to the useless lines around which her fingers roamed.

'Maggie?' I said, pushing myself up onto my right knee and using the boat hook to stand. She glanced back but didn't make eye contact. I hobbled over. The helm was loose, the compass swaying in the slow current upon which the *Buccaneer* drifted. 'Are you all right?'

She muttered something, then looked back over her shoulder. On the seat behind her Colin lay beneath a towel. His body was rigid, his mouth was open and his eyes were squeezed shut. One tiny claw stretched out for Maggie, as if in some last attempt at comfort. He was dead. I pulled the blanket over his face.

'Maggie?' I touched her shoulder and she flinched. Her wound was raw and swollen. Her eyes were red. Her breaths rasped. She blinked.

'You ...' she said, hardly a whisper. 'You're awake.'

'Maggie, your shoulder.' I reached for it, but she turned away protectively. Her eyes fluttered and she frowned, confused. Then she returned to the chart and her mutterings.

I looked up towards the bow. Bryce was sitting halfway up the deck, hunched, with his feet through the guard rail. His shirt was off too, and his great hairy back gleamed a furious red. I couldn't see his face; it had become shrouded once again in beard and hair.

Carmela lay next to him with her head on his lap. Her skirt was hitched up, bare flesh exposed to the sun. I hobbled to them, stopping at the place where the cable had come loose. A rough panel of wood had been hammered crudely around the tether. The mainsail was up and the boom secured for a starboard wind, but there was none, and it hung like a plastic bag in a tree.

Bryce looked up as I approached. He was holding what appeared to be a child's fishing rod with a line dangling in the oily water. He grunted.

'No fish,' he said. 'Nothing biting. 'S like there's nothing alive in this lake.'

He sniffed and wiped his nose. 'Sea,' he corrected. 'Sea, sea, sea.'

'Bryce, what's going on? Is Carmela all right?'

'Aye, just taking a snooze.'

I peered around him, afraid I was going to see her face twisted into something like Colin's death mask but, though she looked far from peaceful, the rise in her chest told me she was alive.

'She's burning, Bryce. You are too.' I looked up at the blazing sun, then shouted across the deck: 'You're all burning.'

Nobody spoke. Bryce sniffed again.

'Just no bloody fish.'

I looked around in horror. Ed was slumped over the bow. I squeezed past Bryce and Carmela and pulled myself from rope to rope towards him. Josh and Danni's bottles were still cable-tied to the guard rail, each one dry as a bone.

'Ed,' I said, shaking him. 'Wake up.'

He gave a start and grunted, looking up. Behind his ragged beard his lips were cracked, one deep welt lined with yellow pus. His eye focused on me.

'Beth,' he said, straightening. 'Thank God. Are you all right?'

He got to his feet, stumbling and steadying himself on a rope.

'No,' I replied, looking down at my missing foot. 'Not really, Ed.'

He put a hot, dry hand on my cheek. 'I'm sorry. There was nothing we could do. If you'd only seen it ... it was like ... it was dead. It would have killed you. That's why you had that fever. Has it gone?'

I nodded, dimly remembering the haze of madness that seemed to separate now from before. I could still see the cartoon loop in my head if I tried, but it no longer ran of its own accord.

He breathed out. 'That's good. I thought ... I thought I was going to lose you.'

He broke into a coughing fit. When it had passed, he stood, hunched and shivering.

'Ed, what's wrong with everyone?'

'I don't know. Fever, bug, dehydration maybe. We only had four bottles of water left, and we ran out yesterday.' He reached into a pocket and produced a flattened plastic bottle. 'I kept my share with yours.'

With no thought I took it, unscrewed the top and threw the contents down my neck. The water was warm, almost hot, but it could have been dog's urine for all I cared; my parched throat no longer felt like it was glued together. From the corner of my eye I saw Ed watching me. I stopped, wiped my mouth and handed him the bottle.

'Drink it,' I said, dizzy with relief.

'No. You need it.'

I shook the bottle at him. 'Drink it, Ed. I need your help.'

He stared at it for a moment, then took it and drank the rest, eyes closed with bliss. When it was done he shook the last drops into his mouth and exhaled. Then he replaced the bottle in his pocket.

My eyes had travelled to the water behind us. Ed knew what I was thinking.

'There's been no sign of him. We've seen nothing since the storm, just flat water. It's like we're floating through a graveyard.'

I searched for memories of engine sound in the delirium of the past few days. 'Have you been motoring?'

'There's hardly any fuel left. We've been keeping it for an emergency.'

'Do you know where we are?'

He shook his head. 'We've been drifting since last night, but we've been keeping to the same heading. It's so hot here, Beth.'

He staggered again and I caught him, relying on my boat hook to take my weight.

'We need to get the others inside or they'll burn. And Maggie's shoulder needs attention. Can you help me?'

He looked up and nodded. 'Of course.'

With some persuasion we managed to tear Bryce from his fishing line and woke Carmela, who looked around, dazed as we led her to the hatch. Maggie wouldn't come at first, but eventually we managed to usher her away.

'Colin,' she lamented, as she passed the stiffened body of her ape.

Ed opened the windows in the cabin, and kept the hatch open when he returned.

'You should go down and get some rest too,' I said.

'No,' he murmured, landing heavily on the bench behind the cockpit. He fell back in the shade and closed his eyes. 'I'm staying with you ... staying ... with you.'

His head lolled and soon he was still, breathing short, shallow breaths. I picked up the dead ape from the seat next to him. He felt hollow and brittle, and without a word I emptied him into the water, where he floated away like dry sticks. When he was gone I found my way to the helm.

There was a peace to that moment I still remember to this day. It was a feeling that had no right to be there, by all accounts, as if it had crept in from some other time and place. It wasn't as if I knew what I was doing, after all. I had no idea where we were. I had no idea how far we were from anything. I had no idea how far off course we had been blown, or drifted, or whether our course had been at all right in the first place.

But surrounded by that searing sky and dead sea, I was somehow overcome by a stillness. I was alone on a boat in the middle of an ocean, sloshing around a recently devastated planet in an endless space. I was in a void, in a void, in a void. And yet still I felt this peace.

If that was possible, I thought, then maybe anything was.

So I put my faith in that feeling, and in a number.

Propped against the side of the cockpit with my stump-grenade hanging, I gripped the helm and turned it port, waiting until the compass needle turned to 263.

Chapter 28

The time I spent at that helm – it wasn't days or nights. Days are like rivers and nights are lakes, and this time neither flowed like rivers or sat still like lakes. It was riddled with eddies that sucked in moments, and running with dangerous undercurrents that threatened to drag you down to thoughts you never believed you could have.

I had to stay focused. Stay awake. Stay present.

263 ... 263 ... 263.

Not days. Not nights. Just light and dark switching like slides in a projector.

There was little wind at first. Time and awareness played tricks on me. One moment I would be staring ahead, eyes flicking between the compass and the water ahead, the next I would be asleep and hanging from the helm. At one point I discovered I had been staring at a bulb of condensation on one of the cockpit's glass panels for what seemed like hours. Snapping to, I made a grasp for it and slavered it into my mouth before it ran.

I moved Josh and Dani's empty bottles to the cockpit, lashing them to ropes and railings with some cable ties I found. I experimented with heights and positions – some in shade, some in sunlight, some at angles, some high, some low – reasoning that at least one might gather enough condensation to create a drink. But they remained empty.

I took to licking the boat. There were places where moisture still hung; in the cracks and crevices beneath seats and wooden runners, and I lapped away at every drop I could find, ignoring the tastes that came with them. It was as I was doing this to the underside of the boom that it began to move. A wind was picking up. I returned to the helm.

263 … 263 … 263.

I grew to love that wind.

I blew kisses to it. It grew steady and strong, but never wild and never malicious.

It's hard to explain unless you've been at sea, but every stretch of water, every wave and every breath of wind, from breeze to hurricane, has a character of its own. Some want to dash you against the rocks, some want to help you, and others couldn't care less whether you prosper or perish. And I know – we see faces in things, don't we? They're not real, just the products of our imaginations. It's a hangover of our infant brains, hardwired to seek the safe image of a mother.

But I dare you. Try it; head out into the ocean alongside those things with no faces, and tell me there's nothing there. Tell me there's no life, no soul, no consciousness apart the one you're having right now. You'll find the opposite, I promise you. It's everywhere, this thing, whatever it is. *Everywhere.*

How I loved that wind.

There was an absence to it, nothing like the gleeful spite of the storm. It was as if it cared nothing either way for what I was doing and just happened to have stumbled into my sail; a bored and stoic westward draught that couldn't have topped 20mph.

I liked the darkness best. It was cooler for a start, and though there was no moon the stars soared over me like a snow globe. I'm sure I could see them turning in their own orbits as I turned in mine, and as they did I thought of my children. I allowed myself little fantasies. Not too much – I didn't want to get dragged into that undertow – just shapeless flashes of hope. Where would we live, once we had found them? Would it be warm? Would there be people, or just us? What would Arthur's first word be?

Just flashes, appearing and disappearing like shooting stars in those milk-sprayed skies.

I woke up to rumbles and a cool feeling on my face. I was surprised to find myself lying on the bench and Ed slumped over the wheel, asleep.

I almost stood on both feet, but froze before my stump hit the deck. As I pushed myself up with my now-trusty boat hook, I realised what the cool feeling was – drizzle.

'Ed, wake up.'

I shook him and he woke, snapping robotically to attention and gripping the wheel. 'What?'

'It's raining! Get the bottles.'

We took all the bottles we could find and offered them to the sky as if in prayer. We opened our mouths but the droplets were so fine that they only coated our tongues.

When the rain had stopped we inspected our haul. There was barely a dribble in each bottle, but we had our share and Ed took the rest downstairs to the others. There had been no sign of them since I had woken.

'I cleaned Maggie's shoulder again,' he said, 'but it's getting worse.'

The pain in my stump became manageable. It screamed whenever it hit something, but mostly it was dormant and I learned how to protect it. That afternoon, as low thunder sounded far away, Ed took the helm and I found fresh dressings in the cockpit's first-aid kit. These I took to the stern. As I peeled off the old bandage I expected to see a mess of infected flesh, but Carmela had done a good job. The skin was neatly stitched, and whatever excess rags of skin had remained after the appendage had been torn away were trimmed and pinched into a squat tube, like a sausage link.

None of this looked like it belonged to me. My calf was withered and pale, like some poor creature cowering beneath a lifted rock. It was dotted with dark specks of blood; the dried spray of some severed artery which, I imagined, had hit Carmela too.

I extended an exploratory finger towards the thing which was not me. It twitched, so I thought better of it and dressed it in the fresh bandage.

We skirted the thunder and whatever storm it belonged to kept its distance. Like the wind it had no interest in us, and apart from its uncertain grumbles the only evidence it gave us of its existence was the occasional drizzle that showered the boat. When this happened we fumbled for our bottles and drank whatever we could catch, splitting the takings with the rest downstairs. I never saw them, and from the look on Ed's face whenever he returned, I was glad.

Whenever the water was gone, we set about licking the yacht. This activity became as commonplace as scratching or sniffing, and whenever a patch of moisture was found upon a rope or a beam, or a section of deck, we called the other over and passed our tongues over it until it was dry.

It was never enough.

One time, as we feasted upon a rivulet Ed had found upon the mainstay, our tongues slipped together in a warm, fleshy collision. We stopped and smiled at this, then finished the job and returned to the helm.

Late one afternoon there was a scream from downstairs. Dani.

I looked for Ed but he was already halfway down the ladder. There were protests, scuffles, more screams and, finally, Dani's muffled sobs. I made my way gingerly to the hatch and hovered over it, already knowing what had happened.

At Dani's request we buried her mother at sea. The only other place she would have wanted to be laid to rest was Gibraltar, she said, and there was no chance of that. We managed to rouse the others and they stood on deck, ragged and pale, swaying like trees. We wrapped Maggie in a sheet, Dani said some words, and we let her slip over the side. We watched as she floated away and finally sank.

The others were too ill to remain on deck, but Dani stayed with Ed and I from then on, taking up watch at the stern.

'How are you?' I said, uselessly.

She stared out at the place where her mother's body had. 'She always thought of herself as this lone wolf, you know? Just her against the world. But it wasn't like that.' She gave me a weak, red-eyed smile. 'I know you think she was a single mother, but she wasn't, not really. I spent just as much time with her friends and cousins as I did with her. That place –' she shook her head '– she relied on it so much she couldn't leave it, even for a holiday, even if I had wanted to go and—'

She broke off, eyes glazing.

'I have a father out there somewhere. She never even considered that I might want to find him.'

After a pause, she shook from her trance, sniffed and wiped away an unwanted tear.

'Anyway,' she said, 'she wasn't a lone wolf. She relied on her friends.'

'And how about you?'

She looked up, eyes brightening. 'I feel like I finally have some. I hope that doesn't sound strange.'

'It's not strange, Dani,' I said. 'Not strange at all.'

On the third day things took a turn. I had been asleep and having a bad dream – not a nightmare, but one of those in which everything is impossible and never resolves. It was about my mother's face, and I woke from it to find that I had kicked out with my stump and made contact with the helm, at which Ed was standing.

I screamed and fell off the bench, and Ed helped me up.

'Fuck!' I yelled into the dawn. 'Fuck!'

'It's all right.'

'It's not all right!' I snapped, and snatched my boat hook.

He looked back at me, swaying, eye drooping.

'Sorry,' I said. 'Get some rest.'

He fell to the bench and immediately closed his eyes.

There was no moisture to lick and no water in the bottles. The storm had slunk off, taking its drizzle with it, and leaving us with a different wind. This one was not so lovely; it was blustery and more aware of us, worrying the sails with vicious gusts that made keeping the compass needle on the magic 263 a far more troublesome task than it had been. By the end of the morning I was exhausted.

'Ed,' I said, but he didn't move. 'Ed, I need to go to the toilet.'

Still nothing.

'Fine.'

I jammed my hook in the helm and used the rigging for support as I made my way astern, where I pulled down my cargo trousers and squatted over the rail.

I had peed over the side many times on the journey, but only passed faeces twice. Neither was what you might call a satisfying experience, but they were heavenly compared to what came out this time.

My stomach cramped and rumbled as an unhealthy, hot squirt hit the water beneath. As a few more similar ejections took their course, I looked grimly down at my underwear – the very same Maggie had given me, what, a week ago? Two? The sight and smell reminded me how long it had been since I washed. Using my elbows to steady myself on the guard rail, I squirmed out of them and used them to wipe up, jettisoning them in the sea behind.

Ed was awake when I returned to the helm.

'Sorry,' he said, rubbing his face. 'I think I slept longer than I should have.'

He took the helm and I sat down, resting my stump on the table. I looked around. Apart from the wind, something else seemed different. Then it dawned on me. My neck prickled.

'Ed, are we sitting low?'

'Huh?'

'The boat. It feels like we're lower in the water than usual.'

He frowned and scanned the water. 'Here.'

Giving me the helm, he walked gingerly up and down the guard rail, looking over the side.

'You're right,' he called back from port side bow. 'And I know why. Shit.'

'What is it?'

'We have a hole.'

'What?'

'It's only small, looks like something hit us, maybe in the storm or the whirlpool, I don't know.'

'Fuck, Ed, what are we going to do?'

He returned to the cockpit and opened the hatch.

'Wait here,' he said, disappearing inside.

'It's not like I'm going anywhere,' I mumbled.

I heard some banging downstairs. About an hour later he returned looking haunted, covered in grime. By this time the wind had disappeared completely and the sun had broken through the cloud with a relentless, sticky heat.

'It's coming into the hull through the front berth,' he said. 'I managed to patch it a bit, but it's not enough. I think I need to get the bilge pump working.'

'What's the bilge pump?'

He shook his head. 'I've no idea.'

He opened the engine compartment and began rummaging inside, then searched papers and manuals on the cockpit shelves. His hands shook as he leafed through them.

'No … no … nope.'

I was nervous now. I felt a chill on my back and glanced behind, imagining I could make out shapes on the dim horizon.

Ed looked up momentarily from his papers.

'I told you,' he said. 'We lost him ages ago.'

'It doesn't feel like it.'

'What do you mean, "doesn't feel like it"?'

I looked back him. I hated this. We had been coexisting quite peacefully for days, and now all of a sudden we were snapping again. It had always been this way, I realised. Our moods swung like pendulums month to month, and I supposed their frequencies and amplitudes were dictated by the chemistry of our bodies, or upon external events that were out of our control. At times our orbits would meet in happy places, other times in gloom or frustration. It was impossible to predict.

But I suppose discovering that you're on a sinking boat in the middle of the Atlantic might be a good indicator of mood.

'It means I think that man will do anything he can to find me.'

His eyebrows twitched upwards. 'Is that right,' he said flatly.

I frowned. 'What's that supposed to mean?'

He shrugged, still leafing through the manuals and shaking his head at every one. 'Why is he so interested in finding you?'

'You heard him. He's insane and he blames me for losing his fight with Maggie. And I stole his boat. Apparently it's special to him.'

'Or you are.'

I narrowed my eyes. 'What?'

'What did you promise him anyway?'

'Ed, what the fuck?'

'You said you asked him to help you, and he said he would in return for something.'

'That doesn't matter. He was lying.'

His hands were a blur now, tearing through the pages with barely a glance.

'But what would you have done if he had?'

I thought about telling Ed of Tony's lies, of all that rubbish he had spouted about loyalty and trust. But no, I decided. Fuck him.

'I would have done anything if it meant finding my children. Wouldn't you?'

He stopped and looked up, right eye wide. His jaw shut tight, and for a second I thought I saw something in him I hadn't before – something free from the shackles of human behaviour. But it left him as soon as it had arrived. His brow softened, and his face was overcome by sadness. He dropped the remaining papers to the floor.

'I'm sorry,' he said. 'Ignore me.'

With that he turned and made his way to the bow, where he sat with his brow on his forearm.

The hatch opened, and I was surprised to see Bryce squinting at the sun. He nodded at me.

'Morning,' he said, and crawled out. He stretched and stood with his hands on his hips, looking about, not quite sure what to do with himself.

'You feeling better?' I said.

He nodded. 'Aye, I am as it happens. What can I do to help?'

'Don't suppose you know how to work a bilge pump, do you?'

He frowned. 'A what?'

'We're sinking.'

He stared at me and blinked. 'Right. 'Course we are.'

He looked around the deck, spotting Ed at the bow. He looked between us.

'Funny time for a tiff, don't you think?'

I rolled my eyes. 'It's not a tiff.'

'What's it about?'

'I don't know. Ask him.'

He nodded and rubbed his chin like a mechanic over an open bonnet. His hair wavered in a breeze. 'Wee man got a touch of the grumps, eh? Well, you've got to remember, Beth, you girls aren't the only ones who have your ups and downs, ken?' He glanced at me and winked. 'Periods and all that, know what I'm saying?'

I made no response.

He held up his palms. 'Now, don't get me wrong, I regard the menstrual cycle with as much fascination and esteem as I do everything else about the female sexual system, and that goes for all those wee fucking annoying mood swings you – and us – have to go through every time you're about to be up on bricks. I mean, Christ, Beth, I've known Carmela for three months so I've seen at least two of those bad boys go off already, and believe me, it's not a pretty sight. But I dinnae lose my fucking rag over it –' he smiled amicably '– so to speak, because I know full well I can turn into just as much of an arsehole at certain times of the month as well. When I'm a little tense, if you know what I mean.'

He waited for me to acknowledge what he was referring to, but I was too distracted by something in his hair. He put his hands on his hips and bounced on his toes.

'When I'm a little *full*,' he went on. 'When the pressure dial's into the red. When there's no more room at the inn. Understand?'

I narrowed my eyes, which he took to mean a warning and raised his palms. But it wasn't a warning. I had stopped listening ages ago.

'I'd be happy to flesh this out with you, Beth, if you like—'

'Bryce.'

'I mean it, I'm not scared of a conversation about how over-full ballsacks might cause just as much chemical and psychological impact as the hormones released during PMT—'

'Bryce.'

'I will *happily* have that conversation with you. But in the interests of the current situation regarding your good self and Mr Grumpy-pants over there, all I'm saying is—'

'Bryce.'

'Have you tried a blow job? Or failing that, a good old-fashioned tug?'

'Bryce, for fuck's sake!'

'Whit?'

'What is that in your hair?'

I pointed and he raised his eyes to his scalp, upon which something was crawling. I had been watching its progress along his hairline since he had emerged.

'Piss off,' he said, swatting at it. It flew off.

'That's a fly,' I said, and as I did, a second landed on my head. I shooed it away. 'Do you usually get flies at sea?'

Bryce opened his mouth to speak but was stopped short by Ed, who was on his feet. I looked across.

'Beth,' he cried. 'Land!'

I peered into the distance, shielding my eyes from the sun's glare. On the horizon was a smear.

'Holy shitbags,' said Bryce. 'He's right.'

I looked closer. I thought I could make out squat, blocky hills covered by low clouds, and some kind of shoreline, but everything disappeared at the edges.

'It looks like some kind of island,' I said.

'Ulrich said that Florida was an archipelago,' said Bryce, uncertainly. 'Funny kind of archipelago, though.'

I spotted shapes flitting above the shoreline. Gulls.

'Wake the others,' I said. 'Get them up. Ed, can you start this engine?'

We motored in on the last dregs of fuel. Everyone was on deck now; Josh and Dani standing at the guard rail, and Carmela sitting with Bryce on the cabin roof with his hand on her shoulder. She had seemed nervous when she came through the hatch, unsure of how I would be.

'Thank you,' I said. 'For what you did.'

She nodded and smiled. 'Not so bad smell now.'

Richard looked the worst of them all. With dark-ringed eyes and hollow cheeks, he held his bandaged hand in a perpetual cocoon.

'I can see people,' said Bryce, when we were about a mile out. Sure enough, a line of figures were clearly visible, looking out from the shore.

If you could call it a shore; it was more of a disordered stretch of rubble, and those hills behind grew blockier and blockier the closer we got. There were spikes protruding from them, geometric shapes that didn't belong on a natural landscape, and above everything was the constant flap and swoop of gull wings.

'Do you think it's a city?' I said. 'Rubble? Christ, what's that smell?'

A stench had been growing as we neared our target. It was a human smell, but not death. Something more familiar.

We were down to the fumes before we realised.

Ed saw it first. 'No. It's not a city. That's landfill.'

The hills were piles of rubbish. Boxes, bags, washing machines, cookers, lawn mowers and vacuum cleaners. The spikes were bicycles, car parts and strips of timber.

And the figures along the shore.

I could see them quite clearly now; there were nine of them. Men and women, brown-skinned, white-skinned, tall and short, with ragged shirts and torn-off jeans. Each one had to be at least sixty years old.

'Think they're friendly?' said Bryce.

We were near the shore now and one of the figures stepped forward. He was black, with a rough fuzz of beard and a high hairline broken only by grey, thick tufts above his ears. He wore a long trench coat over not much else; a pair of orange Bermuda shorts, mud-caked army surplus boots and fingerless gloves. He smiled at our approach, revealing a set of large teeth and kind eyes. In one hand he held a staff of some kind which, on closer inspection, I could see was a rake. With the other hand he motioned to us to steer starboard, to a jetty made of strung-together palettes and tea chests.

Behind him the rest regarded us with the same expression of cautious, almost amused interest.

A bare-bellied white man – he had to be in his seventies – with a long beard, toothless grin, rucksack and wrap-around sunglasses, motioned the same as his friend.

'Over there,' he called out. 'We'll take you in over there.'

My heart thrilled. His accent was American.

We docked at the makeshift jetty and two of them – an old woman with knotted hair and a pale, skinny man to whom she barked impatient instructions in a southern drawl – tethered the boat as we stepped off one by one.

Their seven comrades waited for us on the shore, which I could now see was a stretch of filth embedded with plastic, cardboard and flattened tin cans. The man in the trench coat stepped forward, squinting with a lopsided grin and oblivious to the flies buzzing around his head. I went to speak, but the relative still-ness of the firm land after days aboard the *Buccaneer* put me off balance and I almost fell. He jumped forward and caught me.

'Easy there, girl,' he said. His voice was as light and kind as his eyes. 'Watch your step now, y'hear?'

When the feeling had passed I straightened up and he let me go.

'Well now,' he said, 'my name is Curtis. Curtis Peach. And who might you be?'

'Beth,' I said. 'Beth Hill. Are we—'

I coughed, my throat dry.

'Mikey?' said Curtis, turning round to the bare-bellied man in sunglasses. 'You got some water back there? Come on, man, give it up now. There y'go.'

Mikey had fished a glass bottle from his rucksack and passed it to his friend. Curtis opened it – *pop* 'Whoops! There y'go, girl, take summa that, go on now' – and I drank five long gulps before passing it to the rest. Mikey found more bottles and passed them round too.

I stood, gasping breaths of relief.

'Now,' said Curtis, 'are we what, Beth?'

'Are we in America?'

He paused, mouth open, then smiled. 'Aha. That we are.'

A shuddering sigh escaped my lungs. Ed steadied me, and I looked at him.

Two six three, I thought. *You were right, Ed. You were right*.

Curtis turned to Ed.

'And who's this young man?'

'I'm Ed,' he said. 'Is this Florida?'

Curtis paused again, but this time his smile dropped. He glanced behind him. 'No, sir. This ain't Florida. This is Fresh Kills Landfill – what's left of it anyway.'

'Fresh Kills?' I said, with a glance at Ed. I hovered on the question, not fully sure I wanted to know its answer. 'Where is Fresh Kills?'

Curtis looked at me. 'Staten Island,' he said, and smiled. 'Welcome to New York City.'

Chapter 29

I sat in a three-walled tin shack staring out at mound after mound of human detritus. It was raining, and the corrugated roof hammered above.

'You can have my place,' said an old lady with bright eyes and full, skewered hair. She led me from the shore down a wide, weaving gulley between the rubbish mountains. She smiled as she helped me inside. 'And lucky for you today's laundry day.'

In one corner was a mattress dressed with impossibly pristine sheets and a fluffed-up pillow, and the walls were decorated with pictures, scraps of paper and coloured glass like rough jewels hanging from threads.

'Name's Rhona.'

She patted her wide hips and nodded, satisfied. She wore a blue dress dotted with orange flowers, heavy boots and countless bangles and necklaces. A tattoo – a spider, I thought – peeped out from under the hem of her left arm, stretched with her weathered skin.

I stretched out my leg and rested it on the ground. A bracken of flat cans, bottle tops, smooth glass, plastic, nails and twisted cutlery spread out all around; the terra firma of our sanctuary was just as much waste as the brightly coloured hills that grew from it.

Rhona looked me over, eyes darkening at my stump.

'You had yourself some bad times, I'm guessing. Am I right?'

I nodded. I didn't feel like talking.

'Well, you're safe here. Is there anything I can get you?'

I shook my head. She smiled with a wince of pity.

'OK. All right. I'll get Curtis to bring you some more water. Rest easy.'

The others had been led to similar shacks along the winding road. It was clear our hosts were giving up their shelters for us.

My stump throbbed and my thigh answered with a dull echo. But it wasn't the pain that troubled me.

We had failed.

Ed had been wrong.

Two six three, the magic number to which I had clung all that way, had taken us a thousand miles from Florida, and God knows how long it would be before we reached it now.

I was in a rut between blame and shame. It wasn't Ed's fault, I knew that. He had only said what he had thought at the time. *That maelstrom took us far further south than we should be.*

But he hadn't just thought it, had he? He had been certain.

I promise you.

And through all this, Richard had been right.

Ed, you're not thinking straight.

No. Clearly not. And why had I ever believed otherwise? To give him a chance? Test his mettle? If so, why had I risked our children's safety on an experiment?

Why had I listened to him? Why not Richard?

Rut, rut, rut, went my pulsing stump.

I stared at it, knowing full well that these were not the questions on which I should be dwelling. There was a much bigger one waiting to be addressed.

Why had I listened to either of them? Why hadn't I worked it out myself?

I had put my trust in other people and it had led to this. So if it was anyone's fault, it was mine.

Curtis appeared from around the bend. He stopped and squinted at me, shielding his eyes as a shaft of sunlight broke through the rain. As a brief arc of rainbow crossed his face, he gave a wonky grin, walked to the shack and sat down next to me. He took a bottle from his pocket and handed it to me. I drank from it, and this time I tasted the crystal water as it flooded down my throat. I could almost feel my health returning as I gulped it down.

'What is that?' I said, gasping.

'Pretty good, ain't it?'

I took some more, and offered him back the bottle.

'Keep it,' he said. 'We got plenty.'

'Thanks.'

I ran my hand through the dust around my right
foot. I could feel him watching me, not with suspicion, but interest.

'You're from Scotland, right?'

I nodded. 'That's right.'

He looked pleased with himself. 'I'm, ah, something of an expert with accents. Goes with the
territory.'

I didn't ask him what territory that was, but I
smiled just the same. He watched me again.

'The land of whisky and jigs to the Big Apple,' he
said. 'Hell of a long way to come, if you don't mind
me saying. And something tells me it still ain't where
you want to be.'

I turned to him. He smelled sweetly of dried-in
sweat, charcoal and lemons.

'We were trying to get to Florida, but we were
blown off course.'

He raised his head and made an 'O' with his mouth.

'Florida. Must have been one almighty storm!' His
smile withered when I failed to return it.

'Something like that.' I ran my hand through the
debris. 'That and a disagreement about where we
were –' I rubbed an ancient ring pull, the ones from
before they attached them to the cans, between finger
and thumb, then let it fall to the ground '– in the sea.'

'Ah, I get you, I get you. The good old *navigational
dispute*, right?' he chuckled. 'Boy, if I had a dollar for
every one of *those* little tête-à-têtes I've seen play out
on the sidewalk then I'd be a rich man. Tourists and

whatnot, you know what I'm saying? Woman saying *this way*, man saying *that*. I always used to try to help them, always, I did. A man like me knows New York City like the back of his dried-up hand.' He laughed again, then sniffed, eyes widening. 'But most folks don't want to take directions from an old dude sitting beneath a newspaper now, do they?'

He turned to me, his expression slowly falling.

'I'm, er, guessing this isn't your average tourist expedition. Right?'

'My children are in Florida. They were taken from me.' I fought against the tug of my lips. 'They're very young. If I don't find them, I don't ... I just don't ...'

Without warning my face relinquished whatever weak grip it had upon its muscles and I collapsed into tears. My face shook and I buried it in my palms.

'Hey,' said Curtis, softly, laying a hand on my shoulder. 'Hey, hey, hey. Now listen to me. One of those friends of yours – don't know his name, tall, gloomy drink of water with missing fingers – he told me your boat's in pretty bad shape, but don't you worry, 'cos we're going to fix it for you. We got all kinds of things here just fit for mending boats, cars, bicycles, you name it. Look around you.' His eyes shone. 'We're a veritable *gold* mine. So don't you shed another tear. We'll patch up your boat and you can be on your way in no time.'

He slapped my shoulder. I nodded, smiled, heaved a sigh. 'Thank you.'

'Don't mention it. And in the meantime, just relax and get some rest, 'cos I can see you been beat up almost as badly as your boat, young lady. And actually, you know what?' He glanced at my stump and winked. 'Maybe we can help a little with that too.'

In an instant the rain ceased and the sun sprang from a cloud, as if the weather was merely a bank of theatrical effects. Curtis looked out at the bright, wet pathway and beamed.

'Well look at that, sky's turned.' He got to his feet. 'Know what?' He gave me his hand and helped me up, passing me my makeshift crutch. 'You might even like it here, Beth. Oh, I know, it smells a little, but you get used to it. You can get used to most anything you want to in this life, in my opinion.'

'Not everything,' I said.

He looked a little crestfallen at this, and I felt bad.

'Curtis, do you know where my husband is?'

He frowned and rubbed his shiny palate.

'Skinny fella, tufty hair, missing eye?'

'That's him.'

'He's on the boat. Back thataway.'

'Mister, I told you, you're fighting a losing battle.'

The old – I may as well stop saying that; they were all old – woman with the wild, witchlike hair and the pale, skinny man beside her stared up with bemused expressions at the deck of the *Buccaneer*, upon which Ed was standing, emptying a bucket. He glanced at me and disappeared down the hatch.

'What's happening?' I said.

The woman turned to me and shook her head. 'Sugar, that boy ain't right. He been up and down that ladder sixty times already, each time with a fresh bucket of water, and he just done goes and pours it over the side.' She gave the man beside her, who was still rubbing his chin and looking up at the deck, a sharp-elbowed nudge.

'Hey now!' he barked, gripping his arm. 'That hurt me, Frannie!'

She glared at him. 'Tell her, Harold. That boy up there; he ain't right.'

Rubbing his arm, Harold turned to me with a wounded look. 'Woman ain't wrong. He been doing just as she said for the past twenty minutes or so. Ain't no use in it, no use at all. Whatever he's tossing out just coming right in again.' He leaned towards me. 'Does he got some kinda *condition*? You know?' he tapped his temple. 'In the old noggin'?'

The woman rolled her eyes. 'You're the one with the *condition*, Harold. Now help me up there so we can start work. And miss, I'd advise you to get that boy o'yours down.'

Ed reappeared, heaving another bucket of water.

'Ed,' I called, but he ignored me, throwing the water over the side. 'Ed!'

He paused, cradling the empty bucket and turned to face me.

'I'm sorry, all right? I fucked up. Just one more fuck-up in a long line of fuck-ups. But I'll fix it. I'm going to fix it.'

He hurried for the ladder.

'Ed, stop. I don't blame you.'

He stopped halfway into the cabin, staring down into the dripping darkness.

I hobbled closer to the boat. 'Nobody could have known which way that thing sent us, and I didn't even *try* to work out where we were.'

He looked over, his one eye dark and furious. 'No. You trusted me. And you shouldn't have done.'

He jumped down the hatch, splashing and thumping beneath.

'My, my, my,' said Frannie, shaking her tousled head, around which a permanent swarm of flies flitted and buzzed. 'He got the troubles that one, yes indeed.'

'Mm-hmm,' said Harold.

'Edgar,' I shouted. 'Edgar, you come back up here now.'

'Just what he need,' murmured Harold, 'another *domineering* woman.'

This brought another sharp jab from Frannie. 'Harold!'

'Ow, Goddammit woman!' He performed a little scuttle of frustration in the dust, clutching his arm. 'Stop doing that, will you!' he turned to me, speaking slowly and theatrically. 'All I'm *saying*, is, maybe if you don't raise your tongue at him like that then he'll listen. 'S all I'm saying, nothing more.'

The splashing and thumping continued below deck. Frannie frowned, mulling it over, and finally gave a purposeful sniff. 'Sometimes my husband has a point.'

I sighed. 'Ed, please. Come out. I want to talk to you.'

The noise stopped. A few seconds later Ed pulled himself out of the hatch and stood looking down into the bucket. As a breeze ran through his hair his face creased and he dropped the bucket, spilling water across the deck and collapsing into the puddle.

'It's my fault,' he said, sobbing. 'It's all my fault.'

Frannie looked at me, nodding at him with a 'go on then' look in her eye. I hobbled to the guard rail and put my hand through, finding his knee.

'Ed, it's not your fault. None of this is anyone's fault. And it's not wrong to trust people, least of all your husband.'

I reached further and found his fingers. He tightened them around mine.

'Now come on, because you're kind of –' I looked at the empty bucket and the rapidly expanding pool of seawater '– you're kind of being a dick.'

He snorted and wiped a bubble of snot from his nose. 'Sorry.'

'Besides, I have a feeling these people know what they're doing a lot better than you or I.'

Frannie beamed and placed a hand on Harold's shoulder. 'You got that right, missy. Me and my man here are what you might call the engineering department of this operation.' She looked up at Ed. 'Now are you going to let us do our job, mister, or do I have to call for Leopold to drag you from the deck?'

'Who's Leopold?' said Ed.

Harold narrowed his eyes. 'A great big Texan with an eye for tight pants, if you know what I mean. You don't want to mess with him.'

Ed shook his head and got to his feet. 'No need for that, I'm coming down.'

'Excellent,' said Frannie. 'Gimme a hand up there before you do, there you go.'

Ed helped them both up and took their place on the jetty. Frannie began reeling off orders.

'We'll find them, Ed,' I said. 'I promise.'

At that moment Harold did another one of his frustrated scuttles on the deck.

'Dammit, Frannie, will you please stop hollering at me? I'm doing my damned best.'

Frannie stopped and turned to him. Her shock was replaced with a sudden look of fondness, and she placed a hand on his face. 'I'm sorry, Harold. I know you are.' She gave him a long, tender kiss, than patted his cheek gently. 'Now, are we going to do this thing or what?'

Harold smiled. 'Yes, ma'am.'

There were footsteps on the jetty and we turned to see Curtis again.

'You all right?' he said. We nodded. 'Good. Come with me, I want to show you something.'

Chapter 30

Curtis led us between the garbage heaps. There were voices ahead, and when we turned the final bend I was surprised to see a wide clearing, most of which was taken over by a blue, steaming lagoon. Around it were huts, workbenches and a kitchen in which a small, nervous lady with deep black skin and bottle-thick glasses moved between pots and sizzling platters. The smell was intoxicating, a rich liquor of herbs, spices and fried onions.

'Nice of you to join us,' said Bryce, raising a bottle of water. He and Carmela were sitting in one corner of the lagoon – him shirtless, Carmela still wearing an enormous black bra – and some distance from them sat Richard. He nodded up at us, but said nothing.

Five of our hosts were also in the water; Mikey, the bearded, big-bellied man with long hair and wrap-around sunglasses; Rhona, who had removed her dress and sat like Carmela in her underwear; an enormous, white-grinned black man in a red T-shirt and aviators and, next to him, a muscle-bound, square-jawed white man with spectacularly hooked eyebrows. He seemed the youngest of the lot, probably in his early sixties. He and the man in the red

T-shirt were currently engaged in conversation, while Rhona and Mikey were trying to encourage Dani and Josh to enter the water. They were sitting on battered sun loungers.

'Come on in,' said Rhona, 'we don't bite.'

'Don't have the teeth for it,' said Mikey, laughing. He spoke with the open vowels of a New Englander.

Dani and Josh shared a look, and Josh shook his head. 'No thanks, we're good.'

'Suit yourself.' She turned to us. 'What about you pair?' She exaggerated a terrible English accent. 'Care for a dip?'

This made her and Mikey scream with laughter. Curtis just shook his head. 'Rhona, Rhona, Rhona, when will you learn? Our guests are *Scottish*, north of the border.'

Rhona wiped an eye and shrugged. 'Sorry, my bad.' She affected an even worse Groundskeeper Wully voice. 'Wud ye ceeeer furrra dup?'

She and Mikey collapsed in further giggles.

Curtis looked at us, embarrassed. 'Some of our number ain't so worldly wise.'

I smiled. 'Don't worry about it.'

'You should try the water though,' he said. 'It's hellish good.'

I took in the crystal pool. There wasn't a speck of dirt on its surface.

'How did you do this?'

Mikey slapped the side proudly and pointed to one of the nearby huts.

'Rainwater, triple-filtered, naturally heated and pumped using solar panels. It's what we drink, and it's what we bathe in. Come in and try it.'

Rhona caught my hesitation. 'Oh, don't you worry now, your dignity is perfectly safe. I doubt any of these old boys could muster a hard-on between 'em.'

At this, the square-jawed man looked up, curling one already obscenely curled eyebrow even higher.

'Speak for yourself,' he said. His voice was surprisingly high and nasal, with a little lisp. He looked at me. 'But my pecker don't pose no problems to you, sister, nor your man.' He grinned, looking sideways across the pool at Bryce. 'Can't say the same for everyone, though.'

'Leopold,' warned Rhona.

Carmela scowled at him, but Bryce grinned and raised his bottle. 'Wouldnae blame you, buddy, wouldnae blame you.'

Ed looked at me. 'What do you think?'

'I think it's high time we had a bath,' I replied.

With my stump propped on the poolside, Ed helped me in. The water had the same effect on my body as it did on my throat; an intense relief, followed by near tears of happiness. My muscles uncoiled like slackening springs, and as Ed slipped in beside me, his look told me he was feeling the same.

'There y'go,' said the man in the red T-shirt. 'Feels good, don't it?' He removed his shades and reached across, offering his right hand. 'Name's Johnson.'

We each shook it.

'Beth.'

'Ed.'

'Pleased to meet you. And this is my man, Leopold.'

'He ain't my man,' said Leopold, with a look of scorn. 'My *man*—'

'Oh boy, here we go,' said Johnson, slouching against the wall and sending a bow wave across the lagoon in the process.

'My *man* is far from here,' continued Leopold. 'And a good fucking thing too.'

'What happened?' I said.

Leopold leaned in. 'Caught him ball-deep in our pool boy, that's what happened. Yep. Used to live in a Manhattan condo—'

'Huh,' huffed Johnson, jabbing a thumb at him, 'only fucking soul alive who did. Why d'you live in Manhattan when you could have lived in Brooklyn? Or Queens? Hell, even this dump would have been better.'

'I – I mean *we* – happened to like Manhattan, thank you very much. Besides –' he crossed his arms '– least we had a home. Not like you bunch o' vagrants.'

He chuckled. Johnson laughed and raised a hand, which Leopold high-fived.

'True, true, brother,' said Johnson. 'True, true.'

Meanwhile Curtis had removed his trench coat and slipped in beside us.

'Hoo, there you go, there you go, that's nice. Now, where are my manners. Y'already met these fine gentlemen, Leopold and Johnson.'

They each raised a hand at their name.

'Charmed.'

'Hey.'

'Leopold's our Dallas cowboy, ain't that right, Leo? And I'm Curtis, you know that. Let's see now, there's Mikey from Maine, met him, and Rhona all the way from Calli-fawn-eye-ay. Who else? You met Harold and Francesca at the boat and, ah yes, that little bundle of joy over there in the kitchen is Evie.'

Evie looked up from a pot and gave us a curt nod, pushing her steamed-up spectacles up her nose.

'Evie, well, she don't say much, but it don't make us love her any less. And finally, there's –' he looked around '– where's Suyin?'

Mikey jabbed a thumb behind him.

'Still in the supply shed working on that irrigator. Guessing we won't see her tonight.'

'Huh.' Curtis turned to us. 'Suyin has a technical mind. Not easy to break focus, if you understand what I'm saying. Hope you don't take it personal or nothing if she doesn't join the pool party.'

He grinned. I looked around the lagoon. Smells of the sea were wafting from Evie's kitchen, and the sun was dipping behind the highest trash mountain, sending a cascade of countless diamonds glinting from its summit.

'Who are you all?' I said. 'How did you get here?'

'Like Leo so accurately implied,' said Johnson, holding out his hands, 'we're vagrants.'

'Hobos,' said Mikey.

'Wayfarers,' said Rhona.

'Bag ladies,' squeaked Evie from the kitchen.

'We're homeless, Beth,' said Curtis. 'Least, we were.'

'*They* were homeless,' said Leopold. 'I just wound up here when those things fell down. I was drunk.' His face soured. 'On account of that fucking pool boy.'

They told us their stories.

It had been 11 p.m. in New York when the asteroids fell. Leopold, in a state of woeful inebriation, had left the Wall Street bar in which he had been drowning his sorrows and stumbled onto the Staten Island Ferry. Nursing a brown-bagged bottle of Wild Turkey he watched the spectacle of the Manhattan skyline exploding from the summit of one of the Fresh Kills slag heaps. The landfill – once one of the biggest in the world – had been closed years before, Johnson told me, and its waste mountains capped in protective layers.

But it didn't take much for those caps to burst open when the asteroids reached Staten Island.

It was as Leopold stood with his arms out, shouting, 'Take me, you bastards. Take me to hell!' that Johnson found him, dragged him from the slag heap and down to a bunker by the wharf, where they sheltered as the great rocks tore the island apart.

Emerging later, they found themselves drifting far from where they had been. A small piece of the island, what constituted Fresh Kills, had broken off and found its way out to sea.

This is where the details became shaky.

'That's not how it happened,' scoffed Leopold. 'I weren't that drunk.'

'Yeah, you were.'

'Actually,' said Curtis, 'it wasn't the asteroids that broke the landfills out, it was the breaking apart itself that—'

'Horseshit,' said Rhona, waving a hand at him. 'I was there, I saw the whole thing. Those things burst like boils on a butt.'

'Oh, really?' said Mikey, raising an eyebrow. 'And how did you see all this, Missy? You wearing some protective bio suit or something?'

'I *saw* it from the outreach centre, dummy.'

'Oh yeah? So how come you ended up on Fresh Kills?'

''Cos the outreach centre blew up.'

'Boom!' said Evie, shaking a skillet.

Bryce watched them argue, delighted. Richard seemed less enthused, glancing every now and again at Josh.

'How many times we been over this, Mikey?' said Rhona.

'I don't know.' He gave her a sideways glance. 'But it gets crazier every damn time.'

They ceased their bickering, and Johnson grinned at me. 'All we know is, when daylight came we were here, floating away from the mainland and surrounded by all this trash.'

'That's our truth,' said Leopold, 'and we're sticking with it.'

'Truth.' The others echoed.

'Now we've told you our story,' said Mikey. 'What's yours?'

We told them everything, from Bonaly, the barracks, and the camp at Falmouth to Ed, Bryce and Richard's journey across the country. I listened to Ed recount this part of the story with wonder, as unable to believe in it as I was unable to believe in the lines of muscle definition that had apparently appeared on his shoulders and abdomen. Then I told them of the SS *Unity*, of Mary, of Gibraltar, Tony and our crossing.

When we were done, they were silent.

'Holy shit,' said Johnson. 'And I thought our story was tall.'

Rhona smiled and touched a pendant around her neck. 'Don't worry. You'll find your children. I know it.'

Evie banged the side of a pot with a spoon, crying, 'Service!', and all eyes turned to the kitchen.

'You stay there,' said Curtis, getting out. 'Mikey, do you think this occasion calls for something special?'

'Amen to that,' said Mikey, waggling his palms like a preacher. He rose from the lagoon and disappeared into a shack, from which we heard the chink of glass. When he returned he was carrying a dark, unlabelled bottle with a stopper, which he presented to us as if he were a wine waiter, clearing his throat.

'Sir, madam, a bottle of Staten Island's finest for you. Do you approve?'

I raised my eyebrows. 'That all depends on what's in it.'

Mikey wrinkled his nose and pulled the cork. 'Best not think about that too much.'

As he poured us glasses – Bryce knocked his back and motioned for an immediate refill – Curtis brought us deep tins of delicious-smelling fish stew. Then he raised his glass.

'To friends old and new,' he said, and turned to me. 'And future shores.'

We drank, and while I was expecting some acrid gut-clenching petrol, I was rewarded by a sweet, cherry-like taste that warmed my chest. We drank some more, ate the fish and told countless stories beneath a whirling canopy of stars. Harold and Francesca joined us, and Evie sat with her feet dangling in the water. We laughed, and cried, and laughed some more until sleep took us to our beds, and Ed and I curled up on Rhona's mattress and drifted away to the sound of waves crashing against a metal shore, and wind chimes made of bottle tops and spoons.

Chapter 31

I was woken by Johnson's shadow and a fresh, smoky aroma.

'Wakey-wakey,' he said, handing me a chipped tin steaming cup. 'I know you British like your tea, but all we got is coffee. And there ain't no milk. Hope that's all right with you.'

I sat up and took the cup, breathing in the rich, dark fumes.

'Coffee's perfect. Thank you.'

'Good.' He grinned. 'Breakfast's cooking poolside. Don't be late or you'll miss the bacon.'

'Bacon?'

His grin grew wider and he shook his head. 'It ain't really bacon.'

He slammed the roof twice and disappeared back down the road. It was already warm. I put my coffee down and stretched my leg for inspection. The bandage came off easily and there was no sign of infection beneath it. I retied it and sat for a few moments, enjoying the peace and my coffee.

But as always my thoughts returned to Alice and Arthur, and before I knew it I was out of the shack, hobbling to the shore.

Harold and Francesca were already working on the boat. Francesca was on deck, pulling on a lever while Harold hammered at something below.

'Morning, miss,' she said brightly. 'Sleep OK?'

'I did, thank you. Er ...'

'When are we finished?' She stood straight and wiped her hands. 'Hard to tell, but I believe we could use some help now so you tell your boys, you hear me? And maybe we can get you floatin' by sundown, how about that?'

'I'll tell them.'

'Good. Now I'd get to your breakfast or—'

'I'll miss the bacon. Right.'

She cackled as I turned and made my way back to the path.

'It ain't really bacon, missy!'

Whatever it was it filled a hole, and I had three more cups of coffee, my strength returning with every one. There were eggs too, and when I asked Curtis how this was possible he winked and took me on a walk around Fresh Kills. They had a vegetable patch, tended by Evie and Mikey, on which they grew potatoes, yams, carrots and a peculiar tight-leafed lettuce. They had reclaimed compost from the heaps and built a processing area in which they sorted through the endless mounds of garbage for useful objects. They had to be careful, he told me with a haunted look, because Fresh Kills had been used as a temporary storage area for wreckage after the towers fell. Some human remains still lurked within the mountains.

They had a fuel station, in which they drained and stored gasoline and diesel from the many car engines that had sunk into the mounds, and sometimes even from full spare tanks. It never ceased to amaze him, Curtis told me with shining eyes, what people liked to throw out.

There was a food processing unit where they assessed the many full tins and bottles they found. Corn, beef stew, vegetables, tomatoes, pasta and – to their occasional delight – liquor.

And there was a fishing jetty, complete with a hut for gutting, hanging and smoking their catches.

And they also had a chicken coop.

This was another mystery, Curtis told me as he peered through the fence at the five scrawny hens and a saggy-necked cockerel. But the God's honest truth, he said, was that they found them wandering through the trash the day they realised they had been cut loose from the great American continent. They must have belonged to a Staten Island resident, he mused, and found themselves along for the ride. In any case, they provided regular protein, and eventually there would be chicks.

Curtis kneeled and reached for some of the sparse grain on the ground, offering it to a hen. She came cautiously, head jabbing, and gently pecked at his fingers. His face lit with glee at the touch of her beak, and he chuckled.

'These are my girls,' he said. 'My dad had hens when I was a kid – 1950s, Oklahoma, that's where I grew up. Had about twenty of 'em. Names for all of them. I used to feed them, clean them, collect their eggs, every single day, I –' he paused, the words stuck in his throat '– I had to kill one once.'

With the grain gone the hen returned to her endless hunt for more. Curtis stood, brushing his hands.

'Guess I'll have to again one day.'

From the glistening in his eye, I suspected times would have to get pretty bad before that happened.

'Was it a big farm?' I asked.

'Huh? Naw, naw, we were poor as shit. Fact –' he laughed '– I ain't never had more than a dollar in my pocket any day of my life. But look at me now.' He raised his arms to the mounds around him. 'I'm a rich man.'

We spent all morning walking around the island. It was about as big as a cricket pitch, and my boat-hook crutch made progress slow.

'Let's go see about that leg,' said Curtis.

He took me back to a road leading inland from the pool, and stopped at a larger shack than the others. There was a rugged patch of tilled earth outside it, in which herbs and an anaemic tomato bush grew beneath netting. He rapped on the door and called a greeting, then led me in. It was cool and dark inside, and smells of ginger and jasmine from a small, bubbling pot in the corner mingled with engine oil and burned plastic. The roof was supported by three tall posts, and although I could not make out much in the low light, the space felt as if it was filled with objects. At a workbench beneath a window, hunched over a circuit board with a soldering iron and an eyepiece normally seen on a jeweller, sat a lady in a shawl.

'Hello, Suyin,' said Curtis. She looked around and a wide, studious face greeted me.

'It's OK,' Curtis whispered to me, 'I told her about you.'

Suyin took off her eyepiece and got to her feet.

'You the lady with no foot.'

She looked me up and down, baulking at my boat hook crutch. She slapped it back and forward with her fingers and shook her head. 'No good. No good at all.'

Before I could speak Suyin turned her head like a dog at a distant postman. She growled something, snatched a catapult from her workbench and marched to the door.

'Seagulls!' she yelled, flinging the door open and arming the catapult with a rock in her pocket. 'Go away!'

She launched the rock at the closer of two gulls pecking at her tomatoes.

'Get out!'

The rock sailed harmlessly beneath the wing of the gull, which had already taken flight with its cohort, and pinged against the roof of the opposite shack. The gulls gazed down with lazy smirks.

Suyin let another rock fly. It missed too, but it was enough to convince the gulls to scavenge elsewhere.

She returned and slammed the door, muttering, 'Far-king-gulls.'

She threw her catapult on the workbench and stood before me once again. With a sigh she resumed her assessment.

'Wait here,' she said, and made for a darkened corner of the shack where she rummaged among what sounded like a mountain of bottles and tin cans. The noise was deafening, punctuated only by her cries of frustration as she tried to find whatever it was she was looking for. Eventually the clattering ceased.

'Ha,' she said. 'I found you.'

She returned carrying two things. One was a crutch – a proper one with a rubber foot pad, handle and a soft rest – and the other was a prosthetic foot. It was plastic with brown leather straps, and two of its toes had melted away.

'Where did you get these?' I asked.

'Like I said,' replied Curtis, 'never ceases to amaze, what folks call trash.'

Suyin thrust the crutch at me first. I took it, dropped the boat hook and placed the soft rest beneath my armpit. It nestled into my flesh, instantly soothing the bruised skin. Suyin quickly claimed the boat hook and hurled it into her corner store, where it clattered into the hidden mountain of things. Then she offered me the foot.

I looked at the worn cup in which my stump would fit. Though the pain was less than it had been on that first day, the thought of placing weight upon it filled my mouth with the taste of recently digested mystery bacon.

'I can't,' I said, 'it's too soon. I only … I only lost it a few days ago. It needs to heal more before I can walk on it.'

Suyin nodded, closing her eyes and extending the foot towards me. 'It's better now.'

Curtis rubbed his chin. 'Truth is I don't know the best time to start on a prosthetic, but a buddy of mine lost half a leg when he was hit by a limo on Madison. It was his fault, 'course, full o'wine and running all over the road, but the rich little kitten in the back of the car felt so bad she paid for his surgery *and* all the shit he had to do afterwards. Private ward, personal physiotherapist, the whole goddamn bit. Got him off the booze for a few months too. 'Course he went straight back on it when he left. Anyway, he had a whole half-leg prosthetic on in under a week, on account of his wound healing so quickly. How's yours? Healing OK?'

'It is.'

He shrugged. 'Then maybe it's worth a try.'

I sat on a stool as Suyin and Curtis gently helped me on with the foot. My forehead beaded with sweat as the socket approached, like some grisly space capsule docking with an alien mothership. I flinched at the first touch, but Suyin reached for my hand and smiled.

'Try to relax.'

I tried, and this time when they reintroduced the foot I resisted the urge to tense from the approaching shock. I surrendered to it, and in doing so found that it was not as bad as I had expected. Still, my lungs and heart flew into double-time as Curtis tightened the straps.

'Relaaax,' insisted Suyin, squeezing my fingers.

You relax, I thought, gritting my teeth. *You try and fucking—*

'OK,' said Curtis, 'you're all set.'

They both stood, and Suyin handed me my new crutch.

'Take her for a spin?'

It wasn't quite the spin they had hoped for. I couldn't put weight on it, not fully at any rate, so I let the foot hang like my stump had before and performed a few turns to prove at least that it remained stuck to my leg. Satisfied, Suyin smiled, clapped and returned to her work. I thanked her and we left, making for the shore.

The boat was now a hive of activity, with Josh, Dani, Bryce and Carmela scurrying about under Frannie's orders. Bryce's laughter filled the air, roaring whenever he was given another task and snapping to attention whenever Frannie passed him on the deck. She grimaced, but I saw her chuckle once and dig him in the ribs. Dani was now permanently attached to Josh, seeking his presence even in her work.

I had only known death a few times in my life – unquestionable death, that is, not the uncertainty of my family's fate after the asteroids fell. When my grandmother died the loss I felt had no edges. The empty space she left – like my foot – ached through everything. It had no map, no direction, and no hope of resolving itself. I think this is how grief is for most people; a maze in which you spend your time trying to escape the way you came, until you realise the only way out is through.

But there was an immediate will to Dani's grief for her mother. She knew precisely how to escape the maze and she was going to do it as quickly as she could. Not by curling up, not by weeping and not by asking questions that had no answer, but by spending time with the people around her, whoever they might be.

Her friends.

Richard remained quiet, his injured hand consigning him to the job of carrying wood, tools and other small items from the shore to the deck, but even he smiled at Frannie pushing Bryce around. And watching all of this from a battered camping chair was Harold, enjoying what I imagined to be a temporary increase in his privileges. He had a pipe, and when I asked him what he was smoking he looked up with a gaping, toothless grin.

'All of life is here, missy. All of life.'

Evie served us vegetable soup floating with bits of broken spaghetti for lunch, then everyone returned to work – Curtis to his chickens, Mikey and Evie to their vegetables, and the rest to the boat, while Johnson and Leo sourced parts from the scrap.

This left me to an afternoon to myself, which I spent walking the island.

Gradually I got used to my new foot, assimilating the parameters of its pain. There was a contract beneath me; a solid promise of punishment if I exerted too much pressure, but, although I was far from being able to walk, the empty space below my ankle had been reclaimed and filled. A wholeness was returning.

I met Johnson raking through a waterside scrap heap on the opposite shore to the boat. 'Is that New York?' I asked him, peering into the haze to our west. I could barely make out the shoreline, or any of the lumps which I assumed were buildings. He said yeah, that was New York, although the smog over everything made it hard to tell exactly which part. Sometimes he thought he could make out the stump of the Statue of Liberty, but he might be imagining it.

Either way, judging by what he could see from the top of the highest pile of garbage on the clearest day – which was never particularly clear – they calculated that they had drifted about eight miles out and stopped. It was the same up and down the shoreline, he said; the land had crumbled like dry bread.

I asked him if they had ever tried to get back to dry land, and he shook his head. 'No need just yet. We're happy here. Besides, this water's a minefield of junk and broken land, so there's no way through it on a boat.' He gave me a firm look. 'You'll be heading south, Beth, when the boat's finished. Steer clear of that water over there.'

I walked some more, talked to Curtis at his hen coop and waved as I passed Suyin's shack. I found Bryce and Leopold on the fishing jetty, a bobbing rig of barrels and wooden slats. Leopold was teaching Bryce how to fish.

'Young man, you're tying your bait all wrong,' said Leopold. 'And what in the hell are you using worms for? You need fish, dried fish, here take some of mine. Where did you learn to fish anyway?'

Bryce grumbled that he had never learned to fish, which made Leopold hoot with laughter. 'Boy,' he said, leaning close to him, 'if you weren't so cute I'd banish you from this dock this second, you hear me? There, now cast away, go on, get that sonofabitch in the water. Good.'

His arm was around his shoulder as I placed my crutch on the jetty. Bryce looked up and said: 'Looking good, darlin'.' I said thanks, and asked how the work was going on the boat. It was all fixed, he told me. We would be ready to set sail again in the morning.

'Hell, that's a shame,' offered Leopold, with genuine sadness. Then: 'Oh, shit, look.' Bryce's rod was twitching, and he snapped to attention. 'Pull it in, son, pull it in!'

I left them struggling with the rod and headed back towards the boat. On the way, I caught sight of Richard and Josh sitting outside one of the sleeping shacks. I stopped out of sight and listened. Josh was speaking.

'I'm sorry, Dad. I didn't mean what I said. It's just that you're always telling me what you think I have to do. Otherwise you're punching my arm and calling me *Joshy* or *chief* or *captain*. You never just want to talk.'

'Talk about what?'

'About Mum, for a start.'

Richard's head fell at this.

'You're always with Dani,' he said with a shrug. 'I don't want to interrupt you, cramp your style.'

Josh looked away. 'There you go again,' he said, 'you have this idea of who I am, and it's not ...'

'Not what?'

Josh turned back to his father.

'I speak to Dani because she listens, and I listen to her.'

'Good. That's good. God knows if your mother and I had done more talking we might have been happier. Josh, it's great you've found a girlfriend who you can talk to.'

'She's not, Dad.' Josh leaned in. 'She's not my girlfriend. And she never will be. Do you understand?'

Richard's face seemed to undulate with thoughts, feelings and, finally, realisation. He straightened, opened his mouth to speak, then closed it and returned to his original position. He looked at his son.

'I – I'm not very good at this, Josh. You're right, your mum was better, I know. But I want to learn. Will you help me?'

Josh nodded and they hugged. I took the opportunity to hobble on towards the boat. As I passed I caught Richard's eye, still in mid-hug, and he smiled.

There was nobody there at the boat so I rested on the shore and looked east. I must have sat for two hours scanning the horizon, imagining a white speck cresting it or the far-off sound of an engine. But there was nothing but flat water and a cloudless sky, and as I saw my shadow stretch out before me on the sparkling man-made shingle, I felt a weight shifting; an evaporation of the threat that had been prickling at my neck since leaving Gibraltar. He had failed. The storm had taken him, or the maelstrom, or maybe he had just given up and gone elsewhere. I didn't care. Tony Staines was gone.

I returned to the lagoon and found them all two glasses down of Staten Island's best. Even Dani and Josh were in the water, and they all cheered and raised their glasses at my approach. Evie beckoned me from the kitchen with quick flurries of her hand, and I went to help her prepare food. She talked in excited half-sentences, explaining my tasks. Chop this. Fry that. No, slice it, *slice it*. It's gumbo. Have you tried gumbo? It's tasty, you'll see, you'll see.

Rhona brought out an ancient guitar with three strings, and sang songs with her feet in the water. 'I only know Tom Waits and Joni,' she explained, 'and my Joni's even rustier than this piece of junk so that leaves Tom.' She went to work, growling and rasping and hammering the thick strings as the rest of us clapped along. Mikey roared with her through 'Telephone Call From Istanbul', Evie danced around me in the kitchen to 'Jockey Full of Bourbon', grinning and tickling me in the ribs, and we all joined in with 'Heartattack and Vine'. When her repertoire was complete, Rhona laid down the guitar, gave a theatrical bow and said: 'That's it, all out, done.'

But as everyone called for more and Mikey argued with Rhona about the accuracy of her lyrics, I saw Dani pick up the guitar and pluck cautiously at the strings. Nobody paid much attention, still lost in their own pleas or disagreements, but I watched her, the spoon I should have been using to stir Evie's gumbo hanging loose. Her touch was fragile, but a tune emerged, and then from nowhere she opened her mouth to sing.

Everything stopped. All heads turned. All mouths opened.

It was as if some wounded, exotic bird had suddenly fallen from the sky and bled into the pool. I was sure I had heard the song before, but never sung like this. It was simple enough; she played two strings, walking and reworking the fretboard up and down, and repeated variations of the same phrase. I could hear the words sometimes – something about being dislocated from the world, hiding out in the places beneath its surface – but there was something to her voice that made me forget them and listen to what was beneath. There was another song encoded in there, and there was a distance to it, a terrible space between the words, the notes and even the cracks in her voice that trapped the breath in my lungs. I could not move. And when she finished, all that distance hung there, deepening, widening, stretching out into an in agonising void, and I found that all I wanted to do was close it. So I did. I dropped the spoon and went to the lagoon side, enveloping her in my arms, and everyone else did the same, wiping the tears from her eyes and their own.

Then we ate gumbo, and drank another bottle of Staten Island's best moonshine, and shared more stories beneath that clear, starlit sky until it was time for bed.

They were good people.

Chapter 32

I woke early to grey, mist-muted light. Ed's arm was still around my waist, so I lifted it gently so as not to wake him, took my crutch and slid out into the silent morning.

I made for the lagoon, passing the shacks in which the others still slumbered and snored. The mist clung to everything, pressed down by a cool, wayward drizzle through which the shapes of the lagoon, and its kitchen, gradually emerged. At the far end of the water was the dim but unmistakable outline of Mikey, head back against the side.

'Morning,' I said, and went to the kitchen. I lit a fire in the stove, and while I waited for the pot to boil I got into the water. I would have a coffee, then wake the others. Despite the welcome rest we had had with our hosts, I was eager to get going.

A thought struck me as I enjoyed the cool water for the last time, and I turned to Mikey.

'Mikey, do any of you want to come with us? I mean, I know it would be a squeeze, but we'd manage I'm sure.'

Mikey said nothing.

'Mikey?'

As I peered through the mist I saw something in the water moving in tendrils towards me. I jumped, thinking it a snake, but then noticed it was dissipating. A cloud was spreading across the lagoon. A dark cloud – blood.

'Mikey?'

I clambered from the lagoon and hobbled round to where he sat, but froze halfway as he came into view. Mikey's eyes and mouth were open, his throat cut wide apart.

I tightened in a freezing rush of horror. There was a noise from along the track towards the far shore where Johnson had showed me the coast the day before. Voices. Shaking, I crept through the murk towards them. Not far from the lagoon I saw Rhona face down in the mud, unmoving. Her face was turned to one side, and her bulging eyes and the puddle at her neck told me she had suffered the same fate as Mikey.

I walked on. Another body. Harold lying across the path, reaching for something.

The voices were growing louder. Deep, demanding English voices. I stopped in my tracks. There, outside the chicken coop, knelt Curtis before a tall, bull-chested guard carrying a rifle. I recognised him and my insides heaved.

'No,' I whispered. 'No, it can't be.'

There were other figures with guns, and I thought I could make out Johnson, Leopold, Frannie and Evie standing nearby, their heads bowed.

'Where are they?' said the man looming over Curtis.

Curtis looked up, tried a smile, and muttered something.

'Tell me!' bellowed the man.

Another smile. Curtis brought up his hands. The man smashed his rifle butt into the side of Curtis's head and he sprawled to the ground.

Johnson jumped forward. 'You son of a bitch!' he growled, but the man had already whipped round his gun. A shot went off and Johnson was lifted from his feet as if by an unseen fist. A spray of blood arced from his mouth and he fell in a heap on the floor.

Leopold made a sound I cannot describe but will never forget. He drew Evie close, and she buried her face in his chest.

'Now –' the man turned on them '– which one of you two cunts is going to tell me where they are?'

Shaking, I backed away, my voice hoarse.

'Ed ...'

I turned and ran, immediately hitting a semi-bare grey-haired chest adorned with trinkets. Two hands gripped me. A crocodile's smile.

'Hello, Beth.'

One of his men was behind him. He raised a fist.

More time passing without me. *So frustrating ... I don't have time for this ... this lack of consciousness ... I've got things to do, places to be, people to ... save. Please wake up, Beth. Please wake up, wake up.*

Mummy, please wake up.

My eyes shot open. I was sitting staring at the ground. The compacted mess of bottle tops and crisp packets. I couldn't move my arms. They were behind my back, tied to something.

It was dark and there were voices. Mumbles, sobs, whispers, prayers.

'Beth?'

I looked left. 'Ed ... *ow.*'

Pain shot down my neck.

'Beth?'

I turned again, slower this time. 'Where are you?'

'She's all right, Ed.'

It was Richard's voice. He was closer and behind me. I felt a hand tap my hip.

'It's me, Beth. Richard. Can you see?'

I widened my eyes, tried to shake some sense into them. Gradually the room came into focus. It was Suyin's shack, and we were tied to the three support pillars.

'Yes,' I said. 'Who's here?'

The sound of the voices broke apart, becoming distinct.

'You're with me, Carmela and Francesca,' said Richard.

Carmela was praying in Spanish. Frannie's sobs sounded like an engine struggling to start.

'Ed's on the next post with Curtis, Bryce and Josh,' said Richard. 'Dani, Leopold and Evie are on the third. Josh, Dani, are you two OK?'

They responded with nervous mumbles. 'Yes.'

I paused, running through the names.

'Johnson?' I said.

'Johnson's dead,' said Leopold, voice trembling, from the far post. 'That bastard killed him.'

Frannie made a wet snort. 'Jus' like they killed Mikey, and Rhona, and ... and ...' she broke down again, then composed herself, 'and my *Harold*. Did you see him? My Harold? They slit his throat like he was nothing but an animal. Like he was a turkey! Well –' her voice darkened, and I felt her fidgeting in her bindings '– Ima show dem. Ima treat dem like animals too. Gonna gut 'em. Gut 'em like pigs, one by one, even if I have to use my own teeth! My own teeth! Aw, Harold.'

She broke down into sobs again.

Ed called, 'Beth, are you all right?'

'Erm...' I gulped, checking my extremities. My prosthetic was still attached, I could move my fingers, and aside from my ankle the only pain was in my head, where I assumed I had been struck. I felt a wetness on my cheek. 'I think so. You?'

'Yes. I came to look for you. Next thing I knew I woke up here.'

'Same here,' said Richard.

'Aye,' croaked Bryce. 'Me an' all. You OK down there, pigeon.'

'*Si*,' said Carmela, surfacing from her prayer. '*Si, mi amor.*'

'They arrived on the western shore,' said Leopold. 'Quiet as fuck, just snuck right past us. Must've cut

Mikey's throat before he knew they were even there. I heard scuffling out on the track, and by the time I got up Rhona was gone, and Harold too. Frannie, I'm so sorry sweetheart.'

Frannie sniffed. 'I was … I was taking a shit … if I hadn't a'been, I'd a had my throat cut too.'

Curtis spoke. 'We were sleeping in shacks away from the main track. Rhona's, Frannie's and Harold's, and Mikey's were right on it. That's how they got to them first. Guess they didn't want to kill all of us, for some reason.'

'Who are those sons of bitches?' said Leopold.

'It was him,' I said. 'Tony Staines. The one who was following us.'

'Christ,' said Leopold.

'Well,' said Curtis, 'You were right about him being a – what's that word you use, winker?'

'Wanker,' corrected Bryce.

'That's right. A wanker is what he is, most definitely.'

'How are we going to get out of here?' I said.

'Don't suppose you've still got that tin can, have you, Ed?' said Bryce.

'Nope,' said Ed. 'It was on the *Elma*.'

'Try to reach each other's knots,' said Curtis. 'See if you can untie them.'

We spent some minutes grunting and feeling around the post for knots. I found Carmela's but the rope was thick and tight. It wouldn't shift.

'Hey,' said Leopold. 'Anyone seen Suyin?'

Before anyone could respond there were footsteps outside.

'Quiet,' said Frannie, 'someone's coming.'

The door squeaked open, flooding the floor with bright light. I had a sense that the mist had lifted.

And there in the doorway was Tony Staines.

'Hello, hello, hello,' he said, sauntering in like a CEO late to his own meeting. Beaming, he removed his sunglasses and tucked them in his shirt. Two armed guards stepped in behind and took position against the far wall.

'Well now –' he clapped his hands once and looked between the posts '– interesting place you've got here. Very interesting. Bit of a pong, if you don't mind me saying, but yeah, by and large, I like it. You've done well with your resources; I admire that.'

'Fuck you, asshole,' said Leopold, but Tony ignored him. His grin stood firm as he walked the room, performing figure of eights around the posts.

'You've got your water supply,' he said, counting off on his fingers. 'Assume that's filtered rain, am I right? And absolutely lovely what you've done with that pool, it really is, although – *irk* – we'll probably need to run those filters a wee bit longer for a few days after this morning. Then you've got your generator, fuel, reclaimed from all those old cars and what have you, amazing job, then – good heavens, I could hardly believe this – vegetables! Out here in the sea, on what is essentially, and I hope you don't mind me saying this, I really do, a *rubbish dump*! Aren't you lot clever? And also, I see you've got some chickens.'

Curtis looked up at this.

'Please don't touch my hens, mister. I beg you.'

Tony widened his grin and walked on. 'I do like a nice roaster.'

Curtis hung his head.

'Anyway,' said Tony, 'all great, like I say, superb job, absolutely excellent, and I tell you what, if I was the hat-wearing type then I'd take mine off right now.'

He clapped his hands loudly, shaking his head in awe. When he stopped, his smile became something else, and he raised a finger.

'The only problem is, from where I'm standing at least, this whole enterprise is … how would you say … *unsustainable*. Know what I mean?' He looked around. 'It's only going to last as long as the ones who run it. And please don't take this the wrong way, but I don't think that's going to be too long.' He laughed, a great wheezy laugh, and clapped his hands again. He was close to my post now, and prowling. 'So, here's what's going to happen. My *associates* and I are going to complete our assessment of your little floating shithole, and then we're going to have a nice sit down and a chat. Maybe over a few of those chickens.'

His eyes flashed down at me.

'Maybe have a bonfire, eh Beth? Nice big one. They'll see the flames for miles. Or they would, if there was anyone there.' He knelt in front of me. 'There's not anyone there though, is there, Beth?'

I shook my head. I was bored. I felt no fear any longer. He was just an irritation. 'Just what is your fucking problem? Why do you keep getting in my way?'

He smiled and pushed a ringlet of hair from my face. 'I might ask the same of you, Beth.'

'Don't touch her,' said Ed.

Tony turned. 'Ah, is this the hero? The Great Soprendo? My little *worker bee*?'

He stood and walked to Ed's post, squatted before him and sighed. 'Do you know, I don't have much to say to you. I don't feel like we've, you know, *connected*. Not like me and Beth, eh Beth?'

Ed took a breath through his nose.

'You smell like my grandfather,' said Ed. 'You remind me of him too.'

Tony stood. 'Well, he sounds great!'

Ed shook his head. 'He really wasn't. He used to beat his dog, he never let anyone else speak and he died alone. He still smelled like that, even in his coffin.'

Tony glared down at him. Still grinning, he brought back his hand and smacked Ed across the face. Then he turned to us.

'So, I'll leave you now in the capable hands of Mr Aitkins.' He gestured to one of the guards, who stepped into the light. It was Grot. 'He'll look after you when we're gone. Shouldn't be too long. Oh—'

He turned.

'What happened to Maggie, by the way? Dare I ask?'

He made an awkward face as Dani stifled tears. 'Guess not, eh? Right, I'm off, *au revoir*, now.

He left with the other guard, slamming the door behind him.

Dark and silence reclaimed the shack, though Tony's stench remained in the air. There was a rustle, followed by a click and an orange circle burning in the corner. Grot took a drag and breathed out a great plume of smoke, walking the same route as Tony.

'Whodda rabble,' he said. 'Whoddan absolute fookin' rabble.'

'Buddy,' said Leopold, 'why the hell do you spend your time with that asshole?'

Grot stopped before Leopold's post. 'Who the fuck are you then?'

'Wouldn't you like to know, darlin'.'

Grot sniffed. 'Sound like a bender to me.'

'What's a *bender*?'

'It means a bloke who likes fucking other blokes in the arse.'

'Really,' said Leopold flatly.

'Yeah, really. Good thing you're tied up, ain't it? Or you might have a go at me!' He snorted with laughter and took another drag of his cigarette, still chucking.

'Buddy,' said Leopold, 'even if you were the last asshole in the world ...'

Grot had lost interest and turned to Evie. 'And what are you, then? African?'

Evie buried her chin in her chest.

'Leave her alone,' said Leopold.

Grot ignored him, blowing smoke in Evie's eyes. She coughed, keeping her face as far away from his as possible. 'Hello,' he sang, 'I'm talking to you. Does she even speak?'

Growing bored he stood up and moved on. At Dani, he stopped. 'Now then, now then, this is more like it. Hello, darling. You OK?'

His voice adopted a sickening lilt. Dani squirmed.

'Leave her alone,' said Josh.

Grot sneered. 'All right, easy now. This your bird, is it? She is *lovely*.'

Josh glowered. 'I mean it.'

'Josh,' hissed Richard.

'I'm sure you do, mate, I would too with something this young and fresh. She is absolutely—'

He stopped. Bryce had started chuckling from the other side of the post. Grot stood.

'What's so funny?'

'Oh –' Bryce spoke through his laughter '– oh, you carry on, mate, don't mind me. It's just, I mean, you know, I've met a few wankers in my time and more than I'd care to mention in the last few months, ken? But you, oh boy, you are just the worst, you really are.'

Bryce leaned his head back and shook with laughter. Grot took a last drag and flicked his cigarette on the floor. He loped round to where Bryce was tied. I heard Carmela's whispered prayer gain momentum.

'An absolute –' said Bryce between breaths '– bona fide – fully paid-up – walloper, by the way – yer a' fucking roaster!'

Bryce roared. Grot glared down.

'You'd better watch your mouth, porridge chomper.'

'Away and lick ma fart-box y' radge wee shite!'

Bryce spat on Grot's boots.

'Bryce, please, no,' said Carmela, turning from her prayer again. But Grot had already cracked the butt of his gun into Bryce's forehead.

Bryce growled with pain. Still conscious, he hung his head, taking short, quick breaths, and said no more.

'Bryce!' called Carmela.

Grot turned, fuming now, and marched to our post.

'And who—'

'Hey,' I said. Grot looked up.

'What do *you* want?'

'Come round here,' I said, 'I want to ask you something.'

Grot hovered between Carmela and me. Finally something clicked and a smile flickered on his mouth.

'Oy know yow,' he said, and squatted in front of me. 'You're that one what came into the camp. You 'ad a broken leg.'

He gave a satisfied smile, as if he'd got the right answer in a quiz. There was that fat, protruding tongue squashed between his lips like a slug.

'How did you find us?' I said.

He curled his lip and frowned. 'What do you mean?'

I spoke slowly. 'How did you know where we were?'

He shrugged. 'I dunno. Mr Staines did it, had one of them ... sextant things. You know, like those things you have at school but bigger. He used it to navigate like a compass. Fucked if I know how, I hate boats.'

'But how did you know where we were going?'

''Cos you told us, dickhead. Daytona Beach, Florida, that's where you were going, so that's where we went too.

'That doesn't make sense. We were blown off course. There's no way you could have known we'd gone north.'

The confusion was too much for him now. His grimace had nowhere left to go.

'What are you talking about, *north*?'

'This is New York.'

He hesitated. 'No it's not. It's Florida.'

Time froze.

'What?'

It was his turn to speak slowly. 'Flo-ri-da. Just like Mr Staines said it would be, although you're right, we were a bit far north. We saw some signs on the shore saying Jacksonville, and that made Mr Staines a bit pissed off because it meant we were a hundred miles off, but anyway ...'

Feelings raced through me as he spoke. Hope, dread, joy and despair filled my blood, threatening to burst from its veins. Was it true? Were we only one hundred miles from Daytona Beach?

Had Ed been right all along?

'... and as we turned south again, that's when Mr Staines caught sight of his boat moored in this shit tip. You know, the one you stole from him. He said we should moor on the other side so you wouldn't see us. He's clever like that, is Mr Staines.'

He smiled, pleased with himself again. Nobody spoke. I looked at the ground. My pulse raced and I tried to draw breath. To be this close ...

Grot put his face closer to mine. 'Does that answer your question, love?'

I glanced up and he sneered. The sluglike tongue sat there glistening. I heard Carmela breathing hard.

'*Como un toro*, Beth,' she whispered.

Grot frowned at her.

'I think she knows, pigeon,' said Bryce.

And I did. With Grot distracted, I thrust the top of my head into his chin with all the force I could muster, snapping his jaw shut and whipping back his head. With a startled yelp he stood and staggered away with a hand to his mouth.

We froze as he stood there, eyes wildly roaming the room as he fingered the inside of his mouth. He gulped, then pulled something fleshy from between his lips. He stared in horror as half his tongue hung there dripping, and blood began to gush from his mouth. He turned to me.

'Yewfooshingbish! Ashmoyshung!'

He staggered towards me, fist raised, roaring and spluttering. I braced, willing myself to keep my eyes on him rather than cower, but at the last moment I closed them and ducked my head, waiting for the blow I was sure would kill me or send me back into that terrible unconsciousness.

Moments passed. The blow never came. Instead I heard a whizz and a click.

I opened my eyes to see Grot hovering, puppet-like, with his fist pulled back. His eyes were crossed and his jaw jutted out, providing a small reservoir in which the blood from his severed tongue pooled, spilling like a waterfall. Another stream of blood ran down from centre of his forehead, in which a deep welt was visible.

He made a noise, swatted at something beside him which wasn't there, staggered back a few feet and fell to the ground.

For a few moments the room was silent. Then it filled with the sound of eleven pairs of lungs exhaling.

'What was that?' I said.

'That, missy,' said Frannie, 'was Suyin, I believe.'

'*Psst.*'

We craned our necks and looked up at the open window above Suyin's workbench. Sure enough, there was Suyin, catapult in hand.

'Did I hit him? Can't see.'

'In the noggin', Suyin!' said Frannie. 'Right between the eyes!'

'Good,' said Suyin. 'He was very annoying.'

She swung a leg through the window, balanced for a second, then threw the rest of her body in with it and landed nimbly on the workbench.

She snatched a knife, jumped down and went to work on our bindings.

'He dead?' she said, when Evie was free. Evie ran to Grot's still body and checked his pulse.

She nodded furiously. 'Mm-hmm, mm-hmm.'

Suyin was deft with her knife and each freed pair of hands went to work on the rest. Soon we were standing, rubbing our wrists. Ed came to me and we hugged.

'Are you OK?'

'I'm fine. My head hurts.' I reached for it, wincing as I found two lumps.

'Was he right?' said Ed. 'About being further south than we thought?'

Curtis shook his head, bewildered. 'Can't say, but ... it's possible, I guess. We never made it back to land, and the whole shoreline's been dark and covered in smog since we left. Suppose we could have drifted.'

'But Johnson said he thought he could make out some of the skyline on clear days.'

Suyin shrugged. 'Sometimes we see what we want to see.'

Frannie shook her head. 'I told Harold it was getting warmer, I *told* him. "*We're drifting*," I said. "Feels like the South again." I could even smell it! But he didn't believe me, said it was my hormones. Told him I don't got none!' She made an exasperated sigh. Then her lip trembled. 'Aw Harold ...'

Evie hugged her. I turned to Curtis.

'If we're just south of Jacksonville, how far is Daytona Beach?'

'Can't be more than seventy, eighty miles on water. You could be there by sundown.'

My eyes flashed to Ed. 'Ed, we have to go. Now.'

'She's right,' said Curtis. 'Y'all got to get back on that boat and leave. It's your only chance.'

'What about Tony?' said Ed.

Leopold had found a baseball bat in one of Suyin's junk piles.

'You leave that piece o' shit to us.'

'There's no way you'll be able to take them all,' I said. 'They're armed.'

Evie emerged from one of the piles brandishing a skipping rope, tightening the ends around her skinny fists and pulling it taut. 'So are we.'

Curtis and Frannie found a machete and a metal spike each and stood with the other three.

'Wouldn't be the first time we've had to fight in our lives, Beth,' said Curtis. 'And if we can't beat them, at least we can do some damage for what they did to our friends, and give you some distance in the process.'

Carmela and Bryce shared a look.

'Aye,' said Bryce. 'But you could still use some help. Carmela and I are staying.'

'You can't,' said Ed. 'It's too dangerous.'

'What, compared to the last year? Aye, right fucking *Magic Roundabout* that's been, like.'

'But we need you.'

Carmela smiled. 'No. You need you –' she pointed at me, then Ed '– and you. That is all.'

Richard nodded. 'I'm staying too.'

'What?' I said, 'But you'll be stranded here.'

'Ach,' said Bryce, 'we'll get to shore and down to you somehow. We'll find you. We always do.'

'Beth,' said Richard, 'this was never about us, it was about you and Ed finding your children. And you're almost there, so let us help.'

'Dad?' said Josh.

Richard smiled. 'It's all right, son. You and Dani go with Beth and Ed.'

'No,' said Dani, standing straight. 'I'm staying too.'

'I can't allow that,' said Richard.

'That's not your choice,' said Josh. Standing shoulder to shoulder with Dani, he looked his father in the eye. 'And I'm staying too, Dad.'

'Josh—'

'I want to help.'

Richard gripped his son's shoulder. His breath shook. 'All right, son. All right.'

'Hate to break up the love in the room,' whispered Frannie, peering through a gap in the door, 'but there are two guards outside, each one about the size of Kansas. What're you proposing we do about them, Curt?'

'Hoo, well,' said Curtis, scratching his head. He looked down at Grot's lifeless body. 'Could use that gun, I suppose?'

Bryce snatched up the gun. 'Leave it to—'

But Suyin and Evie had already burst through the door, and screeching like banshees they tore across the dirt. One guard turned in surprise, only to receive a large well-aimed rock from Suyin's catapult directly in the face. By the time he hit the ground the other was in mid-turn, gun lifted, but Evie was already on his back, feet against his spine and rope around his throat. She strained and squeezed and the guard's sunglasses fell from his face, revealing popping eyes. He scrabbled for his throat, fingers barely stroking the rope deep in his flesh, and before long he was still on the ground next to his partner.

Evie whipped off the rope and stood panting.

'Time to go,' she said.

We crept to the shore where the *Buccaneer* was moored, and after fast, fierce hugs Ed and I climbed aboard.

'You got a full tank,' said Curtis. 'Head south and watch for that junk. There haven't been lights on the shore for half a year, but my guess is there will be when you get to where you're going.'

As Suyin and Evie kept watch, the others pushed us off and we let the current take us.

We were about fifty metres from the shore when, with one last wave, the others ran from that metallic beach and disappeared along the track. We had arrived at Fresh Kills in silence, but we left it to the sound of gunshots and screams.

Chapter 33

When we were fifty metres from the shore we started the engine and motored south. I took the helm as Ed watched from the stern.

'Christ, Beth, what are we doing? What if they don't make it?'

'We'll know soon enough. As soon as he realises we're gone, he'll be after us again. We need to get one of those sails up.'

Ed went to work on the mainsail, and as I turned to keep watch something thumped the hull.

'Watch out,' said Ed. 'There's still debris in the water. Keep to port.'

I looked ahead, searching for a path through the plastic lumps in the sea.

'Shit,' said Ed, struggling with the mainsail's cover. 'Who tied these knots? They're like steel.'

Another bump on the hull. Ed fell back on the cabin roof.

'Watch it!'

'Sorry.'

I eased our way from the minefield of junk. Once we were in clear water again, I glanced behind. The island was far from us now and there was no sign of the boat. A nervous smile flickered on my mouth.

'Ed, I think—'

'What's that?' Ed had got to his feet and was back at the mainsail's fastenings.

'I think—' I glanced back again. The smile left me. My heart plunged. 'Oh, fuck.'

'What?' said Ed.

A white shape had appeared to the east of Fresh Kills, turning south towards us with an angry drone.

'They're coming. Ed, they're coming, get that sail up!'

'Fuck.' Ed fumbled with the ties. 'Fuck, fuck, fuck, who tied these knots!'

'Just get it out!'

I pushed the throttle but it was already as high as it would go. The drone grew louder, accompanied now by splashing jolts as the boat scudded, closing the gap.

'Ed, please, hurry!'

'I'm trying!'

Half the mainsail cover was free but there were still six knots to go. I looked back. He was already halfway to us. I scrabbled in the shelf for the binoculars and, as I trained them behind, our pursuer gradually came into focus. Tony's puce and furious face glared back at me from the helm. His white shirt was blackened and torn, smeared with blood from a wound on his shoulder. He was breathing hard, gritting his teeth. There was nobody else on the boat.

I dropped the binoculars and looked back at Ed, now on the last knot.

'Ed, we need to get that sail up now!'

'I *said* I'm—'

He was cut short by a sharp report and the whip of a bullet across our stern. I swung round to see Tony aiming a pistol at us. He was now close enough to see without binoculars, and his eyes were black, boiling with rage. There was no trace of his mask now. The calm waters of the person he had spent his life selling to the world had run dry, and all that remained was the hungry, twisted reptile that had been lurking in its shallows.

He took another shot, closer this time.

'He's firing at us,' I said.

'I got that. Where are those guns that Maggie and Dani had?'

I scanned the deck but they were nowhere to be seen. They must be below deck.'

Another shot. I felt the bullet's breath and screamed. Tony was almost alongside us now, the boat's huge bow wave disrupting our path. With one hand on the helm he glanced between us and the water ahead, waving his gun and trying to find a shot. He aimed, but pulled back at the last minute as he swerved to dodge a lump of dirt.

I had an idea.

'Ed, hold on!'

I swung the *Buccaneer* to starboard, re-entering the dangerous, junk-filled waters.

'What are you doing?' yelled Ed.

'Just hold on.'

Ed gripped the mast. I took us into the minefield as far as I could, leaving Tony speeding along its edge. Our hull thumped and cracked. He took another shot but it missed us completely, and with a snarl he threw his own boat in after us.

Soon he was next to us again, even closer than he had been before. He squinted and aimed at the mast.

'Ed, get down!'

Ed scrabbled to the deck, but Tony had already taken the shot and with a terrible crack, the mast splintered.

Ed's head snapped back.

He fell to the deck, blood already pooling at his neck.

My heart stopped dead. No metaphor. It didn't beat.

'Ed,' I stammered. 'No!'

I stared in horror at Ed's still body, but my eyes were distracted by a huge mass looming ahead. I managed to swerve around it just as Tony let off another shot. This one missed and he hit the obstacle, bouncing to port. He snatched the helm with his right hand, and in doing so his pistol flew over the side. With a cry of outrage, he swung to starboard again, meeting me on the other side of the lump.

This time he didn't stop. His boat crashed into the side of the *Buccaneer* and in a few clumsy steps he had leaped over the two guard rails. I screamed as he landed upon me, pinning me to the cockpit's wall.

'Got you!'

'Get off me! Get your fucking hands off me!'

We struggled. He reached for my throat but I grabbed his wrist. The stench of his breath was so sickening I had to turn from it.

And in doing so my eyes found Ed lying still upon the deck.

I was shot through with grief, a fierce, fierce pain worse than anything I had endured.

Get up, I thought. *Don't leave me, please* ...

I let the thought drift away, and felt an overwhelming urge to go with it – to give up and let that wretched man take my life too. It would be so easy to go limp and drop my arms. His hot hands would find my throat and crush it. It wouldn't take long. Then I could fall into the oblivion that waited behind everything, and I wouldn't have to feel anything anymore.

I think I might have done it too, had it not been for the fact that the foot of that wretched man above me chose that moment to make contact with my stump.

I howled, turned and screamed in his face: 'What is your fucking problem?'

'You, Beth,' he said with hot, heavy breaths. 'You're my problem. You ruined everything. And now you're going to face the consequences.'

'You murdered my husband, you bastard. I'm going to make you pay.'

He grinned and shook his head, eyes wide. 'No, Beth. You're the one who's paying today, not me. And do you want to know how?' He pushed his face closer. 'Fire. I'm going to lash you and that useless corpse over there to the deck of that gin palace, shower you with petrol and strike a match. I'll watch it burn with a glass of my rum, listen to your screams until I'm bored, and then do you know what I'm going to do? I'm going to take a little trip to Daytona, see if I can find your children. Maybe I can teach them a thing or two about consequences too, eh?'

My blood chilled. I said nothing. A stillness had come over me.

He shook me, angry at the lack of response. 'Eh? What about that?'

But all I felt was the churning of a deep and dreadful sea.

There was a glint as the sun caught metal, and my eyes travelled from Tony's rabid face to the chains around his neck.

'Is that all you believe in, Tony? Actions and consequences?'

'What else is there?'

'It's just ... all these trinkets of yours. I wonder what they mean?'

Slow heart thumps like the sway of a whale's tail. Breaths like a thousand-mile tide.

'Totems,' said Tony with a sneer. As his eyes dropped his grip weakened. 'Reminders of the ones who have crossed me.'

I searched through the layers of metal and stone.

'Are you sure that's wise? To carry the belongings of the people you've killed? Some would say you're dealing with something you don't understand.'

Chain after chain, stone after stone, and finally – a crucifix.

'Well, it's a good thing I'm not superstitious then, isn't it?'

My eyes met his. 'I wasn't talking about superstition.'

He frowned. 'What?'

I wrenched his hand away, snatched the crucifix Maggie had given me in Gibraltar and – hoping it would do what I told it – pressed its top.

A blade shot out.

Tony raised his eyebrows. 'Well, fuck me sideways.'

With a scream I drove it into the side of his neck. It went deep and stuck there for a moment. Tony clutched at it, staggered back, and gulped as a belch of blood arrived at the wound and another at his mouth.

At this his face creased with rage and he held out both hands for me, but I had already picked up my crutch and swung it with everything I had against his head. It whipped round and he stumbled right, arms still out before him like a zombie, and my second swing hit him in the throat.

With one last look at me he fell back, hit the guard rail, and tumbled into the water.

I scrabbled to the side to see. He floated away, face down, leaving a trail of blood in his wake until a great pile of rubbish absorbed him and swallowed him down into its oily plastic bowels.

When he was gone, I scrabbled over to Ed. Tears were already at my face when I turned him over.

'Ed, Ed, please, speak to me.'

His face was calm, as if in sleep. There was a wound on his head, just above his left ear, hardened now with blood.

'Ed, please.' I held his head and put my brow to his, whispering. 'I can't do this on my own. I can't, I just can't.'

All I could hear was my own breath and the waves. I stayed like that for some time, just breathing in his smell and whispering the same words over and over. 'I can't do it on my own. I can't do it on my own.'

Our third date was when it happened. We'd been out for dinner, then met with some of Ed's friends in a bar I didn't know in the New Town. There were about ten of us, drunk at a table, but as the evening wore on and the music and laughter grew louder, Ed and I retreated to a corner, sharing our own private conversations, deeper looks and kisses, until finally we became oblivious to the others.

I slept with him that night, and the next day was Sunday.

'What are you doing today?' he asked.

I told him, by reflex, that I liked my Sundays to myself. My flatmates were usually out and about, so

I liked to spend the day reading, tidying, just being with myself.

I detected some hurt in his smile, but he told me to enjoy it and to call him. Perhaps we could meet up in the week.

That day I roamed the empty flat, restless, moving objects and trying to start books but finding myself staring out of the window instead, thinking of his face.

So I called him.

'Hi. It's me. Do you think ... I want to see you. I don't want to be alone.'

I don't want to be alone.

I don't want—

'You're not alone.'

I sat up.

'Ed?'

He turned his head, groaning. 'I said you're not alone. What happened?'

I gasped. My heart kick-started, my veins flushed.

'Ed, you're alive!'

I kissed his face all over and pulled him to my chest.

'*Ow.*'

'Sorry, I just thought you were dead. Christ, don't move, you've been shot.'

He sat up and held the side of his head. 'It doesn't feel like it.' He touched the wound. 'Feels more like a – *aargh.*'

He pulled a long splinter from his flesh and held it up, dripping.

'Fuck, that hurts.'

Suddenly he sat bolt upright.

'Where's that prick?'

I shuffled closer and held his face in my palms. 'He's gone.'

'How?'

I kissed him long on the lips. The taste of saltwater, blood and sweat washed between our mouths.

'I killed him.'

He hesitated, still emerging from the kiss. 'Excellent.'

'Yes, it was. Now let's get our children.'

Chapter 34

We sailed all day with nothing behind us but the wind. It was not the cruel wind that had seemed so intent on pushing us from our path just before we met Fresh Kills, nor the absent breeze that had pushed us there in the preceding days. This one wanted us to move. It was with us, right there on the deck and pushing us every mile of the way.

Ed and I were too engrossed in our tasks to speak. I stood at the helm and hugged the coast while he trimmed the sails and watched for obstacles from the bow, but we shared smiles and glances, and treated each other's wounds when the wind was low.

Hope filled our sails, but as the day wore on we grew nervous. Our threat was behind us, decomposing into fish food, but what lay ahead? The scale of our objective was expanding. Until now it had been merely to cover distance, but soon we would have to moor and scour untold miles of coast for our children. How did we hope to find them? Were they even there?

It was dusk when we saw lights. As Curtis had said, there had been no sign of life on the land since we had set off, but now an orange glimmer clustered upon what looked like an estuary. There was nothing north or south of it as far as we could see, and the water had cleared of debris. We headed in.

The lights drew apart as we approached the estuary. 'They're islands,' I said. 'Just like Ulrich said.'

'They weren't always,' replied Ed, looking over the starboard guard rail. 'Look.'

He pointed down into the clear blue water, beneath which trees and weed-strewn buildings were visible – houses, shops and a car park sailed below, and a street sign that said, to my unfettered delight, DAYTONA.

'Ed, this is it. We're here!'

We dropped everything but the jib and weaved between the islands, keeping our distance. Most of them were small and uninhabited, squat tufts in the water like the ones we had encountered near Cadiz, and others were only sparsely lit.

The main source of the lights was on the southern bank of the river mouth. Unlike its opposing bank, which was deserted and covered with dead trees, this was a series of long beaches backed by dense forest. The lights were flaming torches, between which shadows moved, and a rich concoction of smells floated from the shore; cooking meat, wood smoke and rainforest.

Ed's plan was to find somebody – an official or police – and explain. If this was the safe haven Captain Ulrich had described, then surely they would have some systems in place, a record of who had landed here and where they were.

I didn't like it. The thought of surrendering our search to some unknown bureaucracy – or worse, to be rejected by it – filled me with dread, but it seemed like the only way. The coastline stretched for miles ahead, and who knew what lay behind those trees?

So we drifted, searching for some sign of officialdom.

But life had other plans. Like the wind, something else was guiding us that day – I'm certain of it.

Was it a sound? A smell? Some sensory substrata available only to my subconscious? I don't know, but as we veered towards the second stretch of beach my neck hairs stood on end.

'Ed. Stop. Take down the sail.'

'What is it?'

I made for the guard rail and scanned the beach a few hundred metres from us. There were people on the sand, hundreds of them, and there was no way of seeing their faces. Yet my skin prickled with certainty.

'They're here. Alice and Arthur.'

Ed scrambled from the bow.

'What? Where?'

'I don't know, but they're here, I know it.'

He hesitated, giving me a doubtful glance.

'Beth, I think we should …'

But I was already over the side.

'Beth!'

The water was as warm as the air above it. I struggled for a while until I found my stroke, kicking only with my right leg in case my foot became unfastened. I heard a splash behind me, and Ed's grunts as he caught me up.

'What the hell are you doing?' he said, gasping.

'They're here, Ed. I'm sure of it. Understand?'

I ploughed ahead, leaving him kicking water behind. Soon he was alongside me again, matching my stroke.

'OK,' he said between breaths. 'I believe you.'

The current took us towards some rocks, and we soon found ourselves in shallow, swamplike water packed with weed. There was no way to swim through it, so, with me leaning on Ed for support, we waded the remaining fifty metres or so until, finally, we fell upon the sand.

As I caught my breath, Ed made for the darkened forest at the top of the beach, returning a moment later with a stick. I took it and he helped me up. Dripping, we walked the beach.

There were fires on the sand as well as torches. People were sitting around them; families, couples and old folk dressed in clean clothes and looking well fed. I stared at everyone we passed.

'I'm looking for my children,' I said, voice quivering. 'My children. They were taken from me. Have you seen them? They're only small, please ...'

But they only stared back, pulling their own children close.

Halfway along the beach the fires grew closer together and the groups more tightly packed. Up ahead was a row of small white buildings with electric lights. I felt it again – that tingle. This time it was definitely a sound that caused it, some far-off giggle that set my nerves on fire. I stopped dead, staring ahead.

Ed heard it too. 'Alice?'

'Hey.'

I looked up towards the trees, where a man in his forties with greying hair and a cropped beard was standing. He pointed at me, and I felt a hundred eyes do the same.

'What?'

'Yeah, you. I know you. You're … you were on the *Unity*.' His accent was English. He looked at the woman sitting by his fire. 'Wasn't she? She was on our boat?'

The woman nodded.

Hearts pounding, we limped up to meet them. The man looked us up and down in horror.

'Where on earth …?'

'You were on the *Unity*?' I said.

He nodded. 'Yeah, we got here on one of the lifeboats. But you—'

'Do you know a woman named Mary Higgs?'

'Higgs?'

'She was on one of the lifeboats too.'

His eyes danced around. 'Higgs, Higgs, Higgs … no, afraid not.'

'She's on her own. She has a—'

'Black bob?' said the woman. She stood and brushed the sand from her dress.

'Yes.'

She nodded. 'Yeah, I know her. She has a daughter and a son, they're only—'

'*Our* daughter and son,' said Ed, through gritted teeth.

'Eh?'

'She took them from me,' I said.

The woman's face paled, mouth drooping with horror.

'She told us their parents were dead. She said she was their aunt, she—'

'Where is she?' I said.

The woman pointed ahead. 'She's over there. They always sit close to the track.'

I followed the path of her finger to a crowded area near a path into the forest. People were looking, scratching their heads. I was sure I saw somebody pointing at me, talking to a woman in uniform, but something else caught my eye; a pale, terrified face curtained with black hair darting up the path, and two little legs hurrying after her.

A tsunami of adrenalin washed through me, and I was at the path before I knew it. Ed ran ahead. Voices were raised in protest, and I shook off an unfriendly hand or two. We were on the track now and I was running too, I swear it. There was no pain in my stump or in my leg, there was nothing at all but the hammering of my heart.

There ahead, again. A black flash and two bare legs running down a sidetrack. We followed it and stopped. Insects buzzed and chirped. It was dark in the forest but the way ahead was lit by flaming torches, and at the end was a large metal hut, whitewashed, with a sign above its door that read BOATS.

'They're in there,' I whispered.

We walked towards it. I couldn't see through the windows, so we opened the door.

Inside was a dusty workshop lit by a dim bulb. One wall was lined with a bench, and tools hung from nails above it. A stack of rusty bicycles leaned in a corner beneath a shelf lined with old books.

At the back of the room was a well-worn armchair, and in it, with Arthur on her knee, was Mary Higgs. Alice stood beside her with one hand in hers and the other at her lips.

Arthur looked up, blinked, and returned to the set of keys in which he was engrossed.

I tried to speak but my mouth wouldn't work. I could hardly even move.

Ed leaped forward, but stopped when Mary raised her hand from behind Arthur's head and showed us the hammer she was holding.

She shook her head.

'Shut the door,' she said. 'And lock it.'

I finally found my voice.

'Mary—'

She raised the hammer again, this time with a pleading look.

Shaking, I turned and closed the door, locking the padlock that hung from the latch. Ed was still frozen in the middle of the floor.

'You should move back a bit,' said Mary. 'You're scaring the children.'

Hesitating, Ed stepped back to my side. We stood there, straining like flies on flypaper. It took every ounce of willpower not to rush her.

With a placid smile, Mary looked down at Arthur. My eyes turned to Alice. I tried to smile, and raised a trembling hand.

'Alice ... hi ... hi, darling.'

With one hand still at her mouth, Alice gave me a wary look, swinging at her hips.

'It's me,' I said. 'It's Mummy.'

Mary shot me a look of danger at this.

'Mary says you're not,' said Alice. To hear her voice, even so quietly and with such suspicion, brought untold joy. 'She says you're pretending.'

I looked between her and Mary. Mary's warning look still held.

'Alice,' said Ed.

'And what – what do you think, darling? Do I look like her? Do I sound like her?'

She pulled at her lips. Her mouth trembled. Tears brimmed in her eyes.

'She said you left us. She said you didn't want us any more.'

I glanced at Mary, somehow calmed by the flood of rage.

'That's not true,' I said. 'Mummy would never leave you. Or Daddy.'

She looked at Ed. Her eyes widened, spilling tears. 'Daddy?'

Mary gripped her hand tightly, lifting the hammer and mouthing, '*I'll do it.*'

There were voices from the track outside.

'Mary,' I said, 'it's over. There are people coming.'

'It's not over. It's never over, not when you're a parent. Full-time job, eh, Ally-Bally?'

She winked at Alice and tousled her hair. Alice tried to smile back, but she was shaking now. Her knees wobbled.

The voices outside grew louder, accompanied by footsteps.

'Give us our children,' said Ed.

Mary's carefree expression snapped to vicious fury. 'Your children? How are they *your children*?' She stood, tipping Arthur onto the chair as if he was nothing more than a bag of oranges, and raised the hammer. She gripped Alice's wrist with her other hand.

Alice squealed: 'Mummy?'

Arthur released a doleful cry, struggling to sit up.

'Quiet!' she screamed back at him. She turned back to Ed, crimson with rage: '*I'm* the one who's been looking after them.'

'And we thank you for that,' said Ed carefully, with his palms out. 'But we're here now.'

She shuffled her feet, eyes suddenly flitting around the room. 'Here? Where's here? Where's there? Ha! And who's this, anyway? The husband, is that it?' She looked at me, a nasty smile creeping onto her face. 'Does he know?'

'Know what?' I said.

She winked. 'About you and that tall fella. What was his name, now ... Richard, that's it. You had a little thing going with him, if I remember rightly. Naughty, naughty.'

'What?' said Ed, brow crumpling. 'What little thing?'

I shot him a look. 'She's just trying to confuse us.'

'Not surprising that I was left holding the baby all that time on the boat,' said Mary. She looked innocently around, hammer still raised and Alice squirming in her grip.

'Beth, what's she talking about?'

'Ed, it's not true. I swear it.'

Mary sing-songed awkwardly: 'If the cabin's rockin', don't come knockin' ...'

Ed looked between us, bewildered.

'Ed, please...'

I prepared myself for the indignation I was sure would come. But instead he raised his eyebrows and gave the kind of philosophical sigh that usually accompanies a crumpled lottery ticket. He turned to Mary. 'I wouldn't blame her to be honest. Richard's a handsome man – I mean, I'm not saying I *would*, but if I had to, yeah, probably.'

The room was silent. Even Alice turned in surprise.

Mary's grin wilted, her glee derailed. She didn't notice Ed's right foot shuffling imperceptibly forward an inch.

The door behind us shook. 'Hello?' said an officious, female voice. 'Anyone in there? Open up!'

Mary stared at the door, gripping Alice ever tighter and raising the hammer above her head. Ed gave me a look; an encoded flash that seemed to say: '*Go with me on this.*'

'*OK.*'

My voice shook with fear, but I tried to speak as breezily as I could.

'You're right. He is attractive. But it's not true, Ed, just so you know. We never did anything.'

He shrugged, using the motion to advance his left foot. 'Like I say, wouldn't have blamed you. These things happen. God, remember that girl I used to work with, Laura?'

I frowned, moving my own foot. 'Aye. Worked in HR. Pink hair.'

'That's her. She came on to me once.'

I glanced at Mary. Her eyes darted furiously between us.

'Really?' I said.

'Yeah. It was at the Christmas party and she kind of, just, *pushed* her boobs against me and asked if I wanted to, you know ...'

'No,' I said, with my best attempt at affront. 'What?'

'Do things.'

I raised my eyebrows. 'Blimey, well done. She was pretty.'

'Thanks. I was quite impressed myself.'

Mary's eyes were wild now. She still hadn't noticed our slow advance.

'Hey!' The door rattled and Mary renewed her grip on hammer and child. 'This is Sheriff Hanley, open up in there!'

Mary bared her teeth. The hammer shook above her head.

'Anyway,' Ed continued, 'I didn't take her up on it. Although, I mean ... truth is I might have done.' He looked shamefully at his feet, moving them another few inches. I followed. 'It was during one of our bad patches. *My* bad patches, I mean.'

'We've both had them, Ed.'

Another shuffle. Mary looked ready to burst.

'Get back,' she said, suddenly noticing our feet. She looked at the floor as if was crawling with spiders. 'Get back now!'

'Open up in there or we'll break down this door!'

'The point is,' said Ed, 'I *didn't* do anything because, apart from the fact that I love you—'

'I love you too.'

'It just seemed like too much bother, you know?'

'Aye, right? Imagine the stress of keeping an affair going with all the other shite you've got to deal with. I don't know how anyone does it. Must be an absolute nightmare.'

'Right. Besides, I wanted to go home anyway.'

'From the party?'

Another step. We were halfway to the chair by now.

'Get back or I swear I'll do it, I swear it, don't make me do it. I don't want to, I don't want to, I don't want to, get back!'

443

'Mummy!'

'Yeah, I –' Ed turned to me '– don't really like parties.'

'Me neither. Sometimes I just want to be on my own.'

He smiled. 'Me too.'

'*Get back!*' screamed Mary.

'Oh, by the way, what was the name of that bar?'

'What bar?'

'The one we went to after our third date, that Sunday when I called you.'

'You mean the day before you called me saying you missed me?'

A shuffle. So close now.

'Yeah.'

'That you couldn't stand being apart from me?'

'Aha.'

'That I was—'

'Ed, what was the name?'

'Open this door!'

He smiled back. 'The *Elma*.'

Unable to handle it any longer, Mary screamed. '*Who the fuck are you?*'

We both looked at her, only a step or two away. Her hammer was hanging. 'I'm Mummy, and this is Daddy. Ed, now.'

Ed leaped for the hammer.

'No!' said Mary, whipping it down. I made a dive for Alice, tackling her from Mary's hand and hearing a crack as metal hit bone. Ed yelled, wrestling Mary for the hammer. There was blood on his arm.

'No!' she screamed. 'They're *mine*! You don't deserve them! You don't deserve them! They're *mine*!'

Alice was shaking, her arms tight around my neck.

'It's OK,' I whispered into her ear. 'I've got you. I've got you.'

I pulled myself up the armrest and scooped Arthur from the chair, just as Ed, roaring, pushed Mary down into it.

'And I've got you too.'

I fell down on the wooden floorboards, both children locked in my arms, in an embrace you would have had to snap my bones to break.

The door burst open and the workshop was filled with light and a hundred voices yelling: *'Freeze!'*

But all I could hear was the hearts of my children against mine, and Mary's muffled sobs, and my whispers, endlessly rotating: *'I've got you, I've got you, I've got you.'*

Chapter 35

Sheriff Hanley was a stout yellow-haired woman in her seventies with fierce green eyes and a face that said she could be your best friend or your worst enemy: it was up to you. We were taken to one of the white buildings on the shore, floodlit now and full of baffled faces staring and muttering as we passed. Two of Hanley's men made a brief attempt at prising Alice and Arthur from my grip, but there was no way any one of us would give it up.

'Leave them,' said Hanley, and I think she already knew.

So, while Ed had his arm looked at, Hanley questioned me with Alice and Arthur still on my lap.

Alice did most of the talking.

When Hanley had run out of things to ask, she lit one of her Winston cigarettes and sat back in her chair. She explained that times were different now. There were no more identity databases, and they certainly didn't have any reliable means of testing DNA. Decisions had to be made on trust, she said, and this was a fine thing in her opinion. It reminded her of how things had been when she was a child. She grew up in the 1950s, just like Curtis, though I'd be willing to bet their experiences of that divisive decade were vastly different.

So she had to make her decision based upon the evidence she had, which was the recollections of those who had been on the *Unity*, and of her own instincts about Mary Higgs since she had arrived in Daytona.

'Always thought she was a little cuckoo, that one,' she said.

But most of all she was basing her decision on this babbling girl before her, Alice, who was damn sure this woman and this man were her parents, and that Mary had lied to everyone, but that it wasn't her fault because of what she was.

Which only left me with one job: to describe to Sheriff Hanley what, on God's green earth, a *wanker* was.

Daytona was everything you would expect it to be. Warm and clean, with good food and children everywhere. It was like a holiday camp, only run by the guests. Everyone had a job to do.

Hanley gave us a tour the next day and explained that hundreds of places like this had been set up along the Florida coast as far as Miami, the Keys, the Everglades and up as far as Tampa. She didn't know for sure what was happening elsewhere, but she had heard that Louisiana was even more of a swamp than it had been before, and Texas was to be avoided at all costs.

With no longer any government to speak of, it had been down to local groups to repair the destruction of the strike and the subsequent floods that had ravaged the American coast. Perhaps this was how it had always been anyway, Hanley said.

'Don't get me wrong,' she said, as she led us along a row of small huts in the forest. 'I ain't no an-ar-chist or nothing, but in the end it's always down to people to make things work, ain't it? Here we are, home sweet home.'

She showed us our house, a clean two-bedroom unit with a hole for a toilet.

'No running water yet but we're working on it. I'll be by to talk about how you can help us, work detail and such, but you folks get yourself settled. Better get that boat of yours moored.' She curled her lip at my foot. 'And get that thing seen to at the hospital as well. I don't want no infection in my facility.'

'What will happen to Mary?' asked Alice.

Hanley turned and smiled. 'She'll go someplace safe, sweetheart. Somewhere she won't be able to lie any more.'

'It's not her fault—' Alice began, but Hanley interrupted.

'I know what she is, sweetheart, you don't have to tell me again.'

Some weeks later we were on the beach building sandcastles.

'Was Tony Staines a wanker, Mummy?'

'Yes, darling.'

Of the many facts, myths and conjectures I have drip-fed my daughter, the one she finds most fascinating is that the world's population is divided between those who are and those who are not wankers. I had long stopped trying to prevent her from using the word. There seemed little point.

'How many *are* there, Mummy?'

'You'll have to find that one out for yourself, darling, I'm afraid. But best not to think about it too much, eh? You just concentrate on making friends.'

Friends. Those strange people on their strange islands who one day drift into your waters and wave hello. I have some now, and I scan the shoreline for them morning, noon and night. But there's no sign. Sometimes I stay up after Ed goes to bed, listening to the crickets and trying to convince myself of how lucky we are to have found this utopia. Hanley sometimes stops by on her evening rounds and we'll have a drink or two on the porch. I'll ask her: has she heard of anyone passing through Florida? Someone looking for us? Bryce said they would make for the shore, after all.

'Nope,' she always says. ''Fraid not.'

So I smile and smoke one of her Winstons beneath the warm, safe canopies of the Florida palms, trying not to appear too restless.

But I am. Because we're nothing without our friends.

Alice and I were admiring our sandcastle, and Arthur's attempts to destroy it, when Ed arrived on the beach. He no longer wore the sling the nurse had given him after his altercation with Mary, though he still carried his arm tenderly.

He crouched excited. I shaded my eyes.

'Have you heard something?'

'No. But I met someone.'

'Who?'

'A man who sells cars. They're not what you'd call *new* but they work, and he has fuel as well.'

'We don't have any money.'

'No, but we do have a boat. And he wants one.'

We watched each other for a while. Then I held out my hand and he took it.

So that is how we bid a thankful goodbye to the *Black Buccaneer* and Sheriff Hanley's utopia, and one June morning found ourselves sitting in a rusty yellow 1973 Ford Gran Torino station wagon with five tanks of gasoline in the back.

'Mind how you go!' said the black-haired, gold-toothed man named Edmonds. 'She'll go with you to the ends of the earth, you mark my words. But hey –' he pointed through the open window; crickets buzzed in the field behind '– watch out for Texas, you hear?'

We nodded. He grinned. Then he banged the roof and swaggered back to his yard, where an ancient dog welcomed his return.

We were on a dirt track facing north. Alice and Arthur were buckled into makeshift child seats behind.

'Where are we going, Mummy?' said Alice.

I looked in the rear-view mirror.

'To find our friends, sweetheart. We're going to have a wee adventure. Is that OK?'

She nodded, beaming. Arthur babbled his own feelings on the matter.

I turned to Ed.

'Are you all right driving?'

'I don't have much choice, do I, stumpy?'

'It's an automatic. I'm sure I could manage.'

'No, I'm good. You navigate.'

We pulled away onto a long, straight road. I closed my eyes as the Florida air blew in, and the sun warmed my face, and I let my distance unravel like the road before us.

Just me. Me, a huge blue sky and an old car full of the people I love.

Yes.

I'll take that.

Acknowledgements

The last page of *The End of the World Running Club* produces a mixed response. Some love the ending as it is, whereas others feel a little cheated and want to know exactly what happens next. For my part, I wrote it that way because I felt Ed's journey (at least his inward one) was complete, and this is why I promised myself I would never write a sequel.

I have my editor, Gillian Green, to thank for convincing me otherwise. Her ever-patient persistence finally made me realise that, actually, it *wasn't all about Ed*, and that the other characters needed their stories completing too. Thanks, Gillian, I had such fun writing Beth's (yes, even the bit with the foot.)

Thanks as always to my wife Debbie, who helped me brainstorm (*winestorm* really) Beth's character and story into something beyond the obvious.

Thanks to Katie Seaman, whose meticulous copy-editing skills made such a difference to the final manuscript.

Thanks to everyone with a sailing background who reads this book, for not complaining about the bits I get wrong.

And finally thanks to my father, Norrie, for his enduring love and support, for his advice on the high seas, and for letting me borrow the *Black Buccaneer* ...

Make sure you've read Adrian J Walker's gripping survival thrillers

When the world ends and you find yourself stranded on the wrong side of the country, every second counts.

No one knows this more than Edgar Hill. 550 miles away from his family, he must push himself to the very limit to get back to them, or risk losing them forever ...

His best option is to run.
But what if your best isn't good enough?

The world is going to the dogs...

THE LAST DOG ON EARTH

ADRIAN J WALKER

Author of The End of the World Running Club

Every dog has its day …

And for Lineker, a happy go lucky mongrel from Peckham, the day the world ends is his: finally a chance to prove to his owner just how loyal he can be.

Reg, an agoraphobic writer with an obsession for nineties football, plans to wait out the impending doom in his second floor flat, hiding himself away from the riots outside.

But when an abandoned orphan shows up in the stairwell of their building, Reg and Lineker must brave the outside in order to save not only the child, but themselves …